Praise for *Fly Stone, Fly*

"If Faulkner wrote fantasy, he'd have written something like this... unique, lyrical, and steeped in Americana folklife."
—Sunyi Dean, author of *The Book Eaters*

"A Dark Fantasy that skillfully navigates tropes while weaving homages to Hamlet and one very special fairy tale; every character gets deeper, every chapter gets darker—until the ending which explodes in a bloody, satisfying Tarantino-esque climax where everyone gets what they deserve."
—G.K. Undine

"'Fly Stone, Fly' defies categorization... It is soul music, it is the blues. The further in you go the more you feel its thumping multi-chambered heart."
—Kwesi Dansonne

"A Western Gothic revenge story for anyone who hates bullies and got picked on for being strange."
—Eric Ortlund, author of *All Gods Die and Other Stories*

This is a work of fiction. Names, characters, and incidents either are products of the author's imagination or are used fictitiously. Any resemblance to actual events or locales or persons, living or dead, is entirely coincidental.

Please note: This work of fiction includes mature themes, language use appropriate to period and culture, depiction of traumatic life and death events and immoral behavior. The reader is encouraged to make an informed decision considering personal experience and preferences prior to reading this material.

First Printing: January 20, 2025.
ISBN: 979-8-9919749-0-5

FLY STONE, FLY
A NOVEL

*Dedicated with the greatest respect
to Third Culture Kids and bad dogs everywhere*

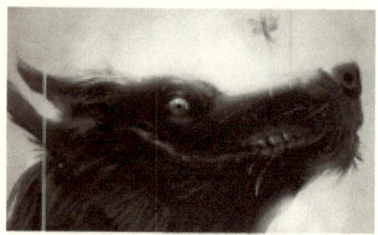

This treatment of stoneflies has been prepared as a guide. Recently, stoneflies — along with other kinds of aquatic insects — have been used as index organisms in pollution studies.
—Stanley G. Jewett, Jr., Monograph 3, Oregon State
College Press, "Stoneflies of the Pacific Northwest"

I will not trouble you here with thrilling accounts of supernatural black dogs, of which there are a great many.
—Gene Wolfe, "The Pirates of Florida and Other Implausibilities"

Memory is not what the heart desires.
That is only a mirror, be it clear as Kheled-zaram.
—J.R.R. Tolkien, "The Fellowship of the Ring"

Prologue

Inventory:

The Qualities of A "Good Dog." He puts his hands in quotes. (Granma says, in my head, *"He was NOT a good dog."*)

Come when called.

Sit.

Stay.

Don't pee on the lawn.

Inventory done.

That's not you, of course, Dammit. We're talking about good dogs.

No laugh? OK. You got other "qualities." Still no laugh? OK, riddle me this: How'd I change from scared rabbit to monster-killer? How'd I get to this storm-tossed hill where I wish I was talking to you?

Granma in my head: *"Don't you DARE toss that penny, 'n TELL your wish out loud."*

All dogs are truth-tellers, sonsa bitches but still truth-tellers, Dammit, so you will understand when I tell you the truth, the whole truth, and nothin' but the truth, so help me God (God—or Gods? If they're anywhere near – more like *when* they're near—I reckon they don't give a damn about strays). Pay attention, it matters when.

Anyway, here's the story. *When wishes were for wishing, aiming was for aiming, and sometimes both came true.* Like you, how I got to be a stray.

Chapter 1

Nose Up

I'll start at the worst part.

A sound like a dull blade tearing canvas.

Big Jim stood on the cabin porch thirty feet from me, legs thrust apart like tree trunks, one giant fist around the neck of my friend, the other with a blade raised above his head. The blade flashed, Doc Ranulf's carcass opened like a red flower, and Big Jim skinned him like I used to skin squirrels (you rip the hide off like a sweater, Dammit).

Big Jim didn't remove Doc's hands or feet. Instead, he left them with their three-inch black claws intact and threw the body on the lawn. Everything mashed into a violent heavy-oiled painting: jabby-greens of grass, stick browns of cabin, yellow-milk sunshine curdled between the trunks of orange ponderosa pines below a burning-blue sky that framed the whole jangly canvas, vibrating as if struck by the hand of a god.

I reached blindly for a handhold. Pop's axe, *Acuere,* pressed down like a thousand-pound tree on my shoulder. The air was dense like a storm coming, filled with the tearing of wet skin, Big Jim's animal breathing, and that indescribable sound from his mouth: shears mashing *click click* in the depths.

A worm turned in my chest: It's my fault, this whole thing. My friend torn; my family destroyed one by one. Did Doc lose heart before he lost his hide? The worm twisted. I told it to go to hell – pretended I was mean and tough as you, Dammit—and walked through the sliding colors until I stood below Big Jim, next to the seeping husk with long fingered-claws that used to be my friend.

Oh, how all occasions do inform against me, and spur my dull revenge!

Big Jim bent to his task as if this was all that mattered. Nailing a wolf-hide.

Bam BAM.

No sign of wings. Just shoulders too-wide for any man, muscles like rock-piles. "Fee, fie, fo, fum.... Mmm." He spoke softly at the wall through a mouth holding nails, almost a whisper. "I smell the blood of George's son." He wiped his drooping blond mustache, nailed the wolf head slowly, working his way around the edges of the hide. One *bam* to start the nail, and the second *bam* to drive it in. "Yet here you are, *boy. Mmm.*" He said "boy" like he meant "worm," and the *mmm* was a sibilant purr.

"In my trap. The last of the Conveners, a sixteen-year-old boy," Big Jim gloated. "I told you I would take everything."

"Not everything,'" I said, my voice rough as an unfiled blade.

He turned his head. Oh, those eyes—*O'er-sized with coagulate gore and large as carbuncles!* The fat on his face rippled, he dropped the hammer and swelled to fill the porch.

"It didn't burn in the fire?" he muttered.

Acuere grew even heavier, a thousand bricks, each the size of Doc's cabin. I felt I would smash through the grass under its weight. I did not answer.

"Boy." *Click Click.* The garden shears snapped behind his mustache. "Give it to me."

Fear in the timbre of his voice, Dammit. Fear!

"You have brought me my wildest dream." He closed a massive fist, each nail a yellow-ragged blade, and smiled. I did not like the smile because it was too big, even for his great face, and the fear was gone. He walked down the stairs, popping his knuckles, a sound like branches being snapped.

Why, what an ass I am, prompted to revenge, to act, I unpack my heart with words. I am punished with a sore distraction. I hesitated.

Big Jim snatched *Acuere* from my hand. "Oh, that's hot," he said with that too-wide smile. His nails scratched the handle as he raised it like a twig. "You thought this could hurt me? Mmm?"

I fell to my knees.

Click Click. The shears mashed in his mouth.

"This is not as fun as I imagined," he said. "Time to die." He swung my grandfather's axe down upon my head as if to split me in half.

Dammit, I realized just now: this is NOT the worst part of the story. The worst part is when your parents climb in a raft to head downriver to get supplies and leave you at the homeplace on the edge of the Idaho wilderness at age twelve. The worst part is they never come back, and you don't know you're a stray. Just waiting. And waiting. Four years of waiting in a canyon by the river. The worst part is not knowing there's a Big Jim waiting too—to end you. Or that Big Jim killed your dad. Or get this: that your best friend is actually your worst enemy. The worst part is living all them years alone having a story in you like a song, and you can't even whistle.

Here I am, trying to untangle this like a snarl of fishing line caught in the river bottom. Find the first loose end. Don't pull too hard.

"Everyone loses parents, Clayton. Only, you started early," Granma says, no-nonsense. "Rub out the fuckin hurt, it's not like you broke a bone."

A boy can't stop his Granma cussin'. And — you know this, Dammit — a boy can't rub away the hurt. It can make you go mad. And there's your first loose end. Don't worry, we'll get back to Big Jim. That was a doozy of a fight, a real dustup. Or, as you like to say, "Nose up, ears back, piss on you."

I reckon I'll start over – and start from the real beginning.

Chapter 2

A Brief Meditation on Slow-Crawling Time, The Nemesis

Here's the truth. It's my fault, I chose to stay. Dad wanted me to go with them, I said no.

"Fine, but don't leave, jackass," he said. "You're safe here." Sometimes he said "jackass" and it meant he was laughing at me, and it was his special name for me. Sometimes he said "jackass" and – if he was mad—it meant he thought I was a goddam jackass.

Time was my nemesis. A slow-crawling beast flaying me alive from the inside out. Three years I lived off fruit, grubs, snared animals — if they weren't dead, I throttled them until they were dead — salmon and venison. The fourth winter I starved. Sometimes I wanted to chop off my cold fingers they hurt so bad. I read my Momma's Riverside Shakespeare (the collected works) and made my own songs. *Of rivers and the chain-ed canyons free, a winding, restless spirit I will be.* I won't talk no more about those years. What is there to tell?

I know a creek that starts high in the Sawtooth's the size of a garter snake and then, after 300 miles under snow melt, turns into a striking rattler. This story is like that. It gets meaner and meaner, fat, snakey, full a poison. It crawled on my chest and bit me. And now vengeance chills my veins. *Come, the croaking raven doth bellow for revenge.* This story starts slow but turns into a helluva bloody ride.

Let's get to the day I met you, Dammit.

Chapter 3

Fly, Stonefly

The sound came from high above the ridge, two pieces a steel scraping against each other, like an iron monster dying. I looked up from the creek — my little river — where I was kicking rocks. In early summer the canyon is a giant stove. The air quivers under the sun and you see things on the hillside that aren't there. Like silver ponds and such. Behind the cabin, the weedy boulder-covered bones of the road lie in patches across the hillside. The road was impassable four years ago washed out by Spring floods. Now the weeds had turned into bushes and little trees. The canyon is so deep I cannot see the top. Its head sleeps in clouds most days in the Winter, and in the late Spring on days like this, the sun presses heat into every crack and the grasses were already turning brown.

"That is the unmistakable sound of a dozer," said MK, and I jumped and squealed.

He loved to surprise me, the bastard. One moment I'm alone. The next, there's MK.

"Whatcha thinkin', Romes?"

It was his favorite nickname for me (besides knave). The first time I met him, he didn't even say that. I looked up, there he was. I screamed and he laughed, popped his knuckles, and said "A fine good morning to you, mkay?"

I scampered inside and it took two days for me to come out and learn that he was kind, in his own way.

After that, I made him say a greeting, so I'd hear him coming. At first, he refused, but then he grinned that slow smile that never met his eyes and said, "how about this. I say '*Ve'achron*', and you say '*Alafar yaqum*.'"

"What does that mean?"

"It's like saying '*Aloha*.' It works — coming and going. Respect, harmony, peace, friendship, throwing away the dirty past, looking up, expecting Good to win." He spread his hands wide, as if to take in the entire world. "*Ve'achron*. Something a friend of mine used to say a long time ago. Not much else stuck. I can't even remember his face."

"I know how that feels," I thought about my Momma and my Dad.

"Let's try it. *Ve'achron*."

"Fine. *Alafar yaqum*."

"There you go. You got it."

Truth be told, Dammit, he liked to surprise me and didn't always stick to our agreement.

The first day I met MK I was still waking up early to wait for my Momma and Dad. Before the food ran out. Before I lived on apples and dried salmon, wild rabbit, and elk meat. MK was shirtless that first day —like always — wearing his long, curling hair free. So long it reached his jeans.

"My only jeans," he explains with a smirk at least once a week, "because they're my own Lee jeans. Get it?" He would pause for effect. "See, here, it says 'Lee' on them. Get it?"

"Yeah, I get it, Hams," I would say, and change the subject with a quote from The Riverside: "*I do wish thou were a dog that I might love thee.*"

"Nah, you don't want a dog," he'd smirk. "They have no sense of humor. And they don't wear jeans."

As you know, Dammit, the first part is dead wrong. And the second is not funny. But him and his ragged jeans thought it was.

I know a vein of pale marble that runs down a cliff in the Frank, that is, upriver in The Frank Church Wilderness, and that is MK's skin. He never gleams or shines. More like someone cut a hard shape in the air in his likeness and colored it with grey mist. Even in the brightest light, his eyes — a shade of blue like the pool in my river — were empty holes, no reflection. His flaxen hair fell over two scars on his shoulder blades. I only saw them once when he first showed up. After that, he kept his hair down.

One time I pestered him, and he grinned, "I used to have wings, Romeo, wings," and I couldn't tell if he was joking or serious. He told me they were mostly for show and that flying had nothing to do with them and that he did not miss them at all.

I laughed and said, "Who has wings?"

"Exactly," he said, and would say no more.

You know how it is when someone close to you pretends a whole part of their life doesn't exist? You get silence, or anger, and you quit asking. When MK got mad, he smelled like before lightning strikes. When the hairs of your arm go up and your hands tingle.

We come down to my river most days to escape the heat, when I'm sick of The Riverside and playing solitaire. The pack is missing the Knave of Hearts anyway, and MK calls me the knave just to be an ass.

"You'll find him someday," he jokes. "Keep looking, knave."

Made me mad as a bag a hornets.

Huge grin: "Someone's not playing with a full deck."

I'd throw the cards on the floor and stomp off to check the trap lines.

Anyone might wonder why I let him into my life. You try living alone four years, Dammit, and let me know. The first winter, I killed the weasel who killed the chickens—and ate him. Chewed the bones, sucked the marrow. But that did not fix having no more eggs. Sometimes you make the best of it and eat the weasel. And what if you decided this new friend needed to leave? How would you get rid of him? And then there's the other thing: what my Momma said about familiars.

"What's a dozer?" I asked.

"Big machine, pushes stuff around." He rose from turning over rocks on the river's edge. "Who you think's coming?"

I realized the far-away rumbles from the night before were not Spring thunder. It would have to work through the rockslide Dad created at the top, then knock down trees and fill in parts of the washed-out road all the way down. The canyon goes up in levels for at least five miles, and every time you think you are at the top there is another rise. It goes on and on forever before you reach the open air above the trees, where mountains rise in grey fists. The dozer rounded a bend high above and shoved a tree off the road.

"There's only one way in: that piece-a-shit road," MK said, smirking. Like he was saying something I didn't know.

The dozer threw up a puff of smoke.

I looked at myself in the water. Brown eyes matched the dark hair that covered my shoulders, crossing my chest. Not as curly or long as MK's — but long enough to dip in the water when I bent to look. Probably longer than my Momma's. Do I look like them? I thought of my parents and felt something rise in my stomach, like when the arrow is drawn tight on the bow and I'm waiting for the elk to step into a clearing.

"Dad, I can clean out the chicken-straw, and trim the apple trees they need it, and bring in the eggs, and wash the clothes and fold them and put them away, and keep the salmon-smoker going, and I'll ... I'll clean the outhouse. I want to stay."

His shoulders slumped, "Get out, jackass."

I tripped on the aluminum frame of the raft in my hurry to climb out, fell in headfirst. A thousand mad voices filled my ears. I screamed, inhaled water and sand, felt my hands touch wide stones rubbed smooth by a million years, and came out of the water in a burst.

"See what I mean, Rose-Marie?" Dad climbed down next to me. "He can't stay."

The raft snuggled on the sand at the edge of our river's pool. A pool so deep even at the end of summer you couldn't see the bottom. I shivered. Down there, bull trout the size of my thigh lay breathing slow. Salmon in waves of silver were coming soon.

"You're twelve, huh?" He grabbed my neck and tripped me over his leg and held me down.

"Dad!" I clawed and scratched. The voices were mad. I vomited water and sand and tried to run away but the water was icy and deep. I thrashed and fell into his chest.

"Ice-Bergmann!" He crushed me in a hug and laughed at his joke.

I squirmed like a wet cat but could not get free.

"Listen carefully, jackass, some people call our family Conveners. We're not fighters. But we are wise, and we are tough. Like our patron goddess, we listen. We wait. We hold 'em accountable. And sometimes — only if we really have to — we fuckem up."

"George! We agreed to wait to tell him. He needs more time."

"Nope," he said, looking down at me. "Not the size of the dog in the fight, size of the fight in the dog."

If you'd a been there, Dammit, you'd a loved that line. I was just trying to wrap my brain around "Convener," and "patron goddess."

"Old enough to stay home?" asked Dad. "Old enough to know what makes a Bergmann wise. It's the waiting, son. All the goddamn waiting." He held my face in his hands and looked at me so long with his pale blue eyes that I looked down. "Well, that. And you *are* the son of a water maiden."

"George!" Mom, again. Scared, pulling his belt loop. "We agreed to wait!" Then to me, changing the subject: "I love you so much, Baby Grizz. There's two pies, four jars of huckleberry jam for pancakes, that big bin of flour, lots of smoked salmon, and a list of chores on the counter. Just because Dad shoved you in the river does not mean you're clean. Bathe every day."

I thought, "No way I'm dunking in the water. Those mad voices want something."

Now Dammit, maybe you think I should have gone with them. How often have I thought that? A million times. But here's the deal: I started hearing those underwater voices calling me two weeks ago every time I swam. And I had not told my Momma and Dad.

Right then, standing by the raft, I was afraid of the voices because they wanted something. Afraid if I kept going under that I would understand them, and it would not be good. I reckoned my Momma and Dad would be home soon from getting supplies and tell me everything anyway, and I would tell them about the voices. Besides, the ragged pine-slat chair on the porch was an old friend calling, "Come sit with me, they'll be home soon." If I knew then what I know now, Dammit, I woulda got in that damn raft.

She blew a kiss, "I put The Riverside on the porch." Like always, she smelled of wild seaweed and the salt-waves of her far-away home. Of course, Dammit, you know that I never seen the ocean, they kept me away from it and never told me much of anything — except vague sayings — about my Momma and her story. You know too that the huckleberry jam didn't last. You know how I prayed every night to our family's patron goddess (the unknown one they never told me about) and she never done a thing. You know I didn't guard the chickens that first winter and they got killed. I wasn't thinking about them making chicks from eggs, keeping the flock going, and how much more food that could be. What a jackass.

"I won't forget, Momma. What if I run out before you get home?

"You won't!"

"What if I get bored?"

"Read," she was back to herself, laughing like a river. "There's no such thing as bored. When it gets too dark to read, tell yourself your stories. You love that."

"Really? You never let me anymore."

Dad *hmphed* and my Momma's brown eyes shone. "Just make sure no one dies at the end like you did to that poor squirrel when you were little. I'll help you learn your gift when we get back. And don't be afraid of your dreams. Let them have their way even when they're bad. Learn to ride them."

"Read or ride?" said Dad. "Christsake. Come with us and get the real story."

She ignored him and spoke directly to me: "If telling your own stories bothers you, read The Riverside. There're plenty heroes to imitate in there," she frowned, "just not Hamlet."

"Ha!" said Dad, "that lily-liver?"

"You forgot their faces," I said to myself.

"What?" said MK and I ignored him.

I started wearing Dad's pearl-button shirt two winters ago, and now I could not button the top three buttons because my shoulders were so wide. But Dammit, when a shirt is one of the only things left from your Dad, you wear it.

The dozer screeched over the last bench and my chest hurt like something shoved through it. I'd been hoping, I realized, without knowing I was hoping, but it was not my parents. A woman with white curls frothing out the back of a blue ball cap walked in front of the dozer, gesturing wildly at a man with hands on its levers. The animal with her was almost wolf-size with wavy black hair and a tail like a flag (ears up, you know who that is, Dammit).

I felt a crunch underfoot. Stoneflies long as my thumb were crawling out of the river like grey-orange monsters, cracking nymphal husks on the rocks, emerging from their casings with glistening wings. Soon, their thick bodies would cloud the air between the porch and the river. I'd stepped on one.

Years ago, when I was six or seven, Dad said, "It's not thinking about you, it's thinking about being itself. Crawling across the stones, the warmth of the water and the hot sun; it's thinking how much it hurts to change, it has no idea what's comin'. See," and Dad held one up as it crawled out of its shuck, opening its peeling new wings, "Watch it fly." He threw it up and it dropped into the water like a pebble, plop. A big fish came up from the bottom and took it in a splash. One moment it was there, the next a ring in the river spreading quietly.

"Maybe next time, Clay," said Dad. "Look around." He pointed at the mare's-tail clouds that whipped the sky, the bronze canyon, and the wafting scent of hot sage and ponderosa coming across the water – the river was a color between jade and blue. "Fishin' with barbless hooks."

I had no idea what Dad was talking about. In my experience stoneflies don't always get the time to learn to fly. Every Spring, I find them on the rocks and bushes and throw them out over the river like Dad did. Many don't ever learn to fly before they get eaten, or crushed by a rock, or stepped on by me.

"Stonefly different than caddis," said Dad. "Caddis grab all kinds of shit, carry it around on their backs." He was talking about the smaller caddis-bugs which are many and numerous as the sand, building bulwarks of fake shell around their squishy caterpillar-like bodies, crawling slowly around the flat tops of rocks on the bottom of the river. "Always glueing 'nother piece of dirt to their home-made shell," Dad said, "tryin' to be safe, Caddisflies just like people. Can't tell you how many times I seen someone rather live in a shithole with piles of stuff, boxes of godknowswhat shoulda tossed ten years ago. They could be free on the road. Fucking and flyin' free."

Dad loved to curse when my Momma wasn't around, and I was used to it. "Aren't caddis light when they break free?" I asked, thinking of the haze of caddis that could fill the canyon in shifting clouds with gauze wings and orange underbellies in the Fall.

"Right before they die," he chuckled. "Yah." He threw another stonefly up and we watched it open its wings for the very first time in its life and chug-chug slowly over the trees.

I thought I saw a look of surprise on its face. "I can fly? Woah!"

Dad interrupted my thoughts. "Focus jackass. Not what they are in the air, what they are underwater. Stonefly or Caddis, what will you be?" I did not tell Dad I seen other bugs in the side eddy up the canyon. I had found the shucked skin of something larger than any stonefly. Monstrous, with a torn hole in its back where it crawled out. I knew Dad well enough to know this was one of his lessons. Best not side-trail.

"I guess stonefly?"

"Yep, friendly, non-toxic. Best way to be, son. On the move." Then he said something I been chewing on for years: "All things change, Clay. All things die. Lasting change is when we become more like ourselves. Like this here stonefly. There is a time to crawl, and a time to rise. There is another change: A change like a cancer that has no end, no limits to its dead growth. That is not real change. The larger it grows, the more it crushes out life, and the smaller — and tighter — the circle it swims."

"I wanna be a mayfly," I said. "They're pretty."

"Not an option."

I did not know what cancer was. I was six years old. "I reckon I'll be the stonefly, then."

"You reckon? I wish you never had to, son." He frowned. "But wishin' never washed out shit-stains." Then he grinned and punched me. "Jackass! You better be a stonefly. It's your Momma's maiden name."

I looked down. Orange blood squirted around the stonefly's legs. The bottom of my foot felt hot from its blood. *"Etu Brute?"* I said for its own sake since it couldn't talk.

"How could you know?" MK asked, and he looked like I caught him doing something horrible. "I don't even remember."

"What are you talking about?"

Then he was back to grinning and popping his knuckles. *"Ech.* You have no idea how *not* funny you are, Romes."

MK does NOT like blood, Dammit, as you well know. Not even bug blood.

"I'm not talking about squishing bug games, mkay? I'm talking about *our* game. 'Etu Brute' is *Julius Caesar*, by the way."

"I'm not playing The TRG, Hams," I said.

"I'm up one, now. Romes." He chuckled. "And we've talked about this, The TRG is redundant. You're saying 'The *The* Riverside Game' when you should be saying '*The* Riverside Game.'" He popped his knuckles, all fear of blood gone. "Here's another for you Romolicious. '*O God, I could be bounded in a nutshell and count myself a king, were it not that I have bad dreams.*'" As he said it, his face clenched like the words hurt.

I thought, "how would I know you have bad dreams? I've never seen you sleep." Instead, I said, "'Hamlet,' easy. And you missed, 'of infinite space,' it comes right after 'count myself a king.'"

"You hesitate, Hams. 'Twill be thy downfall."

"And you know nothing of bad dreams," I said, and shivered at the thought of mine. "''Twill be yours."

His face was a storm, his eyes pure black. "Fuck you, Clayton Bergmann. I have enough bad dreams for a thousand fucking teenagers."

MK loves to curse. *Loves it*. More than Dad, for sure. And only uses my full name when I get him mad — or melancholy – or when he wants me to tell him a story he's forgotten (he forgets things all the time, and I'm always retelling the stories).

"Make it up to me. Tell me about the curse and the prophecy again."

"I've told you a thousand times, the same story over and over."

"I know Clayton Bergmann; I forget the details."

"You're always forgetting, disappearing, coming back and asking and I'm always retelling. No. No more."

"The dozer won't get here for twenty minutes. What else are we going to do?"

"The whole thing?"

"It's like a torn-up Cliff's note in my head," he popped his knuckles. "It starts with that weird-ass quote."

"You mean, '*Time is out of joint, O cursed spite, was I born to set it right?*'"

"Yesss." MK's face went slack, listening in his eerie way. He loves this story.

I get the heebie-jeebies making MK beg, Dammit. I hate to tell the story, but you know what? He asked for it.

"I remember that day well because of the big hatch of mayflies that rolled like a shifting cloud across the river," I said. "Then, the swallows were everywhere, suddenly, tearing the grey sheet in strips, joyful thrown emerald-knives against the sun. Upside-down, falling and rising up the waves, then shooting straight into the blue like feathery stones catapulted from a sling."

"I'm fine without the fuckin poetry," said MK. "Get to the good stuff, Romes."

"First of all, this is the good stuff," I said. "Second, who's telling the story, you or me? Take your medicine."

He flipped me off, but did not disagree.

I continued, and—for pure spite—jammed as much poetry and detail into it as it could handle:

"Momma said I could stay."

"You're going, jackass," said Dad. "We need supplies after all these years. And I got things to tell you. Hand me that tie-down."

Even though it was morning he sweated in the heat as he strapped down the pile in the boat: dry-bags, groover, camp stove, barrel of salt, bags of cured salmon and dried elk jerky and apples, and more. Dad favored his right shoulder broke long ago when a bronc threw him and jumped him red-eyed. He'd worked a hard hour to get the raft "right as rain," like he used to say.

My Momma sat on the dry box in the bow looking at the hillside of *Artemisia Tridentata* (common name, Sage) and massive cinnamon-bark *Pinus Ponderosa* where heat vibrated from the rocks. Momma's dark-honey hair swished against the seat as she tugged it into braids. She turned her face, twisting her hair singing softly, and the silver swallow earrings Dad gave her flashed in the sun.

"Godalmighty, please. The story," said MK, but I just grinned at him and kept going.

Our creek, in a jumble, enters the Salmon River a mile around a bend in the canyon. My stomach flipped like a fish in a pool. I did not want to go with them. Maybe if I had, this whole tangled story would be different. It's my fault. *"The web of our life is mingled yarn."* Then something came into my mind, and I said it without thinking: *"Time is out of joint, O cursed spite, was I born to set it right?"*

Mom's face went white as a piece of linen. The words "was I born to set it right" went across the canyon and came back in an echo like the river was talking to the cliffs.

Dad stared at me and the knuckles on his fingers holding the oars were white as my Momma's face.

Back then, I only knew a bit of The Riverside, and not word for word, line for line, story for story, and rarely did I know the meanings. On that day, I only knew I liked the rhyme of 'spite' and *"was I born to set it right?"* The echo came back from the cliff — soft as a child's whisper, like the beginning of a song.

She blurted, "It's the prophecy about him, how does he know it?"

Dad looked like he was being strangled by a rope. "Goddammit Rose-Marie," he said, and pointed his chin at me while he glared at her. The mood between them transformed like they made a silent arrangement, and she laughed and splashed a handful of water on me.

Dad went back to cinching. "Fucking strap," he grunted, and kicked the boat like it was a mule. "Don't never leave our land. You're safe here. Above the canyon's fine. Not past the timber, not out to the main river, OK?"

I thought of *the question*. The question they never answered because I never asked: "Why are we in a river canyon, just us three? A thousand miles from anyone?" Instead, what came out of my mouth — like a red-tail hawk falling on a rabbit — was, "Tell me why they call us Convenors."

"This goddamn boat," he said, fighting a strap. He rubbed his head with both hands, his back to me. "Fine," he spoke to the rocks across the water. "He's *twelve*, after all." He turned and gave me a long look. "We were gonna tell you about us and our family on this trip. About the calling we've had for a thousand years. And why we're NOT doing it."

"What about the prophecy about me? You NEVER said nothing about THAT. Ever."

Dad's eyes shone with tears, "Prophecy said you kill someone close to you, someone you love."

"George!" my Momma shouted, her eyes wide in fear. "George, what are you DOING?"

My legs felt like sticks of sand. I felt my mind rise and fly over the river like a hawk. I saw auburn-lichened cliffs, Dad and Momma like ants in the raft, me a lonely dot on the sand. I began to tag the different species of swallow – many and numerous—nesting in the cliffs: Grey Bank Swallows, seven. Orange-necked Barn Swallows, four. And of course, my favorites, Violet-Green Swallows named for their bright emerald shoulders and purpley rumps, nine nesting pairs in all, their twig and feather nests clamped to niches in the rock. No, ten nests. One shallow nest, empty as a cup, with a naked open-mouthed bird jerking.

"Ahh," said MK, and I could not tell if he was sad or pleased.

"Shut up, you're interrupting," I said.

"That's why we're here," Dad said, matter-of-fact, like he was talking about rain coming. "It's why we told you NOTHING about the family. We decided when you were a little jackass you need to be away from all that crap until you're old enough.' Dad added as an afterthought, 'Mebbe even keep you from doing it.'"

A pair of violet-greens dropped from the cliff, dove across the water, twisted into the sun.

"There," he said to my Momma. "I told him. After all, he's twelve." He smiled, but his eyes didn't. My Momma looked like she just witnessed a murder.

"I want to know it all," I said, rising to a knee, and I meant it.

"Then you're comin' with us," Dad said.

"What?! No. I can't. I won't go," I said.

"Then you'll find out when we get back. Mister 'I'm Twelve Tell Me Everything About My Family, My Destiny, and the Meaning of the Universe.'"

"Keep going, Romes." MK was impatient. "It's like looking through a curtain, but I remember the next bit's REAL good."

"I don't want to."

MK's eyes darkened to a black that was a lack of any color, "Finish it. Consider this training for what's next."

The dozer screeched, much closer now.

"What are you talking about?"

"Never mind," he said, popping his knuckles again. "Never mind, just finish the story."

"Fine," I said to MK. So, here's the rest, Dammit:

Looking back, maybe my Momma knew something.

She climbed out of the raft and put her arms around me. "Baby-Grizz, your Dad just told you something that may not be about you. An old family prophecy. A thousand years ago an enemy cursed our family as he died. The child of the son of the mountains and the daughter of the seas would be the last of our line: '*When mountain's son and ocean's line betroth, surely water's blood is bloody end, and bloodied end the child of wroth.*' She sounded scared. "He claimed he would come back, even from the dead, no matter how long it took…" her eyes grew dark with tears. "He swore an oath as he lay dying that he would return, take everything from us… everything… then kill us off, one by one." She smiled sadly. "It's just a stupid tall tale that gained pressure over the centuries. Like wind and waves, like water going downhill."

"Tall tales have a way of trueness in them," Dad said. "Living words of wind and wave. Lot a water, lot a pressure. Come with us. Time to tell you everything."

I shook my head and backed up on the sand.

My Momma smiled and the sun came out. "It's fine George. He'll be fine." She turned to me. "There are good reasons we never told you about our family, or about anything that happened before we got here eight years ago." She pushed my wet hair from my eyes. "Here's what you do. Tell yourself all the stories I've told you. You get the stories into a good place in you and then, after a while, you get yourself into a good place in the story. It's like learning to whistle. You think you'll never learn and then one day... "— she whistled a chuckling melody like a red-winged blackbird singing in the reeds by the river — "... One day you just do it. And after that, you know how to whistle."

She held my face in her hands and gazed at me for a long time, long enough for me to get squirmy but she held on. Her dark eyes smiled, and she said, "You are special to me, the very best kind of special."

I always thought she said that because I could remember anything I put my eyes on, like lines in The Riverside, but now I know different. Being special's not about memorizing anything.

My Momma climbed in the raft, light as a feather and darker and more lovely than a summer storm. Back then, she was small, but I was smaller.

"Anytime you're in trouble remember — get in your water," she said.

Get in my water? It wasn't my water, and that was the last thing I was gonna do. Them voices. I untied the bowline and changed the subject. "Dad, water's high, you going through Oriental Spa?"

"Heh," said MK, but I ignored him.

"Clayton, what have I TOLD you?" snapped my Momma.

"Ha ha. No spa today, son."

"Oriental Spa" was a name the river rats gave a whitewater hole downstream that ate a boat of Chinese miners in 1863. "River Rat," as you know Dammit, because this is Idaho, is what they call anyone nuts enough to ride whitewater. One of them Chinese miners twisted for days in the hole before it spat out his body.

When Dad called it "Oriental Spa," my Momma would frown and say, "Inappropriate. You know you can call it something else."

But he'd keep going: "What? It's a pleasant ride." Then he would wait one beat. "With a happy ending." He acted like it was the most serious thought he ever had.

Oriental Spa had a ten-foot standing wave over a churning hole. Easy to miss. But, if you weren't ready, or not paying attention gazing up at birds or drinking too many beers and got sucked in sideways — a dark wave blocked out the sun and you were a gonner like that Chinese miner. You needed to be strong enough and skilled enough to turn the boat one-eighty and face the wave.

"Or," Dad liked to say, "you go in sideways, that bitch'll *flip flip* you like a penny. Happy ending."

Every time he said that I would ask him, "what's a happy ending?"

And he would wink and say, "You'll find out someday, son," and my Momma would punch him.

"Not funny."

He wrenched the last strap tight and surprised me with something new. "Actually Clay, your mom and me busted one of those parlors when we lived in Florida before you came along. We got them out safe. Helped all them women find real jobs. Your mom's doing, mostly. She's the captain and I'm first-mate." He winked at her.

"What's a parlor, Dad?"

"George! Why are you telling him this now?"

"We're gonna tell him EVERYTHING on this trip," said Dad, grabbing the oars with a grin. "Might as well give a teaser." He grinned at me. "See what you're missing?"

"Your dad is right," said my Momma. "There's lots to tell you about our family and what your Dad and I did, all our adventures, before you came along. But not about parlors or inappropriate jokes."

"Aah," MK said. "Here we go."

"The Riverside was calling," I said. "And the silver twilight that begins with the swallows and ends with the jerking bats; dark shadows chasing the invisible insects of the night."

"Again, shag the poetry."

"My Momma said something, cryptic and strange, like a fragment of an old poem:"

Under-wave the stone shall go,
Returning river to its way;
Ever-still the water flows,
Ever-watchful friend of stray.

I shrugged. "Who knows what the hell that means? If I knew that I had four years of long afternoons coming, I would a jumped in that raft. But I chose this, and I got to live with it."

"The fuck you do," he said, grinning.

The squeak and clank of the dozer suddenly filled the canyon.

MK popped his knuckles. "Thanks, Romes, I remember now."

"I can be quiet as an owl on a dark night," I said, hiding behind a big rock. "I can be lost as a rattlesnake in the leaves."

"You are a strange fuckin nerd."

"And you should wash out your mouth."

The woman yelled over the dozer, "GODdamn ASShole cockSUCKin' sonofa bitch."

"Wow," MK said. "Genius."

"Huh?"

"Osmosis. You should have picked it up from me by now."

"I refuse to learn anything from a stranger with dementia."

"Agh... Fuckit," he threw up his long, sinewy arms. "In fact, that's all you need to curse properly. Just say fuck. Or fuckit. Or fuck. I don't care."

"I prefer 'plagues be upon you.'"

"It just doesn't have the same ring, Romes."

"... *Thou art a most notable coward,*" I said, "*an infinite and endless liar, an hourly promise breaker, the owner of no one good quality.*"

"Worthy your lordship's entertainment!" He shook his white-gold hair across his shoulders laughing. "*All's Well,* Act III, Scene VI! I'm up, two to one!"

"Shhhhh," I said. "They'll hear you!"

MK just stood in the river grinning like an idiot. "Only the very best curse like that old woman, Romes. Years of practice." He kissed his fingers.

Then she went off. "SHITeatin' DungHISTIN' COCKsuckin'...," she took a breath and finished with a yell: "...MOTHERfuckin' TIEwhacker!"

"Wow," MK said, "An artist. With a penchant for lumberjack slang. Hey! Down here, we're down here!" MK started waving.

"Shutup!" I moved behind a big rock.

He mouthed "knave" and headed up to the chicken shed. Down the hill floated, "*Ve'achron,* Romes."

"*Alafar yaqum,*" I said without thinking and felt a surge of anger at myself.

Chapter 4

Sorry Jackass

Before we follow MK to the chicken-shed, Dammit, where I met you and my life changed and never went back to the way it was like an egg broke into a hot pan, I should tell what happened in the river. Or should I? I'm not sure it really happened.

From the deepest pool—robed in azuline, translucent as a mayfly—there rose a creature. Its wings were gems, trembling with the colors of dawn. Its body intertwined as if two creatures embraced, gold and silver; its lashing tail and turning body split the air like a knife.

BOOM.

If I'm making it up, I want to make up more. If it's not real, I'd rather not be real. If it *is* real, then everything — all of it, every moment of this whole fucking story, as MK would say — is worth it. This is why I'm talking to you, Dammit. The more I think of it — and let me tell you I've thought a lot — this is for you mostly. But not all of it. Some of this is for me to make sure I'm not mad. What if I am? All I can do is use the best words I know to describe it to you, to give you a semblance in human language of what it said to me. Maybe dogs see things like this all the time. I never have.

Water rose on either side of the winged creature in a silent fall going up against all gravities. The cliffs were a garment ripped by a mighty hand. Rainbows leaped on its face like swords dancing. Yeah, I know, swords dancing, just go with it, Dammit. Like I said, I can't find other words. It folded its wings like gauze, turned its many limbs into its chest, and twisted between water and sky like a cottonwood seed on the wind. In a voice like a multitude's—but also a lion's, and another like that of a sea-falcon—it cried to me.

Ve'achron!

In its mouth was a ravenous red wolf with eyes of fire. Like MK's eyes when he is angered, but black as obsidian and limitless. If that were possible. In the mouth of the wolf was a sword which breathed as if alive. Above the river silhouetted against the tallest ponderosa, they rose and rose, looking down upon me. I stepped towards them. Unable to draw back, drawn like an ember to the swirling heat of the fire. Waters rose to my knees.

I felt my hand rise, as if to say, "here I am." I went to the creature like the river is drawn to the sea. I stepped deeper, felt water rise to my chest.

Child, thy doom and joy, in word and sound
To the powers: it is done, home! Feast arrayed;

The creature's three tails lashed like a pellucid storm-tossed kite. Its voice was singing wind in the canyon, a thousand wildfires.

For blood spilt on earth's sweet, hallowed ground,
Wander no more. Thou a kiss, Our folded blade.

A sound like the thrumming of the wings of wild geese surrounded me. Every cell in my body vibrated. My heart was a wick. I felt a gentle hand light the flame as the winged creature spoke again:

Alas, the cleaving of your heart!

Its eyes were the beginnings of stars and the endings of worlds. I felt a deep sadness—deeper than any black hole—pouring from them, and the sadness was for me. It spoke softly; I was unsure I heard it right.

Everything will be made new.

I trembled like a seedpod on the wind.

We have more for thee, child. Hearing, thou shalt forget. Lest, overcome by sadness, thine heart rend afore time.

I felt my knees crash onto the stones — and I went under. The horror of the water voices was nothing compared to the Mayfly Creature telling me what to remember. I pressed my face into the stones, seeking to hide. I heard rocks clicking, the infinitesimal claws of the stonefly nymphs crawling, the fins of the bull trout touching the sand. I drew in a breath, and the river surged through me like the mouth of a howling red wolf. I fled the water, but a small child stayed. I crawled to the edge, retched, lay in the sand. The circling of the air — like a hand in a pool stirring — was gone.

I vomited water. Beneath the largest ponderosa across the river through my water-filled eyes, as if looking through melted glass, I thought I saw the figure of a man tall, broad-shouldered, with close-cropped hair. How striking he looked with wild eyes and one hand raised as if to wave.

A *crack* like a gunshot came from the yard and I turned and saw the dozer smash through a fence post with you running beside it. I looked back across the river but the dark figure was gone. If I had ever seen it. I reckon I was seeing things; things brought on by breathing too much water and not enough air. I coughed, shook myself like a dog, and trudged up the hill.

By the time I caught up to MK, I almost decided this had not happened. Why do I tell it to you, Dammit? Maybe, the further into this sound and fury of a story I go and the more I change—the more I feel I must try to remember the Mayfly Creature and their words. Words that disappear and flash in my memory like far-off signals at night. I see them in my dreams like the faintest stars. Like gazing sideways at the Pleiades dancing. Have you seen them, Dammit? Have you seen them dancing like maidens in black waters?

"What fuckery is this?" MK turned from peering around the chicken shed.

"I slipped coming out."

The dozer smelt like burnt rubber and screeched between broken fence posts where the old road enters the yard.

"I thought you couldn't go under water?" he said.

The water dripped from my clothes and turned the dust into mud.

"Agh, forget it. Check out this moron."

The man stopped the dozer, two dust devils rose on either side. It was real big; like it could push our biggest boulders into my river. (Only the winged creature could push them out. Or make new ones, Dammit.)

"Craig, you GODDAMN assHOLE get the HELL off my land."

"This ain't your land. Move!"

She put her hands on her hips. Big hands, small hips. "Was my son's land, and NOW it's mine." Her orange T-shirt had a line of sweat down the back. Wisps of white hair curled out of the cap, sticking to her neck.

"I can't see," said MK. "You're in the way, I'm going to the other side."

"Lina." Craig put his hands up like he wanted to stop her from jumping over the front of the dozer. "I GOT to do this. Orders."

"You. Of ALL people. Should KNOW better." She said it like he was an animal that stole something from her, and she had dragged him out of a hole. "Besides me, YOU were the only one knew where George's place was," she said, and spat on the dozer. "Traitor."

Craig had bags under his eyes like he hadn't slept for days. Sweat ran down his face. "They made me. Big Jim told me if I didn't do it..." His voice cracked, and he wiped his face. "Lina, if it's NOT me, it'll be someone else."

The blue hat tipped at the sky. Her boots ground into the dirt and her stance slowly widened.

The dozer *vroomed*. "Get OUT of the way," he yelled.

"SO HELP ME YULL HAVE TO SQUISH ME UNDER THAT GODDAMN MACHINE."

And then you found me, Dammit.

You cocked your head. Fresh fighting cuts on your face, and that nasty open-mouth grin. You were covered in dust from chasing the dozer. You grinned, but it came off like a scowl because of that old scar that runs from chin to ear. Later, you told me about the five-dog fight. How you tore throats and pissed on their carcasses, shaking the blood from your jaws.

I wasn't sure if you were friend or foe. I reckon you didn't either.

"Hey," you said. "Friend or foe?"

"Friend, I guess."

You wagged your tail and the scar on your face pinched your eye and it was like you winked at me. I liked you right away. I could see you liked me too. Sometimes, you just know.

"This is not going to end well," I said, thinking I was talking about the dozer but as I look back on it now, kind of a prophecy.

"No shit, Sherlock," you said, and made me smile. Dad used to say that.

"You gonna bite me?" I asked.

"Nope." You scratched your ear. "Piss on you." Then you proceeded to do that to the chicken shed. It was you taught me how to act cool. Pee on something, look at the sky. Make a joke. Keep your nose up—and ears back.

Craig revved the engine – I learned about this later on, there is a thing by your foot makes the engine go— and between engine revs he would yell at her.

VRROOOOOOOOM.

"Bitch!"

"That ALL you got?" she yelled.

Craig revved the machine every time she tried to speak.

MK came around the corner, and you saw him for the first time, Dammit. Your hair went straight up, your lips pulled back from dripping fangs, and you backed away.

He waved and smiled like old friends, but you backed around the chicken-shed. Come to think of it, it's the only time I ever seen you back away from anything.

Then, everything changed in a moment.

MK jumped like he was snake-bit. His face twisted into a mask of pain. In the crashing and revving of the dozer I thought I heard him say, "*That goddamn asshole.*" He clutched my arm, bent down, wrote something in the dirt, and walked from the shadow of the chicken-shed into the dust-devils and blinding heat of the yard.

Scrawled in the dust was, "*Sorry Jackass.*"

I yelled at MK and jumped after him. Then thought better and came back. Then looked at what he wrote and fell on my knees.

Lina pushed on the front blade of the dozer like she would send it up the hill by sheer force. MK climbed up behind Craig and put those thin arms around him. He leaned down. His long, wavy hair hung over Craig's face, and I couldn't see what he was doing. Maybe saying something in his ear? The engine stopped and silence fell on the yard.

Craig's hands dropped to his lap. Like two animals working together, they crawled up his sides, and started gnawing on his chest. I know, hands don't do that. Craig sat there, under MK's hair, with his hands digging slowly. Like living things. Scratching at the spot where his heart was.

Lina stopped cursing. Her voice was a whisper, but I heard it clearly in the silence. "Craig, goddammit, put your hands down."

Instead, he tore his shirt.

You came to stand beside me, Dammit, your face a grimace of fangs and spittle. Every hair on your shoulders straight up, and a low snarl came from your throat and wouldn't stop.

MK shuddered like he drank from a freezing mountain stream and leapt from the machine. He moved silently. And very, very fast towards the cabin. The only sound was the far-away voice of the river. Then he cursed: "*God-dammit I can't hurt them, Big Jim. They're like family.*" It was his voice, but someone else's sentences. He walked up the steps of the porch, past the dog-eared Riverside sitting on the table between Dad's split-pine chairs and disappeared through the open door into our one-room cabin.

A breeze, smelling of cool river and hot sagebrush, stirred the yard. It felt like a kettle on a fire waiting to explode.

Craig looked into the sky, right at the sun. His hands scratched his chest slowly. His mouth opened like it was too hot.

Lina screamed, a sound I'd heard before only once. I had to shoot a cougar up in the snow because there was no deer, they had all left, it was too cold. I shot it in the face in a tree. It fell out and came at me screaming and I had to shoot it again on the ground just to make it stop.

Craig fell off the dozer into the dust. Red eyes turned directly at the sun streaming tears. Mouth open like it was too hot to close. A fingernail ripped off against his shirt in a smear of blood.

"Craig, what the FUCK you doin?" She pulled his hands down — it took a mighty effort — and knelt on them. Even under her knees, they struggled like twisting snakes.

She looked up and saw me.

Dammit, have you seen the green ledge on the big Salmon River?

Jade-colored water sucks the raft forward in a slick "V." No going back. You hear the roar, but the drop over the green ledge in the distance is so sharp all you see is a line of river—and a blue sky clouded with the chugging wings of a thousand stoneflies. The narrowing "V" is faster than a galloping dog, the roar is a stampeding herd of Aurochs. Under that green ledge is a rock. And then the wave opens over your head like a frothing mouth.

The river moves slow at first — what's that word my Momma used to say? —*inexorable*. Here's what inexorable means, since dog vocab is pretty much riddles and dirty jokes: there's no stopping it and no matter what you do, that slick "V" sucks you in. Over the green ledge and down, down, down.

Chapter 5

Old Women and Dogs

"*Flaming baga,*" she muttered and stood up.

You watched me silent as death. That nasty half-smile, half-open pant, dared me to move. You weren't friendly no more.

Craig's hands crawled up his chest.

"Dammit back off!" Her voice was gravely, and she coughed. Later, I found out it was the smoking. "Who are you?" she said softly.

I backed away but she followed.

"What're you doin' here?" Her skin hung on her like she was getting ready to shuck it off and come out like a river bug.

Her eyes were a pale, pale, blue. Lighter than the sky. There was only one pair of eyes I knew looked like that. King of the Jackasses. I thought about all this faster than she could talk, which was fast. Then you leaned against her, Dammit. You got golden eyes with that liner like you been at a beauty salon. Lovely, and mean. "Pretty as a goddamn butterfly," Granma used to say, "asshole of a skunk—and the heart of a fuckin lion."

I'll never forget how, when you were thinking, your head would cock to one side.

"How long you been standin' there?" she said. "Answer me. You talk?"

Of course, I talk. Just not to you.

"You look like someone I know." Then her eyes widened. "Tall as his granpa, those hands. And them shoulders." She stood there in the sun next to the chicken shed and cried. The wrinkles in her face were coulees. Tears ran down both sides of her nose through the dust and freckles. I wondered — like I was a red-tail flying high above Frank — if the river looked like that. All that water following wrinkled canyons down to the sea.

She grabbed a package from her back pocket, put a stick in her mouth, and lit it with the flame from a small brass box embossed on one side with a double-bladed axe and on the other with fading words, *Coeur De Montagne.* Above the words, an engraved face. You know, Dammit, I never seen a lighter until that moment? I barely remembered what a cigarette was. Sometimes Dad would smoke while we fished. But he was careful with his stash and never let me try it.

"Oh this?" she said, waving the cigarette. "Call 'em cigs." She closed her eyes and sucked in the smoke. "Aaah," opened her eyes, coughed, and spat. Smoke swirled from her nose around her head. "Clayton." Her hand reached to touch mine. "You 'member me?"

I shook my head and stepped back. But the eyes, Dammit. I remembered, then, reaching with little hands, how those eyes laughed at me and twinkled.

"Clayton," she said. "I'm your Granma Lina."

Ants crawled up my foot. The small dark ones that come out in the sun. Each on a mission. If I was ant-size they'd be monsters trying to eat me. I'd be running scared. Their mission: eat Clayton. I stomped on one, heard it pop, then crushed a whole bunch with my heel. She was old and slow. I would run up the coulee into the forest. If her dog chased me, I would hit it with a rock. She grabbed me. She was faster and stronger than she looked. The last time I been touched was my Momma four years ago. When that old woman grabbed me, it felt like I was a lone pine, and the sky touched me with a lightning bolt. I jumped two feet in the air.

"Clayton!" She pointed with her cig, holding on with her other hand like a vice. "Don't you run." She looked like a tired juniper after a bad fire. "Thirteen years been lookin' for you and your folks, lookin' since '86 — folks disappeared RIGHT off the fuckin grid," she said. "Did not know about this place back then." She smoked the cig down to a tiny grub in her fingers watching me like a hawk.

I watched her like a marmot from the rocks.

She said to herself, "Do I say it?" Then she seemed to make up her mind. "Clayton — your folks. Your folks're dead." She threw down the cig and grabbed my arms. "Four years ago, in a car wreck on 101, since I known. They told me it was in flames. I could not go to see." Her face crumpled.

Up on the hill across the river, the sage that was grey yesterday had transformed overnight — I noticed it shining in the sun — into an iridescent green. I wondered if it was *Lamicae* or another kind. Rarely does sage shine like this.

"You hear me?" she said.

I could not meet her burning eyes; I looked up at the hillside.

"I'm all you GOT," she said.

Porter — I used to read him all the time because he was the only other book I had besides The Riverside — says, *"...the aims of plant taxonomy are two-fold: (1) to identify all the kinds of plants; and (2) to arrange plants into classification to show their true relationships."* I reckon you must know what things are before you can figure out how they relate. Or is it that you need to see how they are related, then you can know what they are?

Porter went into the fire — page by page — last winter in the cold time. The ice was on the inside of the windows, and I could not feel my hands. I can't help it; I'm always making lists. Porter called it inventory. Thanks, Porter. I burned you, and here you are, still inside me: *"...even the fully explored and more civilized parts of the globe still present problems in plant identification because the inventory is not complete."*

Problems? Will the problems go away once the inventory is complete?

What did she say about my parents?

"You don't 'member me." A statement. "Your ma an me never got along; she kept you from me. Never stopped by after Pops — your Granpa — died." She sounded defeated. "She thought I was a bad influence."

Did Lina say she was looking for me for thirteen years?

"I *am* a bad influence. But I love you. And now I'm here."

That would mean this is 1999.

She reached out to me again.

This time I let her touch my face. Her hands were calloused and warm.

Craig stumbled around the chicken-shed, his eyes staring at the sun. They were red — bright red — streaming tears. He wrapped his arms in a bear hug around Lina. Craig bent down his head and shoved his open mouth against her ear. His hands, stronger than hands should be, ripped her shirt, clawing at her heart.

You snarled, leaped at Craig's throat, missed, and latched onto his shoulder. Lina yelled, *"DAMMIT!"* All three of you fell backwards.

Craig would not stop ripping at her chest. He was stronger than her, me, and you put together. But slower. I grabbed her and pulled her up, and he started to roll over. You let go of his shoulder and latched onto the side of his face.

"Dammit, get the fuck off!" she yelled, and you let go.

I kicked Craig in the face and kept kicking until he passed out and lay there face-down in the dirt.

"What a goddamn FLAMIN' bag a nuts," said Granma Lina and pulled me away.

Looking back, this is probably when you and me got to be friends, Dammit. And why I'm telling you the whole story so you and me know it from top to bottom and inside-out. I reckon it might be a bad habit — talking to you. But I can't quit. You loved her. So far as you were concerned, anyone who fought for Granma Lina was your best friend, pack mate, and pal.

I figured out pretty quick you were one helluva dog. Which is like a coyote but more loyal, less magic, and dogs like to be scratched until their back leg goes "thump."

"Dammit you fuckin stray!" she yelled. But I could tell she was relieved. "You didn't have to bite him."

You sat panting, with that nasty grin and blood all over your face and cocked your head. *"If a bird does not fly, it goes to bed hungry,"* you said. *"Hargh."* Which came out like a quick snarl, but I could tell was your way of laughing. Turns out, you like a good riddle. It was when you were quiet, I learned to watch out. The quieter, the meaner.

Granma didn't answer you back, and that is the exact moment I figured it out—only I could hear you.

"Foe?" You asked.

I shook my head. Craig was just an old man who lost something. Something real important, I reckon.

"What same thing—dog and tree?"

I shook my head.

"Bark. Hargh."

It took the rest of the afternoon to stop Craig's bleeding, tie his wrestling arms to the dozer, and tell you to watch him while we went to get Granma's truck. She asked me questions non-stop—"Your wet, boy. You fall in the river?" —but I kept quiet.

It was a long walk to the flat area a mile up where a rusty, red pickup with big tires was parked in a patch of fireweed. She had to grab the handle to pull herself up. I couldn't tell where the red ended on the truck and the rust began. It smelled like dog. The seats were ripped, and the floor was littered with crushed cigs.

She jammed a big knobby stick with a grinding sound, and a *"Sonofa!"* curse. She cursed every time the gearstick jammed, or the brakes didn't work (which happened sometimes), or the wipers stuck, or the heater-fan didn't kick in. The radio blared — I jumped. I hadn't heard a radio in years. A man wailed about a gang of robbers waiting in the dark for some guy. Real comforting, Dammit. Sounded like he was one day from dying.

"Tape a Pop's stuck, plays same songs over 'n over. Every one sadder'n an armless carpenter," she said. "This truck belong to my Beaumont, your Dad's Dad, gone a long time."

By the time we got Sonofa down the hill, Craig was clawing through the rope. His eyes turned way up in his head trying to find the sun which had passed over the ridge. Tears streamed down his cut-up purple face. Blood congealed in the bite spots. One loose hand scratched his chest; it was raw and bleeding. You were a foot from his face, waiting for him to get up so you could latch on.

"Tie up his hands, again. Tight but not too tight," Granma said. She leaned her driver seat forward. I pulled and she pushed until Craig was in the back, his head in a corner.

"Get in, let's go."

I shook my head and turned to walk away.

"Goddammit Clayton. *Get yur JACKASS in the truck.*" (That is when I knew she was family, Dammit). "I ain't no monster. I'm family. Get you cleaned up. NEED a haircut." She tugged my hair. It hung down my chest, wavy and darker than my Momma's. She touched the fresh scars that ran across my chest.

"I can take care of these. Got E oil, make 'em better."

The last thing my Momma and Dad said was "stay here, you're safe."

As if she knew what I was thinking, Granma said, "This not the only land in our family, Clayton. Got land in Junction City, Pop's house. Just me an' Dammit there now. Our homeplace." Her voice choked up. "Talk to me," she said.

Something inside me opened like a dying flower and I said, *"There is much music, excellent voice, in this organ; yet cannot you make it speak."*

It was the first thing that came to mind. I read it that morning.

Her eyes shone. "You talk!"

Then I said, *"...I will tarry, the Jack will stay, and let the wise man fly."*

"Talks like a parrot" she said to herself in wonder, "or like he's from somewhere else. Been too damn long. Talking like this to himself."

"Of rivers and the chain-ed canyons free, A winding, restless spirit I will be," I said.

"Sonofa bitch!" she said softly.

I wanted to tell her it wasn't all there was to say, and that MK was here. But I also thought it is better to be silent. When you say things, it's like taking a walk in the forest at night. You have no idea where it will go.

Her shoulders straightened and she reached up and grabbed my shoulder. "Claim you," she said proudly, "Your mine. My boy's boy. That's all there is to say."

I turned and strode to the cabin. My Momma and Dad would come if I stayed.

"You need family. Me." She'd followed me to the porch. "I'm all you got," she said. "I need you too, Clayton. You don't know. Bad stuff going on. I got something of Pop Beaumont's, family axe he gave your Dad, now belongs to you. Best to be with family, not alone."

I went in and tried to close the door, but she had the knob in her hand.

"You not hear me?" Her blue eyes burned. "Your mom 'n dad are D—E—A—D. DEAD. They are NOT coming back. You hear me?"

I slammed the door and threw the deadbolt.

MK sat by the woodstove, his eyes two holes with nothing in them, just what's left after you shoot the gun. *"George was a badass and my guess is like father, like son. I wouldn't knock down their place for a million bucks. Beaumont taught me all I know about logging."* It was MK, but it was Craig's phrasing coming from his mouth. MK's face squirmed, *"With his grandfather's axe in his hands, I know Big Jim, you told me, if he exists, he's a problem."* He squirmed and squeezed his knees. *"What if Rose-Marie finds out?"*

"Finds out what?" I whispered.

Granma banged on the door, "Come ON Clayton, godDAMit open the door."

MK squeezed his knees. *"What IF the boy really is alive? I know that family,"* his voice trembled, *"we should not mess with them, even if there's only one left. O God, they're a mean bunch."* His voice dropped to a moan, *"Except Rose-Marie. She'd never forgive me."* MK got a look on his face like he heard something horrible, *"Leave my boys out of this."* His voice trembled, *"I'll knock down anything you want."*

I shook MK, "A plague upon you! Where is she? Where are they?"

"Who you want to talk to?" His eyes were fiery obsidian. "I got lots of people in here. Lots and lots."

At the back of what seemed like an endless cave, a voiceless multitude wrestled under the sepulchral light of his gaze. The vertigo made me retch.

He grinned, popped his knuckles and was back. *"Call me what instrument you will, though you can fret me, yet you cannot play upon me.*" He rubbed his face. "Name it, Romes," he said, "Extra point for the character."

"I hate you, I HATE you, I wish I never MET you." I yelled.

"Too bad. I'm up 3-2 now."

"What's goin' on, Clayton," Granma yelled. "Open the door!"

"Plague be upon you," said MK with a smirk. "It's starting to grow on me."

I jammed my fists into my closed eyes until I saw flashes against the darkness. What if my Momma and Dad come back and I'm not here? Dad said, "never — don't ever leave." Momma said it too. My chest felt like Craig was ripping out my heart.

And that's when the first waking vision come upon me. Well, a memory, I think, but clear and strong like I was living it all over:

Long ago, me—age five—getting tucked in. "Momma, where are all the people?"

She laughs, "Our homeplace sits on the edge of a big wilderness, Baby Grizz. People call it 'The Frank.'"

Dad grunts. "Nope. 'Frank' is all you need. He's just a dude. He won't eat you alive like the nemesis of our ancestor that creeps in the night, the justice for the murdered ones that eats your heart while you watch. Pops Bergmann — your Granpa — used to call it Das Ungeheuer." Dad's face darkens, he pauses, and I pull the covers up to hide.

"I'm kidding, jackass!" He's laughing. "If anything, 'Frank's' just an A-hole. '*The* Frank' is wild, strange, nasty. Like a monster. Something that comes at you in the night when you ain't lookin'. BOO!"

I jump and squeal, and he laughs so hard he can't breathe. I must have been four, or maybe five.

"Tell me about Pops."

"Some other time," Dad says rubbing his face. "Go to sleep."

He never did tell me, Dammit. He always said, "some other time, Clay."

"Ok, then tell me about The Knave of Wind and Wave. I heard you and Momma talking about him this morning." (When they thought I was outside feeding the chickens.)

Dad's face is grim; he recovers quick. "That's a different R movie, jackass. Our ancestor – one who started the family—destroyed our nemesis, Sengrim."

Momma, from the porch: "*Steer, angry Nemesis, the happy helm.*" (She was always quoting The Riverside, Dammit. Dad called him Shakesbear, though. Got a kick out of it.)

"How many nemesis do we have, Dad?"

"We're their fuckin nemesis." His big hands curl around an invisible handle. "Don't ever forget."

"It's *nemeses*, Baby Grizz." Tonight is Momma's night to read late. The moon is bright, and the sky is clear which is why she's on the porch.

"I wanna be tough like you, Dad." I hug him. "I wanna act fast."

He clenches me tight. "I was like you, once." His breath warms my neck. "You'll meet the family someday and learn to be strong and quick. In the meantime," his pale blue eyes gleam in the shadows, "don't be scared of 'Frank,' he's nothing like Sengrim. Or Das Ungeheuer. All our ancient nemeses are gone and dead. Be thankful. That one's *never* comin' back. It chased our family a thousand years until your Great-Granpa and Pallas sent it to monster-hell."

I shiver and hug him close.

"Who's Pallas?"

"Sleep, son." He pulls the covers up and ignores my question. "Frank's' just trees and rocks and beasts and river. He's wild, but he ain't bad."

I survived next to Frank, wondered about nemeses, read Shakesbear, played the TRG with you-know-who making stupid jokes and disappearing for weeks. Do you know how long four years is when you're waiting? I'll tell you Dammit. It's more like twenty. Being alone—trying not to die—is hard to describe. In the crazy bits, wild animals stalked me, and I stalked them. MK would pop up and scare me clean out of my pants. The real crazy was freezing nights and seeing things. Sometimes you wake up sweating after someone murders your Dad with a long, pale knife. Or you feel Das Ungeheuer in the room with you, but it is a black room you can't escape.

"You have a terrible gift, Baby Grizz, you need to learn how to live with it."

My Momma believed I have a gift, wanted me filled to the brim with stories.

I don't want it. No story-telling for me. I learned to sleep little, do inventories to stay awake, and — when that didn't work — to play all the parts in *Hamlet* to keep away the dreams.

I opened my eyes and saw MK was gone.

You sat by the door; your tongue hanging out the side of your face and that nasty scar-faced grin. You must have snuck in the house before me.

Me and a dog who picks too many fights. I felt like I was drowning, or being stabbed, or both.

"Good woman," you said. "She feeds kids."

I reckon, looking back, that is what helped me decide. A dog with a conscience. A badass, riddle-making dog who thinks he's funny. You're not funny by the way. Just a sonofa bitch with too much attitude like Granma says.

"Piss on you." you said. I could tell you wanted me to come.

My choice to leave the homeplace with Granma was like throwing a bag a hornets into a locked house. Because MK tagged along, and MK got involved. And, slow as I am to take action, I got real mad and I got involved. And all hell broke loose in Junction City.

But you know this, Dammit.

What you don't know is how I got away from Big Jim and that axe coming down on my head. All the way to this storming hillside where I'm telling the story. So, listen.

I unlocked the cabin door. Besides Granma's blue eyes and you, Dammit, what made me decide to go was the thought that my Momma might still be alive. I'm always doing the opposite and getting in trouble. I should a listened to Dad and got in the raft. And I should a stayed at the homeplace no matter what Granma said.

"Poop on you," I said. "How long will it take to get there?"

You sneezed, shook your whole body from front to back which I learned later is how you laugh.

"How high can stone fly?" you asked.

Without waiting for an answer, you said, "It don't. Hargh."

Chapter 6

I Leave The Riverside

I opened the door. In the blue of her eyes a figure in dark fire gleamed like a shadow in the heart of a wave.

Granma Lina reached her big hands around me and pulled me close.

The canyon smelled of cigs and underwater rocks smooth as glass, of stonefly nymphs long as my thumb splitting their skins and launching off the rocks into the haze.

It was at that moment I had my second waking vision, which, best as I can describe it, is like breathing – the in and out of it, Dammit. You feel the breath coming *out* of you. That's you in your body and feelings, right now. And then, like the blow of a hand to your face, you feel the breath go *into* you, invading you. That's the vision of where you been, memories like silver fishing line, and how it lives inside you still.

Dad climbed from the raft to stand next to me on the sand. "Son," he said. "Anything ever happens to me; I don't want vengeance." He ruffled my soaked hair. "Not worth it. Live your life." He changed topics quickly, like usual. Like he asked for salt on his eggs. "Listen. Fear keeps your edge. But Fear's a thief. You let him in, he'll shove you in a trench in your soul, eat you. Put on your skin like a jacket."

He squeezed me in a hug that cracked my back.

"Evil's happy to fuck up shit. It don't need a motive." His face twisted, "It'll come up with some reason, for your own good. Watch for the fruit."

"Dad, how do you keep from being scared?"

His face hardened. "Look Fear in his red eye. Tell 'im, 'go fuck yourself,'" he said.

"George!" My Momma shook her head, frowning.

Dad's hands turned to fists. "You'll know Fear when you face your enemy. But you don't have to show it." He grew impatient. "Long ago we had to change our family name to escape the old country and fit in here; it used to be *Coeur De Montagne*, and "Coeur" means "heart." Where's your heart?"

"Right here, Dad," I rubbed my chest.

"Not bad, Flipper." He grabbed my hand and rubbed the calluses (when I wasn't Jackass, I was Flipper on account of how long they were. My Momma said I would grow into my hands, but I never did, Dammit. Every time I grew bigger, they did too.).

"You'll need hard hands, like knobs on an oak branch, for your Grandfather's axe." Dad squeezed my neck. "I'm bringing *Acuere* back; you're gonna learn how to hear her."

It was the first time he mentioned Pops Bergmann in years. Or his axe.

"How would I listen to an axe?" The only axe I knew was the maul in the woodshed. And my hands were already calloused from all the work splitting rails for the fence line.

Dad ignored me, ruffled my hair. "Woodpile better be HUGE when I get back, Flipper."

When I was learning to split wood, age six, Dad told me he didn't have a double-bladed axe no more. Almost good as a gun in a fight, he said. A double-bladed axe was called a labrys. One blade of the axe was kept sharp enough to shave your face and take down a tree and the other blade slightly dull — better for splitting. "Don't trust cast-steel axe heads, forged is magic," he said, scraping the maul's edge with a file, disapprovingly, as if it would never be as good as his old axe. Which it wasn't.

I asked him how he could tell.

He said, "Easy. Forged shows winding topo lines that prove it's seen fire and water and the hard edge of a file a thousand times. And here," he rubbed the center of the maul's head, "it will have a secret mark made by the smith." He sighed a long sigh, and it sounded like "*Holdfast.*"

"If there is a name," he leaned close, "it is not the name of the maker — as the cast axes made in factories display the stamp of their maker — no, it is the name of the axe, itself, which carries its destiny." His voice changed, deeper, as if reciting from a book. "It takes great skill for any smith to forge a labrys of this nature, greater skill for the smith to inscribe the name, and the greatest skill of all to forge a destiny to the name." He sighed again, as if he couldn't help himself: "*Acuere.*" This time I knew he was speaking a name, felt my forehead tighten and hair rise on my neck.

"What is *Acuere*?" I asked. "How does he do it?"

With a blow, Dad split a round of dry maple. His muscle bunched in a hump over the old break in his shoulder as he lay down the maul, picked up the split and tossed it at my face.

"'Nough questions, Jackass."

"Clayton!" She waved her hand in my face. "Hey! We need daylight to get out!" Granma had the same speech as Dad, like a summer storm spitting hot drops. She pushed me down the steps and into the truck and told you to get in back with Craig.

"Leave him on the blankets, plenty soft," Granma said, started the pickup and turned up the radio. "Gonna be a rough ride."

The singer on the radio sang about pain like a corkscrew in his heart.

The road — or what was left of a road — turned like a corkscrew back and forth across the hill. Every time we got to the top, there was another ridge. We ground over boulders and through washouts. Trees that used to be silhouettes on the ridge — that took me a day to climb to — were outside the window. First, stumpy junipers. Then, dark firs and bronze ponderosas that smelled like vanilla on the heat. Finally, in the high-altitude air, tamaracks with needles so light green and shiny, the trees vibrated. I wondered if Porter saw trees this way, like they were alive, like a person. Like they had legs under the earth and walked nightly. Even sometimes in the day when the sun is a golden rope pulling them? Or did Porter only keep them in a notebook with crimped letters and lines drawn with a straight edge? I reckoned I'd like to talk to Porter someday. I'd tell him I can do both. Like Sonnet 24: "*Eyes this cunning want to grace their art, but don't know the heart.*"

If MK was here he'd make some dumb joke about trees actually being people with gas and rhyme it with "fart." It was right about then I realized I left The Riverside on the porch. I tried to open the truck door.

"No, Clayton — NO!" Granma pulled me back. Sonofa churned over a rock. My head banged off the roof, *chunk!* "Goddammit, George made it hard to get in here," she muttered through her cig. We bucked across what was left of the rock-slide Dad created years ago with an old stick of mining dynamite.

I thought we were going over the edge a hundred times that day, Dammit. I'd imagine I'd feel air for a moment, it would shudder and lean, Granma'd yell "*Sonofa!*" Then we'd be bouncing downhill in a trail of dust between the ponderosas. Loose chunks of metal and glass and people and dog flying into the air. We'd smack into the river like a falcon into a rock. A falcon who can't pull out of a dive. I've seen it, Dammit, and it ain't pretty. The sound is the worst.

We passed a parked truck and trailer. I reckon that's how Craig got the dozer out there. Sonofa clambered onto a ridge of speckled granite. A mantle of beargrass fell from the ridge's shoulders on either side. Every beargrass had a stalk the length of a man's leg with a nipply cream-white flower the size of a small woman's breast (Don't laugh at me, Dammit, that's an MK description. He used to bring it up on the long walk up there hunting in Spring.). The beargrass nipples were almost ready to open.

Burnt trees like matchsticks marched over saddles. The mountain's spine rose before us like the back of a speckled lizard. Snow filled the north-side crevasses on the lizard's back. I never seen the ocean, but my Momma used to say it was waves far as you can see. More and more mountains like waves rolled into the distance in the East. Their jagged crests shone in gold; their troughs rolled in late afternoon darkness.

We'd come a long way from the heat of the canyon. The sweat between my shoulders started to freeze. I shivered and looked into the shadowed coulees below and searched for our homeplace, but it was gone. The meadows, the fences, the cabin, the chicken-shed, the outbuildings, all gone. In the bottom of the canyon, the river was a silver trail. It ran through the mountains like a road. Maybe under them. The man on the radio whined about the sun sinking like a ship.

And it was. Though I never seen a ship, I reckon it's like a raft only bigger. And not filled with smoke because my Granma smokes more cigs than her muttered words. She talked to herself, but I couldn't make out the meaning. The sun dropped over the mountains, sure enough, like a raft going over waves into a whitewater hole.

We stopped a couple times in the dark to fill Sonofa's tank from gas cans in the truck-bed. Long after midnight the truck groaned over a pass, then towards glimmering lights around a dark lake.

"Clayton, I don't mind you don't talk." She blew smoke at the windshield. "Almost home."

"Yep," you said from the back, "Home."

"Junction City," she said. "Not really a city, Clayton. Couple thousand."

"Dogs too," you said.

Granma's smoke must have got out of Sonofa because it was everywhere thick between the trees. Sometimes in the Spring and Fall, my river does that, and mist comes off the water. Sonofa's headlights hit a mirror two feet in front of the truck, bounced back and blinded us. Mist beaded our windows and ran in streams. Sonofa slid sideways and almost went off the icy road.

"Goddamn fog!" Granma switched the lights to low and cranked up the heater which squealed and then settled down to a soft grind. We crept into Junction City with Craig's fingers scratching like rats and Granma peering over the steering wheel, cursing "*Sonofa!*" every time the wheels slid.

A smell like unwashed body entered the truck. Like something good gone rotten. Two summers ago, I waited all Spring for the peach tree to fruit and I couldn't wait no more and picked a fuzzy peach and cut it open. Inside was a mash of writhing caterpillars. They were full on the pith and threads of shit curled from their black bodies.

"Stinkin' all Spring," said Granma. "Like summer's never gonna come." The red tip of her cig lit her face. Dirty snow under streetlamps lay piled in parking lots and driveways melting in streams that looked dark as blood. A breeze blew a clearing in the fog. I heard the voice like the cry of a hawk.

"Jackass. Took you long enough to get out."

He stood under a streetlamp. The slumped shoulder gave him away. Because of the clearing in the fog, I saw him coming for a while. You growled and Granma said, "shutup Dammit." She did not see or hear him.

As we drew near, close enough to see the lightness of his eyes he raised his hand, and said it clearly in that rusty voice, *"Jackass! Save your mother. Avenge me. Stabbed in the back."* Then his eyes bulged, his lips pulled back in a grimace. *"Look for the silver sword and the man with the shining eyes. And the whisperer. Finish this."* He raised his big hand towards me as we passed, close enough I could have touched him if the window was down. *"A tale of vengeance,"* he whispered, *"Vengeance and death."* The shade of my father stepped backwards. *"And blood. A lot of fucking blood."*

Then, he was gone in the fog.

Craig's hands thumped like rabbits in a snare. The man on the radio wailed about getting somewhere called Kansas before the snow thaws, and I swear in that moment all I wanted to do was go there. How can I feel two things at the same time? It's like a rattler bit me. Then, bit me again. I knew I would never see my father alive.

"Ya hungry?" Granma patted me on the shoulder. "Almost home. First, get Craig to E.R." Granma pointed at a massive house with her cig. "They run everything," she almost drove off the road pointing. "'Goddammit! 'Cept us poor folk. Cleanin' condos. Wipin' asses."

Rankness filled the truck, and I rolled my window down.

She spat past me out the window, a rocket-of-a-hawk that disappeared into the fog. "Fuckin richers." Granma didn't seem to mind the unwashed body smell.

Or notice the soft, childlike voice outside my window: *"Mmm."*

She just kept talking, but her voice faded into the mist around my head.

I saw a hand like that of a baby, but maggot-white, crawl slowly over the edge of my door, one finger at a time. Long, long fingernails. Too long for any child's. I realized the hand pulled at the edge of a window—inside me. It was a warm, pleasant voice, vibrating every vein in my body. Meaner than anything I ever heard, yet kind as a friend, a low whisper:

"Welcome, boy. Mmm. You will let me in."

We pulled up to a stoplight and the hand pulled away. The rotting smell cleared, the cool fragrance of Spring in the mountains flowed into the cab like a river and the man on the radio wailed about standing in a doorway. After listening to him all night his strange voice had worn a groove in my brain. Like when someone tells you the truth.

Scritch Scritch. Craig's fingernails ripped at the seat.

I was a stone clasped in some unseen hand dangled in this river of fog.

Granma had not seen Dad and that was weird. (He was a ghost, not everyone sees ghosts. Or talks to dogs. Except me, I reckon. And besides avenging Dad, I would have to find my Momma and save her. Save her? How would I *find* her?) Granma had also not heard the whisperer. Then I realized there was someone else Granma could not see or hear.

Swish, swish. The mist-river closes around me. *Just drop me. Let me go home.*

Granma had not asked about MK. It was like she could not see him at all.

Chapter 7

Weirdos

Dad says people are assholes or weirdos. If you got to choose — be a weirdo.

I reckon, some dogs are assholes. Act friendly, then latch onto your face and don't let go. Bad dogs. Some are the very best kind of bad dog. That's you. *The sourest natured dog that lives.* Living wild like a hobo for nothing but the truth. A weirdo who enjoys pissing on car tires in public, but also a good lie in the sun. Which is why I'm telling you, Dammit. The only way to untangle my heart.

Please remember this: Granma don't listen, and the kids in town don't care. We got nothing to talk about. I don't know TV and movies and clothes. They don't know Shakesbear and survival and being alone. We are from different planets. What do they know about the hurt? If I talk to you, what does it matter? I have learned people are ashamed of who we are. We talk and talk, weaving fake clothes with words of nothing. Everyone likes the sound of their own voice. No one listens. *By our ears our hearts oft tainted be.* Why should I talk, it only makes it worse?

I seen what we do with words, and it is gross. Like cleaning a shit-stained floor with a dirty rag.

I would dare them to know me — there is a lot to know, but probably not much to like — but I reckon they're afraid. And not just because I don't look like them or think like them. They sense something. Who wants to get inside the head of a weirdo?

Let Hercules himself do what he may, the cat will mew and the dog will have his day.

You like me and that is all I need.

We got sucked over that wild green edge. Down — way down — into the whitewater churn of someone else's story. I hear them crazy voices and I cannot get out.

Chapter 8

Perchance to Dream

After you and Granma tucked me in and went to sleep in the other bedroom, I lay watching the long axe in the corner watching me. It was a waiting person, full of moon-shadows, a labrys razor-edged on one blade, dull on the other, with letters inscribed in a flowing script by some lost art. The name Dad spoke in a whisper years ago: *Acuere.*

"Hold fast," she said.

So, I did. The handle snapped into my hands like a magnet. *A great perturbation in nature, to receive at once the benefit of sleep and do the effects of watching.*

In the dream, Dammit, I had no axe, and couldn't feel my fingers in Dad's leather work gloves. The snow was crusty. No new snow had fallen in weeks. I watched my breath come out of my mouth in clouds. My hands were shoved as far into my armpits as I could shove them. My stomach twisted like a rabbit in a snare.

"'Tis the cold, damnable cold that makes us men," whispered MK, just to make conversation. We whisper when we hunt so we don't scare the animals away.

"Guess that one." He wasn't wearing anything, the bastard. Jeans like usual and no shirt.

I frowned. "I got nothing. Why aren't you cold?"

"All in your mind." He chuckled, perched on the branch above me, long hair swinging.

"I can't feel my feet, or my hands."

He cracked his knuckles one by one. "C'mon, guess. '*Tis the damnable cold* — you know this."

"No idea."

He covered his mouth, laughing, trying to be quiet in the woods. "I made it up."

I started to smile. I couldn't help it.

"Got you good," he said, picking the frozen bark from the pine and throwing it down at me.

"Plague upon you."

"If Clayton did it with a potato, what would they call the baby?"

"That's gross."

"Hesitater. Get it? Hesi-Tater. Like you, thinking too much. And freezing. The Hesitater."

He is not *that* funny, Dammit, but he is all the funny I got.

"I am freezing," I said.

We sat there, quiet, a long time.

Acuere cut my finger. Pain flashed, and I woke to see a drop of blood squeeze from a paper-thin cut. I will never forget how it felt. Not the cut, which was shallow and burned like fire. Something deeper: like I was being taught a lesson, told to remember who I was, and asked to *do better* all at once. I imagined Pop's hands on the handle, and Dad's hands. And put her back.

"Hold fast," she said.

I sucked my finger, closed my eyes, and let sleep fall.

I felt the rough tree behind my back. Heard MK chuckle. I was back in the dream; this time the snow blew sideways in gusts like being slapped over and over. It melts and drips down your neck. I shoved my hands in my armpits and started to think on my usual thought — hiking out.

The salmon had come in ragged numbers as if they had forgotten how to return. No deer or elk — they all decided to move somewhere else. Nothing on the trap lines. Thinking of fried venison and eggs made the dying rabbit in my stomach start scratching its way out.

"*When we both lay in the field,*" I whispered, "*frozen almost to death, how he did lap me even in his garments and did give himself, all thin and naked to the numb-cold night?*"

"Richard," said MK with a grin. "K-Pow! 1-0. *When blood is nipped, and ways be foul, then nightly sings the staring owl, tu-who; tu-whit, tu-who.*" He paused, then said in his most ghostly voice, "*a merry note.*"

I ignored him and turned away to look uphill through the pines. It was "Love's Labor's Lost," but I was tired of playing the game.

"Times up," he said. "2-0, me."

I saw myself crossing the ridge, and I knew—because I'd been to the top a few times—when I crossed that ridge there would be another one. After that, spires of rock and screes, ridge after ridge. Waves of bone, cold rock rising on and on and on into the wilderness. I knew then I had only enough in my legs to get down the hill to the cabin and roll up, freezing, under the blankets. I would ball my hands between my legs and wait for the hunger to finish me. The rabbit in my stomach would gnaw its way out.

"C'mon, I'm bored," MK groaned, "tell a story about the cougar we're waiting to kill. Pass the time."

"I will if you shut up."

"Cougars aren't that smart. This one's starving worse than you. You're skin and bones, with skin being the majority. What you do to it — pulling the trigger — will be merciful."

"I don't know about that," I said. But I was hungry, and the last dried salmon ran out two weeks ago. Actually, salmon skin. I started to think about salt, what it tasted like on meat, and spit filled my mouth.

"Have you the lion's part written?" he said. *"Pray you, if it be, give it me, for I am slow of study."*

"Easy. 'Midsummer Nights,'" I said.

*"*Heh, did you get what I did with lion?" MK chuckled. *"Do it extempore, its nothing but roaring."*

"An you should do it terribly," I grinned. *"You would fright the duchess and the ladies that they would shriek. And that were enough to hang us all."*

"Yep," he agreed, *"that would hang us, every mothers son."*

The TRG was fun but sometimes we were too good at it. So, I told the cougar story. It was better than listening to him butcher Shakesbear. "A cougar was going there. But when he arrived at his perch where the trees come together and the wind is high and quiet and far away, he found a bear curled in the roots of the tree, sleeping. And the cougar knew the smell had scared away every deer for miles."

"Good! Only, more action," He popped his knuckles and leaned forward.

I told the story, and it *was* a good one — as if I already knew it, even though it was brand spanking-new. For a moment we forgot the cold and the hunger, rode the cougar's back from one escapade to another. A lonely, badass cougar looking for a badass cougar family and finding none. Fighting bears (a great bear-paw swipe nearly killed him), picking off baby wolf cubs, getting in scraps with other cougars — just for shits and giggles like Dad used to say — getting into all kinds of dustups. Until he grew tired and came slumping over the hill above us. Starving, tired and alone.

"There. Hear it?" MK whispered. "I knew you could do it Romes."

A crack in the woods. Anything that walked on the snow right now would make noise. Curtains of snow wavered in the last light of a winter sun already gone.

The trigger lay under my finger. I was too cold to feel the steel. It was as if a lead blanket pressed me to the ground. Then I saw it. The cat was a big male and so alone. I knew the aloneness it carried because everything changed. The woods got quiet, and I felt like I feel when MK is gone, and even the air feels heavy enough to crush me like an ant. Except ants are never alone, they always have other ants. On the cougar's chest, three unhealed deep scars ran diagonally like dark zippers. MK was right, pulling the trigger would be doing it a favor. But not in the way he meant. Pulling the trigger would just take away that alone-hurt that runs so deep you can't scratch it out.

The big cat walked down the hill, looking left and right, sadder and more silent than anything I'd ever seen before, even me. Then he saw me. He stopped. I could tell he hadn't figured out if I was real or not.

I didn't know if he was, either.

He lifted his head and sniffed the air. His eyes were larger than I expected, light brown like honey. He moved quickly, but with a hitch in his gait that had to be from the open scars.

The bear fight!

I stopped breathing. The air drifted down the mountain towards me so the cougar could not smell me. Snow moved and shifted in the twilight between the trees. It was right about then I wished I had not made the cougar such a badass in my story.

"*A very little, little let us do and all is done,*" said MK in my ear. It was Henry V, of course. I pretended not to hear.

I lifted the gun to my shoulder and the cougar saw me, jumped six feet in the air, and climbed a low branch on a ponderosa. It crouched there, hissing. A low, deep mewling that made the hair on my neck stand straight.

I had two choices. I could try to get closer, or just take the shot and hope the aim was good and the buckshot was enough. The third choice was even stronger. Let him go.

I hesitated, and MK whispered, "I'm gonna stop calling you Romes. Always considering every option, WAY too slow. Hams the Hesitater. Just pull the trigger, goddammit. Kill it, Hams, you only have one chance, kill it, pull the trigger Hams, kill it, kill it."

I found the cat in the sights and pulled the cold trigger.

Felt the gun pound my shoulder, heard the thunder and watched him fall. He screamed like a woman stabbed in the stomach and there was blood on the snow. He pushed himself onto his front paws and jumped, faster than anything I'd ever seen. Before I could pump the shotgun, I was on my back. His face snarled against mine, blocked by the gun.

I felt claws ripping across my jacket, through my skin and the bones of my chest. His hot jaws spat blood from the other side of the gun barrel, the only thing keeping him from my throat.

I was way too slow.

He knocked the gun away, bit my face, and killed me. I choked on the blood coming down my throat. I screamed, knowing I was dead, and woke myself with a rattling gasp, my blanket soaked with sweat. There in the extra room in Granma's house, I remembered what really happened:

I slipped in the snow, fell on my face, and banged my chin on the shotgun. I rolled over in the snow, pumped a fresh shell into the barrel, and sat up with my legs sticking out in front of me.

For a moment he crouched where he fell, looking lost like a house cat. He looked around through the blood in his honey eyes, crying. Searching for his momma. I had something in my eyes that felt like I was looking through the river at him. So I wiped my eyes with my left hand. When my hand dropped, there he was — coming through the air at me.

I shot him in the face from three feet away. One moment his face was there and the next there was a mist of red and he slumped at my feet. Blood pumped from a gaping wound in his neck. Most of his head was gone.

I slit his abdomen with my hunting knife and put my hands in his red, steaming belly until they warmed. It wasn't until I thanked him for his life like Dad showed me — Dad would place his hand on the head of the animal, looking up — that I realized I was crying. There was no head for me to place my hands upon. Tears and snot covered my face, fell on my hands and the entrails. Was I crying for my own wounds across my chest that burned and bled? His aloneness? How easy it was to pull the trigger? Or something I could not say.

I did what Dad taught me. I leaned over the body with my hands in his warm gut. My face pressed into his wet and bleeding shoulder, and I blessed him. Under the blood, I smelled the snow and the sap of the tree-limb he had climbed.

"Thank you for your gift, that we may live."

His claws were as long as my thumb. Some held shreds of my flesh.

"Come to us brother, make your home with us. When all things are made new. We shall meet on the great plateau beside the river under the healing tree."

MK was gone, that bastard. He really does hate blood. I didn't see him for days.

The house was so quiet I could hear you and Granma snoring back and forth through the walls like a two-man pull saw. I couldn't help it, Dammit. After rolling around some, I picked *Acuere* up again. Felt her cold iron press against the hot scars across my chest.

And fell into the darkness of vision, a black snake of static charge that squeezed around me and crushed my chest. Five miles away, a pale hand like a fat baby opened a door. A hand with too-long nails. *Click click.* On the lintel of the door. Then, it was there in a rush, at my feet, crawling up my leg.

A small nail tapped my chest. *Click click.*

"Ahhhh. You have finally come." A high voice like a child's, quiet, sweet.

I smelled breath like mud and rotten bodies, the bottom of a swamp.

"Open. Let me in," the child-like voice asked softly.

"No!" I whispered.

"Oh, you will." It was very happy, very soft. "Give it. Mine. Your grandfather's axe. Bring it."

Was it me wishing, or did I feel a shiver through *Acuere's* handle and up my arms? My chest burned, and my mouth opened like some other person's: "Go eff yourself."

Indrawn breath. Wheezing. Soft little fingers. *Click click.* "Boyyyyyy. You just started a war. I will take everything from you. You will see, you will bring it to me."

I shuddered, it crawled on my chest, and I turned my face before I could see its face.

"Who's there?" It said.

"Ve'achron," said a dry sarcastic voice.

The axe blazed, a shock-wave. My chest burned like fire; the creature slammed against the darkness. Blinding flames shoved it through the aperture from which it crawled, slammed the door shut five miles away. I heard its fingernails scrape on the lintel *click click* before the door closed with a snap. A fresh wind blew the hair from my face, drying my tears. I smelled a familiar scent, the smell after the lightning has come.

I clutched *Acuere* to my chest, hot as steel in the sun, rolled over, and – as is my practice when I cannot breathe or think straight from the night terrors—started Sonnet 102 in my head, with *"My love is strengthn'ed, though more weak in seeming,"* and by the time I reached somewhere close to Sonnet 146, *"Poor soul, the centre..."* I entered the realm of sleep, leaving the realm of visions with its dread far behind.

She called me in a language I did not know, nor did I know her. But somehow, I understood her. It was a tug low behind my wuttus. She had a name that no one could say because she would not let them say it.

I went to her across a meadow carpeted with flowers — *Gentiana detonsa,* the wild violets that clamber high places, under the peaks near green estuaries fed by snow — I ran to her down a steep bank to a dark pool. Found her lying on a bed of white waterlilies, surrounded by swans. The fragrance of the lilies was a mist, it surrounded me, and I fell to my knees. She laughed, bade me rise, and — though I did not know how — she held me against her wild chest like a gosling.

She told me it was not personal. When she sent the dozer, she was unaware I was there and that I would bring her the axe and serve her because I owed a debt for my father's disobedience.

I said of course: my axe, and all I have is yours.

She smiled, and touched my face, and I knew I would scourge the earth for her if she asked me to. She laughed at me and said We are already in hell in this godforsaken town where She was banished so it didn't matter. But if I wanted to help Her get out, I would do as She said. She would call me, and when She called me, I must come. She said, if I would come to Her, and follow Her, She would give me one true love to last my life.

"You are my one true love," I said, and She laughed. It was the sound of the waves and the gulls and beneath the waves the sound of fanged creatures. She put me on the back of the largest swan, and it rose from the pool where She disappeared — skin like fresh cream — under black waters.

I wanted nothing but to lie with Her, that chest, that wild and white-fragrant bed of undulating lilies. But the white-feathered back of the swan rose inexorably.

I woke to *Acuere* on my chest — red-hot, smoking — burning a hole through my shirt. I threw her on the floor and twisted the bed covers, panting like a dog in the sun.

"Hold fast," she said.

I feared I would never see the Swan Lady again.

I swore, "If She calls, you will go."

I finally slept, and I wished I had not. I know this dream. I try to hold it back when I feel it coming, that sour taste in the mouth.

When It wants to visit, It wants to visit.

I could smell the cesspool rising in the corner of the room, a dark and festering hole. It always comes from the water. I could not see the thing. But you know how dreams work, Dammit. I could see IT.

A creature of the darkest waters — no, a terror, blacker than the blackest night — of dragging, stinking, yak-hair and spider legs with a mouth like a cave with swords in it. And a back end like a shag carpet covered in filth and crawling with maggots and ticks. It had no eyes, or nose. But it did not need them to see me or smell me. It spoke to me, and the sound was like a woman being attacked by apes.

"*If thou givesssst me thy heart to eat,*" it said, "*thine enemy I shall conssssume.*"

It wanted to talk to me more. I stuck my fingers in my ears. It came at me backwards and the carpet of filth crawled slowly up my face. I woke with a muffled scream and fell on the floor scrabbling to find *Acuere*, which I clasped — cold as ice — again to my chest.

I lay there crying and hoping Granma would not hear me. I lay there for a long time trying NOT to fall asleep.

You scratch at the door, Dammit, but I am stuck in some dark place and cannot return to let you in.

I am not sure what happened next is a dream or what my Momma calls "the visions." But I saw it so clearly, Dammit, it was as if I was wide awake and in my right mind.

Dad ran around a corner as if pursued, stumbled, and leaned his broken shoulder against a fence, his face shrouded like a cloud, his eyes sparking blue. I felt a pang shoot through me, all these years in the cabin I had dreamed of him and seen his face slowly disappear as I forgot it. Now he was here. More real than ever. I knew that face even though it swirled behind curtains I could not pierce. But his eyes pierced it.

Dad held a foot-long file — like those used to put an edge on an axe — in front of him like it was a knife. I watched him falter and look around wildly. Then his face changed, went slack. He looked up at the sun, dropped the file to the ground and clawed at his chest. Behind him on the other side of the fence I saw a shadow rise. Wide and tall as a bear, with many-mirrored eyes you see underwater on some insect.

The fence exploded. A thin sword pierced Dad's chest from behind like a licking silver tongue. He cried a great cry and fell.

I gasp in the cold. I feel morning coming but all is dark; the moon is gone. My chest feels like a hand squeezes it, closing tighter and tighter. I cannot breathe. *Acuere* is no help. She no longer speaks.

You scratch the door, whine, and this time I rise. I let you in. Granma snores through it all.

You enter silently and jump on the bed, lick my face, snuggle up under my arm and lay your head on my scarred chest. I touch your own scar, the one that writhes across your face and through your ear, and you lean into me. Your heavy head is musky, warm, like an animal in a cave. Your scar a knotted rope.

You breathe slowly through your nose. The sound of your exhale matches the drop of your deep chest. Slower and slower. Warm as a wood-fired stove.

I feel my breathing ease.

Sometimes, the snuffle of a dog falling asleep — well, you know, Dammit — it is the sound of the whole world getting better.

Chapter 9

The True Topography of the Heart

Inventory:

One light switch in the hospital room, flick it on and off, wow. Did that thirty-four times until Granma made me stop. Speaking of which:

Granma made me take off my shirt after I growled at the nurse. So here I am, half naked doing inventory. Porter would be proud. Morning Inventory, Dammit. That's how I start every day at the homeplace. After inventory — Shakesbear. But always, first, Morning Inventory so I don't panic.

One boiled egg from Granma's cold fridge. In my pocket. For later. I miss eggs. So much food here, Dammit.

One dog who likes me. I like him too. That's you, Dammit.

One Granma — aged-crone, harpy-like, wild as the furies and warm as a quilt. I like her.

One furnace came on this morning, banging. Warmth from a hole in the floor. I laid on it.

One warm boy. Clayton Solomon Stonefly Bergmann.

Too many dreams to inventory. *Dream on, dream on, of bloody deeds and death.*

Inventory done.

Last night Granma touched one of the framed black-and-white photos of Pops holding *Acuere* in his big hands, head of thick silver hair, and a thin mean smile like Dad, and she said, "There you are, Beaumont. Look. I brung him home."

This morning, she came in and saw the axe on the floor. "What the hell I tell you, Clayton? That thing is dangerous. It is NOT what you think. I don't got time to tell you. We're late, breakfast on the table, let's go."

"Hold fast," the axe said.

You jumped off the bed and I picked up *Acuere*, felt the weathered ash handle click into my hand. The double-bladed head was flat and mean as a big rattler.

Granma pulled her blue cap over her eyes. "They left me a note yesterday. Summons about my house. That's why I didn't talk on the way home. All goin' ta shit."

I reckoned something was wrong. She could've told me about our family last night, but just smoked and muttered.

"I GOT to get you to Doc, make sure you're OK."

She grabbed the axe from me, leaned it blade down in the corner. "Now there you go, *Acuere*, don't mind him. He's your own blood." She turned to me. "You don't know nothin'. Story so long I don't know where to start." She ran her hand through her curls and across her sweating face. "Why in God's green earth — we're not even to June — does it feel like it's gonna be one a THOSE days?" She hmphed and tugged on her cap. "A dog day."

"Every day is dog day," you said, and went outside to pee.

"Hold fast."

"You looked like your Dad just then," said Granma, her face twisted.

All I could see of Dad was his broken face last night. It was his broad hands, the twist of his shoulder and pale eyes told me it was him. Someone killed him then stomped his face in pure spite.

The windowless hospital room smelled like soap and sores. It smells nothing like where I am from, Dammit. Later that day I learned schools smell even worse if that could be possible.

"He can talk, Doc, he just don't like to," Granma Lina said to a man in jeans and a green shirt who stood at the open door. I could tell she trusted him.

"I am not understanding you, Lina," Doc Ranulf said. He had a thick accent. Later that day Granma told me Doc lost his family or left his family. She wasn't sure, it was all rumors. He smelled like soap, and the rotten smell of sick things. Under a nose like a granite outcropping, his jaw pulled the edges of his mouth down, so he never looked happy.

"Funny talk too. Old timey, when he do it," Granma said.

"When nurses said you were here with your wild grandson, they trying not to smile," he said, entering the room. "Young man, these scars how you get them?"

"Craig OK?" asked Granma. "How's his heart?"

"I am not sure. Many things go wrong with the heart, eh?" Doc rubbed his long nose. "The heart is simply this: A pump the size of your fist...." He clenched his fist into a knot, and it was a very large fist. "... A pump, resting at the center of circulatory system, moving the blood through a network of vessels."

He looked through the wall to somewhere far away.

"As you know, the true topography of the heart is vast, wrinkled with rivers and layered mountains. It is a most dangerous country. Those who venture there must be foolish, unafraid, or...." He shook himself, seemed to realize he was speaking out loud, but continued. ".... Or willing to suffer the trials of loss and grief far beyond any hope of return. The nurses are getting Craig ready for the med-vac to Boise. Soon he will go." He reached out and touched my scar.

I growled.

"NO Clayton," said Granma. "NO! Sit still. Remember I told you before we got here, sit still. Let him do his thing."

"I am not afraid of him," Doc seemed to return to from a faraway place. His lips drew back in a ghastly smile, then he wrinkled his long nose. "You are still eh, in the smoking, Lina?" He sounded disappointed.

"Yeah," she said. "Down some."

"Two packs per day is not down some," He said. "You need to quit."

"No shit Sherlock." She rolled her eyes at me behind his back. "Quit tomorrow."

He probed my stomach gently with his long fingers. "How long was he there?"

"More'n three years, Doc. Maybe four." She sounded worried. "His parents, my son George and Rose-Marie, left him only I didn't know they left him when they did because we wasn't on speakin' terms at that time, and I heard last month they died in Portland, so O & S said their property belonged to the corporation because of the foreclosure and all that bullshit. So, I went up to their place to stop Craig from tearing it down."

He made me get up and walk around in the room. "Anyone on his own this long displays certain trauma-associative disorders, eh how you say, issues, it is common," he said. "We do not see people like this anymore." He held my wrists in his hands, looking at me, "If the silence is the only presenting symptom from the solitude — all these years of being alone — you should be grateful. There are much worse things than this."

"He was talkin' to himself an' he locked the cabin door," she said. "I KNOW he can talk," she said fiercely. "Said somethin' to me, only can't remember, it was old timey, King James."

He stretched my hair in his hands and sniffed it.

Granma raised her eyebrows at me behind his back.

"The old medical journals," said Doc, "they speak of these Jeremiah Johnsons, the trappers, the mountain men. Two hundred years ago, they come in after the winter, and you find the hair growing through the underwear."

I didn't know what he was talking about. I cleaned myself most days, it was something my Momma drilled into me. "Cleanliness is readiness," she used to say.

"He OK?"

"He is not OK but... that is OK," he said, and he spoke quickly, in bursts, with pauses between each phrase. "The scars under the scars," he whispered. "*Die narben unter den narben.*"

"Do these hurt?" he asked, touching my scars. "How did you get them?"

I remembered last night, and the dream of the cougar and I started to shake.

"Do you have bad dreams?" he asked me, eyes glinting.

I looked away. Yes. Bad dreams. Very bad dreams.

"In these dreams, sometimes do you see the kin-hunter *Das Ungeheuer* — the terror? First it speaks with you, it seeks the heart of the guilty... then it eats you?"

"Doc!" Granma smacked him with her cap. "You cannot scare this boy like that!" She patted my arm and squeezed my shoulder.

How did he know? I managed to shrug my shoulders and look like I did not understand him.

"Never mind, never mind. A stupid, er, *unvernünftig* question," he said, still looking deep into my eyes. "Fight or flight or freeze," he said as if that closed the current topic.

"Least he didn't starve to death," she said, fiddling with her cap.

"This is true. He is skeletal, also eh — how you say?—lanky, but he seems physically healthy. But Lina," he paused. "Lina, the starvation comes in many forms." He wrote something on a piece of paper. "Get the blood work done. I want to look at the levels." He held up his hand, like he wanted to shake mine.

I took his hand and shook it. Dad taught me that.

He held on and kept looking at me in the eyes. His were brown pools. Like a wolf, I couldn't shake the feeling. A wolf that seemed about to cry any moment. No reflection there, except for hunger and sadness.

"You should not be afraid," he said to me directly, "of being slow to act. When we lose those we love, we may fall in love with losing." His deep voice cracked. "And this is the slowing."

I did not understand the words, but I understood the sound.

"You should expect eh, the development, to be frozen, in more than one way," He said to Granma.

"He's sharp as Pop's axe, I know it," said Granma.

"I have no doubt he is sharp, he survived alone four years. It's not about smart, it's about the development. You will need to be, eh, patient with the behavior, some of it will be very strange."

She pointed at me, "Say your old-timey talk. Strange but not stupid," she said to Doc.

"Everyone develops at different speed," said Doc. "When the trauma, you know, that which hurts us on the outside, or on the inside, when this happens, it can — how you say it? *frieren* — freeze our development. Not all over, or always. This freezing happens in spots." He paused and let go of my hand and started sniffing the air. "This takes time to warm up. You need the right conditions."

"Didn't freeze him, you know, down there?" She sounded alarmed.

He laughed, cold, like someone hiding in the snow in the dark. "No, Lina, he is fine in this area. You get the blood work done and we will know more. Physically, he seems like normal boy minus the fat. Your son was tall?"

"Nope, George takes — I mean, he took — to my husband's side, all them stocky and strong as a mustang, 'cept for Beaumont. Clay's lanky like his Granpa—my husband. Rose-Marie, she come from slim folk too, so he might take to her. Got his ma's eyes."

"Nez Perce?" he asked.

"No. The isles a Scotland. Smart and pretty. Went to college in England after George met her. Why he stayed away so long. Hmphh. Her and me never see eye to eye."

"The physical development seems fine," said Doc. "It is the psycho-social development, the stuff in his head. It takes time."

"Let's go Clayton."

"Wait, Lina. You must see the developmental specialist in Boise for kids like this."

"NO fuckin kid like this, Doc."

He scribbled on another piece of paper. "For his sake. Please see this woman."

"Nothin' little love can't fix," she hooked a finger in my belt loop and pulled me out the door.

I saw a sharp tool on the counter by the door, like a handle with a little knife on the end. I grabbed it and put it in my pocket. I don't think Doc saw me because he didn't say anything and I'm quick.

There was a sound like a tree-branch shattering. A woman screamed. Two nurses ran from the next room with blood on their hands and faces white as the floor. The bloodiest nurse — her whole uniform soaked — walked slowly towards us.

"Doc-doctor Ranulf? Ohmygod."

"What is it, Amy?" His mouth opened, his tongue long and rough.

I smelled it too. It was the blood.

"He got loose." Her voice trembled. "The buckles on the straps, they didn't hold." She said again like she was in a trance: "He got loose."

"What is this?"

"We gave Craig the max dose of the sedative. It looked like he was going under. We left the room to get the transfer paperwork. Ohmygod. We thought we'd get the extra straps because he's so strong – slow but strong. We gave the max dose, we were only out of the room for 20 seconds, maybe 30 at the most, but when we came back... Ohmygod." She rubbed her hands together and the blood on her gloves made a sucking sound.

"What happened to Craig?" His voice was so soft, I almost couldn't hear him.

"He... he was loose. Sitting up. His hands were free." She whispered, "The max dose, we gave him the max dose."

"We tried to restrain him. He's so strong," said the other nurse.

"We pulled on his hands, we tried," said Amy. Her hands rubbed one another over and over, ripping the blue gloves, her eyes looked through the wall at something that was not there. It reminded me of Lady Macbeth rubbing and rubbing, except this woman had real blood dripping from her hands, soaking her blouse.

"Lord have mercy," Granma said. "Good Lord, have mercy."

"He shoved his hand into his chest, ohmygod. He cracked the ribcage, ohmygod the sound."

Then I heard the sound. Like someone ripped the wall apart in the next room.

I turned and saw Craig through the open door on the bed. He was not done. His streaming eyes gazed through the ceiling at a hidden burning sun. His hand plunged into his chest, blindly feeling his organs one by one. The other hand grasped a slab of his ribs and held it open.

The blind hand felt for something. It moved slowly, pushing deep between the broken ribs. His chest made a sucking sound. His bicep tensed as if it would tear from his shoulder and Craig ripped out his heart.

His mouth gave a shuddering "*guuuughh*," and the heart came out in his hand — jerking and splattering from his chest, veins like shorn ropes quivering and dripping red across the floor and the white sheets. His eyes became calm like the pool of blood on the floor. The hallway smelled thick of blood. Metallic and tingly. The smell when you gut a deer.

Chapter 10

The Smile of Achilles

Granma cried silently as Sonofa threw gravel across the hospital parking lot. "Sweet Jesus. Why Craig? Flamin bag a nuts." She pointed her cig at me. "He was a GOOD man workin for BAD people, Clayton. That's all." She muttered to herself, "What is WRONG with this fuckin world?" She shifted in a crash of gears, "Clayton, law's gonna get involved." She started to sing in a husky voice,

"Hurt can't hurt my heart always.
Under skin and silver star..."

You howled like a pack of coyotes. Your tongue flapped in the wind. Granma Lina lit another cig, and said, "Dammit, you sonofabitch." But she smiled.

We sped past dirty snow-piles and tamaracks like giant toothpicks waiting for Spring. Lime-green color buzzed their fingertips. The man on Pop's radio whined and Craig and the blood took over my brain. I saw his body on the bed and the nurses slipping on the bloody floor. One hand shoved deep into his chest like it was pounded in there with a hammer, and the other hand clasped something raw and dripping. It was smaller than I expected. Veins hung from it like blue spider legs.

Two kids my age walked slowly across a parking lot towards a long, flat building, and I pointed. They looked like they would rather be anywhere but there.

"That? High school. Eat you alive." Then Granma had a change of mind, I reckon. She pulled over. "They got books in there,

Clayton. Stuff to read. More'n old copies of *Loggers World* I got lying around. You want some books?"

I nodded my head. Ever since I left The Riverside on the porch at the homeplace I felt like I did not have my right arm.

I remember my Momma and Dad talking about school long ago, I must've been three or maybe four. Dad said I needed school, and she said we were fine, that she would teach me everything I needed to know.

"Everything he needs to know is in here," she said, patting The Riverside.

Dad said, "Doubt it. How's he gonna learn to NOT tell stories? He storied that squirrel to death yesterday. 'Once upon a time, a squirrel was my friend and I fed him so many nuts he ate them all and then he exploded.'"

"We'll keep him here, away from people. I'll teach him."

"Looks like I lost another battle, though."

My Momma pulled his hands down, kissed him, and rubbed his stubble. "Yes," she said, "you did."

Of course, he kissed her back.

My Momma and Dad had their own game. My Momma won a lot.

I opened the truck door and got out.

"Stay!" Granma said. "Some people here don't like Bergmanns."

I wanted to find The Riverside. And I wanted to stop thinking about Craig's jerking spider-heart.

Granma leaned back in the seat. "This is a bad idea. Your Dad. He was always jumping headfirst into..." She paused, "...Jumping

straight in... like your ol' Granma." She sighed, then winked her
blue eye at me, lit a cig, took a long suck, and sat looking at the
school. "I got a meeting about our house. Can't take you. Don't
want 'em to know about you." Tendrils rose to the ceiling until her
hat floated in grey clouds and her blue eyes were like sparks in the
distance. The man on the radio sang about the darkest hour being
right before dawn.

Then she made up her mind. "OK, dammit. But remember:
you're a Bergmann." Smoke drifted from her mouth. "Don't you
EVER back down." She turned the truck off.

Three dogs stiff-legged, fangs bared, crept slowly towards us
across the road. The biggest dog in front was the color of a pale
turd. His pig-eyes shone in a skull like a rock ledge. Muscles rippled
over his shoulders. The other two were ill-fed strays. Gobs of spit
fell from bared fangs. But you know, Dammit, scared dogs still bite.
The big one had to be twice your weight, broad across the shoulders
and he watched me like I was a rabbit.

"Watch and learn," you said to me. "Then do what I do."

"Hey, catfucker," you jumped out the window, and swaggered,
silent as a black ghost into the middle of the road. "Get lost." Your
tail went up like a flag on a pirate ship, and your hair crested from
shoulder to tail. ("You and that goddamn tail," Granma used to say,
"lifting up the world like a carjack under an Oldsmobile."). It is a
nice tail, Dammit. Mighty fine. I thought of The Riverside, then,
and that old line came to me: *Cry havoc, let slip the dogs of war.* "This
must be what it's like," I thought, "*the dogs of war*," and felt my back
scrape against Sonofa.

A gun hammer pulled back *CLICK*, Granma climbed from
Sonofa with a six-gun bigger than her forearm. Her voice was quiet.

"Get the fuck outa here Achilles." She pointed it at the big dog. "You, Dammit — Get in the truck."

You backed up next to me and stayed — but did not jump in the truck.

"Achilles, I swear. I'll blow that grin off your face. GET!"

Achilles wiggled his head side to side like the spade-head of a rattler and snarled at me.

"Don't you lay a fang on my boy! Knew you when you was a puppy. A stray, squirming pile a wags and wiggles. I've fed you, fed you with milk from my own hand. Why you turn on me? And of all the masters — Big Jim? You listen to me. GET outa here!" She shook the gun again.

Achilles whined. For a single moment the face of a puppy who wants to be loved flashed, and then it was stamped out. He snarled, and spit dripped from his fangs. But he backed away, hate blazing in his eyes.

"Dammit, you DO NOT go after him," she said, and you whined but stayed.

Achilles paused at the corner — along with his two mangy friends — and watched us with his fat, pink tongue hanging from his mouth.

Granma waved the gun, "SHOO!"

He stretched and sauntered off slowly.

You walked to the edge of the road, lifted your leg, and peed where Achilles had peed.

"Found that boy, Achilles, when he was a pup more dead than alive. Big Jim stole him away and fed him babies — fawns, kittens, even pups — turned him into a bully. Or worse."

Granma shoved the pistol under the seat and pointed at you, "Good boy," she said. "Stay."

"Piss on you," you said and scratched your ear.

I was glad you were on our side. That was before I learned for dogs it's not about sides. It's about the pack, a good lie in the sun, and sometimes a dustup. Just to find out who's first — and who's the catfucker.

"*Cry havoc,*" I said. "*Let slip the dogs of war.*"

Granma bark-laughed. "Sonofa bitch! I KNEW you could talk, Clayton."

"Dammit loves the boy. Like the chase, the leap, and the blood."

I thought that was mighty fine, so I rubbed the chain-like knobs of your backbone.

You grunted happily.

My hands were shaking, and I felt like I was going to throw up.

"You boys done with your lovefest?" The cig in Granma's mouth stuck up like a smile. She made up her mind. "Well, two bad choices. Neither's great."

"Don't go," you said, and jumped in Sonofa.

But Granma never seemed to hear you like I could. Just slammed the door and headed towards the school like a dozer with no brakes. I wish I listened to you, Dammit. But I blew you off and went to school. Although "going" to school is a big lie. It is more like school goes all over you.

So quiet I barely heard, you said, "Ears back."

Chapter 11

Penny for My Thoughts

The school smelled like armpits and cleaning solution. Long lights flickered. I wanted to turn off my sense of smell, but you can't do that Dammit. If you asked me if I would take the hospital or that school, I'd take a bed next to Craig with his hands crawling. I felt the cold of the long-handled knife in my pocket — the one I took — and felt better. I could smell books somewhere, so I stayed.

"Half the day's gone, Viola." Granma leaned against the counter. "Can he get in?" It sounded like she was checking me into prison.

Viola was white-haired and wrinkly like Granma. Unlike Granma, Viola looked like she quit caring thirty years ago. "Fine. Fill this out," Viola pushed papers across the counter. "You hear Big Jim kicked out them vagrants?"

Granma smacked the counter. "Viola, don't EVER trust a big man who talk that smooth."

"Hmph," said Viola. "You're the last one in Junction City thinks that about Big Jim." She walked away.

"More like Big Asshole," said a voice behind me. "Make that two of us left in Junction City."

"Penny!" said Granma looking up with a smile.

I smelled flowering sage and cigarettes. A wild forelock hung over grey, flashing eyes — one of which did not look exactly straight at me. A little left of center, not enough to be lazy, but not straight either. Later, Doc told me about divergent strabismus. I was not sure which eye watched me. I felt dizzy. A line from The Riverside came to mind, "*Though she be but little, she is fierce.*"

83

"This is a girl," I thought. "They got bigger." Then, "Do girls smile?"

She did not smile. "Greetings, dark stranger." Her voice was warm and raspy, her brown hair short. "What errand brings you unto our desolate gates?" She wore a black T-shirt that said "Grateful Dead" with turtles and sunflowers.

I, of course, said nothing. Later, I learned this can be a wise approach when conversing with a girl.

She had full lips like a smile was coming but the edges turned down. Later, Dammit, it was her smile-frown I missed so much. Right then, she looked right through me. My stomach felt hot like I was hungry.

"Um," she said, and waited. Then she said to Granma, "What's up Elbedee."

"Haven't seen you in forever, sis. This is my grandson, Clayton." Granma sounded like I was the best thing she had. "Penny's down the street from me. Known her a long time. She calls me Elbedee. Stands for 'Lina Bergmann Don't - somethin' - somethin' — I can't remember the rest. Penny's a good kid, good heart."

When Granma said, "good kid," Penny's eyes flashed, but she said, "Jesus, forget much? Elbedee's your acro-name. It's not that hard." Penny said to me, "The full version is Lina Bergmann Don't Fuck Around."

"No, she don't," snapped Granma. "Specially when she's being interrupted, goddamit give me a new form Viola." She turned to me. "Kids use to call me Elbedeefa. The Strays from down the street that sometimes come to dinner." She chuckled. "An it stuck."

"Me and Cress made that one up a long time ago," said Penny. "When we were little and lived with you." Her face went vacant, and I watched her eyes turn inward on a memory. I was not sure I had ever seen a smile more beautiful, more distant, or sad. "L.B.D.F.A," she said, remembering.

"Where you been, Penny?" Granma asked. "Your friends come over. Even Cress. Haven't seen you in months."

Penny shrugged, her eyes flickered, and she was back with us again. I couldn't tell if Penny had a bruise or a shadow under her eye. She tilted her head sideways as she looked at me. It was a bruise.

"Clayton's been living on the Salmon," Granma said. "Well, near the Salmon."

"Waaay out on the Salmon, from appearances Elbedee," said Penny. "I've driven your rusty pile of crap. How did you get there and back without breaking down?"

"Lucky, I reckon."

"You still call it *Sonofa*?"

Granma kicked the counter. "That is *your* name for it. Now stop interruptin'. I got to start this over."

Penny wrinkled her nose. "What *is* he wearing?"

"Pop's clothes," said Granma. "He was the best goddamn thing ever happen to me. Sorry Beaumont." She paused a moment and closed her eyes, then said quietly, "Did not like me cussing."

"Hmm," said Penny, watching me like a hawk watches a squirrel. The late-morning sun caught her eyes through a window, and they were no longer grey. They were violet-green like the backs of swallows against grey cliffs, first to arrive in Spring. One eye gazed into mine, the other looked past my ear at something coming. When she shifted her gaze, I found she still looked me in the eye—but now it was her left eye that kept contact, and her right eye bore straight into my chest as if looking at my heart.

I put my hand on the wall to steady myself.

"You." Granma pointed at Penny, "Talk to my boy, OK?" She bent back on the counter quickly, pulled down her hat, hiding her face.

The phone rang and Viola sniffed at us and went in the back to answer it.

Phones. Granma has a light blue one hanging on the wall. She talked to the hospital this morning on it. Inventory time: Colored phones. Small to big? I wondered what color and kind was the phone Viola was talking on back there, and who was she talking to? What mechanism causes the sound to flow so quickly? Is it like rivers going downhill from the mountains? Could I pick up a phone and talk to my Momma somewhere? I was thinking about how I was going to ask Granma about that later when Penny cleared her throat, loudly.

"Ahem." Penny was staring at me with a strange expression. A combination of surprise, curiosity, and maybe anger.

I'd been staring at her the whole time. Inventory done.

"What are YOU lookin' at," she said. "You should see yourself, Mister long-haired lumberjack. Kids here will think he's *woo*," she said to Granma. She drew a circle with her finger by her ear.

"He's not dumb. He just don't like to talk. Show him around?"

Penny laughed. It was that sound I already loved, water coming off hills after a storm. She wasn't smiling. "Maybe I'll show him around Elbedee. Maybe not. I got stuff to do."

Granma hmphed.

"You should *not* have brought him here," Penny said. "This school is dangerous. Especially if they find out he's a Bergmann."

"Can't," said Granma. "Need him safe, and not at home."

"Well safe is *not* here," said Penny. "Anywhere but here."

I did not understand what she meant, but I could feel it in the lights and in the smell.

Penny sighed. She must have known you can't make this Granma change her mind unless she wants to. "Tell you what Elbedee — I agree," Penny said. "He's not dumb. No matter how much he looks like a bony, Abercrombie football player. He's not stupid." She winked at me. "I'll tell you something else. I bet I can make him talk." She took a step closer to me. "I'll make you talk *today* Clayton Bergmann." She smiled for the first time, and I felt something in my stomach again, but lower. I must have been real hungry.

"Doc says he's froze and needs to thaw," said Granma, bent over the paperwork.

"Hang around me, you'll warm up fine," said Penny, and her eyes flashed, "Though my appearance disarming, actions alarming, for long they're brewing—I know all my doings."

"Hmph," said Granma, but she smiled.

I had no doubt. The fire in Penny's eyes I'd seen only once before. You, Dammit, facing down Achilles.

"You look ridiculous," Penny said, "take off those suspenders," and her hand slipped inside my wool pants, cool and quick, snapping off the brass clips. "Is it really you?" she muttered. "What are you doing here? Do you know how fucked up this town is?"

The smell of the earth after a quick rain surrounded me. Like a fire put out by a sudden storm. I did not understand her, Dammit. Not at all. I never met her before, but she acted like she knew me. Her chin brushed my shoulder. Something stirred down there in the wuttus area that I *never* felt before.

"I've been fighting and fighting," she whispered. "No one will believe me, CS, and I can't talk here." She glared towards where Viola was still talking on the phone in the back room. "He has spies everywhere."

"Elbedee, it's bad enough you got him in wool pants and fucking plaid," Penny stepped away. "Fresh from logging camp."

Viola sniffed. "Language young woman."

"Fuckedy fuck."

Viola's face turned to stone.

"Go ahead, kick me out," said Penny. "I'd rather be home."

"You've got no home." Viola grinned a mean grin. "Guttersnipe. I think, young lady, that school is exactly where you belong."

Penny shrugged, but I could tell it hurt.

"She always got a home with me, if she wants it," said Granma. She shoved the paperwork at Viola like she wanted to punch her. "He likes reading like you, Penny. Book-smart like his ma. Never took George for likin' that kind a girl."

"I'm that kind of girl," Penny said. And then blushed.

"I know you like readin'," said Granma. "Just get him somethin' to read. No classes, you hear?" I thought for sure Granma was going to put the suspenders back on me, but instead she took them from Penny and started filling out another form.

Penny pulled a purple book with worn gold letters from her back pocket. A woman in a big dress leaned back in the arm of a muscled, shirtless man. His other hand held a rifle. "Here you go." She handed it to me. "To get you through the day. Meet me in the school library when the last bell rings, Fifty-six and Wabashaw. Ha."

Granma hmphed, *"Penelope Lyle,"* she said.

"We'll have a book date," Penny said, ignoring her, reached up and rubbed my ear lobe.

Her touch was warm and yet I shivered.

"For goodness sake," she said. "Tie up the fuckin hair." She took a piece of twine from her pocket and reached up around my face, pulling my hair together. She squeezed her bushy eyebrows as she concentrated. Her eyes were swallows flashing green across the river under a soft rain. And Dammit — you know when it takes you over. The smell of a powerful woman.

I could not breathe.

She whispered, so close her breath was all around me, "*Your crafty design precedes you, ODCS, And your fame, which reaches high, even to the heavens.*" Then she stood back. "Don't worry about the name, CS, I give everyone I like new names. There you go, MUCH better."

I can name twenty-five birds by their silhouettes and calls alone, but I could not name what I felt.

Her eyes blazed, and as she reached up to push a stray hair behind my ear, she spoke so quietly only I heard. "Look, someone in the O & S is after my sister Cressida. She got wrapped up in their shit. I had to get on the inside. It's a mess. If they find out, it's over for her."

I must have looked surprised. Pretend what? I couldn't imagine Penny being anyone but herself. Granma looked up sharply, then bent back to finishing the form.

Penny frown-smiled and the sun came out. "I have to find Cress," she said loudly. "See ya Elbedee. Just send him to study hall until school's over."

"Oh, good idea," said Granma.

"See ya ODCS," said Penny, flashing that turned-down smile. She walked down the long hallway, her back straight as a board. Until it curved. I found myself watching the curve and how it connected everything.

"Keep a sharp eye for monsters," she called over her shoulder, dead serious.

I realized I did not smell the lights anymore. Just her.

"You should see your face, Romes."

He was there like he had walked away to get a drink and missed a part of a conversation. It was only a night and a day since I'd seen him but felt like a lifetime.

"*Ve'achron,*" he said, his usual greeting.

"Alafar yaqum," I said without thinking. That sonofa bitch had me trained well.

"Huh?" said Granma, surprised, waggled her finger and grinned at me and bent down to her work.

"Who was that girl?" said MK. "And how do I meet her? A little scraggly, but delicious."

I felt all kinds of feelings from mad to happy. I did not want to be around him because of Craig. But I did. He knew something, he knew about my Momma and Dad. I could see now Granma was interested in him, wasn't sure what he was. All he had on, still, was the dirty jeans.

"Young man, where is your shirt?"

"You can see me? Wow," said MK, looking at me and shaking his head at Granma. He was genuinely surprised. I was surprised too. "Peculiar. Wow," he said again. He waved a pale hand like he was brushing off a fly, then changed the topic quickly. "In that outfit you look just like your Granpa. Only with long hair, and your mother's eyes. Come to think of it, you don't look like him at all." He grinned. "I missed you Romes, where you been?"

"How you know about my Beaumont? Who're you?" asked Granma.

"I'm MK, the new student teacher," he said, waving his hand again.

Her eyes fluttered like she was passing out.

"You like my blue shirt?"

She pushed back her hat, "Yeah," she said. "Yeah, looks good."

He nudged me, grinned, and said to her, "I'll take him to his first class in this shithole."

"Teachers are not supposed to cuss," Granma said, sounding confused.

Viola walked out, MK waved his hand, she fell against the counter, pulled herself straight, then said to Granma, "Big Jim sent us a new teacher." She smiled at MK who grinned back. "Like I said, Big Jim's making this town great again." She handed MK a folder. "Here's his schedule. He can go to class; he can go to the library. Whatever." She wandered back to talk on the phone.

"You know how to get home?" Granma pointed through the wall. "Two blocks that way," she grabbed my hand, put some paper in it. "Here's three bucks if you miss lunch."

"Wow," said MK. "A whole three dollars."

"Clayton," she said, like she hadn't heard him. "Don't forget you're a Bergmann. Means somethin'." She hugged me.

I nodded. I heard that from Dad before.

"You look like your mom, that ain't good in this town. Too many rednecks."

"You're right about that," said MK. "Foot taller, five shades browner than everyone else."

She didn't hear him or didn't want to. She waggled her finger, "Clayton, don't you get in NO fights." Then she grabbed my hand. "But... if you do — you be LAST one standin'. You take this BIG hand and squeeze it into a BIG ball like this and hit HARD, OK?"

I raised my fist.

"Good, good!" She started to walk out the door and stopped. "Don't feel right to go, but we'll lose the house if I don't get to that meeting." She shook her head and seemed to make up her mind. Maybe it was MK's presence. Maybe it was she did not know how evil school is.

She walked back to MK and stuck a finger in his bare chest. "Keep an eye out for him." It was not a request. "You and your blue shirt."

He laughed and put his hand solemnly over his heart. "Pleasure."

"Here. Right here, boy," Granma pointed to her chest. "I got love for you. Do what the teacher says, Clayton. Then come home."

She gave MK a last withering look on her way out the door. *"You better take care of him,"* she said.

He raised both hands with a shrug and a grin. "Aye, milady." That grin that never looked like a smile — ever — Dammit.

Chapter 12

A Lighter in My Chest

"Phew! Your Granma stinks like ash tray and old woman."

"Where are my Momma and Dad? How do you know them? You said, in the cabin ...." My throat closed like a trap door.

He ignored me. "How about it, Romes, you gonna do what I tell you? Granma says 'do what the teacher says.'"

My hand was still closed in a fist. I raised it at him, but he kept on blabbing as we walked down the empty hall.

"And Penny. Whoo! That scent after a rain, what do they call it? *Damn*!"

My face betrayed me.

"Romes has a crush! Your class, according to this, is around the corner. I thought for sure you'd cut your hair before going to school." He was rambling and happy for some reason. "Least you smell OK."

"Granma wanted to, and I said no. Where are my parents, and what did you do to Craig?" I asked.

He pretended to look at the class schedule. "I, uh, you... you know how it is, Romes. I feel better than I did yesterday."

"You killed him," I said. "He broke open his chest and crushed his heart."

MK had a look on his face I'd never seen before.

"You did something to him, you took something from him, he's in your head somewhere," I said, "and you know where my folks are."

He scratched his head, and the smile came back, "Up in here? Nah."

93

"You got to tell me where my parents are," I said. "Craig knows. Knew."

MK smiled, and it was only then — for the first time ever — I saw how sad he was. How lost, how alone. More alone than that cougar ever was. And tired. Alone and tired in a place with no friends. It was in the smile, and in the sound of his voice. Full of so much darkness and pain I couldn't believe he could smile.

He just looked at me and smiled that smile and popped his knuckles absently.

"You know I'm your friend, I won't leave you," I said. "You can leave me anytime. You leave me all the time, anyway. But I won't ever leave you."

He put a hand on my shoulder, just like Granma, and the look I got was a black waterless well with no bottom. It passed and he grinned and was back to himself. "Oh, you'll leave me someday, Romes. I have a bad habit of ruining friendships. *Hope must, in despite of fearful change, play in the strongest closet of my breast.* Easy one. Name it."

It was a horrible joke, but also good. Sneaky. I will not always explain these things to you Dammit, but maybe just once? The TRG is not about scoring points, only. It's about the tasty bits and the right timing and a good inventory.

For example, in this case: The joke starts with knowing what is "inside the closet of my breast" — a heart. Second, what was inside Craig's breast, and why it is not in there anymore. Third, that we had been looking at a young breast too. And fourth, we did not get caught in the looking. And for me, maybe there was a fifth: the hoping. About the breast. (Later, Penny explained to me about staring at girls' chests and bad manners, but I did not know any of that when I met her). The sneaky bit was that it was not in The Riverside, so it did not count, and he loved to do this to me at the worst moments to win a point. Extra five points if you can pull it off. Extra ten if you get caught. Inventory done.

"It's not in there, I know that for sure," I said. "I caught you. Ten points to me. Pizzle."

"Still good huh, Romes?" He grinned again, "Sneaky good. I will tell you this, I didn't make it up, it's for real, just not in your stupid book."

"Not in the story, not in the game," I said, hoping I was right.

"You have no idea how true you are just now," he said.

A bell rang, and the hall filled with boys and girls. MK shuddered and said, "People. Ug. You need to be in room 207. Oh, and you are now officially ahead by three." I wanted to tell him he was wrong — it was four. But he was gone.

Students rushed around me pulling books out of metal boxes in the walls. I kept my eyes on the ground and steadied myself, one hand on the wall. I will describe them to you, Dammit, particularly the girls who come in every shape and size. Some are round like river rocks; some tall as willows. All of them softer than I remembered, when I saw them in the store with my Momma when I was little. The hallway sounded like flowers that talk. They smelled wonderful.

What is going on with MK? He and I were friends. For years it was just us. I thought I knew him. Days — no, months and months — of playing The TRG, looking for the knave of hearts, hunting wild game, and flipping rocks in the river. Does all that time with someone mean you actually know someone? Sometimes with friends, I reckon you think you know everything about them. But it's not that way, is it, Dammit?

I am learning not to stare at girls now. But you need to understand that on that day in the hall I was only good at three things: Shakesbear, fishing, and tracking wild game. From Shakesbear I knew how to talk to girls. You must be forthright with your thoughts and treat them like equals, and sometimes they like it when you speak a pretty line or joke with them. Still, I did not know *not* to stare. From tracking I knew about walking through new timber over a ridge or crawling slowly in the thick grass. Either way, you're looking for sign and trying not to be seen or smelled. It's pretty simple when you fish or hunt. You learn to be curious and move slow. You take everything in. You keep your eyes and ears peeled.

Inventory:

I heard Porter pose a question in my head:

"One wonders if a taxonomy has ever been built for girls." I could see that some looked like *Rosaceae* and I wondered if they had thorns. Some like *Aceraceae*, gangly, and some shone like *Solidago* and *Helianthus*. I could not figure out what Penny was. She was a girl that did not fit any inventory, and that was a good thing.

I wished I didn't burn Porter's *Taxonomy* in the coldest winter, page by page. That winter everything in the canyon died except for me. If I still had it, maybe I would know more about how things fit together. I do remember *Phytography and Its Terminology*, the eighth chapter, and the classifications of each inflorescence. I wondered if girls had stigmas, styles, anthers, filaments, petals, sepals, and ovaries like hypogynous flowers. Where do you even start with this kind of inventory, Dammit?

Since I was already portering, I reckoned I would start with the sounds of their voices and calls to one another, or maybe the size of hips and how the butt pops. But where are the thorns? Some are flat, some wide, some are round and strong. Or maybe eyes and hair. Breasts is not a bad idea. Or lips....

Someone grabbed my pants from behind.

I reached down, but it was too late. Hands ripped my pants to my knees. Everybody stopped and stared at me in Granpa's red briefs. A boy laughed. Then everybody laughed.

"Red underwear! Ohmygod it's Superman!" someone yelled.

I was an animal in a hole and the hunters stood on the edge. I wanted to run but I was caught. I covered my wuttus with Penny's book and everyone laughed. Girls were pointing, boys grabbed one another and bent over with laughter.

"Fag's got a steamy chick book, and he won't let it go!"

I dropped Penny's book and reached down to pull up my pants, but someone behind me stepped on them, pushed them down to my ankles. I grabbed them with both hands to pull them up. But the foot was there on my pants. My legs got tangled in my pants and I fell. More shouts. The hunters closed in.

"Stop it!" Penny was on the floor next to me, pulling up my pants. "Fucking assholes. Leave him alone."

It didn't stop the laughing.

Someone sang in the crowd, "Penny is a ho-bag."

Someone else pushed her from behind, and she fell on me.

"Wear a belt," said the guy whose foot held my pants down, and he kicked me with the other foot. "Go back to the rez."

Someone in the crowd yelled, "Teacher!" and in a flash, they were gone. It was like nothing happened. The bell rang, everyone took off and the only way you could tell they were still watching me was the laughing didn't stop, it just got quieter.

Penny grabbed my pants, pulled them up and shoved me through a door and into a dark room. "What the FUCK are you DOING?" she whispered. She wrestled with my pants. Somehow the button had come undone. "Didn't I tell you to watch out for monsters?"

I nodded my head. She stopped buttoning my pants and reached up. She had to pull my face down, she was so short. Or was I tall? Her hands were on my face and her thumbs rubbed the tears from under my eyes.

"Don't cry, NO. Don't let them see you cry," she said fiercely.

"No." I said. *"I will be the pattern of all patience, I will say nothing... I am a man, more sinned against than sinning."*

"What?!" she whispered. She kissed me like a fighter, like salt water in the darkness. I felt her all around me. If there were any words to say, after that kiss, I had nothing. Something like Granma's lighter went "pop" in my chest.

After a long time, she leaned away panting. There was grey light coming through a small window. We were in a storage room. Her eyes were shadows. Her nipples were hard points under the sunflowers on her T-shirt. I couldn't catch my breath. With one hand, she tugged my pants together and with the other pulled her long belt out and ran it around my waist through the loops.

"Now you're in MY fuckin story, CS."

I tried to grab her, but she was already moving to the door.

"I want to — but I can't," she said. "Besides, I'm NOT the one with outsider tattooed all over my face." She kicked the door open like she was mad at it and pushed me out. "Get going, you ... you nimrod. They're assholes — but this is a whole new level. They obviously know who you are." Her face twisted with frustration, "I can't be seen with you." She waved down the empty hallway. "Go!"

I took two steps and looked back. Light from the long tubes above us, a pale and unnatural light, flooded her face. I guess my tears transferred. Because my face was dry and hers was wet.

"CS," she said. "I'm tired. So tired. I been fighting these fuckers way too long. I can't remember half the time who I am. I can't remember what it's like to read a good book anymore." She rubbed her face. "I had to become someone else to get close enough to bring them down. And now Cress got sucked in and I can't do this without her being free. I can't, I can't!" She looked fierce and sad and tired all at the same time. She backed away. "I don't know why I just told you that," she said. "I don't talk to anyone anymore."

I still couldn't breathe. The lighter in my chest was burning up all the air like a torch.

"Go away," she said, but she was half-smiling. "Your mom told me you'd be like this. You don't need me to find the library, nimrod."

I didn't move. The hallway was completely empty. Did she mention my Momma?

She pushed back a strand of dark hair, her finger travelled around her ear, and an earring flashed. It was a silver swallow. "Yeah, I said your mom. She gave this to me. And the magic of her gift, so far, has kept me safe. They can hurt me, but they can't kill me. There's a fuckin boatload you don't know. Where's the book I gave you? I hid it ALL in there."

I pointed to where I fell in the hallway.

Her smile disappeared. "You lost it? You HAVE to find it." She pounded the wall. "The assholes TOOK it. They CANNOT see what I wrote." Without realizing it, she had walked up to me and was glaring up, her nose inches from my chin. "That book was on loan from the Penny Library of Classic Shit, and you are GOING to get it back." She shoved me in the chest, "GO FIND IT. You just don't lose books."

Then she changed her mind and grabbed my hand. "CS, this is all you need to know for now." She looked around quickly. "I know about you. I know about your family. Your mom made me promise not to tell your Granma. *She said you were safer if you stayed hid a while.*"

My face must have been pure surprise.

"Yeah, your mom. She was kind to me after your dad got killed, and her kindness is keeping me alive." Penny rubbed the swallow earring absently, and her voice dropped to a mutter. "I'm close, real close to figuring out what Big Jim is doing. But first, I got to get Cress out."

A sick-looking girl walked down the hallway to the office and Penny and me stood there looking at each other in silence until she went around a corner.

"There's SO much you don't know," Penny whispered. "Junction City is in the cross-hairs. Something bad is coming. Real big and real bad. Not just Junior, or Big Jim. Go! Find my book."

I heard it, Dammit, but it did not sink in until much later.

She started walking away, like she did when we first met. Her hand pulled up her shirt to wipe her face, exposing a pale shoulder blade, thin ribs, and that curve that made me lose my breath all over again. I ran after her, grabbed her hand and held it to my chest where the lighter burned, and said,

"*I am no pilot;*
Yet, wert thou ... wert thou as far as that vast shore
Wash'd with the farthest sea,
I would adventure for such merchandise."

Then I saw her smile, really smile, and it was like the sun after the storm. It was like the first day of Spring when the snow is gone, and you wake up in the morning to the song of the first bird singing out his heart. The varied thrush, I reckon. Singing till his chest would burst. Her smile was bright as the sunflowers on her T-shirt.

She slapped me softly and I grabbed her hand and held it.

She tried to pull away, then stopped, and leaned close, whispered in my ear.

"Nerd! Told you I'd make you talk."

"*I would adventure for such merchandise,*" I said to her again.

She whispered, *"Dost thou love me? I know thou wilt say 'ay.' And I will take thy word. Yet if thou swear'st thou mayst prove false."*

I'll tell you right now Dammit, when that girl quoted The Riverside, I knew she was the one for me and I was for her. She could have ripped out my heart and stomped on it and — still — I would have wanted her. I wanted to kiss her again. Instead, I stood there with my mouth hanging open.

She laughed and the lighter burned even hotter. My whole chest felt like it was on fire.

"Yeah, well, you know how *that* one ended, don't you?" she said. "Two teenagers who *thought* they were in love." She sighed. "Nerd. You're not the only one in this town who can quote Shakespeare."

"Hey Worthless," said a deep voice, "why you talking to him?" It was one of the boys who pulled down my pants, the one with shoulders like a bull and a neck to match. He was a head shorter than me, but muscles bunched everywhere. He pushed his head forward an inch from mine and looked at me through his eyebrows.

Her voice changed, "It's nothing, Junior."

"Get your fuckin hands off her," he said.

Junior? I thought: if he's Junior, what's Senior like?

I took a step back from Penny but kept holding her hand. Somehow it had slipped into mine. It felt small and cold.

"I said, retard, get your hands off her." He was right between us; I could smell his breath and see the red lines in his eyes and the hair starting to grow on his upper lip. He had a bottle of water in his hand, and he opened it and reached up and poured it over my head.

I felt it run over my eyes and lips and down my neck.

He stood on tiptoe and stuck his nose against mine. "Hey big chief, let Worthless go. Or I'll give you the same treatment she gets when she talks back." He tossed the empty bottle against the wall.

"Fuck you Junior," she said, "you're not my boss."

He slapped her, and I stood there holding her hand, frozen. I couldn't move. A red blotch sprung up on her cheek.

"Word of advice, chief," he said to me. "Never drop a dollar to pick up a penny. Why I call her Worthless." He grabbed her ear, twisted until she gasped, and he hissed, "Fuckin don't EVER talk to me that way again."

She pulled away from him, rubbed her cheek and leaned against me. "It's OK, he's my boyfriend CS, do what he says."

I did not understand why she wasn't mad. I heard the tremor in her voice, I knew she was trying to stay calm. I did not understand why back then, Dammit. If I only knew then what I know now—about why she chose to stay. She was the bravest of us all.

"Oh, I am *not* her boyfriend, CS," he said mocking her voice, "She's been giving me attention this week, so I stay away from her sister. Oh yeah, I know what you're up to, bitch."

"I'm not your bitch," she said, but took a step back. I could see Junior had rocked her.

"Who the fuck are you?" he asked. "What does CS stand for?"

"He's new, Junior, he can't talk, and I'm helping him get to class. It's fine." Her voice was strong, but shaky.

"Well, chief, no touching the goods." He leaned in, like he was saying something funny, and whispered. "Damaged anyway, ya know. That weird eye. Spooky! I try not to look at it when we're, eh, you know...."

What was he talking about, I wondered.

"You know what I'm talking about. I stay away from full penny-tration." He grinned at his joke. "Partial penny, OK. Just be smart, use the mouth. I never go full penny. Har." He grabbed his wuttus, rolled his eyes back until only the whites showed, made a fist, and pumped it back and forth in front of his mouth and pushed his tongue in rhythm against the inside of his cheek.

I didn't understand what he was doing. He looked like he was going crazy. I looked from him to Penny, who was silent, rubbing her cheek and looking away.

"Besides," he touched her lightly on her nose, "my job's to muzzle her. Get this bitch-dog locked up in the pound."

Penny's hand squeezed so hard I felt mine would break. "Don't do it, CS," she said.

I saw the bruise above the red mark on her cheek. Dad used to say a phrase sometimes when he was talking himself into something — you'd a loved it, Dammit. So, I said it, nice and loud and slow: "In for a penny, in for a pound," I said.

Junior's eyes got wide.

I pushed Penny behind me.

Junior tried to rip her away.

I felt my right hand — slippery with the water he poured on me — reach out as if it belonged to someone else. My hand pulled his shirt into a knot on his chest, so tight that he could not breathe. My fist, Dammit, it is a bigger fist than I thought. I twisted his shirt and lifted him off the floor. His arms banged against mine trying to let him go, but I wouldn't.

"Let him go! CS, you fucking idiot!" Penny yelled.

I let him go. It was more like something in me that was very, very strong pushed him. He banged off the wall and fell on the floor, groaning, holding his back. He seemed OK, just didn't want to get up.

"Get OUT!" She shouted at me.

"You're dead," Junior said quietly. "You just picked the wrong guy to fuck with."

I reckoned it was time for me to go. So, I started walking.

"I saw your dad die, he was CRYING," shouted Junior behind me. "And you just made things real bad for your mom, you fuck. I know where she is."

I'm not a fighter, Dammit, as you know well, or I'd a gone back and made him tell. I rubbed my shaking hand where I could still feel Penny's cool fingers.

Junior's fist smashed against the metal boxes on the wall, but I kept walking.

"Don't touch me! I'll kill his fucking ass.

Chapter 13

I Am A Salmon

"Listen Jackass, the river drops over a big rock and takes a turn against the cliff. All you're trying to do is *not* flip. Coming off the cliff is a surge of water the size of a house. The wave hits you like a giant's fist. The raft crumples. You're in darkness under ten tons of river and you can't breathe. What you gonna do now?"

"I'll turn into a salmon, Dad."

That is what school is, Dammit. Ten tons of river and all. And it was the river side that I returned to in my mind – that same day they left me—as I swam the halls looking for a way out:

"Clayton Solomon Bergmann!" The only time my Momma would get mad is when I zoned out. "Mind me! It's OK to hide in the Riverside, but it can be hard to understand. It's Shakesbear, after all." She smiled at the fact that she was using Dad's nickname for it. "If they make you feel strange – wait. We'll talk when I get back."

"Momma, my wuttus feels weird." All the standing in the cold water had made my wuttus shrink in my pants. When I was little, I made up words like "wuttus," and Momma used them like they were real. We had lots of words in our conversation that I never heard anywhere else.

"That happens sometimes in cold water," my Momma said.

Dad grinned, "Haha, now what you gonna say?"

"Also," my Momma said, ignoring him, "you're the age when sometimes a spirit comes to a boy. Usually, a friend."

"Let's go," said Dad, cutting her off.

"Anything weird happens," Momma said, "don't be scared. Tell us when we get back."

"Don't want to hear about your wuttus, though," Dad said.

She ignored him again. "Trust the river. I've prayed for your familiar to be strong, like you. Who knows what it will be."

My Momma told me about familiars while Dad was out checking trap lines last week. Some people where she is from across the ocean get spirit-friends to help them when they are young. That is a familiar. Then she said something real weird:

"Most people can't see the Nisoi, the non-humans, or even talk to them, but you might. You should know there are three tribes of Nisoi. 'Rivers' are what my people call them, because of what happens if you step in their flow. They draw you in. Humans call them Gods, In-Betweeners, and Monsters. We call them The Three Rivers. There is a fourth River, but I don't know if They are a tribe, a Nisoi, or what. I've never met one, and I'm not sure where they stand on the war. Don't tell your dad I told you."

"The war? And what River are we?" I asked.

"Another time," she said, picking up the Riverside. "Let's read *Hamlet,* less drama." And she would not speak of it again.

That hot morning when they left me, I was an unbroken story-jar filled to the brim. I was a twelve-year old daydreaming on the mystery of Sonnet 146: "*Then, soul, live thou upon thy servant's loss....*"

"Fuck familiars." Dad tightened a strap on the raft. "Keep it simple, Clay."

Mom grinned at me.

"Anything not family is monster," he said. "Don't talk to 'em, don't touch 'em. If you run out of food, do what I showed you. Take the gun. Set the traplines. Pick the fruit. Close up chickens at night. Salmon start running, put out the lines and get the smoker fired up. You know what to do. Be back in ten days."

"What about wolves or cougars? What about bears?"

"Monsters, jackass, not animals. You can handle animals, you're twelve." He threw a leftover strap at me. "You're all grown up now, you'll be fine." He grinned. "You'll read that god-awful Shakes-Bear book on the porch, eat like a baby grizz, and forget to mind the place. We get back, you'll be ten feet tall, fatter'n a cow, and the chickens'll be dead."

"Shakespeare, dad, it's Shake-SPEARE."

"What? Wild Bill?" That's the other name he called Shakesbear, Dammit. "No," he said, "I coulda swore he was a grizzly bear." He said it with a straight face. I'd heard that stupid joke a hundred times.

"Baby Grizz," my Momma smiled at Dad, "don't mind him. Remember, we don't talk like The Riverside these days. When you're around other people, anyone but us, if you talk like that — they won't understand."

"He won't be around anyone else," snapped Dad. "He's staying home."

"You mean talk like this?" I said:

"Of rivers and the chain-ed canyons free,
A winding, restless spirit I will be."

Dad muttered something to himself about a gottdamn-good-for-nothing-book-learning-wife who teaches sons things they don't need to know, but I saw him smile. I have forgotten so many things that come back to me in my dreams like songs. But I remember this: He was proud of her, and proud to be around her. Every word — even curse-words — was "I love you."

"Well done!" Her wild eyes shone. "Best remember that's not how people talk anymore." Then, my Momma frowned and leaned forward over the bow. "Sometimes the wave looks big, son. But if you face it head-on it will be fine. Sometimes you have to go under to get through."

Looking back, Dammit, I'm not sure she was talking about a wave on the river.

Dad pushed off my shoulder, climbed in the raft and took the oars. "Let go the rope, Clay."

I threw the bowline in the boat.

Those pale blue eyes stayed on me as the boat turned in the current. Then, a quick smile. The smile that flashed when he was proud of you. "Do what I taught you. No matter what, don't leave our place." His teeth shone in the sun. "Listen to your Momma — but for godsakes jackass don't read ALL fuckin day."

"George, language!" Then, my Momma called as the raft spun away. "Read all day if you want Baby Grizz! You're safe here." The raft paused in the eddy before the turn, she raised her right hand, and her voice came across the water: "'Of rivers and the chain-ed canyons free, A winding, restless spirit I will be.' Lovely, son."

The last thing she said to me, Dammit.

I wish I never made up those stupid lines. I say them to myself all the time, as you know, I can't help it. They're all I got. If only I'd gone with them. It's the extra hurting we do to each other — because of the fear, I reckon — that makes us so goddamn sad. Like a scared dog that bites a kid in the face. Not you, Dammit. You were never scared, and you would never, ever, bite a kid. Except that one time when he deserved it.

A family of swallows chased each other, dipped the river, and shot into the blue, wings flashing in the hot sun like flecks of fool's gold. Our canyon filled with the desolate smell of wild river: fish, warm rocks, sage and the faint vanilla of ponderosas upstream. I almost swam after them. Instead, I stood there like a stone. A little stone under a big one, at the bottom of the river.

Poor soul, the center of my earth.

Why dost thou pine within and suffer dearth?

What the hell does *that* mean, Dammit? Sonnet 146 is molten-silver tied around my heart. The hurt is not from the cougar's claws, not from eating so little for so long that I feel my shoulder bones against this shirt. It is deeper. When the kids laugh at you in the hall; when you lose your parents, then lose the hope after that; when the topography of your heart is vast, wrinkled by nameless rivers in mountains you cannot climb.

So shalt thou feed on Death, that feeds on men,
And Death once dead, there's no more dying then.

I remember Dad's neck, burnt and sweaty as the raft spun away under his pumping arms. He needed to make the chute. I remember the freckles on his hands. How his right shoulder bent inward from the old break. I remember my Momma's eyes through blowing dark hair as the raft disappeared. But I cannot remember their faces. The sand in my eye would not come out, no matter how hard I rubbed and rubbed.

I know the sound my river makes in the canyon when no one is there; it is not the sound I hear in these halls, a sound like the roaring of a flood. Like the voices underwater that call my name.

MK said I should go to room 207, and there it was. I walked in the door peeling the boiled egg I put in my pocket that morning, dropping the shells on the floor. Everything went quiet. Snickers in back.

"It's the new kid."

"Superman undies."

"Who eats an egg in the middle of the day?"

"Pick up those shells," said the teacher in a tired voice.

When I just looked at her, the teacher picked up the shells herself, threw them into a big can, and told the whisperers to pipe down. Then she asked me what my name was.

I pointed at my throat and shook my head, so she told me to write my name on the board. *Clayton Solomon Bergmann.* Of course, I could have added *Stonefly*, but my Momma once told me that it was better to keep it hid — she never said why — and "anyways, that is just the English version of my name; it is *not* how to say my real name, which is pretty much unpronounceable. Maybe you didn't know this," she smiled a crooked smile. "... But the 'stone' in 'Stonefly' is silent." She laughed and laughed, and I didn't get it. Momma jokes are the worst, Dammit. Besides, stones make noises. Especially when you roll big ones off a cliff and watch them crash through trees.

There was an empty seat in the front and the teacher told me to sit there.

"Tard, you stink. Like rotten eggs." Snickers and giggles.

Ten tons of river. I was a Chinook salmon, and I found a place to hide. *Of rivers and the chain-ed canyons free, A winding, restless spirit I will be.*

Inventory: Let the current flow around me (hold the pencil like my Momma taught me, do math, and my other thinkings). Be the salmon — or a silent stone that cannot fly. What made Craig want to tear out his heart? How did Penny get that earring, where is my Momma, and how does Junior know? How do I get more kisses? I've made a real enemy now, haven't I? What happened to Penny's book? Inventory done.

Not really. Just a bunch of questions with no answers, Dammit.

Porter was wrong. The more you know — the more you organize — the more mess there is. Like building a dam with twigs. But Dammit, I cannot help myself. My brain porters everything together. That day at school, I talked myself out of revenge: *If* I did find my father's murderer, how would I kill him anyway? I'm no killer, I puke every time I harvest an elk. I sat at that desk and wrote it down on paper just to make it real.

Deareste Momma (and Dad, too, I guesse).

I will finde you. At leaste Momma.

Love, Clayton (Silente) Fly

I didn't have an answer for where to start finding her. Other than the Craig that MK was carrying in his head. I wrote:

PS. I want to go home.

But like Granma says, "wishin' don't wash out shit-stains, Clayton. Only washin' does that." I was stuck in the first act. Every time the second act started I got booted back to the beginning. The bell rang and everyone moved but me. The note had turned to mush in my fist from the sweat. I wish I kept that letter and I wish I never went to school, Dammit. But wishing don't wash out shit-stains.

I fell in love ten times that day. And fell out of it too. Every girl was a constellation, every boy a flame. *Golden lads and girls all must, as chimney-sweepers, come to dust.* Let me tell you something, Dammit. They are so full of colors and fire — I could not look away. Lovely and cruel. Shining like mountain lilies, *Lloydia Serotina,* that die the next day in a Spring snowstorm. I know this happens; I have seen it. When you are that high anything can happen.

"*Love is merely a madness and deserves a whip for madmen,*" MK would say. I never understood him until now. "*None of us is whipped,*" he'd mutter, "*and cured by the whipping — because the whippers are in love too.*"

I get it now, Dammit. But it is too late. By the time the last period was over, my eyes hurt from getting whipped. Like needles were stuck in them. I had to get to the library. Penny would be there.

Chapter 14

The Quick Brown Fox

"Watcha want, lil bruh?" Sharp eyes like copper flames watched me curiously. The nameplate read, "Librarian," but hand-written on a piece of white tape over it was "Mister R.F. Brown." His bronze mane barely cleared the counter.

"Mister Brown take that scowl, turn ya wise like an owl," he rubbed a scraggly white neckbeard. He looked in his thirties, but something about his eyes felt very old. Very, very old. Like being alone in an old growth forest where you can't see the tops of the trees and their roots clamber under the duff with folded fingers. He wore an over-sized red shirt splattered with green fronds, purple parrots and splotches of something dark I could only assume was food. Which explained the meat smell. From the back I caught a whiff of old pages, crayons and pencil dust.

"Heard ya met Mister Brown's buddy. You know, Doc?" He leaned his armpits on the counter and folded his twiggy fingers under his chin. "Big nose, little weird in the eyes? Heh. Means well, though." His eyes closed halfway like he was listening to a conversation down the hall. "Watcha want, lil bruh," he asked again. Mister Brown pulled a meat stick from the back pocket of his jeans and started chomping.

What do I want? What I wanted would take all day to tell him. What I wanted was Penny. What I wanted was my Momma. What I wanted was vengeance for my father. I wanted a family ranch shadowed by ponderosas, cooled by a river. And a smart-ass friend. I wanted to go back. What a weirdo.

I heard Dad in my head: "Weirdos make the world go 'round." My Momma had old surf magazines at the cabin (which is how I know what the ocean looks like). In one grainy photograph a man held a surfboard, and Mister Brown — in his flaming shirt covered in purple parrots — was dressed just like him. That is, if you shoved a wild fox into man-skin, gave him a bad haircut and sandals, jeans and a big flowery shirt.

"Tokens and tools, lil bruh," Mister Brown scratched his ear with the meat stick. "Misers and rules. It's the man who makes mantles, and mantles makes fools."

Not Shakesbear. Weird. But not bad.

"All the info in the world does not make Dick a wise boy, heh heh." He tapped his nose. "Dick saw Spot run — but did he see Spot shit? Heh." This to himself: "Well said, Mister Brown, heh."

He made no sense.

"No lawn sign against dog shitting will keep the dog from shitting on the lawn. There's your sign. Another good one Mister Brown, heh." And he actually patted his own shoulder.

I picked up the pencil on the counter and wrote on a pad of paper, *"Looke for Pennye."*

"Just missed her! She came in with info, but she can't be seen with Mister Brown — or with you, lil bruh — had to run. She said, uh, what did she say? Oh yeah, 'find my book, dumbass.'" He banged the meat stick on the counter. Mister Brown wrote below my words, *"The quick brown fox jumped over the lazy dog."*

Mister Brown reached up on tiptoe, pulled a small coin from behind my ear with and showed it to me. *"Walah!"* he shouted. "A penny for the penny-lover. Heh." He pushed the penny against my chest with his finger, it was hot as a cinder. "Names got power. Who are you?"

I wrote on the pad, *"Clayton Solomon Bergmann."*

"Hallelujah!" He snapped his fingers, tossed the meat stick.

He danced a jig like he had to pee real bad, caught the meat stick (which seemed to have gone through the roof for fifty feet before it came back down) and took another chomp. "Mister Brown got more nuts for you than a chipmunk in the Fall. Heh. And by nuts, I mean info, lil bruh. Son of Rose-Marie Stonefly and George Bergmann, yes?"

My mouth must have dropped.

"Mister Brown turn your frown upside-down," he grinned, and started rolling the penny across his little twig-knuckles like it was riding the whitewater on the Salmon. *Slam!* His hand hit the counter. He was still grinning snaggly and stinky from ear to ear. He lifted his hand. *"Zimilia Zimilibus!"* He exclaimed like it was a piece of gold. But it was just an old penny. Brown, a little dented on one side, with a grease stain across the face of a severe-looking man with feathers in his hair — who looked nothing like Penny.

"Take it," he said.

I shoved it across the counter back at him. It was hot as a rock under the noon sun.

"No, take it." He chuckled, "Trust me, you're gonna need a penny at some point lil bruh, and not just your new kissin' buddy, heheh. Now listen. A cousin a mine, Mister Bay, gave that penny to me — *that* penny." He tapped the penny. "Said you'll need one or two. Not the size, lil bruh, it's how you wink it, huh?"

Dammit, I did not understand a word. A lot like MK, though Mister Brown seemed friendlier. But sneakier. I didn't have to look away from his eyes like MK's.

He pushed the penny back. "Learn quick. How to wink n' roll. This leads to stokage." He shrugged his shoulders and popped his fists at the air like he was fighting. "Which reminds me." His face changed, and he leaned forward. "Your ma, Rose-Marie, she ever tell you the Clackamas Chinook story, *'Skukm and the Wonderful Boy?'"*

I shook my head. How did he know my mom?

"Who ARE you? Where do you think we live bruh?" His voice dropped, and I had to lean in to hear. "Look. A skukm over here is like what your family on the other side of the pond calls an ungeheuer, ya know, a terror, the thing from the water that comes from behind in the dark. Blacker than night, no eyes because justice is blind – but has long teeth."

He slammed his meat stick down *BAM* and I jumped a foot.

"Heh! You ever seen one?"

I felt a chill go through me, but I shook my head — No. I seen one in my dreams, Dammit. A lot. But I wasn't going to let this weirdo know that.

"Hoo bruh, yep. I see by your face; you know what I'm talking about. You ain't from here originally, Bergmann. Honor stories from *this* ground." Mister Brown pressed down his finger on the penny and looked at me like he was truly — and for the first time completely — a librarian, and said,

"Ground is ground, earth is earth,
She makes us certain of our worth.
Her garments woven ever new,
But who's the weaver? Maybe You."

"No? Never heard it? Un. Be. Leavable. And she ain't — leavable that is. This lovely earth. Heh. This folded plain." He rubbed his eyes like he couldn't believe I did not know about skukms, then slapped his meat stick on the counter absently. The *WHAP* brought him back. "Of course, there are folds within the folds. So." He tapped his long nose significantly as if I got every nuance of what he was saying — which I hadn't in any way, shape, or form, Dammit — and he leaned forward, beckoning. "Mister Bay my cousin, who gave me this here penny, told me this story. Wanna hear it? Course you wanna hear it!"

He didn't give me a chance to answer.

"Hope I do it justice, though." He cleared his throat, pulled out a fresh meat stick, and ran his small hand down its length like he was preparing to conduct an orchestra. "*Long time ago, when wishes were for wishing, aiming was for aiming, and sometimes both came true.*" He paused as if waiting for me to say something.

I was thinking about Penny and where she might be; her lips and how she felt pulled close.

WHAP went the meat stick on the counter and I jumped a foot.

"Focus lil bruh! Long time ago—long before diseases and wars and aggressors who brought them—A skukm of some kind, maybe the worst kind (that is, the ones that don't seek justice but only blood and souls) this skukm come out of the cottonwoods where the Willamette river — you know, the big one runs up the valley over by the Great Ocean – that big river, it falls over a great ledge, they called it Wallampt. Anyway, that skukm, lil bruh, he ate a whole village there by the falls right by the giant cottonwoods. I mean this skukm was a badass motherfucker."

I started to walk around the counter towards the books, but he grabbed my wrist. His nails cut my skin.

"Listen, bruh." His lips pulled back from pointy teeth; he wasn't smiling.

"The skukm kills everyone, right? Eats 'em all. Except the pregnant wife of the chief. She jumps in the river, turns into a salmon — *poof* — gets away." He leaned closer, I choked back a sour taste in my mouth. "The kid gets born, grows up, his mom takes him all over — to different spirits of the lakes and the rivers and whatnot — bathes him in the spirit-waters of all the streams. Gets him trained up. By the way, lil bruh, the training parts are always the best parts. Meet up with the old fighter, struggle, learn kung fu bullshit. I hate to cut that out, I got no time. Trouble comin' like a slow train, and I got to finish quick."

"Anyway, the fish that turned into a baby turns into a little boy, and that little boy grows into a young man — maybe about your age, grown up but not full grown-up — and he goes back *with an axe* to the old village at Wallampt. Nothing is left there from his village. Just wet stones and rotten logs from the Spring floods. He swings that axe 'THWACK' deep into a giant old cottonwood felled by a storm lying there on the cold shore of the river. Can you see it? It's sand and river-rocks on the shore with that fat muddy river swole from Pacific winter rains, and that axe stuck in that downed tree right there by the falls. You see it, lil bruh? Vengeance, heh heh."

He licked his teeth with a long, red tongue.

"The axe makes a sound like a bolt of lightning hitting the ground and it echoes through the forest up from the river, across green hills covered in old oaks naked in the winter, and the wild evergreen mountains to the East. In one of them dark lonesome valleys full of ferns and water and big boulders covered with moss — that same water, by the way, that runs all the way down into the Willamette and over those falls past the axe-tree — in the half-light of the darkness under the trees the skukm lifts his head up in the cold under old growth trunks as big around as a house, he rises up in a deep gully, and he sniffs the air and listens." Mister Brown's eyes burned. "Oh yeah, that fuckin' monster hears the sound of the axe, he feels it in the water, he smells it in the air, and he knows it's not thunder. It's something made by a man. A strong man. But he's not scared of strong men, they taste better anyway. And he's hungry."

"The cottonwood that the boy sunk the axe into is one of them old-growth mothers like nine feet across. Used to be a forest of them where the three rivers come together. The Willamette, Clackamas, and Columbia (only that wasn't their only names in those days). Anyway, the boy sticks his axe in the downed tree, and leans up against it and waits. He waits a long time listening to the roar of the falls with his back to the water, watching the woods. Waiting — and scared of waiting because he can't hear anything coming in the roar. So, he will have to see it coming."

"He waits a long time, and his eyes start to close, he's so tired. And he has to fight to keep them open, lil bruh, he slaps himself and pinches himself. And it starts getting dark and cold, there's a storm coming, and the drizzle starts to fall. You know the cold rain – almost a mist—you get in late Winter that comes off the Great Ocean? So, he decides he's not waiting any longer, and just as he stands up and stretches, the skukm comes walking out of the woods." Mister Brown shivered. "Like fuckin' darkness. Like hair with teeth on it. Like a grizzly bear and a walrus did the nasty on a seashore and then a humpback whale came and jizzed all over it, and this is what you get: a big, fat, hairy, toothy monster all arms and legs and mouth with a hump-back. And lil bruh, ya know what? That skukm smelled like a whole village died and was rotting inside him." Mister Brown paused for effect. "Which it was."

Kind of like you, I thought, and tried to pull away.

But he grabbed my wrist again like his life depended on keeping me there. "Listen!" His voice rose. "The skukm looks at him like he's an appetizer, and thinks to itself, *That's it? That's the man who made the thunder? No problem.*' The skukm chuckles, a little self-laugh, like he does sometimes when he's alone and telling himself stories of who he ate and what he did to them before he ate them. And he says to the boy, *'Hello boy. Perfect timing. I was thinking I was hungry. I can smell the shit in your guts and the blood in your veins. I'll mix 'em into my favorite kind of man soup and across the top I'll squish your milky brains.'* Only what actually comes out of the skukm's mouth is a sound like a baby getting crushed by a car tire far away in the woods. So far you can barely hear it scream but you know it's bad."

I shuddered. He let go of my wrist, and leaned in.

"The boy pulls the axe out of the cottonwood trunk — I told you it was a big axe, right? — and the skukm just laughs. A deep laugh like rocks rolling around in his stomach bashing people who cry out, and he says, *I'm too powerful for you kid, don't you know I ate a whole village back there?'* The skukm raises a long arm big around as an oak tree and all crooked and kinked up, and he points downstream. But all the kid sees is the arm and the fingers and jagged fingernails like swords with rotten meat hanging off them and old dried blood under them from the killing."

"The kid thinks about running at this point, I mean, wouldn't you? He grips the axe which feels like a broomstick in his hands, looks around, and thinks, *'Oh dear god what the fuck do I do now?'*"

Mister Brown paused.

He knew I wanted to hear the rest, and he grinned and slowly continued, speaking each word carefully. "The boy sees the cut in the cottonwood he made, and he gets an idea. Quick and as powerful as falling water he swings the axe deep back into the cut *'THWAM,'* so far into the tree that the axe-head disappears into the cut—and sticks there."

"The skukm grins a mean grin, I mean the kind where you see his teeth and then you see the teeth behind the teeth. He's thinking now the eating just got easier. The kid's a chicken, and stupid too. Won't even try to use the axe, doesn't know how to fight."

"The kid looks the skukm in the eye, right into that dark well-hole of nothing. That black pit of an eye with dead people moaning at the bottom, and the kid says, *'You're so all-powerful and strong, then fuckin' help me do this. I been choppin' on this tree. Hold this crack open for me while I take another cut. I don't think you can, though. You ain't strong enough.'*"

Mister Brown grinned a mean grin.

"Yeah."

I wasn't sure what was coming, but I wanted to know, Dammit.

"The skukm gets mad," said Mister Brown, "because the kid is telling him he ain't strong, and he thinks to himself, *I'll show this little fucker how strong I am. Then I'll eat him slow and dirty, rip off his arms first and watch him beg me while I eat his feet, and then his knees, and then his legs, and then his dick, and finally when he's almost dead — but not quite dead and still watching me — I'll rip out his heart and eat that too – right in front of him.'*"

"The skukm is SO pissed off about how this kid doesn't think he's strong enough, that he just does it without thinking: He sticks his long dirty fingers — all fifteen of them with their long nails like fuckin' jagged spearheads — into the cut in the cottonwood. He shoves them way in there to pull it apart, and '*WANG*' the kid pulls out the axe, and the crack in the trunk slams shut.

WHAP. Mister Brown cracked the counter with his meat-stick. I jumped and squeaked, I'm not afraid to say so, Dammit.

"The skukm's fingers are caught in the crack like a bear-trap, just for a second, you know. Just long enough, and, heh, heh, he's leaning over too because his fingers are caught. You see, in the perfect position with his neck exposed. A thin neck under that head the size of a Volkswagen bug. The kid sees the pale hairless neck like a skinny baby seal and hauls back with that axe and swings as hard as he can—and chops off the skukm's head."

WHAP. He slapped the counter with the meat stick, and I jumped again.

Mister Brown paused to let it sink in. "Then he chopped off the other two heads that grew out of that one. And then he grabs the little skukm fucker that came out his ass. He was waiting for that one because of what his mom told him in the dark nights getting him ready: '*Be sure to watch the ass, heh heh, that's where the last one comes out. You don't watch the ass, fucker'l come back at night and crawl inside you, right up YOUR asshole, and kill you dead and then YOU'LL be the skukm. Heh heh.'*"

Mister Brown rubbed his hands together. He loved that story, I could tell. "That's how people turn into skukms, by the way," he said. "Hoorrrible way to go." He shuddered and wasn't funny anymore.

It *was* a good story, Dammit.

Mister Brown popped the last of the meat stick in his mouth. "So, he watched and waited. When the ass-skukm came crawling out — it was almost too dark to see — the boy was ready. And he killed that one too. Right there at the butthole the size of a little cave he caught it as it came creeping out looking around with its beady red eyes covered in wet shit. He grabbed it with both hands as it squirmed and squealed—twisted it until he popped off its little hairy head. Then he cooked that little skukm – body and head—and ate the whole thing. Right there on the wet sand and rotting leaves, with the great waterfall at his back, that boy ate that skukm."

Mister Brown pulled a fresh meat stick from his back pocket. "That's how you finish a skukm by the way. Eat or be eaten." He chuckled evilly and tapped the penny on the counter. "Take it, lil bruh. You rub that penny and wish for me, I'll be there. By the way, that's the best way to get out of jams anyway. Tell a story."

"*Hide fox and all after,*" I said to myself, thinking of the young prince in The Riverside, his back to the wall. Whose very friends were not to be trusted. I picked up the penny, wiped off the meat grease, put it in my pocket, and wrote on the pad, "*I looke for The Riverside.*"

"Why didn't you say so! Over here." He pointed down a long shelf towards the back. I left him at the counter and walked up the row pulling down books. It did not take me long. I saw it, Dammit, like finding a lost friend. Its weight felt perfect in my hand.

"Books are like guns," said Mister Brown at my elbow, and I jumped. He grinned. "Be ready to fire, lil bruh. Or someone will use it against you. How 'bout this," he said, and pulled a very old book from a shelf. The worn title said, *Dragonflies of North America*. "My recommendation if you only had one book for this town."

I pushed it aside and turned to leave.

He put a small warm hand on my chest. "Mister Brown got debts to pay, don't walk away!"

I didn't care. The Riverside was heavy and perfect.

"Mister Brown knows your parents told you nothing, lil bruh. For better or worse. He knows your Granma don't want to tell either—she has her own reasons. But we're in a war and pressed for time. By my count, we got about a day. So, Brown's gonna lay it out, like the monkey said to his butt. Heh." He paused a moment to enjoy his joke, then got serious. "There's a stalemate in the war. Been this way at least four years. They got everything screwed down so tight this town is popping screws loose. But they don't have the axe. So, they can't finish. And they can't get to it because it's in that house of your Granma's, which is, itself, hallowed ground. That house was built on love not blood or bodies."

Acuere was special, I felt *that* last night. And Granma's house was a sanctuary. But nothing else made sense.

"Same thing with Penny. Yeah, Mister Brown knows about that too. That earring was given in love, and she's protected. Least, for now." His voice lowered. "This bad cat, everyone calls him 'Big Jim,' but he isn't a big One yet, She made him Her right hand. She promised Big Jim something in return." Mister Brown raised an eyebrow. "Can't say Her name, lil bruh. Gets hairy real fast if you say Their names. You'll know if you're ever around Her: your knees'll buckle, your heart'll stoke, you'll beg a favor, and your ass'll get smoked. Heh. When it comes to the big Ones, you step in their current—they'll suck you in and change you forever."

He studied the meat stick, deadly serious. "Two kinds of change. One: you change into something completely different, tear the fabric of the world, make yourself into God. That change does not give, it only takes. It's not turtles all the way down, it's blood and bodies—all the way round."

"The other change, the real kind, is become more like yourself. That's all. Simple. *Good things afoot in the groaning earth. Good things givin' birth.*" He stopped suddenly. "Mister Brown's talking too much, lil bruh, wish I had more time. More everything. Heh. That's what the snake said to the lizard about his legs."

He suddenly sounded so sad I almost patted him on his rusty head.

He squinted at me like he would bite me if I did, wiped his greasy hand on his neckbeard and down his purple parrot shirt. "Me and Doc don't know what She promised him, or put in him, but Big Jim's changing — and if he ever gets to the full change, it will be something to see." He whispered, "If that happens, though, none of us will be left to see it."

Whoever this Big Jim was, Dammit, he had nothing to do with me. I started to walk away, and Mister Brown's fingernails dug into my arm, and he spoke solemnly:

To catch a dragon that flies,
You got to deal with its eyes.

He smiled kindly but it looked like a grimace. "Can't say Mister Brown didn't tell ya everything when he first metcha. Everything will be made new, I tell you now, so later it's true. Take the book!"

Dragonflies of North America felt like it could fall apart. A yellowing page held a drawing of a beast I had once seen underwater devouring the heart of a tadpole.

I shook my head, handed it back and held up The Riverside. This is all I need.

He sighed, shoved *Dragonflies* on the shelf and winked, "Browny-decimal system. Heh."

Yes, I get it Mister Brown. Right there: third shelf, back wall.

We walked to the front desk together, Mister Brown stamped The Riverside, leaned on the counter rubbing his neck-beard, and said softly, "Word on the street, lil bruh, is there's a creepy dude with you. Cold. I don't know what he is. And that's saying somethin', 'cause I know EVERYbody."

I ignored him, but I must have looked horrible. When I looked back as I walked away, I saw it mirrored in his face—how do you tell someone that your friend, the creepy dude, is a murderer?

Mister Brown's eyes crinkled in another attempt to smile. It was like a man-dog-cat with a scruffy white neckbeard trying to do something impossible with his face. He started to apologize, but instead, he sighed and wiggled his meat stick at me. "*Her garments woven ever new, but who's the weaver? Maybe You,*" he said.

Mister Brown pointed with his meat stick down the hall at the front door.

Being the jackass that I am, I chose the opposite.

Chapter 15

Eat Like Wolves, Fight Like Devils

I walked out the back door and counted five of them. The sky was a mean blue, scraped clean of every living thing. MK, with arms crossed, leaned against the school gazing up at nothing like he hung out behind schools all the time. "They want to hurt you," he said. "If a potato had its way with you, what would they call the baby?"

"Hesitater," I muttered.

"Exactly," said MK. "You better get inside."

But it was too late.

"It's lumberfag," said Junior, blocking the school door, "No Dad here to help today."

"No Dad anywhere, no cops," said a boy taller than me with a huge belt buckle and shovel-hands. "No axe either. Like clubbing a seal."

They all laughed.

Junior ripped The Riverside from my hand and gave it to Shovels. "You have no idea who you fucked with, chief," Junior said. "Where's your Dad's axe?"

Shovels smacked The Riverside, and it cracked like a gunshot. "Junior's dad makes him look like cinderfuckingella."

"I AM cinderfuckingella," said Junior, and he pulled Penny's book from his back pocket and ripped out page after page. They floated across the parking lot like giant snowflakes. He threw Penny's book against the brick wall of the school. It burst open; pages flew everywhere. "I lied. I didn't see your dad die but I heard it was *the shit*. But I wasn't joking about your mom." He flexed his hand into a fist, looking at it. "When I'm done with you, I'm going

126

to find her, and hurt her." He grinned coldly. "And tell her it was you made me do it."

I knew I was supposed to do something, but everything felt far away, like I was at the bottom of my river. I shouted, "WHERE IS SHE?!" All that came out was, *"Graaahgh Arhga Sheee."*

"Fuckin mute," said Shovels, and they all laughed.

"Look chief," said Junior. "If I do what he wants, my fairy godfather'll make me more yoked than any 'roids could, trust me." Junior's arms were twice as big as his neck, and his neck looked twice as big as his head. He said the next thing slowly and it echoed between the school buildings. "I'm gonna kick your ass, chief, and when I'm done, he's gonna kick your ass, and when he's done, we're ALL gonna kick your ass, and when we're all done," he took a long breath, "we're gonna make sure you NEVER walk again, or make more Bergmanns — dumbfuck. Your line ends here."

MK popped his knuckles. *"Nefariams nefarious, n'est pas?* The lanky one wants to castrate you, Romes. I think he does it in his free time on a ranch. You should go."

I shook my head. I wasn't going until I picked up the pieces of Penny's book and got answers about my Momma.

"We could go nuclear, Tater," MK played with a curling strand of his hair. "I can't do it unless you ask, though. Just ask for help."

I wasn't about to ask that bastard to help me, Dammit. I wished you were there. I wasn't about to watch him suck one more person's soul, or whatever, out their ear, no matter how much they deserved it.

They circled me like wolves. I itched for *Acuere,* but she leaned quietly in the corner of my room. I had no sword, no halberd, no dagger, lancet, falchion, hangar, cutlass, or seax. Nor did I know how to wield such things (though I do know how to shoot, trap, net, hook, gut-out and skin pretty much anything). My mind began to work on the problem, Dammit. I'd give my left hand AND a bucket of gold for *Acuere*.

Left hand? I stuck my left hand in my pocket and the small blade I took from the hospital fell into it. Mister Brown's cold penny was there at the bottom too. I chose the blade and pulled it out, moved it from my left to my right.

"Scalpel me to death?" said Junior, and the others laughed.

No, I shook my head. I just wanted to go home. I pointed towards the road with the knife, and muttered, "*If we do meet again, why, we shall smile; If not, why then, this parting was well made.*"

"Oh, he CAN talk!"

"He brought the right blade for a nut-job," said another, laughing.

"Sweet partings!" yelled another.

"Gimme that," said Junior. "I'm gonna part your balls off."

They were all around me. Shovels started thumbing through The Riverside. "Jeezus, I can't read this shit."

"He can't either," said Junior. "He's a retard."

On the ground I saw an ant by himself. He woke this morning in a pile of ants. The first one out the door, maybe. I put my toe down on him. I pushed hard and felt him pop. You don't thank an ant for giving its life, do you? He was alone anyway. No one would know. I heard a high-pitched sound, like a mosquito. At first, I thought it was the ant crying, but it was air coming out my nose.

Junior knocked the knife out of my hand.

I pinched the penny in my pocket between my thumb and finger, tried to make myself wink. I'd rather be anywhere but here. How do you wink at a penny, Mister Brown?

Two of them grabbed me from behind and held me. Later, Dammit, you taught me to go for the leader first. Cut his throat and the rest will run and all that.

I wished I could squeeze that penny and wish to be on the river by the ranch in the sun. I smiled sadly. I was wishing to make a wish, which is the stupidest thing ever.

"What you grinning at, ya fuck?" said Junior.

Shovels raised The Riverside over his head and hit me in the face with it as hard as he could swing. Everything blew up in a fire in my head. I slumped in their arms. Something burning shot out my butt. Shovels was so close I could smell his breath. It was like mud where something has crawled in to get away and then died. I felt blood running into my mouth. My eye would not open.

"You wanna be friends with us?"

I nodded my head. My mouth tasted bitter. I began to gag and retch.

"Pussy," someone muttered.

Shovels threw the Riverside on the ground and punched me in the face. I bent over groaning and Junior kicked me in the wuttus. I felt the pain shoot up and pierce my stomach and blow out my head. I yelled and collapsed in their arms. They were laughing. I couldn't see anymore, my broken eye clouded with tears.

I threw up chunks of boiled egg, and they dropped me on the ground.

"Ugh," someone said. "He shat himself."

"Dude. You just kicked the shit out of him. Like for real."

Junior picked up The Riverside and smashed it on my face. I curled into a ball. Then he kicked me again. The pain shot across my body and into my head. It felt like I was going to split open.

I heard MK in the mist, "I'm here to help, you know. Just say so. You've got to say so, I need you to say so."

"No!" I screamed.

"Oh ephemeral qualities of man, how prideful, how meritorious thy preening," MK said. "Guess who said that?"

I groaned, *"...the fault lies not in ourselves, we are underlings."*

"Gross, shit's coming out of his pants," said Shovels.

"God, you stink." I heard Junior clear his throat with a sucking, ripping sound. Then he spat onto the back of my head. I felt it drip down my hair. They laughed, and I heard them closing in, taking their time.

"Pull down his pants," someone said.

"This will only take a second," said Shovels.

"Dude. Romes," said MK, and he sounded sad. He sounded far away on the other side of the universe. "For Godsakes. Just ask."

They kicked me. Over and over. A ball of fire stabbed my chest, my wuttus, my face, my side, my hands. I couldn't stop retching. Wetness dripped down the back of my legs. I heard someone crying and realized it was me. Me and that dead ant on the ground.

"A wolf comes."

The words came from my swollen, bleeding mouth in a mutter. I must tell you the truth, Dammit, I saw the wolf before I ever told it. A wolf covered in black hair, lank and with teeth like knives, ravenous as time. A wolf who looked like a man.

"Hey, stop! He said something."

I reckon it was a concurrence that I imagined the wolf and he came. Fate, serendipity, or something like that. It doesn't matter, I wasn't thinking. I was hurting. Something deep inside me wasn't held back no more.

"*A wolf comes, a wolf comes, a wolf comes....*" I said it, over and over.

"Did you hear that?" Shovel's voice trembled. "What's that sound?"

I heard it too. A snarl, far away and coming closer. The story inside me broke open, and from my mouth came words, ancient and strong: "*The wolf was going there, and on the way, he saw a traveler waylaid by robbers. A wolf comes.*"

There was that snarl again. Much, much closer. Deep, and long. Dark as the shadows under the Douglas firs in the twilight of the valley of the skukm. I thought I heard you, Dammit, howling far away: "*YES.*" But you were not the snarl. It was something else — not you — moving faster than a car and snarling as it came.

"*A wolf comes,*" I said.

Shovels yelled, "What the fuck is that? Run!" Someone kicked me in the head and darkness fell.

One voice was foreign. It sounded like a wolf, mean and hungry. The other voice sounded lighter, familiar. Pain shattered my head and I groaned.

The wolf voice said, "Be gone." I thought he was talking to the lighter voice, but then you said, "Nope." The single best thing I heard all day, Dammit. Everything hurt so bad, and my left eye would not open. So, I closed my other eye and tried not to hurt.

"All is fair in love and war," you said, and nuzzled my face.

"Called me," said the wolf. "Who is it, this *pisskopf*?"

"Yes, I know bruh. Didn't you meet him earlier?" The fox-voice sounded frustrated. "I wish you could remember your other self. It's Rose-Marie's boy. He needs help, and we are it."

"Eat is better." The wolf was angry, and still hungry.

"You already did. We just put what you left in the dumpster. Grab his legs, no, bruh, not there, his feet," said the fox. Someone leaned over my shoulders and lifted me.

"I *beriechen* death messenger." Long, hairy arms with claws held me as if I was a child.

"It's an old story, the death messenger isn't real."

"Ha. Like us? He is here. No *gestank* like this," said the wolf.

"Monster stink?"

"Nah. Something else."

The fox asked, "You know what makes a monster a monster?"

"Let there be light." You sounded curious, Dammit.

"Two things," said the fox. "One, they want to live instead of die, even though sooner or later, all things die. We all want to live, eh? But monsters will do anything to extend life. Anything. Two, they want to be something they are not. When these two purposes breed together — you get the stink of cancer. That which grows uncontrolled beyond its nature."

You asked, "How can you tell if a monster likes you?"

There was complete silence. A long waiting silence. I heard you lift your leg and scratch your ear. They were not going to take the bait. Instead, they began to walk, carrying me away from the school.

Then you spoke, and I could almost see the grin: "He takes another bite."

Silence.

I get it Dammit. Sometimes no one wants to play.

"Kill the death messenger?" asked the wolf hopefully.

"It's death messenger bruh, no one eats him, he eats them. Then they eat themselves. Anyways, we're OK. There's blood here, and you know — the old stories — how it goes if he's here. He can't stand blood."

"Fighter," you growled. "The boy can fight."

"Yep, my fine prince of a dog. I agree with you," said the lighter voice. "Lycaon, the boy called you, didn't he? Anyone ever call you before?"

"No one calls the wolf. The wolf calls himself," said the wolf. And he spat.

"Hargh," it was your bark-laugh. "How does that work?"

"Oh, he called you," said the fox. "But the boy knows nothing about what's really going on."

"Diamond with flaw better than stone," you said. "Dad's ghost asks for vengeance."

"*Wachst der mut auch feigen hunden*," said the wolf.

"The fourth path is what we chose, eh? Not fight or flight — or freeze. You wouldn't be here otherwise, no matter how grumpy."

I felt the wolf shrug. "Bah. '*The dog, he is brave when he sees the bloody bear paw in the snow*.'" And he spat again. "This fight we are having, this is fight to the death."

"All is fair in love and war," you said again. "I prefer war. Hargh." I could sense the grin across your face; a statement of fact, like so far as you were concerned, the conversation was finished.

"Well said, prince. Well said, but still, we try for peace."

"Not me," said the wolf.

"Hargh," you said, and it sounded like you agreed.

I felt my body squeezed in those hairy, sinewy arms and I fell into a dream-valley of stabbing pain. There were skukms; I fought them many years in the twilight under ancient trees. Always watching for them by my fire on the sand. But one came from behind from the river. It tore out my heart and ate it.

Chapter 16

Child of Sadness

"You have *got* to be kidding me," said Mister Brown, helping me up the five steps of Granma's porch. My head felt like someone stuck a rod through it. The wolf was gone but its bloody scent was on my skin. Or was that my own wounds?

Granma lay sideways on the rough-hewn floorboards, a thin trail of smoke rising from a cig in her mouth.

"Be careful passing the hippo in a canoe," you said, and leaned against my leg to hold me steady.

"You're gonna burn down your house, Lina." Mister Brown sat me in the canvas chair next to the front door. Then he threw the cig — and the bottle she was holding — onto the lawn.

"No shit, Sherlock," she mumbled at the wall. Granma sat up slowly, her blue cap lopsided on her head. A crumpled piece of paper stuck out of her fist. "Gonna take my house," she said, and then grabbed her head. "Aagh. Brown, they're taking it all. Everything." She waved the paper at the house. "All O & S did was give me this paper. Assholes."

"Clay's hurt bad," said Mister Brown.

She turned her face from the wall and saw me.

I closed my good eye. I did not want to see her looking at me.

"Clayton?" she said in a whisper. Then, in a low voice to Mister Brown, "Get me HELL off this porch, you red-headed cocksucker."

"Get inside lil bruh," he said to me. I opened my eye. That toothy grin almost split his face in two. "Told you to go out the front." He clucked his tongue.

I tried to stand up, the pain mashed my head in flashes, I threw up on the porch and passed out.

When I woke, I was in the bath, and they were cleaning poo from my legs—and I passed out again. Next time I woke, I lay on the couch in warm, dry clothes with The Riverside heavy on my chest. Everything spun.

"… they beat him an inch from the hospital," said Mister Brown.

"Nah," Granma said, "no Bergmann ever stay in no damn hospital."

"He could use some stitches above that eye. Call Doc, he'll make a house call."

"Them boys'll need more than stitches when I'm done. Kill 'em all." I heard the false pump of an empty action, *shick-shick*, followed by the click of shells pressed one after the other into a shotgun. "Kill those fuckers. All a them. Woh." I heard crashing and opened my eye. She leaned against the shelf that held all the plates and cups. They slid onto the ground in slow motion, piece by piece, and every crash felt like a kick in my head.

Mister Brown took the gun from her and put it behind the front door.

"You won't find out who they are," he said. "No one talks."

"Clayton," she said loudly, then grabbed her head. "Ow. DAMMIT, come HERE."

You let her lean on you. "Fight?" you asked.

"Clayton, who hurt you?"

I shook my head. Even if I had words, I wasn't going to tell her. I didn't want her gunning around in Sonofa looking for Junior and his buddies. Lady Macbeth with a shotgun. I almost smiled. MK would have made a joke. That bastard, always gone when I need him.

I looked at you, Dammit, and you looked at me. "Yup," you said. "Kill 'em all."

Mister Brown said, "You like that Riverside, lil bruh? I picked it up after the fight."

That was no fight—that was a beating, I thought.

"Hmphh," Granma said. She got a glass of water from the sink, sat in her armchair, pulled her hat over her eyes, lit a cig, and smoked it all the way down. Then she started a second one with a second glass of water. The smoke swirled around the ceiling and out the open front door. I reckon she didn't want me to see she was sick. Why else would someone lie on their face?

I pulled The Riverside to my chest, closed my one working eye, and tried not to hurt.

While she smoked, Mister Brown carefully opened the wadded-up paper — like he was touching something bad - and read out loud:

To the Tenant, Mrs. Karolina Bergmann:

This is notice of eviction due to failure of your landlord to make mortgage payment over a period of one year. On April 25, 1999, you are required to vacate the property premises in the presence of our executor. If you do not vacate the premises by the date stated above, you will be forcibly removed, as the property is slated for removal to another site on the 25th day of April.

If you have any questions about this notice, please contact us at any time. We live to serve all our residents in Junction City with the utmost care for their wellbeing.

Helping you thrive,

The Oyster and Swans, Inc.

Executor, Rev. Dr. James Y. Sengrim, Esq.

"That's tomorrow," Mister Brown said, and he was angry. "How can you not know about this?"

"Found out at the meeting," she said. "I'm not moving. O & S own the house, not the land. They own all the other plots in town. Fuckers stole house out from under me when Beaumont died. Legal bullshit. They can't get the land, it's protected. That fuckin snake Big Jim bought the house from them and I pay him rent and he pays them. They run Junction City."

"But this says he hasn't paid them in a year. It's obviously a scheme between him and them to get you out."

"Don't matter. Jim needs my rent and I'm paid up. He's a scheming asshole, but he won't do it. He can't take the house. I'm protected. *Vengeance mine and rolling flood.* Something that belonged to my Beaumont protects me, so long as it's here."

"Mrs. Bergmann," Mister Brown's voice was tight with anger. "Love alone and your husband's legacy can't keep you safe anymore."

She shrugged and her eyes sparked blue. "Them and whose fuckin army?"

Mister Brown spoke slowly. "Adverse possession law, my dear, changes everything if they can get you, or the house, to move. Do you know the nature of the object here which they want but don't know how to access? If they get the house moved – or destroyed—they can take possession of the land legally. And the object too."

"Over my dead body," she said.

"Yes," he said. "Exactly. They own the judge and the cops. It won't matter."

"They won't do it," she said, "Been tryin' for years, and they can't. Anyways, Jim needs my rent money."

"Did you hear me?" Mister Brown's voice rose. "He has not paid them for over a year. There's a back-alley agreement. They have legal right. What are you going to do?"

"Nothin'. They can come and try. Fuck 'em all." She walked zig-zag — still smoking — to the bathroom.

Granma stayed in there a long time.

When she came out, she had a pill bottle and a glass of water. "Take these," she said to me. "Damn ALL those cockSUCKERS to hell." I could not tell if she was cursing the boys who beat me, The Oyster & Swans, Inc., Reverend Sengrim, or all three at once.

"Clayton, you're a mess. They use a baseball bat?"

I pointed to my foot.

"Fight back?" Her eyes blazed.

I did not have the heart, or the voice, to tell her: about me, about fighting, about my Momma somewhere getting hunted down by Junior. Whatever Bergmann strength she kept talking about, whatever courage to stand up tall when things got rough, was not me. I was the ant; they were the foot.

Granma's eyes were red, her hands gentle as she cleaned my face with a warm towel. It hurt, and I'm not talking about what hurt on the outside no more, Dammit.

She sang softly:

"Bruise turn green, Cut turn scar,
Mister nut-man and the bay,
Breaking bones and holey jars..."

She coughed, lit another cig, and kept singing:

"Hurt can't hurt my heart always.
Under skin and silver star,
When all things new be made."

"Old family song, Pops taught me and I sung to your Dad when he was little," she said. "Anytime he got hurt. Somethin' about a prophecy but Pops never told me what." The words ran together until everything was a voice, and smoke, and an old woman's eyes. And the voice was two hands holding my heart. You whined and came close and licked the bleeding cut on my face, and she did not stop you but continued to sing:

"Living words, wind and wave,
Comes the one who kills his blood.
Curse of death and open grave,
Vengeance mine and rolling flood.
Child of sadness, sings to save,
When all things new a-bud."

Comforting, Dammit, in a strange way. Like getting your head shoved in cold water.

"Take this." She gave me water and more pills. "Help you sleep."

"Look at your face," said Mister Brown. He held out a small mirror.

"He's never used one," Granma said. "Never seen himself."

I wanted to say, yes, I have. Sometimes the river is still. You can look into it and see yourself moving. Sometimes on the edges — when the sun is right — you can see your full self in the river like a dark cloud with light around you. I wished MK was there. He would say something like, *"'Make thick my blood; stop up the access and passage to remorse,'* — who said that, Romes?" I'd say, "Lady Macbeth in the fourth scene, I reckon. Though for this day of woe and betrayal I prefer Lear." And MK would laugh and say, "you moron, it's the sixth scene." And we would fight and call each other "Hams" and "Romes" and make up wild lies.

"Look, lil bruh," Mister Brown's voice was gentle. "Look in the mirror."

A ragged wound under my eye bled like a mouth. Blood trickled from its torn lips. My other eye glared back like a dark spring, water seeping down my gaunt cheek. I was in a storm, looking through the rain.

Where are you Momma?

My hair hung matted over my shoulders. It must be drenched from the storm. "*Blow winds,*" I thought. "*Blow and crack your cheeks. Rage, blow. You cataracts and hurricanoes spout....*" Yeah, that about says it.

Everything started to spin. I closed my eye, and felt the mirror fall.

Chapter 17

Ms. Swan

If you're wondering how this works, Dammit, it's simple. Every time I tried to open my one working eye; I fell deeper. Though visions happen rarely, I knew the feeling: rushing forward, falling deep. It was morning of tomorrow – tomorrow—and I was in a big truck with a big man. *I was watching what was yet to come.* And was, somehow, inside of it.

Her messenger seemed more beast than man. Snakes for arms and worms in his gut. When I looked straight at him, I saw only this: a large man with wide eyes and a thick mustache drooping yellow over his mouth, and a tendency to "mmm" like he was tasting something good. Like a cat purrs deep in its chest after eating a mouse.

It was Big Jim.

His chest was deep as a barrel and touched the steering wheel. His head leaned forward to miss the roof, and his shoulders were so broad they crushed me against my door.

"Mmm." He purred and looked at me, eyes glinting – eyes too big even for that head. "You have been summoned by Mistress _____." He said her full name. Something like a hand squeezed my stomach, or lower, my wuttus. The closest feeling I knew was when I saw Craig holding his jerking heart. Scary and weird and you cannot take your eyes away. A line from The Riverside came to my mind: "*Rank corruption, mining all that is within, infecting what is unseen.*" Hearing that name was like being crushed by gravestones and suckled by a mountain lion. It must have shown on my face.

"She's got that effect," said the giant, grinning, and I thought I heard a faint *click click* from his mouth.

"Boy, mmm. Your grandfather's axe? Where is it?" The "mmm" habit made my skin crawl. Like he peeked at a naked woman without her permission.

Even if I could talk, I wasn't gonna tell him a thing.

"Never mind. Here we are," said Big Jim.

We pulled up to a storefront downtown on the lake. I felt no pain from my wounds. Gotta love visions for that, Dammit. Also, I wanted to meet his Mistress. Wind rippled the lake with a thousand knives. And yet that overpowering smell: mud and a rotting peach full of worms.

Big Jim unlocked a door with gold writing, *"The Oyster & Swans, Inc."* Above the door, carved swans danced around a ponderosa. A bell tinkled as the door opened. It smelled like the den of a pack of women. Shafts of sun crossed a room full of racks of sweaters and skirts of brilliant colors. Rings glinted in a glass case. A woman with short silver hair worked behind the counter. Long ago, something hot had been poured across her face leaving a burn scar. Her eyes stared through a film like the second eyelid of an owl. She did not look up. Her fingers seemed to know where everything was.

Big Jim kissed her roughly. She gasped for air, grabbed a knitting needle from the counter, and slashed blindly at his throat. Big Jim chuckled — sidestepped faster than any fat man should move — and caught her arm. He twisted the arm. She cried out and dropped the needle.

"How long you been waiting to do that?" he murmured and slapped her so hard she fell to the floor. His voice dropped to a whisper (the meaner he got, Dammit, the quieter). "Get your ass to work before I twist your other arm."

She crawled to the counter and pulled herself up.

Big Jim gazed at me as if he expected a challenge. "Mmm...."

I said to myself, "You're dreaming, you're dreaming, just wake up." But I knew different. It was tomorrow, and I was seeing all of it.

"My lady, mmm what can I say?" he chuckled. "She keeps me warm, yes, the long cold nights. Let me tell you, a real firebrand."

Big Jim pushed me through the door at the back and we walked down a hallway hung with thick curtains. I felt I was crawling under a mile of earth. I couldn't breathe. A musky scent drew me through the drapes and down, down, down to the center of the earth. Big Jim pushed the last curtain back, put his hand on a door and turned to me. "This is a great honor. Don't screw it up." He opened the door.

I smelled perfume like something large had lived in too small a space all winter and was waking up. Stairs rose to an ebony throne encrusted in black gems. It was empty. Two swans sat on either side of the throne sleeping, heads tucked. Lamplight shone on the edges of the room. Curls of incense rose from jeweled boxes. The stairs behind the ebony throne disappeared into shadowed distance, as if they never ended. The never-ending space behind the throne echoed with fervent rustlings, whispering lovers in the dark.

MK — out of nowhere — grabbed my arm. "Smells like a hundred secretaries jammed in a conference room at the Holiday Inn." He grinned at me. "Romes, this One will eat you alive, mkay? Don't mess with golden wenches on a warpath." He cracked his knuckles. "How good am I Romes, really? Finding you in the future? In a fucking *vision?* They should write a play—about me. *Make dust our paper and with rainy eyes our sorrow.*"

I thought, "Easy. Richard the II, Act Three." But I could not speak in my vision. And he knew it, and grinned even bigger, the plague.

"Point to me, Romes. Point to me."

Then the world changed and has been different ever since. A golden light came from fifty paces away in the depths behind the throne, moving towards us — time stood still — and down the steps, one by one, She came. Slowly, the room filled with a smell so different from anything I'd ever known, so strong and overpowering, I fell to my knees. It was She. The one who called me in the dream on that first night at Granma's.

I felt my chest blaze again as if *Acuere* laid upon it.

"*Kyvernisei o erotas*," She cried, and the two swans beside her ebony throne raised their wings wide and called in fell voices. Down Her upraised arms rippled violet flames.

I struggled to lift my head to look upon Her, but it felt like a dozer under the dirt. Unbidden, a phrase from The Riverside came to my mind, for I believe I knew Her:

Forc'd to content, but never to obey
Panting he lies, and breatheth in her face.
She feedeth on the steam, as on a prey...

Surrounded by gentle winds, still strong enough to mar the surface of Her form, all I could sense was the Most Beautiful Creature the earth had ever born. Because I could not speak Her name without losing my senses—indeed, my whole self—I chose the closest thing I could find that worked: Ms. Swan.

"Welcome Clayton," said Ms. Swan. "Welcome unto Our lands, son of George and grandson of Beaumont. We saw thee in Our sacred vale. We called, thou hast come. Still, thy father has been much trouble to Us."

I would give myself away, piece by piece. In words, and in deeds. In stories, in lies, in truths, in any way that I could — and I would do it because She demanded and not because I wanted. But I did want it, Dammit. Because She wanted it.

"Welcome fair stranger," She raised a lovely hand to MK and sat upon her throne. "What shall We name thee?" (I wanted to go to the mountains, mine the purest of gold for a thousand years, and smelt a ring to fit upon a single finger of *that* hand. Just so the ring might shine with Her radiance). Her voice was warm and heavy like a thousand nights under a thousand velvet blankets, and the scent of Her was like the source of all the women in the world.

"I go by MK, just MK," he said, with that chilling grin.

I couldn't help smiling. My head was starting to clear because Ms. Swan was not gazing at me. It was like moving from hot sun to shade.

We needed to get out. Something was not right.

MK bowed. *"Who ever loved, that loved not at first sight?"* he said.

"Only me," She said, and silence filled the room like incense. "Be welcome Death Messenger. Though others will not give thee welcome, We say 'Welcome to Our lands. Be at peace.'"

MK trembled, his voice a mutter more to himself than to Her, "I am never at peace. All fear me. All tongues cleave in my presence, all hearts die at my touch. None speak to me of their free will, none freely but this boy."

"Free will?" She said. "Free will is for The Nisoi. And fools who pay *no* price. All others pay the toll."

"The shadow of memory is a shroud upon me," said MK. "I wander in bleak and lonely lands accursed and forgetting myself. A friend to outcasts and orphans. And worse." Hope rose in his voice. "Tell me You know me. Do You know me?"

"Never have We seen a thing like thee," Her lovely voice quivered.

"Show me how to find myself, and verily — with all my soul — I shall give You service," he said and there was not a hint of a joke in his voice.

"Mayhap, We shall unveil this. In due time." The voice had command to it, but also, something deeper. Was it fear? Did She really know who he was, Dammit?

MK's face twisted and his voice swelled, the sound of his words was a room of people all talking at once. "I carry many voices. I cannot hear my heart."

"You fear it," She said flatly. "What thou hast done."

MK gazed somewhere past Her shoulder in the dark corner of the throne room and did not speak, his face etched with pain.

She turned Her gaze to me; its weight pressed me into the floor. "Tell Us, Clayton, how dost thou find Our town?"

MK bowed, "If I may: he cannot speak, your gracefulness." I'll tell you one thing, Dammit, he could recover faster than anyone I ever knew. He grinned, "To be brief, on his behalf I must tell You he has found Your town... unwelcoming."

"Unwelcoming?" said Ms. Swan and laughed and it was like the sea being born. "This news of Our lack of hospitality has come to Our ears." Ms. Swan rose from Her black-pearl throne: "No more attacks. We have need of thy service, boy. Small tasks, of the lowliest and easiest kind, which, if thou completest, thou shalt receive thy reward. We will tell thee all. And thou shalt come to be with Us, and We shalt give thee what thou seekest."

I tried to crawl to Her, but MK held me back in his cold hands.

"Ah Romes," he whispered, "Quests? That old herculean labor gambit. I advise shrewdness."

I didn't care. I wanted to pierce Her veil. I wanted to see that Face and receive all She was. Yes, I wanted my mother and father. But here — with Her presence heavy as a cougar waiting for a kill — I wanted more, much more than that. Her love for me made the room ripple and bend.

This was the moment in the vision, Dammit, when I saw something I did not see later. There were two of Her. The one present in the room, and a thin and twisted shadow on the stair behind, babbling quietly in an unknown tongue, as if possessed. Then, the babbler bloomed from gibberish to full sentences, speaking to Herself:

"It is a lie: Love and all it rests upon," She murmured. *"I sent Craig to tear down. I begin the work that tears the world. Anything built by love."* She stepped forward into Ms. Swan and they became one, and She cried, *"Let Agdistis come!"*

I never saw the babbler again. Ms. Swan's power was so potent I kicked the small voice in me that cried *"don't trust Her!"* into an iron chest. As the two became one, She raised her ivory arms over me in blessing and I caught a vision – a vision within my vision—myself raised in purple flames and power to that ebony throne to rule. Her presence behind me, hands around my chest, and the promise of much, much more.

I groveled; face pressed to the floor.

She held those perfect hands out — as if nothing had just happened — and I felt Her presence spilling on me. "If thou doth act as We require, We shalt give thee word of thy Mother and Father. Even more, We shalt give the greatest gift. One true love to last thy life."

Dammit, these old gods, they love to twist the dagger. She could have directed me to tear out my heart with my own hands and I would a done it.

"Trust me, Romes, the opposite of love is not hate—it is rot," whispered MK. "I would know. And thus, known by its fruit, the decayed fruit of a twisted tree."

"The first task is simple," She said. "There is a buffalo hide in the house of Our lover. We are estranged. Bring it to Us."

MK laughed, "I suppose you want us to steal apples from Atlas too?"

"This is harder," She said. "The second labor is this: A girl in this town, Penelope, her heart is most courageous. Bring it to Us."

"Why is this girl so important?" MK asked. "Why her heart?"

"She is protected from Us by a gift of love. She is a thorn, unmoving."

"Ah, I see it now," said MK, tapping his nose. "Your original vocation, though now forsworn, prevents You from breaking what love has given or born."

Ms. Swan moved restlessly. "It matters not why. She is adamant, she cannot be moved."

"Ah," said MK, grinning. "She asks too many questions."

Ms. Swan cut him off, "She is a danger. Our servants have no power to take her life. Her time is up. Bring Us her heart, boy."

I'll tell you what, Dammit, I wanted to walk away. Nothing could make me hurt Penny. Ms. Swan turned her full gaze on me like the noon sun, and I forgot everything – everything but wanting to do what She wanted.

"Clayton," She said, and my body vibrated with Her warmth. "The girl is an obstacle. The love We give thee will crush her memory to nothing." She smiled at me. Smiled at *me*. I nodded my head and bowed and felt the lighter blow out.

"Don't worry, we got this," said MK. "I know you're addled."

Ms. Swan's voice was a low register like a river in a canyon. "The third labor is easiest and least important. Still, in your grandmother's house there lyeth an axe. Bring Us the axe, We shalt give thee what thy heart desirest most."

"There's a lot of heavy promising going on," MK observed quietly. "Notice, Romes, the conditional statement: If you do this, then this will happen. Always thus are great religions founded. Of course, as you know well, it all hangs on the trustworthiness of the one making the conditions."

MK stepped in front of me. "If I may suggest an alternative?"

The room filled with a new scent. Goddess waiting. Like fresh-turned earth in the rain and burnt flesh.

MK took another step forward. "It's a bit much — don't you think? To ask a boy to fetch the heart of a maid?" He popped his knuckles so hard I thought his fingers would break off. His smile widened, it was his crazy grin, the one that matched his eyes. "Especially a maid he finds attractive?" He whispered to me: "*I am punished by a sore distraction*, Romes, I'm going full-crazy Dane."

The One on the ebony throne leaned forward.

"What if there were another way to do this?" MK asked. "To get what You want and help the boy. What if it's me instead of the boy? What if I get something?"

Ms. Swan gripped the arms of her throne.

MK licked his lips, looked at me, and cracked his knuckles. Then he did something so strange, I will never forget it. He knelt. In that moment the whole world with multitudinous seas turning incarnadine felt like a sharply drawn breath in the lungs of a frightened child. The room spun. All that is green turned red. He knelt looking up, with his arms wide.

"If I vow, here on this ground, upon my own name to serve the ruler of this town, in return, You tell him about his parents, get his mother back to him, after I have served You for — say — a day."

Ms. Swan tapped a single lovely nail on Her black throne. "Agreed. And for thee?" She asked.

"For me? All this poor fool wants is to know who I am, what I've done, and how to stop." MK turned and smiled so sadly at me I thought my heart would burst. "That's all. Just a little info in this great big world. *I am but mad north-north-west, Romes. When the wind is southerly I know a hawk from a hand-saw.* Name it."

You know who it is, I thought to myself, and you know that's perfect.

"Oops," he said with a shrewd look. "I forgot you can't speak in this vision, Hesitater. Hah! Point for me." He smirked and turned back to bow before the black-pearl throne.

"You ask this, knowing the outcome?" Flames played down Her fingers. "Two days of service shall we take," She said. The throne had become the mouth of the lioness, and within the mouth there was a Woman, purple fire in Her eyes.

"This I cannot do," said he. "One day. Just one. Going twice, going thrice...." He knocked the floor with a fist. "This is a once-in-a-millennia offer."

"So be it. One day," She said.

The room expanded and sighed. Light entered from some unnamed meadow where ran many girls. All of them beautiful as Her. Some of them more fey.

"We will take thy one day," Ms. Swan said. "For this boy, and for what thou asketh of Us. Thou shalt serve Us, Nuncio."

"On what shall I swear?" he asked on his knees with his arms wide. His flaxen hair spilled down his back over his ankles to the floor. "On your throne? On my name?"

"On the very name of That which first sent thee as scourge."

"This I cannot do," said he. "I remember Them not. You think I remember what I am or where I have been or what I have done? Why you think I'm doing this? No! I will swear upon the Ruler of this town."

"So be it," She said. "Swear. On the Ruler of this town. Let vows be made, let blood be spilled."

Then I saw something most strange, Dammit: threads of white silk seeped from uncut holes in his hands and feet.

"I vow," he said. "I give my service for one day. I give all of me to the One who rules this town," he swore, and he bent his forehead down and touched the floor. "To know who I am and what I have done." He raised his face and lines of white-silk blood ran from his black eyes.

The room rang like a brass bell, and She groaned in pleasure. "This blood is a pleasing gift," She said.

"And how to stop," he said.

The lamps blew out. The room went black.

"It is done," Her voice sounded in the darkness, deep and triumphant.

She lit herself on fire from within, a firefly in purple flames, and rose from Her throne and came past MK, still entranced and kneeling, to me. She kissed me. It was like being pulled underwater, losing my direction in the woods, getting a foot chopped off to save my leg, and being buried alive. She bit a fingernail like a hook from the tip of her perfect thumb.

"Forget not. When We will it, We shall call thee."

With one hand on my chest — warm as the sun — She opened my shirt and pressed the fingernail under my skin. "You will come to me," she whispered. It only hurt a moment. Something cool slipped between my ribs. Then, it was gone, and Ms. Swan rubbed my chest and ordered: "Ours thou art."

In the dark behind me a great beast expanded its chest. Big Jim had been in the room the whole time in the shadowed doorway. Listening. *Click.* It was a strange sound from under his mustache, large shears snapping shut.

"Done, yes," said MK, and I turned to see him rise. A light shone from his face, illuminating every line and crevice that ran from his black eyes. He shone. A lighthouse, silver in a sea of darkness.

"Milady, our service is not transactional, it's personal," he grinned. "We go the extra mile. Thine achievement is our success."

Was his wink for Her or me?

Ms. Swan shifted disapprovingly on Her throne, I heard the *click click* of Big Jim's shears behind me, and the room began to spin slowly.

"We listen, we care, we deliver," MK said. "I'm trying out mission statements. What dost thou thinketh?"

"Enough," She said.

"Thy satisfaction is our number one priority," he said.

The room spun, then dropped into a swirling river. I fled like a salmon to its natal stream. Swimming as hard as I could away from that black-pearl throne towards a golden-lamped kitchen that moved further away with every stroke.

Chapter 18

A Seat With The Strays

My chest felt like a fish lying at the bottom of a lake. The fishhook wiggled and I felt a cold pain. At the table in my mind where we — I mean, I — meet together I heard a new voice. She laughed and said I was Hers.

"Big, fugly fish," She laughed an icy, hard laugh, "We pull thee in anytime."

I hated Her for the leaden fingernail twisting in my chest. But I also wanted Her in my arms.

She whispered fiercely, "Don't come now! We will call when We desire."

I will say this, Dammit, there are other voices in me besides Her. Not like MK. These are my voices and — though usually quiet, like snow falling in an open field — I do hear them. Unlike Her, some of them sing.

The smell of bread baking. The soft *clack* of dishes set on a table.

The wound under my eye cracked; something wet rolled down my cheek. The lamp over the table was gold syrup lapping against the darkness at the edges. Granma moved in the light like she swam in a yellow sea. A tiny woman in a white nightgown covered in blue flowers sitting at the table spoke directly to me:

"Brute beauty and valor and act, oh, air, pride, plume, here..."

She pounded Granma's table. "Walter was so angry with me, he kicked the dog, but he ate another helpin', uhuh. *Buckle! AND the fire . . . ."*

"Well, Sophie," said Granma. "Your hubs had a fuckin temper. Almost bad as Beaumont's brother, Gipfel. You know, him who moved to Hailey and won't talk to me no more."

I closed my eye and, in the darkness, Sophie twittered like a bird,

"Breaks from thee then, a billion
Times told lovelier, more dangerous, O my chevalier!"

I felt her next to me and opened my eye.

"Hello, I'm, I"m ..." the little woman smiled gently and paused as if remembering.

"She don't remember a lot no more, Clay," Granma said. "Best to play along."

"This one is full of words," said the little woman. "Brute beauty and valor."

"Nah," said Granma pushing back her cap and smiling at me. "Welcome back, you been talkin' weird, rollin' about. That's Sophie — Sophelia's her name. Been my best friend too many years. Since your Pops brought me here and built me this house."

"Fall," Sophelia said to me in her bird-voice, *"gall yourself, and gash gold-vermillion."*

"She talks a song sometimes," said Granma Lina. "Don't mind her. Lots of her been gone somewhere else too long. What's left likes to say the things she knew when she was young."

Through the blood in my cracked nostrils, I smelled dish soap and something else most powerful: night air in mountains. You know about this, Dammit. When the air gets cold and quiet, and the vanilla from the ponderosa bark is the first smell. Then, a layer of fine dust and pine pollen, followed by the bitterness of the young needles of tamaracks and ponderosas.

Granma started humming and turned to the stove.

"...bruise turn green, cut turn scar... hmmm hmmmm...."

Sophelia took my hand in hers. "You're the gold-vermillion, the dapple-dawn-drawn falcon. No one should ever kick a dog. Hello, I'm, I'm. What am I?" she said. "I know you, you're the wimpling wing."

"Sophie," said Grandma Lina moving a pot from the stove. "Your Sophie."

Sophelia clenched my hand so tight I gasped, "He is filled with light, yea, stronger than ten thousand warriors, than a storm in the mountains with wings on the wind, than the lions in the caves of the mountains in their roaring."

Granma Lina put her hands on her hips, cap tipped back, her broad shoulders filled the room. "Weirdest fuckin thing I ever heard you say, sis."

"Hello, I'm Sophelia," said Sophelia to me,
"You'll lack neither courage nor sense from this day on,
So long as your father's spirit courses through your veins."
"Godalmighty," said Granma. "Let him be."

I was on the edge of a cliff. The emptiness below me had no bottom and I could not step back. All this talking and talking. I started to do inventory, Dammit, like I always do when I can't make sense.

Inventory:

Is Craig still inside MK, and can I make him talk?

Why can't I say Her name?

Did Ms. Swan really ask for Penny's heart?

Did MK really swear to serve The Ruler of Junction City?

And the question under all the other questions. The one I asked every morning when I rose, and every evening before I laid down. The question that drove me to re-read The Riverside as if there was a clue between every line. The question that hurt every time

I wrung the neck of a rabbit or slit a deer's throat: Why did you leave me alone? *How weary, stale, flat and unprofitable seem to me all the uses of this world.* Everything hurts. Where are you Momma? Inventories are supposed to be about what you know, not what you don't.

Inventory done.

A bark, and you came in the door, tail like a flag. Behind you, Mister Brown looked like he'd be waving his tail too if he had one. You laid your heavy head on my chest and looked at me for a long time.

"He sleeps sound who feels not the toothache," you said.

I sat up, groaned, scratched your ear, and wished there was a way to tell you about MK making the vow.

"Good conscience is a soft pillow," you said.

"Hello," said Sophelia, "I'm, I'm..."

"Sophie," said Granma.

"A real pleasure, Madame Sophelia Ethenoe." Mister Brown used her full name, and it made her smile and clap. He bowed over her hand, his scruffy hair flashing like the setting sun. He pulled out a chair for her and waved his hand in front of her face. Out came a shiny thing he unfolded, a little crown with glitter and glass. "For the queen of wisdom," he said.

She put it on her head, "Ooh!" and her eyes flashed grey and keen.

There was a knock, Granma said, "It's open," and Doc Ranulf came in. Well, he entered the doorway and stood sniffing and looking around with a leather bag under his arm. "I see, even from here, my patient requires mending," Doc said.

"Clayton been layin' here all afternoon — cryin' out in dreams," said Granma. "Cut over his eye won't stop seepin'. Close the door," Granma said, "Stay for dinner?"

"I have big lunch today. But again, I am hungry like..." He paused, smiled at some secret joke, forgot to close the door, pulled a chair up next to me and opened his small leather bag. He frowned at Granma. "Stop the smoking, Lina. You smell like the ashtray."

"Quit tomorrow," she said, and winked at me.

Through the open door I heard voices singing in the twilight interrupted by yells and what sounded like an argument. The voices came onto the porch.

"Get this shit right. Do it again," said a tall girl who had to bend to come through the door. They entered one by one and stood in a row, four of them, their voices rising like a wave of hot afternoon sunlight up a cliff-wall. It was a sound like swallows weaving in and out.

"There will the river whispering run
Warm'd by thy eyes,
More than the sun . . . ."

Your clear voice, howling, rose to the dark ceiling. Three of them started whooping, and the one with glasses grabbed you and hugged you. "Yeah, Dammit!"

"Whatsup Elbedeefa? We're practicing," said the tall girl with splotches all over her face like a trout. "Think we got a chance?"

"Sure," said Granma, setting the table. "Take the dog, secret weapon."

They laughed and everyone spoke over everyone else. It was like a hive of bees. Somewhere in the conversation, I heard they were an honor ensemble going to State, whatever that is.

The one who looked like a squirrel with big front teeth and cheeks like nuts in them said, "Holy thit what happened to you?" I never heard a lisp before, Dammit, she was hard to understand.

The third girl — big glasses that made her look like an owl — shut the door, "Is it possible to be any ruder than you?"

The fourth girl, quiet as a deer – except when she sang those sweet, high harmonies—jumped wide-eyed when the door banged. I thought right away of a fawn with some kind of stomach problem. Gaunt, beautiful, overflowing brown eyes.

Trout said to Deer, "... It's not that Junior doesn't like you, it's that he wants your bush, that's all, don't take it personal, just your bush, not you." Trout, Squirrel, and Owl stopped talking all at once because they saw me on the couch.

Silence. Nothing like being stared at by four pairs of girl eyeballs.

"Let's eat," said Granma Lina, lighting a cig and giving Doc a grin when he shook his finger. "Clayton, these're MY strays. Been watching 'em since they were little." She pointed at each in turn. "Des, Feebs, Hel, and Cress."

"Don't forget Penny," said Mister Brown

"Fuck her," said Deer so quietly only I heard her.

"Yes, yes, Penny too," said Granma.

"We're not strays, Elbedeefa," said Trout, waving her long arms. "Being called a stray implies a parentless progeny, and we do have parents. Asshole parents. But parents nonetheless."

"Smarty-pants, Desdemona. This is my grandson, Clayton. Beat up today. Know who?"

"No." They said, all together, with a sigh, like they practiced ahead of time.

Trout said, "We hear things, but no one's saying for sure."

Squirrel said, "People thay he tried to thtab Junior."

Owl nodded her round face solemnly; the light made her glasses shine yellow.

Squirrel poked my arm, "That hurt? How 'bout there?"

I pulled it back, grimacing.

"What about here?" she asked, poking again.

I closed my one working eye and pushed her hand away.

"What the fuck," said Squirrel.

Doc said, "This should not hurt too much." He pressed the wound under my eye. I jumped off the couch, growling, and you leaped beside me with your hair raised. He lied, it hurt. Something was wrong with my ribs. I fell back on the couch grabbing my side. My arm hurt bad too, it wouldn't bend, and never mind about my face. I was like Henry after Agincourt, but without the fire.

"*Schnitt nahen.* We should X-ray the arm and the ribs, but eh, you are strong, I think OK."

Your hair raised, Dammit, lips pulled back from your teeth.

"Are you peeing the blood?" asked Doc.

I nodded my head. Yes, before Granma made me lay down when I first got there.

"If you pee blood tomorrow, come see me."

You bared your teeth and moved between him and me. "Small streams make great rivers," you said.

Doc bared his teeth; they gleamed long and yellow in the lamp light. "I know. *Sitzen.*"

You sat. I reckon you knew he was doing good to me, or maybe you finally found someone to respect, Dammit. I know your ears went back. But you did what he said.

"Better for this dog to know the proverb: 'lie down with dogs, get up with fleas,'" said Doc, and I think the grimace on his face was a smile.

While he bandaged the cut with thin strips, he spoke quietly to me of my condition. What I will say here, Dammit, you heard too. But I'll say it because I'm still trying to understand: He said it was not my fault, the stealing of items (he knew about the knife from the hospital), and hesitating. That this came with the territory and that there are lots of people who pick stuff up like packrats for their own reasons, or who freeze and can't do anything, like rabbits. But that I was definitely not a rabbit. And what I am is still being revealed, and so forth. He said "freeze" was a good word for it, because if I waited in the light long enough, I would warm up and move faster. I'm still waiting, Dammit, I can see things and I know what I should do. But I don't do it.

The Strays wanted to eat, but Grandma and Sophie made them stop until Doc got me to the table. There was meat in a brown sauce with potatoes. A dish with green beans. Leaves and red tomatoes in a glass bowl with raspberry dressing. And bread. Crispy-brown on the edges, steaming from the oven. The girls broke off pieces, knifing up square chunks of butter. Some of them spooned honey from a jar. Steam rose under the light.

"Slow down. Grace, grace." said Granma, her voice rose as she poured wine into coffee mugs.

"Mister Bakeolus at school says praying doesn't work," said Owl. "He says god is the leftover part of our brains that hasn't finished evolving."

"Well, he's a dipshit," said Sophie, folding her hands primly.

"God or the teacher?" asked Trout with a big grin.

"Sophie! Watch your language at the table," said Granma, seemingly unaware that she was rule-breaker number one. "We're prayin' to that leftover brain right now."

"Ohmygod," said Squirrel. "Then, pray already."

"You give teens the spirits?" asked Doc, sniffing and leaning back in his chair.

"Yep. Little wine don't hurt." Granma looked like she was going to say something, thought better of it, and then said it anyway. "Their folks drink too much. Here, it's different. Sue me," she said, and winked at Doc.

Somehow, we all fit around the little table, elbow to elbow, and there was still an extra chair.

"Shall I move the chair?" asked Mister Brown.

"No," said Granma. "Always leave the extra chair."

Every face turned to her.

"My Beaumont always did it for the stray, an I'm gonna keep doin' THAT till the day I die. Hold hands," she directed. Then she took off her hat. The wrinkles under her closed eyes ran in rivers of darkness. "God of the strays," she said. "Thank you for bringing back my Clayton. Hmmm." She drank from her mug. "Bless those cocksuckers, pardon my French."

A giggle from Trout, a *"jeethuth"* from Squirrel, and a *"shush"* from Owl.

"Them who beat up my Clayton, you know I would put a slug in 'em." She paused, took another drink, seeming to wrestle with what to say.

The table got restless, and we all opened our eyes.

Well, I opened my one working eye, let go of Mister Brown's hand and grabbed a slice of bread. It was warm.

"Dammit, Clayton put that bread down. Look, if he's real," Granma said to us, "then he, or them are big enough to not worry about my mouth. If he isn't, don't matter huh?" She shrugged. "Supposed to pray for enemies. God help me. I'm trying." She closed her eyes, and I put the bread in my mouth anyway. The warmth of the crust became a memory: My Momma held my hand on one side, and Dad held my other. I could see the waiting faces of my parents at the table.

"You know I got lots a questions," Granma prayed. "We kept the chair. See. Be with my Beau." Her voice became rough. "Tell him .... I'll see him by the river under the healin' tree."

Mister Brown's eyes opened and looked up to the ceiling, but he said nothing.

"OK. That's it," Granma cleared her throat. "Gimme that song, girls. The one reminds me of Beaumont."

The strays began to sing:

"... *Our storm is past, and that storm's tyrannous rage....*"

"Amen! Stop," said Trout. "My stomach started singing." She rolled her eyes, grabbed the roast pan, and we loaded our plates.

"Excellent, so wonderful," said Mister Brown with a slice of bread half in his mouth and half in his hand.

"Hrggh," said Doc, his mouth full of meat.

"Now listen Cress, think about this, for once," said Trout to Deer. "If you give your snatch away that easy, they think you aren't worth the fight."

Squirrel chuckled through her food, "Haha, like the redneck dad. Put the thnatch in a gift bag and keep it behind the thotgun."

"Huh," said Trout, "I can't understand you, lithper."

"Cunt," said Squirrel.

Owl said, "Hmphh," like she was the conscience, but quit trying long ago.

"What kind?" said Trout.

"I'd go with the 12-gauge, buck thot. Haha."

"No, I meant the gift bag," said Trout.

Everyone laughed. I didn't understand, so I just watched them.

Deer's face under the light was unreal, like a painting of a woman too beautiful for Granma's table. Her eyes were large and when she reached across the table for the bread, her arm moved so smoothly it made all the other girls' look like something I drew when I was a child. Deer spoke little, just laughed along with the others and looked sideways at me.

Squirrel said, "You gotta keep boys withing for more."

Trout scowled, "Whad'you know about that, fatty?"

Squirrel held up a middle finger, smiled happily, showed her two front teeth, and kept eating.

Grandma helped Sophie cut her roast into pieces and ignored The Strays. Mister Brown and Doc piled their plates and bent over them eating as fast as the food would go from hand to mouth. Chunks fell on the floor, and you were underneath to clean them up.

Granma pointed her fork at my plate. "Girls, more food. On there."

I ate everything but the leaves. Three times they loaded my plate. I drank wine, tart as late-Spring cherries. I ate and drank and forgot and was forgotten. And remembered you under the table with scraps. This is what home is like, Dammit.

Mister Brown cleared his throat. "Ahem." He rubbed his white neckbeard thoughtfully. "Ever hear the one about the ogre, and the boy who stole his treasure?"

"Who cares," said Trout, and the girls giggled.

Mister Brown continued as if he did not hear her. "It goes like this...."

I like these stories, Dammit. They're better every time I tell them.

Chapter 19

Table Fables

"Long time ago, when wishes were for wishing, aiming was for aiming, and sometimes both came true, there was a boy and his mother who lived poorly on a piece of ground that would grow nothing. There was no husband because he had died early, a wastrel and drunkard. But the boy was sharp as a fox's tooth and just as wise. Heh heh."

"The mother and son starved until they were skin and bones. For the fields they worked were destroyed by a hailstorm, and all they had left was an old goose. The youngster told his mother not to worry, he took some of her leftover nail polish — from an earlier life when she was a young woman with riches before the good-for-nothing husband wasted it all — and painted their last boiled egg a shining golden color."

"On his way to market with the old goose under his arm, he ran into a fantastic traveling circus magician who was actually a real magician who had stolen three beans from the queen of the fairies, and the youth got him drinking and talking about the beans and all their possibilities. He excused himself to go to the bathroom, and while there, shoved the golden egg up the goose's ass, and upon returning, set the goose on the table. Heh, heh. At which point, the goose — who could hold it in no longer because it was a BOY, heh, a boy goose — promptly laid a golden egg that was not only golden but cooked and ready to eat."

"The magician got seriously excited by the possibilities. As drunk magicians always are. It only took a few minutes of sweet-talk by the crafty boy and the magician was magicked out of his magic beans and gave them in exchange for a goose that laid golden cooked eggs. A great deal from the drunk magician's perspective, to be sure."

"Boring," said Trout. "I know this story."

"Shut-up," said Squirrel, "I like the thtory."

"The egg wasn't an egg," said Sophie matter-of-factly. "Just a painted river stone."

Mister Brown looked at her in surprise but kept going. "The young man returned home to his mother and showed her the beans, and she cuffed him and threw them out the window with many tears and groans. For she knew that they would now die a slow, painful wasting death from starvation."

"Yeah, we know," said Trout. "Then the beans grow, and Jack climbs up the beanstalk and there was a giant, blah blah, princess, gold, blah blah blah, ax chop down beanstalk, blah."

"Shush," said Granma, suddenly fierce. "Enough."

Trout didn't mind her and pounded the table. "Blah. BLAH." The strays giggled, and she asked, "How come there's no 'girl stories?'"

"Ah my child," Mister Brown said, "Ask, and you shall receive. Mister Brown, like you, thinks the world too long has shoved golden over-cooked eggs up its arse when it comes to female heroes. So, here's one you might like."

He waved a hunk of bread as he talked, jamming it into his mouth between breaths.

"Long time ago, when wishes were for wishing, aiming was for aiming, and sometimes both came true, there was a clever, wily peasant woman, whose tricks could be much talked about. The best story, however, is how she once got the best of the devil and made a fool of him. One day the peasant woman had been working in her field, and just as it was getting dark, she was getting ready to go home when in the middle of her field she saw a pile of burning coals. Filled with amazement she walked toward it, and sitting on the top of the glowing coals there was a little burnt devil."

"Strange is as strange does," said Granma.

Mister Brown barreled on like he hadn't heard her. "You must be sitting on a treasure," said the peasant woman.

"Yes indeed," replied the devil, "on a treasure that contains more gold and silver and precious stones than you have ever seen in your life." And he scratched back the coals, and underneath, in a very large pot was the treasure.

"The treasure is in my field and belongs to me," said the peasant woman.

"It is yours," answered the devil, "if for two years you will give me one half of everything your field produces. I have more than enough money, but I have a desire for the fruits of the earth, and I — by my nature — am unable to steward them so I must rely on others."

The peasant woman entered into the bargain, saying, "To prevent any dispute from arising about the division, everything above the ground shall belong to you, and everything beneath the ground to me."

The devil was quite satisfied with that, but the cunning peasant woman had planted turnips.

Now when harvest came the devil appeared and wanted to take away his crop, but he found nothing except the yellow withered leaves, and the happy peasant woman dug up the turnips.

"You got the best of me this time," said the devil, "but it won't happen again. Next time what grows above ground shall be yours, and what is under it shall be mine."

"That is all right with me, you foxy devil," answered the peasant woman. When planting time came, she did not plant turnips again, but wheat. The crop ripened, and she went into the field and cut the full stalks off at ground level. When the devil came, he found nothing but the stubble, and in pure disgust with himself and anger at her, he turned around four times, stamped, and jumped into a chasm that opened.

"That's the way one has to deal with foxes," said the peasant woman who then carried away the pot full of treasure.

"That is the lamest, stupid-ass story I ever heard," said Trout.

Granma hmphed but did not disagree.

"Ah, but there is one last little thing to tell, my lovelies," said Mister Brown. "The two years of waiting per the agreement was over, so the peasant woman moved the pot of treasure home and began to use the gold, silver, and precious stones to buy all the things she did not have. But every item she purchased only made her feel worse because it was devil's gold. By the time she finished with the treasure and lived in a mansion with servants and horses and carriages, her heart was as empty as the empty pot that sat on a pedestal in her living quarters in the great northern wing of the mansion."

"It was then, on a dark morning with barely any light and many mists across the moor, that she heard the devil say, 'you thought I was gone, and that you won. But I am here, and I have been here all along, hiding at the bottom of the pot. Every piece of gold you used to purchase something for yourself also purchased a piece of your heart. For the pot and your heart are one and the same now. When you completed all your purchases, not only is the pot of treasure empty, but so is the space where once dwelt your heart. And that is where I have come to live. Now, soul, you are mine.'"

'And that,' said the devil, 'is how foxes deal with souls.'

"WHAT?" The strays were angry and started to yell all at once at Mister Brown. Even Deer joined in with a low voice like melted butter.

"She doesn't win?"

"Double-U. Tee. Eff!"

"Male chauvinitht fucking pig."

"You are lame. The story is lame," said Trout. "This peasant woman is lame. And your stupid soul-stealing devil is lame."

"I'm sorry!" Mister Brown yelled. "Devil's strike bargains, bargains that end badly, that's why they're devils."

Doc Ranulf pushed his chair back from the table and folded his arms and glowered. He was not going to say a thing, but something had angered him, and he was silent for a long time as Mister Brown continued.

I thought of the recent bargain struck by MK with Ms. Swan in my vision and how it might turn out, and which one was the devil. But my thoughts were interrupted by Mister Brown.

"GOOD GOD you are hard-asses. OK. Hold a moment, my lads and lasses." He pulled a fresh meat stick from his back pocket and started to draw circles and figure-eights on the table with it. Then he grinned. "Alright, I got it!"

"The peasant woman was not sure what to do, and truly, lost hope as she considered an eternity with the devil living inside of her. For he had climbed in there, and let me tell you, it hurt like the devil. Heh heh. But then she had an idea."

"'That is fine,' she said to the little devil, 'you have out-foxed me for certain-sure. I can only hope that you will take away that damn pot from my house, for all it does is trouble me with its presence, it makes me think constantly about how I lost to you.'"

"The devil, of course, took great joy in doing the opposite because devils, as you know, love to see us in pain. He left the large pot sitting in her mansion to torture her and moved into her heart to live. And she endured great trouble and pain, like nothing you will ever understand or I can describe. The closest I can get is to say that it is something like having a splinter driven under your fingernail, over and over. Then pulled out again. And done again. Or, like having an itch on your back that you cannot scratch. That turns into a spider you cannot catch."

"How 'bout just crabs," said Trout with a snicker.

He didn't slow down. "The crabs crawl in, the crabs crawl out, the crabs play pinochle in your snout."

"Ug, not inside?" Trout winced.

"PG-13 please," said Owl. "Continue."

"Ok, well," he continued with a nasty smile and a thump of his meat-stick, "the peasant woman did have a plan. Every day she ate as much as she could, because, of course, she was still rich and could order all kinds of foods to her table. And with all the food she was imbibing, and so much of it rich meats and sweet cakes, she had to take the biggest shit.'"

"Uh, are we allowed to tell stories like that here?" asked Owl, pushing up her glasses.

"Go on," said Granma leaning forward, "Go on."

Mister Brown grinned. "But she did not want to shit right away, no, no, no, she wanted it to build up, heh heh. Really build up. So, she paid three of her stupidest men-servants to put a cork in her ass, sit her on the pot, and feed her for days. It was painful, but no more painful than the devil in her heart. And certainly, there was the joy of knowing that she was working on something that might be worth it."

"So, wait." Owl raised her hand, "This is not possible, you can't just put a cork in it."

"Hey stupid, LET HIM TELL THE STORY." Trout thumped the table.

"You're stupid."

"And YOU need to put a cork in it, cunt."

Silence descended, except for the rustle of Owl's arm as she flipped off Trout.

Mister Brown took a chew of his meat-stick. "So, they fed her. And fed her. And fed her. Until there came a day when even the stupid menservants could see that something bad would happen if they did not pull the cork. But even they – simple as they were—were wise enough to know that no one – no one!—should be close to the 'vent site' when THAT happens."

"So, they put their heads together, and one of them had an idea. 'I've got a monkey who loves pulling on ropes, strings, pretty much anything he sees, he pulls on it. Especially, anything yellow, like bananas. We could use him.'"

"Oh, sweet Lord Jesus," said Granma and put her hand to her mouth.

"Hee hee," said Sophelia. "Pray, praise, and give thanks!"

Mister Brown raised his meat-stick like a baton, and straightened his back like he was going to cast a fishing-line to the other side of the river. "So. The three menservants tied a long yellow cord to the cork in her butt and laid it out along the floor, very easy to see. Then, they hid behind a couch. And let in the monkey."

He paused and popped the last bit of his meat stick into his mouth, chewing slowly.

"Please, finish the story!" It was Trout, and she threw a napkin at his head.

"It is at this point that I must pause," he grinned. "To remind all of you that it is good to have a plan, better to have two, and best to have three or four in your back pocket," said Mister Brown with a wink, pulling a meat stick from his back pocket.

"GODALMIGHTY just finish," yelled Trout.

Mister Brown grinned, slowly wiped his mouth with the napkin, nibbled on his meat stick, and then continued: "The monkey walks in the room, and right away, why, he sees the rope. He runs up to that yellow rope and grabs it and tugs. As haaaaard as he can." He paused again, wiped his forehead with the greasy napkin.

"He sets the fox to keep his geese?" It was you from under the table, but Mister Brown ignored you and kept wiping his face.

"What happened, dammit!" said Granma, smacking the table.

Sophelia clapped. "The cork the cork the cork, out comes the cork, pop, pop, pop," she said.

Mister Brown sighed, and frowned as if he was very sad. "In the aftermath, they interviewed the three menservants, one by one. They asked the first one, 'what did you see?' and he said, 'buckets and buckets of shit, just pouring out!' They asked the second one, 'what did you see?' and he said, 'wagonloads and wagonloads of shit, just pouring out!'

They asked the third one, 'what did you see?'

Mister Brown paused. The table was completely silent, he grinned and took a bite of his meat stick.

"... And he said, 'I saw that monkey trying to shove the cork back in her ass!'"

Everyone gasped and laughed and pounded the table. Granma Lina cried and laughed at the same time and blew wine out her nose. You crawled out, Dammit, and howled like the world was on fire. Finally, everyone calmed down, Granma shoved you back under the table, and Mister Brown said, "You forget. There is still more to this story."

"Yes, oh yesssss," said Trout.

"That day, the day of the monkey," he grinned, "the peasant woman shat so much of that shit, the shit filled the pot to the brim and over. Great heaping mounds of shit. Rolling rolls and thundering explosions and curling curlishes of shit. Whirling dervishes and splatting splattishes of shit. Whole turds like fat little boys taking cannonballs into a diarrhea swimming pool of shit. She SHIT SO MUCH that it came all the way, right to the top, and over the edges. She filled that pot to the brim and over."

"Yettthhhh." Squirrel was excited. "Would you rather drink a cup of thitty diarrhea or eat a turd," asked Squirrel, completely out of the blue, and Owl yelled "gross," and threw her spoon at her. When silence finally descended, we were ready for the ending.

Mister Brown said, "A full pot meant a full heart. The devil had nowhere to live, and that little sonofabitch moved out faster than a spider monkey can tug on a rope. Heh heh. 'And that,' said the peasant woman to the devil, as he jumped lickety-split from her heart and ran out the door, 'is how ass-souls outfox the fox.'"

"Ass-SOULS, hah," said Sophie.

"For the rest of her life, the rich peasant woman was wise, and caring, and giving, which is the best of all possible combinations for anyone. She lived frugally and cared for all of her people, gaining favor in all the community by judging wisely between them when conflicts arose. Providing for their needs in every way, beginning, of course," he paused and smiled with those snaggly teeth and took a bite from his meat stick, "with the monkey."

"He lived to a royal old age and sat on a little throne."

Mister Brown grinned so big, his copper eyes closed, and I thought his face would split. "But anytime he saw a yellow rope...."

He paused for one breath. ".... that little monkey would shit himself and run for the hills."

Granma poured another mug of wine for herself after the laughter died down. "'Strange is as strange does.'" She took a sip. "Haven't laughed like that in years. Only one thing."

"Hmm?" asked Mister Brown.

"Your first story. Didn't finish."

"I was reading the room," said Mister Brown, grinning.

"Well. Let me tell you somethin'. I'll finish it. It's a story dear to the Bergmann's, we tell it all the time," said Granma. "But I don't tell long tales."

"You don't tell long anything," said Sophie, and everyone laughed.

Granma pushed her hat back. "That boy's mama did the right thing because them beans WAS magic beans and needed to grow. Like any beans do. The beans grew into a vine and the vine wouldn't stop growing night and day and curled up into the sky with a trunk the width of this here room, and it curled all the way up into a giant's house up there."

She smacked her cigarette pack on the table. "That smart-ass kid climbed up there quietly and saved a lovely maid from the giant and stole his axe and when the giant tried to come down to kill the boy, why, he took that axe and chopped down the tree. They say that no monster – or any creature of the Three Rivers—wants to be near that axe. They all fear its edge. Which can cut any creature no matter what power it's got. But others say the boy killed the giant some other way, with some other kind of magic he stole from him."

"The heart-bone, that is, *Os Cordis*, it is interesting phenomena," said Doc Ranulf suddenly.

Granma shuddered, took a big drink from her mug, and Mister Brown looked frustrated.

But Doc kept going, "It is a medical fact that certain creatures — particularly the large ones — have a heart-bone which supports normal function of the valves in a heavy heart."

"Hmm," said Mister Brown. "I heard the boy did not steal the axe at all. That he was a wiz with fire, and he forged a double-bladed axe-head in the giant's own forge from the links of the chains in which the giant imprisoned him. Chains made of the bones of a dead monster, the ancestor of all the giants. It is said he named the axe *"Sharpen"* on its Water Day when he took it from the fire to plunge it in cooling oil in the trough. Except..." Mister Brown paused and looked around. "...Before he could assuage the axe-head, he was attacked by a god. A mad god who desired the axe. The boy fought with a coal-glowing axe, and – against all hope of survival—plunged it deep into the chest of a god." Mister Brown's voice filled with wonder. "The axe-head went from red-hot to ice-black. Cooled in the blood of a dying god. In his weariness following the battle the boy spoke a single word, *"Sharpen,"* and fell in a trance. When he awoke 40 days later, he spoke a prophecy, a phrase of only seven words." Mister Brown paused to bite from his meat stick.

"Well, what did he say?" demanded Trout.

"Sharpen whets the edge of a greater," said Mister Brown. "No one has a clue what that means."

Granma's eyes got big, and she pulled out a cig and lit it and blew out a giant plume of smoke. Her pale eyes shone like blue sparks. "Where the hell you hear that?" she said.

Mister Brown winked and took another slice of bread. Granma's smoke rose above her head to the ceiling. "Mister Brown hears all kinds a things," he said. "I even heard its name *'Sharpen'*

was forge-scribed on the axe-head — if it still exists — by good ol'
Jack O' The Montagne himself."

"Shush, we don't speak that boy's name around here," said
Granma. "Besides, that's not what us Bergmanns call him, and
that's not how we tell that story." She pushed her chair back and
went to the kitchen sink.

Mister Brown shrugged. "Like the shark said to the baby
dolphin when it asked him why he was swimming so close: 'this
water's big enough for both our tales.'"

"Hmphh," she said, focused on filling a water jug.

"The best swimmers often drown," you said, scratching your
ear.

Doc, with watering eyes, said quietly, "I have one."

The stray's jaws dropped, and Granma said, "I'll be."

Sophie smiled and patted Doc's arm. "Of course you do. *Nor
mouth had, no, nor mind, expressed what heart had heard of, ghost
guessed: It is the blight man was born for, it is Margaret you mourn
for.*"

At "Margaret," he leaped to his feet, as if to run, teeth drawn
as if he had been whipped. But he did not take his arm away from
Sophie, and Mister Brown touched the other one gently.

"Lycaon, she is gone, she is gone," said Mister Brown. "They are
gone, and you are here. You are here."

Doc's shoulders slumped and he covered his face. Then, he
leaned into the light of the lamp, placed his hands back on the
table. He was no longer Doc, or a doctor. Like a thing from my
father's tales when I was young. Whatever the case, the lamp
seemed to dim when Lycaon spoke, the table glowed like a fire and
we sat before it at a dim age in the early life of the world, when the
forest was vast and young and very hungry.

"Long ago when the world is young, when the forests are dark and the meat is scarce, a wolf meets a dog in the forest."

Doc's lips drew back from his teeth. "It is indeed a very long winter the wolf has suffered. He is famished, gaunt and weak. Indeed, feeling badly about himself and his situation, and his great heart becomes downcast. Lo, while the wolf sits there under this oak in the frozen snow, waiting to die, along there comes a well-fed dog who has escaped that very day from the house. He is out taking in the air, chasing the squirrels, running through the snow, pissing on this and that, and enjoying himself very much indeed."

"This one I like," you said.

"The wolf says to the dog, 'By the eyes of my mother, my friend, you are looking well, very *gepflegt* ah sleek and the lovely ears.'

'By your permission, let me smell you,' begs the dog.

The dog is indeed well-fed and goes on and on about how much of the food he receives all the days, how well-cared for he is, how warm is the fire, how soft is the bed, and so on and so forth.

When he is finished, he says to the wolf, 'My friend, let me smell you more. Ah, this must not be! You are smelling of the forest, and the dark caves, and the hunger of many days. Come with me, you will see, my master will take you in for he has always been a friend to the wild things of the forest. Trust me, come back with me to the house, surely the master will give you some of the choice cuts or at least a soft bone or two, he will comb the fur, warm the shivering bones, he will pull the thorn out from you for I see you are lame in the leg. He is a good master, surely, he shall do this for you.'

'Let me smell *you*,' says the wolf. 'Ah now this is a fine invitation, you are fat like a yearling in a meadow, and sore tempted I have become. Fire and bed, food, and to be led, this is a sweet promise for this cold day, with so many more of the cold ones to come.' Now tell me, let me ask you just one question, so I may know my way.'

'Ask me anything,' says the dog, 'I am your friend, only let me smell you more.'

'Enough with the smelling,' says the wolf. 'Is this always what you do upon the meeting of the other?'

'Yes, indeed it is the custom of those of us who live with the men,' says the dog, 'this is how we show the friendliness and also know who is the first one, and who is the second one, and so forth.'

'By the fangs of my fathers, shall I ask my question, or shall you smell more?' asks the wolf. "I thought you already asked it," says the dog, and the wolf almost leaves him then and there, for wolves, though patient in the hunt are not patient with fools. But he says to the dog, 'I am wondering about this line on your neck where I see the fur is worn away. I am wondering why the fur, it is gone, why this is a ring around your neck? There is no creature I have ever met has one of these.'

'Oh, the fur,' says the dog, 'this is the easy question! I escaped today from the house and, as I ran out the door the collar around my neck it was *weggezogen*, ah how you say it, pulled away from my neck. This collar I wear at the house ever and always while I am there laying at the fire. The master will give you one. I am sure of this. That is how he claims you. You will love the collar, for all those who see the collar know that you are his.'

'Well, well. All this, and a full belly too,' says the wolf.

'Yes, yes!' cries the dog, jumping up and bouncing about, 'let me smell you more!'

'By the fangs of my fathers, these full bellies you speak of.' Doc paused for a long moment, as if he was finished with the story in the middle of the sentence. But then he drew a long shuddering breath. "'These full bellies. They are a poor price to pay for liberty,' says the wolf. And he ate that poor dog there and then, felt much better about the state of his downcast heart, and went off to the mountains in a blizzard, shaking the snow from his black neck-hair to hunt for the rabbits. For his heart was once again wild and strong.'"

Doc shook himself as if waking from a deep slumber and looked around. "Ach. Never mind. The heart...." He wiped his eyes, and muttered, "As you know children, the true topography of the heart is vast, wrinkled with rivers and layered mountains. It is a most dangerous country. Those who venture there must be foolish, unafraid, or willing to suffer the trials of loss and grief..." he choked, and stopped a moment before going on, "...far beyond any hope of return."

The table was silent except for the sound of Mister Brown's chewing.

"Now I go," said Doc Ranulf. He was moving to the door before anyone could stir.

He paused on the threshold.

"Young Stonefly." In the shadows cast by Granma's kitchen's golden light, it looked like his watering eyes finally overflowed. "Remember what I said. It takes time, this topography of the heart. The wounds, the wounds." His face became dark as a storm. "They may heal. But the scars remain. Do you understand this?" Before I could nod, he was gone.

"No collar for me," you said, and I noticed it was true. Your hair lay untouched, black and thick around your neck.

"A poor excuse for a story," said Mister Brown smacking his stick on the table with a crack, "but an excellent reason to ask for another slice of this most, err, magnificent bread."

"That was horrible and sad," Owl said. "Why is that guy so weird?"

Mister Brown buttered his bread slowly, making sure the butter went to the very edges of the crust. It seemed he had not heard her. He laid down the knife, held up the bread and looked at it carefully.

"Ah," he said. Then he took a bite, chewed, and pieces flew across his plate. "First of all, weird is relative my dear. You would be very weird to many of Mister Brown's friends. However, you are correct, he is weird. Or maybe strange is a better word. Although weird used to describe that better, back in the day. I digress. We'll use 'weird.'" He grinned and chomped.

"Second and to the point: He is in pain, my dear. So much pain. He was weird before the pain, anyway. Hard to understand, and most vicious and, eh, changeable. Now he is even more weird, of course, because of the pain. His wife, his children — two daughters, you see, young and fair-skinned with long waving hair, black as raven's wings — taken by a murder most foul in his own house while he was on a journey. Their hearts removed. As if ripped from their chests by a great hand."

"Stop!" said Granma, slapping the table.

"I was there to see it." Mister Brown ignored her, as if in another place, "But too late to stop it. The murderer, we searched for him a long time."

"Not the time for this. Enough," said Granma sternly, but Mister Brown kept plowing on.

"He cut his hair off. All of it. Of course, it grew right back. But that's what the ancients did to mourn. And he mourned a long time. He kept cutting his hair every time it grew back overnight."

Mister Brown scratched his white neckbeard, his eyes deep in a memory. "There will be a reckoning," he said. "Just this morning, I finally heard from a trustworthy source. Someone on the inside. Someone unknown to the murderer. They told me WHO did it. Verified! Mister Brown needs to tell Lycaon, but I'm not sure how.

Until then, Lycaon heals all of us because, eh, you know the old saying about the physician?"

"Heal thyself," you said, Dammit.

"Just so." Mister Brown sighed a long, deep sigh. Then tossed his last bite deep into his gullet, swallowed it like a frog swallows a fly, and shrugged. "He heals others. He cannot heal himself."

"Keep friends close?" you asked, crawling from under the table. "Enemies closer?"

"Yes my prince," Mister Brown chuckled. "Thus, we all do when we fear ourselves." Then he spoke directly to me. "Clayton, Mister Brown has something to tell you."

He pointed at me with a fresh slice of bread.

"These stories are more than info. They're stoke. Sometimes, you're *inside* the story, very cool, heh. But sometimes," he said, looking deep in my eyes, "if you're lucky, lil bruh — like a magic penny in your pocket — the story finds you, gets *inside* you."

Granma interrupted him, "Not now. Too much too soon." She glowered at him. "Help me clear the table girls."

Mister Brown didn't seem to care what Granma thought. He slapped the table *CRACK* and everyone jumped. "If that happens and the story gets inside, WOOWEE! Watch out!" he dropped his voice to a whisper. "If it's inside you, lil bruh? No telling where *that* vine grows! Where that line goes." His eyes were molten copper and I felt something burning in my chest very much like Penny's lighter. A white-hot furnace under a rushing wind. I looked away from those burning eyes. Something in how he spoke sounded a lot like my Momma, but I didn't understand a word of his stupid gibberish.

"Go big or go home," you said, and you were dead serious.

The door slammed open. Penny stood in the doorway her arms crossed over her chest, her eyes on fire. "CS where's my book?"

One eye straight at me, the other at my chest as always. She looked hopping mad.

I felt the lighter go *pop* in my chest, and it was a different fire than Mister Brown's story-fire. It was warm like a coal in my heart. I felt as if I could touch anything and make it burn. The room got dark, and Penny started to glow. I know, Dammit. You told me later it was my wuttus talking, she did not glow, and that all dogs go crazy at the sight of a good bitch. But I disagree: she's no bitch in heat, we humans have something more in us. Like she was a part of me that got pulled out and I needed her back. Like she belonged under my skin (I mean, she already was because she was always on my mind). I saw Penny standing there with shadows cast on her face in the golden light, and all I wanted was to be with her and to work the homeplace together.

Two burning coals are all you need to make a fire.

It did not matter that she was angry like a storm. It made it better.

"Come in, Penny. We got plenty food left," said Granma.

"Where's my book?"

Deer slammed her mug on the table. "You're not wanted here," she said in a strangled voice. "Bitch."

Granma clucked her tongue. "No way to talk Cress, not to your sister."

"Do you have it?" Penny asked me. She was wild with fear. "Where is it? You don't have it." She looked everywhere in the room but at Deer.

"Can't you thee? He's had the thit kicked out of him." said Squirrel.

Deer pushed back her chair and stood up. She was shaking. Her beautiful face was like a painting of a woman screaming, but she said it so softly again I could hardly hear, in gasps and bursts.

"Get the fuck away... from me. You fucking thief. You fucking bitch. Fucking... man-stealer."

Penny's face crumbled. "I'm s-sorry, Cress." Her face convulsed, she stepped back and disappeared in the darkness of the porch, and I heard the sound of her feet running down the stairs.

"Romes, guess I showed up just in time for the cat fight." MK sat in the stray chair, grinning like — well — like a cat. "*Fortis Feminam Est*," he said and leaned back in the chair between Granma and Deer, his hands behind his head. "Let the wild rumpus begin, or as I prefer to say, (and he changed his accent to "Earl Grey English" as he likes to call it) '*he which hath no stomach to this fight, let his passport be made.*'"

Your lips drew back above your fangs, all your hair stood up, and you backed against the fridge.

"Henry The Fifth," I said, and MK clapped his hands as everyone stared at me like I'd grown a second head.

Mister Brown jumped up from the table like he was stung by a hornet and spat on the floor. "Mister Brown must leave." I blinked and he was gone in the darkness with Penny.

MK shone silver-gold like the summer moon, distant in wildfire haze. "Remember, Romes, the vow doesn't kick in until tomorrow morning. I'm harmless."

It wasn't until later that I understood, Dammit.

He leaned over, somehow keeping balance on two legs in the chair, and, grinning, put his hand on Deer's thigh.

I thought, "the next thing he's going to do is whisper in her ear." Something blew up inside me like a rotten tree struck by lightning. I was mad at him and his smile that was like the lid on a coffin, at his long fingers on her thigh, at the whisper he spoke into Craig's ear, at myself curling in a ball like an animal as they kicked me. At the memory of my Momma, and the ache that she was somewhere close, and I would never find her. At rottenness plunging dark roots into the wrinkled rivers and layered mountains of my heart.

I leaped across the table scattering plates and mugs of wine — you barking, girls screaming, and smashed his chair on the ground. He wasn't in it.

MK sat on the counter, waggling a finger.

With no memory of how I got there, I was standing over Granma on the floor, a chair-leg in my hand. She looked so small.

The Strays jumped up, screaming.

Sophelia alone remained in her chair. Still as a wax figure, hands folded, looking down.

"*Shall you eat like wolves and fight like devils, Romes?*" MK waved a finger. "I came for the catfight, not your breakdown."

You growled, "birds of a feather flock together." I reckon you knew exactly what you were doing, Dammit, because MK shot you a dirty look.

Granma didn't move from the floor, her hand shaded her eyes but I saw tears on her cheeks. I leaned back, and howled until there was no more air. Then, you took over. Your nose turned up, a howl deeper and longer than mine. Rising from the depths of your great soul, climbing like a waterfall of sound — up, up, up — through the roof. Then, silence. And your shining eyes.

I grabbed Granma's hand, pulled her up; she threw her arms around me. I grunted as she squeezed, and she whispered, "It's OK Clayton. It's OK."

I threw the chair leg at MK, and ran up the stairs to my room.

The bedroom filled with pictures of Pops working in his shop, building tables and chairs with his own two hands, smiling over his shoulder at the camera. Pops holding, in one big fist, a salmon as long as his leg. Pops standing on a felled tree as big around as a dozer, with Sonofa parked next to it, tiny and brand new. Standing stern-faced, *Acuere* in his hands.

Hands the size of hubcaps wrapped around the handle. Hands like mine, only they actually did something.

I laid there a long time, quilt stuffed in my mouth, looking at those old photos. Wondering if those hands could pull out these cankering roots.

Hoping MK would *not* come to sit on the edge of the bed and play the TRG.

Hoping he would.

Chapter 20

It's Not How Fast You Run

I don't want to wake from the dream because I'm with Dad before him and Momma left.

He moves quickly with little wasted motion up the scree, sweat-stained shoulders wide as fence rails. "C'mon son. One last push." He pulls himself through a crack between two boulders.

My legs scream in pain, sweat drips from my nose stinging my eyes. I'm breathing so hard that I'm seeing lights. He will not slow down the pace he's kept for three hours, and he will not let me stop.

"Dad, I can't. I can't keep going."

No response. His ragged jeans disappear over the top of the boulder, and I grab for a juniper branch.

And miss.

My feet churn in the loose pebbles. My arms flail. I feel a bottomless depth behind me; wide, unending space a mile above our river. I feel like I am on a swing — and falling — all at once. My stomach clenches into a ball, bangs into my wuttus, and I feel it all twist and suck up into me.

"HELP, Dad!"

"C'mon son, almost there."

The smallest hint of a breeze — a zephyr from across the vast canyon — pushes against my back and I fall forward, banging my shin. Pain screams up my leg. I'm weeping. I sweep handfuls of gravel and dust and dry grass into my chest in a choking embrace. "I can't go anymore," I say to a juniper root.

"It's not how fast you run..." the voice floats down past the boulders and gnarled juniper like a gritty whisper, the echo of the breeze at my back. "It's not how fast you run... It's how long you can go. Get the fuck up here."

It takes one agonizing minute of clawing, blinded by sweat, choked by dust. But I find my way up the chute. I bang my elbow twice before I emerge into bright sun.

The tamaracks are turning yellow on the heights below peaks covered with an overnight snowfall. Green-gold aspen shot with white bark encircle meadows where hidden springs rise. Some nameless bush in pale purple grows along the mountains' knees; hidden by the leaves of summer and now revealed in Autumn like a new species. I have the fleeting thought that Porter would know what they are. *Tongues in trees...good in everything.* But I am not sure Porter saw anything this lovely.

Dad sits, serene, on a rock, rubbing his old broken shoulder, wiping sweat from his face, and looking into the distance. He is not concerned I almost died. He pats the lichened boulder beside him.

"Siddown. Look, son. Just look."

So, I do. Rub the sharp pain in my side, wipe the snot off my nose, and try not to aggravate my skinned knee and elbows.

"You made it," he says proudly. I know he's happy when he grabs my neck in his thick fingers and squeezes, grinning close to my face. Those light blue eyes — almost grey — sparkle in the sun.

My eyes follow the bends of our little river as it curls and twists like a shoelace, then disappears into the canyon of the Salmon River.

"I'm only going to say this once. Every mountain is worth seeing from the top. And every mountaintop is worth seeing from more than one spot."

I don't understand, but he keeps going on.

"You were born of water; it pumps your heart. No river should make you afraid."

It did not make sense. I reckon I'll always be afraid of rivers. So no, Dad. You're wrong.

"Don't ever crush anyone. Be curious, especially of women. Listen to them. You'll learn them — and yourself — better."

"Dad, what if they don't want to talk?"

"Ha!" He grips my shoulder. "Last thing. Sometimes people are just assholes."

"Why?"

"Don't matter. We know mountains and rivers, what they give. But assholes? You can't get to the top, or swim to the edge of an asshole. Sometimes only one thing you can do."

"I like mountains, but not rivers."

"Wipe it! Ha." He moves on quickly, like always. "Kidding. With assholes you got to do three things, not just one." He rubs my neck, and we look across the canyon, feel the sun, watch it touch off reds like candles in the trees.

"Out last 'em, Jackass." He squeezes my neck again. "Out loco 'em. Out love 'em."

I tried hanging onto that boulder ledge where Dad and I sat because I desperately wanted to ask him the questions I never did. When I was nine and he was alive. But you know how dreams work, Dammit. You're there, age nine feeling fine. And then you're not.

Chapter 21

Loco Loco

You hold your pillow over your tear-stained face and call, but your father does not come. The dream is a weight on your chest. His axe – the one he didn't want—snaps into your hand.

"Hold fast," she says.

I hear you whine at my door.

"C'mon, Dammit," Granma says quietly, "get your butt in here. Let him be. Best thing for that boy is sleep."

"No man is an island," you say. But your claws scratch down the hall behind Granma.

In my heart there was a kind of fighting that would not let me sleep. Inventory.

Who are my friends?

One dog. Never backs down.

One granite-colored killer. Disappears every time I need him, like a bum leg.

One Granma. Mean. And good. I scared her tonight and I need to say sorry.

One ghost of a father wandering in the mist calling my name.

One Penny. I want to see her again. Help her find her book. Run away together.

One Mister Brown and one Doc. Just plain weird.

One Momma: not a friend, but alive somewhere close. Find her. Keep her safe from Junior.

Inventory done.

You can only do inventory for so long, Dammit. Or play all the parts of *Julius Caesar* and *As You Like It* in your head against one another, with Hamlet entering, madly, to jackass it up.

So, I went looking for Dad. Well, his shade. Hoping against hope that Dad's ghost would find me in the dark and tell me where my Momma was. I reckoned *Acuere* would come in handy if Junior found me, so I dropped Pop's axe out the window, hung from the sill with my one good hand, and let go. When I was six, Dad taught me to land and roll if I fell from a tree when we were hunting. *Acuere* was heavy as a log when I picked her up with my good hand, so I changed my mind about walking around town with an axe on my shoulder and hid her under the low-spreading branches of a blue spruce on the corner.

"Hold fast," she said.

"I'll come for you," I said, and meant it.

Porter didn't cover evergreens in his taxonomy, but Dad had drilled me on the basics: "Someday you'll understand trees are a family thing," he said. "You need to know all a them, jackass." I reckon a blue spruce with pokey branches is alien enough in this town. Like me. Easy to find, even in the dark.

How good is it to be alone looking for your Dad — but identifying trees instead? Pretty damn good, Dammit. They smell different at night. Very satisfying. I got to twenty-three species before Big Jim found me lost under a streetlight as I limped the back streets of Junction City dragging a foot from the beating like a lame beggar.

I will say two things now, Dammit, because I will forget them later: I am not sure if Big Jim is a "He" or an "It." I'll usually say "He" but sometimes "It" pops out. I thought, "*I have sworn thee fair, and thought thee bright, who art as black as hell, as dark as night.*" Mostly I see him as a gigantic fat man, but sometimes I see something else; to say it out loud is too hard right now so I won't. The second thing is this: I had already been with him before in the vision. But when it picked me up that night, it did not know me. But I knew him. In case you're wondering, it doesn't help knowing ahead of time. It's worse because I don't have the guts to change anything.

A large hand adjusted the mirror of his black truck. "Hey boy, I'm Big Jim. Get in."

"No shit, Sherlock," I thought. Granma is starting to influence my vocabulary, Dammit.

You know that feeling when a predator is near? The hair on your neck stands up, and you know you're being watched. Its eyes were knives thirty feet deep in a lake. I reckon I never seen someone with that much fat, like a bear eating anything it can get its dirty paws on, non-stop, for months. Wrinkles across its puffy face folded in on themselves.

He spoke so softly, I had to lean in to hear. "Boy, I know you touched that axe of your Grandfathers. I smell it on you. Where is it? Mmm."

I almost nodded. How did he know?

"Rich reward for that — what you like? Girls? Boys? I can even give your Granma's house back. You know we own it, mmm?" The hand moved the mirror. Muscles the size of my leg bunched in his arm. He was bigger than anything I'd ever seen. "Mmm," it said again, looking at me.

I felt like I was being tasted. With its eyes. Like babies with long fingernails were crawling into me. There, I said it.

"Glad I found you," Big Jim murmured. "Mistress wants you."

I did not want him to touch me, so I got in on my own.

"Junior didn't have time to get Penny's book, so we will." He looked at me like I was good to eat. "Mmm."

Quit it, you're imagining things. He's just a big man who owns a big truck for his big butt. The truck smelled like cinnamon and leather and — down underneath — muck. The back seat was empty except for a pile of flappy books with girls on the covers, and the girls were not wearing much of anything. In the vision before, I did not see this. Lots of details I don't see in my visions, Dammit.

"Go ahead," said Big Jim flipping on the interior light. "I keep 'em for the boys mmm."

I reached back and picked up one with a girl who looked a lot like Penny, only her mouth was open, and all she wanted was me. Definitely not like Penny who mostly looked at me like I was a joke, and she was holding back a laugh. I flipped the pages, and there they were, one after the other, with no clothes on.

"We're at the School, boy. Go find the book she gave you." Light poles shone like islands in the dark lot. Big Jim took the magazine, orange fingernails too long for any man.

Something rose up in me and I swung at his head as hard as I could, but he caught my fist in a giant paw and squeezed until I cried.

"There'll be time enough later to fight me, boy."

My hand hurt like he broke something, a grinding pain up my arm.

Big Jim chuckled and shoved me out the door. "Don't throw up in my truck." He pointed at a dirty snowbank against the back of the school, "Go look."

I pushed my legs to move, I did not want to find out what would happen if I said "no." I wanted the book too. I limped to where they beat me up. Big Jim turned off his lights. But I could feel those mirrored eyes watching.

"This fucker. Avenge me. No going back, she asked for justice." His voice was clear behind my left shoulder, mad as hell.

I jumped and turned. Only snow crystals shining in yellow islands in a black sea.

"Dad! Where's ma?" I whispered. My voice cracked and felt unnaturally loud.

Behind me, hoarse and low: *"You been sent. For blood. Fuckem up."*

I spun again. Dirty snow glimmered against a brick wall. No Dad—anywhere. You know the smell of snow, Dammit, when it's melted in the sun and then froze? Nobody anywhere, just that smell of old, tired snow. I rubbed my neck and remembered how Dad used to grab me by the neck when he was happy — with a grip like a bear-trap — and make me squirm. I'm not going mad, Dammit, I'm not going mad.

I saw a loose page stuck in a snowbank.

"It wasn't as if Roy didn't know what Volusia McTavish wanted, after all, he was a man and she was a woman, aching with unmet needs. Her voluptuous thighs tightened with a thick heat as he removed his sweat-soaked chamois, hung the shirt and his holstered ivory-inlay pistols on the back of the chair. With his armor removed, his steel-grey eyes were gentle like a lost boy's, and a wild humming filled her ears like bees in a hive."

Then, a blank page covered in silver pencil lines like spider webs:

Dear Lina,

I can't get out. I won't share this with you, anyway. I'll burn it. If you ever read it, it's because I killed myself.

I hope you don't believe the rumors. I've been trying to help Rose-Marie, you see? Maybe you don't see. You have no idea what really happened... maybe, like the others, you believe the lies about

George and Rose-Marie dying in that flaming car wreck. About what I've become. I had to get close to find the truth.

The least I can do after Rose-Marie hid me from Big Jim and George fought him, gave his life, so I could get away. You taught me you got to fight for family. I know you wish they told you they were here; they had their reasons. Rose-Marie's not family, but... she IS. So, I went back in the snake pit.

I have to get her out.

They're trying to bring something, someone real bad. I prayed for justice, like you said to me a long time ago about a smoldering wick, but nothing happened. I am not strong enough to kill myself, or to leave anymore. They can't kill me because Rose-Marie's gift protects me. But they can hurt me. I'm so tired. Cress started hanging out with Junior, and I HATE it...

It ended abruptly.

Big Jim revved his truck.

I shoved the hand-written page in my back pocket. None of the other pages I picked up had writing on them. Dammit, I know – I know. I should have let it ALL sink in. Instead, all I could think about was, *"I prayed for justice...."* Was that who Dad was talking about? *"She asked for you,"* his ghost had said.

My foot slipped in a patch of my old blood and I fell where they beat me up. My face banged on the pavement. I lay there, Dammit, and waited for Big Jim to crush me dead under his tires. I could smell what I left on the ground yesterday. *Blood.* I opened my eyes, saw my hands in front of me had become fists. *Blood.* I heard words in my head from The Riverside. *I must be their scourge and minister... I must be cruel only to be kind. This bad begins and worse remains behind.*

Dad said he rode a loco-bronc once, and it changed his life. "Only way to get to love sometimes, son, is go through loco. That jackass bucked me off four times. It wasn't the ridin', and it wasn't the riggin.'"

"What was it?"

"It was me. Wasn't as crazy as he was. Got to be loco to fight loco."

"What'd you do, Dad?"

"Punch him in the face, rode his ass till he stumbled. He never did buck me off ever again."

"DAD! You said *never* harm animals!"

"That punch? Didn't hurt him one bit. Hurt me more n' it hurt him. Fractured middle finger, see?" He held up the still-twisted finger. "Not like me gettin' thrown four times and bustin' this shoulder! I got his attention, though. I looked him in the eye, said, 'go fuck yourself,' though I didn't mean it. Then I rode him. 'Loco Loco' was his name; guarantee he earned it."

"That's a silly name, Dad."

"Not as silly as jackass, Jackass."

"But you were mean to him!"

"That mustang loved me till the day he died. And I loved him back. I was his scourge *and* his fuckin minister."

"Shakesbear! You were listening when Momma was reading!"

"Maybe, son. Maybe your old man knows a thing or two about Wild Bill and loco princes."

"But Dad, you hurt that horse."

"Butt Dad? No 'butt Dads' around here!"

"Dad, I don't like to hurt things."

"'Butt Dad' knows a thing or two about horses, jackass. Sometimes only way to get to love is through loco."

Lying there on the cold ground, I heard Dad one last time — or thought I heard him—because it was a whisper, like the sound you hear when a mouse burrows under the snow: *"Out last 'em. Out loco 'em. Out love 'em."*

Sometimes, Dammit, you got to turn into someone who hears blood's rhythm like drums in a song. *Essentially, I am mad in craft.* Get real quiet, put on a disguise, climb into the blood. If the disguise don't work, go plain loco. I felt my heart pumping, *blood-blood*, rose to my knees, brushed off the snow, *blood-blood*, and walked to the truck.

My Momma was alive, and seemingly, somewhere in town. I was gonna ride this loco bronc until it took me to her.

Big Jim smiled too wide for any man. I saw its mustache quiver, heard the *Click*, and something sharp draw back behind its yellow teeth. "You find it?"

I nodded and handed him the loose pages (but not the one in my back pocket, Dammit).

"Mmm," he turned on the cabin light. "Where's the rest?"

I shook my head. He looked out the window at the blackness, squeezed the steering wheel so tight it creaked. "Pity you can't be more helpful." He was not pleased, those hundred prism eyes flashed, but he turned the wheel and pulled away.

I picked up another flappy-book and disappeared into their gazes.

Chapter 22

Blood, Blood

Sharp ridges to the east stood out like fins in the early morning twilight, like some ancient lizard rising from the deep.

The home place was over there, somewhere. I felt it calling, you know Dammit, buzzing like the dial on Granma's old telephone. *Home thump-thump. Home thump-thump-thump.*

"I'm taking you to a ceremony, and I must quickly teach you many things," said Big Jim. He rubbed the steering wheel. "Sometimes a shepherd's got to crush the flock mmm for its own good, you see?"

I did not see. "If this guy is the shepherd," I thought to myself, "I reckon I don't wanna meet the bear."

I thought a shepherd takes care of the sheep, each one, gives them pet names like *shnookabay* and *wooky-wook-wooks*. And sometimes, if one gets lost, he leaves the others and goes after it. My Momma told me that story one time after I would not go fetch the chickens in a storm. She said, "even chickens need a shepherd, Clayton. Especially the little ones. Stop crying about the thunder and go get them."

I picked up another flappy book. It was pretty easy starting up a conversation with the girl.

"So you don't like to wear clothes?"

"No, silly. It's warm here. Why would I wear clothes?"

"I'll tell you a secret, boy. Here, let me turn on a light for you so you can see her better," said Big Jim.

"You really shouldn't be here in this truck. You should run."

"I know. But I'm going loco to catch loco. Anyways, if I ran, he'd catch me. I like talking to you. Where do you live?"

"What about your dog? Can't he help?"

"How do you know about him?"

"Never mind, I just know."

"He's sleeping like a log back home."

"What a goodfornothing sonofa bitch."

Really, Dammit. That's what she said. I tossed the flappy book on the back seat. I'm not going to listen to anyone who talks about you that way.

"Folks call me Pastor Issen, mmm but I am not him. I am Sengrim. I wear this man. I came to him indigent, *bettelmonch*, and he ate up my devotion." Big Jim made the snipping sound, like scissors closing. *Click click*. "Then I ate him."

I imagined what that must have sounded like and shivered.

He laughed softly. "I did it quietly, from the inside. But it was easy, and I was patient. He had been very alone. He ceased to love people, even his wife, choosing to love the ideas mmm? Big Jim's fingernails clicked against the wheel. "With his measly academic battles and his online chat rooms. He taught me, and I learned, at first in order learn your language. But then I learned so I could learn him. Mmm." Big Jim sighed as if he remembered a good meal. "I learned all his words and theology, and you know what? Though he knew the concepts and the sophistries – see what big words I learned?—he did not know what was hidden there." He sighed. "Do you know what Skylos—I *hate* to quote him, but in this case he was right—says about dogmatics?"

I did not know about dogmatics, unless it was something about you, Dammit.

Big Jim grinned, *"Dogmatics is too many dogs pissing on a single hydrant. The issue is neither the dogs nor the hydrant nor the piss. It is the residual effect in one location."*

As Granma would say, like every villain, Big Jim tried too hard to sound fucking awesome. I know all about dogs and hydrants because I seen you do that; and I don't see the worth of peeing all over the same spot. Though you've explained it to me more than once.

Big Jim tugged on his mustache. "Issen gazed ever more deeply at the jewel-encrusted ark instead of the mystery it held." Big Jim turned its face toward me and its eyes glittered. "One night we were in his study, and he was lecturing — passionately, I might add — on the verisimilitude of the office, staring into my eyes. He should have been visiting the sick and widows, or clothing orphans. Or home with his wife. Something. Instead, he was with me. I saw him in there, in his eyes, and I climbed in mmm."

My neck prickled.

"I see you know me, boy." A voice, like that of a baby, came from Big Jim's mouth. *"Give it. Mine."* He chuckled and his voice returned to its low rumble. "Mmm. Where was I? Ah yes, the love of ideas that lowers the gate. It did not take me far to catch him. His mind had become rigid. He could not run far. When I found him, he was dangling his legs over the edge of a trench he'd dug, staring into its ideal depth. It was easy to push him in. A small push? Mmm. And bury him within his soul. The trouble — or value, in my case — with ideal depth in you humans is there's no bottom."

Big Jim smiled *click click* and its eyes gleamed like fiery candles. "When you're that alone among people, who knows when you're gone? No one. Not your wife (I ate her. No, no, I see by your face you think I climbed inside her like I did to Issen. No, I did not eat her soul like I ate him. I just ate her. Every bit, starting with her stupid, prying eyes. Then I told everyone she'd run off with the plumber). Who knows when you're gone, mmm? Not your parishioners. They think he still exists, only more mmm confident.

I tell you a secret. They like me better. They do whatever I tell them and pretend everything is fine. You know what FINE stands for, boy? I told them I changed my name to Sengrim, and they didn't blink. They just kept coming back, sopping up the drivel and being fine. Boy, listen to me. Mmm."

A purple tendril licked his mustache like the flash you see when you shut your eyelids too fast. "It is a wonder what people will do..." he smiled too wide for any human, "...for a big man *click click* who is sure of himself. Mmm."

I thought he was going to rub his belly.

"I learned Issen's ways, kept his gentle voice, squeezed into him like a suit (these people pretend I remain his size because they will not accept the alternative) and buried him deep in his own self. You should hear the screams, mmm? In truth, he is helpful to me. I was streetwise but not man-smart. This lonely fool gave me the conceptual vocabulary to open all the doors that had been theretofore shut."

I did not understand, and I did not want to.

Big Jim turned the steering wheel, and we entered a silent street. "We only want one thing. We Nisoi—you call 'monsters' – we will do anything. Anything to be you. Yes, mmm I am a very good speaker of words *now*. Maybe, you smell the ripe scent of something resembling – but not actually – a wolf. For that is what I was." He pounded the dash. "Those were bad days for Sengrim. A thousand years ago, someone convened my presence at a gathering of the Nisoi, and when I refused...." Its voice trembled with rage. "Threw me to swine in a pit. They chewed my flesh from my blood-weeping body – old pigs, very old and very fat – they gnawed my skin away with broken teeth. They flayed me alive." He shuddered. "Slowly. Even now I hear the squeals." His gentle voice never changed, but the menace made the hair on my arms rise. "For *that* I will make Reynard suffer. And of course, you."

Did this beast ever stop talking? I turned the pages and found someone who looked just like one of the seven sisters in the river.

"It was your ancestor who flayed me. And I cursed him:" His voice turned into the whining tones of the baby's:

"When mountain's son and ocean's line betroth,
Surely water's blood is bloody end,
And bloodied end the child of wroth."

His voice returned to its deep timbre. "Remember that one? Your ancestor threw me to the pigs. And as I fell under them, skinless – do you know the pain of having your skin ripped? The unending pain of the air touching every opened nerve?—I promised him I would return one day and take everything from him."

A chill took hold of my bones; everything went dark.

"It took me years mmm?" Big Jim's voice became the soft baby's whine. *"I crawled a thousand years amongst the worms, rolled in filthy sewers of rats, a slug, a baby-maggot, a larva. I transformed in their guts to a shape that suited me. And then I found my way here, by the scent of your family alone. For that is all I had that remained. The sense of smell."* The deep rumble came back. "And my Mistress gave me a new life. More than this man-suit. Into me She planted mmm? Never mind who She is you'll meet her later, eh? Into me She planted new life, Cold Blood mmm — from somewhere I shall not say, cold, dark, with no air — that I may be her protector."

Blood, blood. I felt it rising in my eyes. I fumbled at the door, but Big Jim pushed a button and the locks clicked shut.

"I have too much still to say. Mmm I'm growing, boy." His hand squeezed the steering wheel, and it squeaked as if it would tear in two. "Why do I tell you? To show I have NO FEAR (he whispered it so softly I could barely hear him, but it felt like a shout) ... NO FEAR of you — the son of my enemy, mmm? That is why."

Dad says that anyone who talks to hear the sound of their own voice is the worst kind of jackass; the kind that don't know they are a jackass.

"Something in me changed, mmm? I awakened like a dumb animal to speech — you see, I spoke before, but it was a second language not my mother tongue — I awakened and I found this new self's sweet pleasures mmm. Of the flesh." He chuckled, and it sounded like a rutting elk.

He had been hunting our family a thousand years. I tasted something sour in my mouth.

"Reynard cannot capture me. Long he and that man-wolf hunted me, and before them, your ancestor." His voice dropped again until I could barely hear him, the sickly baby: *"And as promised, I will take it all from you. But first, I skin them alive. Flay them like the beasts they are. And nail them to a board."*

The nausea passed, but my head buzzed.

"I have digressed, there is much teaching mmm that you need, boy. As I catechize all my followers. Not even my Mistress knows of my followers, you understand? She thinks I guard her. She's a fool!"

I reckon I knew who She was, Dammit. And I reckon She does know, and I knew that before the day was done, he was taking me to see Her.

"You know you're filthy? Filth requires an intermediary. Me."

I felt like one of those ants in the school parking lot.

"Your Granma – filthy. Your dog – filthy. Your mother—filthy. But I made her mmm holy." He smiled at the look on my face. "I set her apart — 'set apart' means 'holy,' boy. I catechized your mother." A soft laugh. Big Jim touched my hair with a sharp nail. "I will catechize you too."

I felt a crushing weight on my chest.

"Pay attention," Big Jim said. "You know, you can curse god? Mmm? That's what I'd do if someone stole my mother. Raise a fist. Curse."

Dammit, you know how Porter says we are a long way from achieving the goal of a completely phylogenetic system? Did you know Linnaeus who originated the system brought back 537 specimens from his first exploration of Lapland, was made a Knight of the Polar Star in 1753, and when they went to his home after his death, they found his herbarium filled with more than 14,000 specimens? What did Big Jim say about my Momma? If the most-high God would come down, if They would present Themselves to me, maybe I would speak, but I doubt it. I can't speak to a normal human, let alone a god. What if there are 14,000 of them?

"I have learned so much about you humans since my awakening." Big Jim traced symbols on the windshield, his nails scraping. "People don't like to go to the source, it bothers them. They put innocuous men like Little Issen into buffering offices so they feel better about their nakedness before the void. Mmm. They wrap themselves in grave clothes of their own making to keep from seeing the grave. Sheep."

I thought, *beings like Big Jim don't want to go to any source, they want to be the source.*

"Anything you need to get off your chest, boy, you know, anything you can tell me about your grandmother, what she's up to?" I heard anger. Or was it fear? "Where's the axe? What did she do with the axe?"

Like Granma would say, I'm not gonna tell you about no fuckin axe. Especially now that you're revealed as our ancient enemy. I heard my father's voice long ago, tucking me in: "Our ancestor – one who started the family—destroyed our nemesis, Sengrim."

We turned onto a dark gravel street with houses on each side.

"Boy," he said, placing a paw on my arm, "I will now teach you of worship."

I forced myself to keep looking at the black mountains above the trees.

"These magazines," he pointed to the back seat, "are a form. First, we gather the congregation."

He pulled up to a house surrounded by aspens shining silver in the dark and a small boy, maybe eight or nine years old, dropped from a window, scampered across the lawn and climbed silently into the back. The boy did not act like we were there at all. He stared out the window, his thumbs played with his fingernails, clicking. Sometimes he would hum to himself, but it was more like a low moan. Big Jim drove a short way, stopped, and another boy ran silently from a porch. He kept driving and stopping, and by the time we left Junction City, the truck was full of little boys in pajamas, tense as cats in a window watching a dog go by.

Big Jim drove faster, dark trees flashed. "Listen carefully," he said. "Some people say only god gets worshiped mmm but it's not true. It's not about him, her, them, they, it, whatever. It's about us. Mmm? We worship all the time. Some people say we don't worship but mmm. Fools! Ignorant of the condition of beings. We all worship. All of us. Question is what mmm." He smiled, *click click* broad teeth shining under the yellow mustache. "This is catechesis, boy."

He patted my arm kindly.

"I prefer the warmth of flesh, hot flesh, as my worship. And breaking things. Take a boy for example. Very elastic, usually mmm? These things in the boy that bounce back — breaking them. This too can be a form of worship. Mmm. To help a boy turn on himself, to help him stretch the band to its limit, yes. Then you put your finger on the band and .... mmm."

He snapped his fingers *CRACK* like a tree snapping in half. He sounded so kind.

"Maybe you will worship me someday mmm? Today I show you."

My neck felt like ticks crawling. *Blood, blood.* I remembered the girl who looked like Penny in the flappy book and realized I forgot what the real Penny looked like. I had no lighter in my chest, only a skewer through my wuttus every time I gazed at her.

"You know there's something rotten in him?"

"Yes, shutup, yes I know."

"Why don't you look at me more? I'll be your girlfriend."

"I have a girlfriend." (I lied, Dammit, but what else was I supposed to say?)

"Mmm," Big Jim said, noticing my eyes. "Best of all. The worship when you break a girl. This, you know nothing of. But I will show you."

The smell of fearful boys, leather seats, and the faint and irregular *click click* in Big Jim's mouth filled the truck.

"Mmm," Big Jim said, and its great hand curled over my knee.

It was right about then I wished you were with me, Dammit. Nasty grin and all.

"Where is that turn? Ah." He peeled onto a narrow dirt road without slowing down. High grass grew down the middle, swishing beneath us. Pine trees leaned above, darkness on either side.

The road became narrow and full of weeds.

He's taking me somewhere out here in the middle of nowhere. He's going to kill all of us and there's nothing I can do. Blood.

The road ended in a pile of rocks. He stopped and the boys tumbled out, still silent and tense, and we walked past where some bikes leaned in the twilight and through a stand of scrubby pines.

The boys rushed ahead in a silent pack. I tried to walk behind Big Jim, but he grabbed my shoulder, and pushed me forward. The trees were so close we had to push through, and I felt their fingers catch my hair. I saw a glow in the distance.

"My boy will be here," he said. "You will see him baptized in blood to be my one true son. You will see," he whispered, "with him, I am well pleased." I tried to turn but he held my shoulders and pushed.

He was strong, Dammit, like ten men poured into his hands.

"You know he's not my real son?" He said. "I adopted him as a tyke. Fed him on things little boys should never eat mmm. Unless they want to not be a little boy—ever." He pushed me into a shallow depression, a glade surrounded by trees that leaned in overhead. "But he will be my son soon, like me with Someone on the inside."

The depression in the ground was deep in the middle, covered in pine needles that muffled every sound. A group of boys sat in a circle. Slicing through the middle was an old railroad track on rotting rail ties. "Up there," Big Jim pointed into the darkness where the tracks disappeared under the trees. "Up there's an old mine, boy, and let me tell you it is still producing, it's open like a wet cleft mmm a honey rock, to me. Copper. Gold. But also, a place to stash a body."

Big Jim's blond curls dripped sweat across his forehead.

He did not notice, or see, MK on the edge of the bowl sitting cross-legged, a light shadow under the dark shadows of the pines. MK's teeth shone, and that grin felt like getting the fire lit on the darkest night of winter. I didn't wonder why he was there, Dammit. I was just glad he was.

I swear I saw a dark tendril flare again under Big Jim's mustache. "Ah, here he is."

"What the FUCK," said Junior.

"Relax. Mistress told me to bring him."

"This idiot fucking called up the wolf-thing that ate Emmet."

"Pretty sure he didn't mmm? It's been in town biding its time like me."

"Whatever." Junior kicked a boy in the wuttus hard enough to make him bend over, retching. "I'm telling you dear Father, he's bringing back the old ways, he's dangerous." Junior picked a dead stick from the ground. "You told me we're crushing all that out."

I hoped Junior was right about me, Dammit, because he sounded scared. I had *not* forgotten he hurt me.

"He's a Bergmann," Big Jim got quiet. "Be dead already no thanks to you, but She wants him tenderized, mmm? That is why we are here."

Junior poked my bruised face with his stick, "Goddamn, did we do that?"

I jerked my face away.

"Lookin' good — chief shit-my-pants."

I forgot how bad my face looked—and felt.

"Haven't got to your ma... yet," Junior smiled. "Before this day is over, I will."

Blood, I thought. *Blood-blood* said my heart. My hand turned into a fist.

"MY MOMMA," I said.

"Quick," said Junior. "He's gonna call that thing again."

Big Jim twisted my arm behind my back and I blacked out. When the light came back, I was crushed in a hug, held against his massive barrel chest and Junior was patting my head.

"So, you CAN talk! Don't worry, I'll make her talk too."

In the center of the circle on a rotten railroad tie was a statue no higher than my hips. Just blobs on bigger blobs.

"First, we light the beacon," said Junior. "It's time to land the plane." He took a wild-eyed rabbit from Shovels. In one hand he held it by the ears. In the other hand he held a knife, sharp on one side with jagged notches on the other. Some of the boys knelt, others began to sway back and forth. The rabbit jerked, trying to run in the air. Its legs thumped against Junior's chest. The youngest boys were crying and tried to leave, but the biggest ones held them until they were still.

"We got to do this before sun-up," said Junior to everyone. "QUICK."

He knelt and crushed the rabbit's head under his knee. It squealed like a trapped girl.

"Mmm," said Big Jim behind me. "Keep your mouth shut."

Junior's arm rose and fell. The blade jaggedly ripped through fur and bone. *Blood.* There was blood and white fur all over the statue and he held up the screaming rabbit by the hind legs and by its ears and let the blood drip from its living body across the smooth face of the statue, which seemed to smile.

"Aahh," moaned the circle of boys all together, and I tried to break free but Big Jim squeezed so hard I felt my ribs creak. MK rose and stumbled down the tracks, rubbing his eyes. He never could handle blood, Dammit.

"No!" cried a boy. A bigger boy slapped him and took a drop of blood off the statue and wiped it across his eyes, into his ears, and across his lips.

Something said, *"It is good, it is very good,"* and it was not any of us there. Just a deep voice that sounded like a man and like a woman all at once that came from the ground and the trees. *"Blood, blood,"* said the voice.

Something in me started yammering in harmony with the voice. The fingernail Ms. Swan shoved into my chest felt like a sliver of hot lead, and I could tell – as twisted as She had become, even if She welcomed this new beast—She hated this too.

"*Blood, blood,*" murmured the voice, mixed with the smell of rabbit and the sound of crying boys.

Something is coming, something slouches.

"Accept this gift, Mastress," intoned Junior. "Erased in your unity, the polarities."

"Watch," said Big Jim, a sharp fingernail on my neck. "I saved this last secret for you. We are bringing Someone. Someone the ruler of this town—Someone She does not know. One long gone, more ancient than all of us. It has promised to serve me and raise me up. It needs to enter through a living being."

"Come Mastress," whispered Junior. "The blood of animal, the blood of boy. Come."

"The Progenitor," said Big Jim, his deep voice full of awe. He knelt and pulled me down.

The boys rubbed their hands across the head of the statue, rubbed them up and down in the blood, from the base of the statue to its smooth head, moaning. Then one of them, the tallest one, took the knife and cut himself in the arm and poured it over the statue. "Drink. Drink us," he whispered.

Big Jim breathed hard; his thick fingers circled my upper arm. "See. This is when the band stretches tight, and I touch it. Gently. Mmm. And it snaps." Blood welled from where his orange nails pressed my skin. The smallest boy — the first who climbed in the truck this morning — broke and ran down the tracks, but three others chased him, tripped him, and brought him back shaking and crying. They pushed him to the front until he laid against the bloody statue. Blood covered his face and chest. He tore off his shirt, embraced the statue.

"LIGHT THE BEACON," Big Jim said softly, but it sounded like a shout.

They pressed in.

"See, boy?" Big Jim said, "This mmm. This worship," and his smile dropped down from under his mustache like a dark cave. "This beacon of broken children." The shadow of tendrils flickered and sucked back in. *Click Click.*

The voice was in the ground and trees and railroad ties and vibrating air in our veins, *"Not enough. MORE. Where are the girls?"* It groaned and the ground shook.

A scream came from Junior like a stab straight into the heart of the sky. I thought his throat would tear open. He threw the jerking rabbit into the trees, tossed boys away from the statue, and laid both hands on its blood-soaked thighs. He cut himself, then pressed his hands up and down against the lubricated and bleeding stone curves of the statue.

"MORE," said the voice.

One by one, beginning with the biggest boys, they passed the knife, cut their arms and chests, and dripped blood on the statue.

"MORE," said the voice.

The glade was thick with the smell of blood, and the sweat of unwashed, heavy-breathing boys trying to make something come that was close but never arriving.

The dark voice vibrated against me. *MORE. Where are the girls?*

I broke from Big Jim's grip, ran to the edge of the glade and puked. *Blood, blood.* I could not scrub it from my ears. The sound of flesh being cut, the soft gasps of pain. The shuddering moan of the dark voice that vibrated my flesh and within my veins – against every blade of grass, every stunted mushroom, every tree and stone in the murder glade. Above it all, the smallest boy crying like a rabbit in high pitched sobs.

Chapter 23

If You Can't Quit, At Least Quit Trying

Trees scratched like wires against steel on the sides of the truck as we headed back to town.

"You'll get used to it, boy," Big Jim patted my arm *click click.* "Don't worry, it IS a lot of blood, mmm."

"No shit Sherlock," I heard Granma say in my head, "And fuck-off, he's no boy a yours.'" When she popped off in my head like that, I started breathing slower.

"We did not please It. But we shall. We need a different beacon. Female." His hand moved up my arm and squeezed my shoulder until the joint moved. "One more stop mmm before we get you home."

My muscles spasmed. Not from his grip — which felt like a meat-clamp — but from how close his hand was to my neck. I squirmed out and grabbed a new flappy book from the back.

"Oh, so you're back. Now that you need comforting."

"Shutup and just let me look in peace."

Big Jim said, "Your grandmother know you're with me?"

I shook my head.

He squeezed my shoulder again, every part of his large face moving except his globby eyes, too big even for *that* face. "Time to introduce you to the ruler of this town, the Mistress." *Click Click.* "Don't tell her what I'm doing, or..." The force of his grip gently pulled my shoulder from the socket, snapped it back, and I cried out.

When I could see straight, I turned the page – don't let him see you hurting, Clay. New girl. Red head.

"Sister says you got a dog."

"He thinks he's funny."

"Dogs are funny!"

"No, he tells riddles. Stupid ones."

"Riddle me this: what's the difference between vision and reality?"

"Why, what an ass am I! This is most brave, that I, the son of a dear father murder'd, prompted to my revenge by heaven and hell, must, like a whore, unpack my heart with words." So much for going loco.

In the vision I had not seen scared boys, or blood, or Junior going nuts, or felt that Presence that vibrated my skin. Whatever Dad thought I would do to avenge him was a fading dream. We were on our way to see Ms. Swan. I would do nothing.

I reached for a new flappy book, maybe this girl wouldn't ask questions.

MK was in the back seat, riffling through one, and smacked my hand. *"Rain added to a river that is rank, perforce will force it overflow the bank,"* he said. "Name that one, Romes, and I'll get you out. Extra points for why I chose it."

I knew exactly what he was talking about. But I wasn't playing his game no more, Dammit. I smiled grimly. It hurt my face. I realized I could see through both of my eyes, a new development. I reckon I heal pretty fast. Also, this: Big Jim could not see or hear MK. I mean, MK was back there flipping his long hair, popping his knuckles, rustling pages and talking. Like always, being a Jackass. Nothing—Big Jim just kept driving and squeezing the wheel like it was the neck of a rabbit.

It was right about then, Dammit, in that tomb-of-a-truck that I made up my mind. I was quitting The Riverside and quitting MK. Something is rotten in the state of Idaho. No more trying to make order from chaos with someone's lines not my own. No more scourge, or minister. Lay back and go with the flow.

But my heart wouldn't quit trying. *Blood, blood,* it thumped. *Blood, blood.*

"Boy, it's simple. I want that axe, mmm?" Big Jim pulled up to the Oyster & Swans, turned off the engine. "Your Grandmother will suffer if you don't bring it to me."

One time when I was little and had not yet become afraid of the water, I was floating like a log on my back in the pool in the river and looked up — and saw all kinds of wild and lovely creatures, Nisoi as my Momma calls them. Well, maybe you don't see them, Dammit, but I did. Just that one time. Some even told me their names.

I found Mom on the porch reading Shakesbear.

"Momma, what do I say if one a them (I pointed up) asks me to play?"

"Who!? What did you see?" Her eyes flashed. "I told you to not go in the water without me."

I described what they looked like and that they all waved.

She got a strange look, "Clayton, you be careful. Not everyone can see Nisoi. If anyone of The Three Rivers ever try to talk to you, you run the other way. Except for one." She made as if to say more, but I interrupted her.

"What if they're faster?" Still a good question, in my opinion. "And what if they're friendly?"

"Don't tell your Dad," she said. "Not yet. Your peculiar gift. I need time."

I am a broken branch, Dammit, from a broken tree floating in a river of blood.

All I know is when you're in this river — before you feel it pick up speed and the green ledge coming — and you look up and see Nisoi, you wonder, "did we drive them up there with our killing?" I wish I knew enough back then to ask Momma, Dammit. But I knew nothing. I thought of the beast that Big Jim and Junior lit the beacon for in the murder glade, the Nisoi that was coming. God, Monster, or something else? Whatever blocked it was not the killing. No, it was the killing that was bringing it. It felt like a spider just crawled in my shirt.

I wish I could go loco like Dad. I wish there was a way to get out, Dammit. Or die. But my heart won't quit. *Blood, blood,* it thumps. *Blood, blood.* Sometimes you're just stuck. In this dream I can float. But I do not know how to swim.

The little bells jangled as Big Jim pushed open the door to the Oyster & Swans.

Chapter 24

Just A Simple Inventory for Us, Dammit

Porter says, *"...The aims of plant taxonomy are two-fold: (1) identify all the kinds of plants; and, (2) arrange the kinds of plants into a scheme of classification that will show their true relationships."* You tell me, Dammit, what's more important: relationships or schemes?

I prefer Inventory:

Ms. Swan. Extra powerful goddess. How do I know? The Name I can't say and how the fingernail twitches in me. I would tear out my heart right now if She asked. But She's not in Her right mind. I know nothing – nothing—about women-goddess-types, but I know when someone's not right in the head. Like MK said: *"the opposite of love is not hate, it is rot."*

Ms. Swan's "labors" One, Two, and Three:

Bring the buffalo hide from Her ex. Steal it, actually.

Bring Penny's heart. Which means ... no I can't say it.

Bring *Acuere*. I get it, OK? She's real scared of it.

MK. He makes a deal with Her to help me. No, actually a vow to serve the Ruler of the town for one day. Plague upon him.

Big Jim. Now, this part I did not see in the vision, Dammit. On the way back from Ms. Swan's to Granma's, Big Jim tried to touch my wuttus. I jumped out of the truck. He chuckled *click click* and told me they didn't need me no more and took off. I walked home.

Me. Flaming Bag a Nuts. This I picked up from Granma.

Relationships. I can't stop thinking about Ms. Swan. To be wanted by someone; it changes everything. *Oh, what a rogue and peasant slave am I!* If She tugs on the nail in my chest, I won't be able to help myself. I will go.

Inventory done.

Chapter 25

I Write A Sonnet, And So Forth

I found Granma's note on a napkin in the kitchen. Words like knife strokes:

Welcom bak. Pee bld, SEE Doc.
Gon wrk. Eg, mlk in frj. NO scool. REST!
Lv yu thr n bak,
Gma
Ps. Get me new chr—HA! Reed yr BIG book.

A plaid curtain over the sink fluttered. The kitchen was an oasis after the coils of Ms. Swan's throne room and the weight of Big Jim's hand. It was cool and grey and smelled faintly like bread.

The only reminder of my rage the night before was a scuff on the floor and a missing chair. I was tired from being awake all night, but my head was clear. My body felt like a bad tooth trying to heal. Let me tell you, Dammit, a bad tooth makes everything bad until you pull it out with a pliers and a kicking tree (the tree is for kicking while you pull).

I noticed The Riverside on the table with a broken spine and my blood on its edge like an old rusty sword. I had to pee and did it with one hand. The other, my right one, curled like a claw. It hurt like a knife was stuck in my back. No blood though. *Courage, man, the hurt cannot be much.* I got mad because saying it made me hurt. Then I got madder because I had promised myself I was quitting Shakesbear.

I grabbed a half loaf and ketchup from the fridge, Pop's brass lighter – Granma must have forgotten it—and a pack of cigs off a shelf and walked out on the porch.

216

There you were, Dammit, laying above the top step.

Your tail wagged but you didn't move. Your eyes followed me as I sat in the camp chair.

"Piss on you."

"Poop on you," I said.

It is always easy to talk to you, Dammit, so I told everything that happened: "After we left Ms. Swan's place, Big Jim asked me about *Acuere*, but then he said they didn't need me no more. MK was doing the job for Ms. Swan. What does "expedient" mean?

"Dunno. I'm a dog."

"He said I was 'expedient,' whatever that means."

I felt a weight leave my shoulders as I told you, Dammit. "He tried to touch me, but I jumped out. He said, 'Run for home, boy. I'm sending a friend to finish you. Achilles.'"

"Show that catfucker who's a friend."

"Pretty sure he's the enemy."

"Smart enemy better than dumb friend." You came and licked my purple-claw hand. "Makes the battle better."

"I thought *you* were my friend."

"Yup," you said. "Ear. Now." By which I assumed you meant "scratch me," so I scratched behind your ear. You liked it, groaning low.

"Being happy is better than being king," you grunted as your chest hit the floor.

We watched the morning sun touch the ponderosa needles.

"Let that sonofa bitch come," you rolled over, showing your underparts. "Bigger dog, harder fall."

Granma's house sits on a gravel street five blocks from downtown, surrounded by overgrown lilac bushes and decaying buildings. Some houses on the street are built with red or green-painted logs. Others have flaking white paint, small windows, and yards covered in dead weeds. In between them stand ponderosa pines, a few firs, and aspen groves in the low wet spots where the snow remains. A lone blue spruce with branches to the ground sits, alien, down at the end. Across the street — where Sophelia and the strays live — an old car sat in weeds, and a few trailer houses hunched like old women in rusting skirts; paths through the snow-killed grass between them showed where people's feet tracked from rotting porches.

I remembered Granma said, "richers moving in, only a matter of time before they doze the street and throw up condos."

The whole street felt like it had been holding out for years and if you blew on it wrong it might crumble like a dandelion. Granma's house looked like a fighter that lost too many fights against too many winters and dug a hole and hunkered down behind its lilacs.

"I know what that feels like," I said out loud, startling myself. The sound of my voice, rough on the edges, made me drop the pack of cigs.

You turned your belly towards the sun which was still behind the ridges in the east. The air was clear and slightly blue like a jar of lake water. It smelled of rain coming. Not right away, but by sundown, I reckoned. I stuck a cig in my mouth like I'd seen Granma do. Then I lit it with Pop's lighter on the first try and breathed in. It was like a campfire in my lungs. I coughed and pain shot from my wuttus through my eyeball. I squirted ketchup on the bread and took another drag on the cig. That sweet and sour on my tongue was like I was five again. I watched the last brown snow melt off Granma's lawn into an oily lake in the street.

Something crinkled in my back pocket. Penny's page from last night.

My head buzzed like a bee-filled tree as I read it again (was it the cig or something in there I could not understand?) I tried to think about it, but all I could think of was her: leaning forward and looking at me, one eye looking into my head and the other gazing at my heart, those long fingers to pushing her forelock back, speaking Shakesbear like she knew him by heart. What did she say to me? *"If thou swear'st thou mayst prove false."*

I would prove I wasn't false.

It is easy enough, Dammit, to compose the first lines of a sonnet. I pulled a pen from my pocket—taken from Big Jim's truck, don't ask me why, I just take things—and wrote slowly with my left hand on Penny's page pressed against my leg. With you breathing slow, and the soft creaking of the pines with the birds waking up, it was easy enough:

In every light your eyes so constant shine,
With clear unwaver'd purpose to my thought.
Of rays and waters mix'd they do combine
And make my heart to grow from what is not.

If I sit long enough the rest comes to me. So, I looked around. I started thinking there, on the porch, how I like mornings and evenings best. When the light is coming in or going out. When the quiet is like a person who listens, and sometimes even talks back.

Quiet came and sat next to me. I knew it was Quiet because we did not have to talk to understand each other. The sun crested a ridge to my right, golden; a flame of vermillion fire touched the dead lawn, light painted the trees and houses as if a great hand turned us upside down into a bucket of sunshine, and the aspen were covered with shaking golden coins. The microscopic birds who creep upside-down the ponderosas cried out, buzzing back and forth, and the rest came to me like a hidden spring after a long hike:

As growing is what living things may only be,
As dying, every sun must ebb, your light the greater light;
I your virgined moon and you, my mirrored sea;
Still, all these darker eves grow soft to morning bright.

I cry — and vaunt my skiff upon the watered skies
To reach you in the night; where into you I rise.

I did not understand why I made up that last bit, but it felt right, Dammit, so I spoke the whole thing out loud to you.

"What do you think?"

"Wisdom is a baobab; no one person can embrace it," you said, and went back to sunning.

I felt sick. Every person—good like Penny, bad like Junior, ugly like me – was a diamond. *The beauty of the world.... what is this quintessence of dust?* Even Junior and Shovels and their gang were a new country. Each of them, canyons and hills and alpine lakes. And further waters. I searched all the things I knew from The Riverside, and—though there was much remembered—still, I had no words for how it felt to see people. Real, living people. Then I thought of Big Jim and the glade with the crying boys and did not want words.

"I'm gonna die, aren't I?"

"Death is not the enemy," you said. "The river calls to the rain, and it is the ocean who answers."

"You and your stupid riddles," I said.

"Proverbs, dumbass. Not riddles," you said.

"How come I talk to the dog, but not people?" I asked, and you grinned that nasty, scarred-face grin.

"Birds sing because they have songs—not answers," you said.

"If only I could sing," I said.

You growled, and the hair on your back shot straight up.

"Nose up," you said.

A familiar dry voice said, *"Veachron."* MK strolled out from under the trees. *"O, how bitter a thing it is to look into happiness through another man's eyes.* Care if I join you, Romes?"

I grunted and shrugged my shoulders. Alafar Yaqum, asshole.

"You don't have to be silent with me," he said, "I know. You talk."

"*Friendship is constant in all things, except you,*" I said. "'As You Like It' by the way, plague."

"Oh, Hamlet-my-sandwich, MK like!" He grinned, looking across the roof of the house like he could see Jupiter a million miles away in the dark. Or Uranus. I grinned to myself. How about you can't see my thoughts and I like it that way. I decided this one time I could let myself use a little Shakesbear. I was quitting, but a little bit won't hurt—right, Dammit?

"*Tis an ill cook that cannot lick his own fingers,*" I said. I was thinking of friendship.

"Easy. 'Romeo and Juliet,' Act IV, possibly scene three? Romes, what a juicy pair of lovelies Penny and Ms. Swan are, eh?"

I felt a fingernail wiggle in my chest. "What nefarious deeds did you do for Ms. Swan? Where have you been?" I asked.

"Me? Nowhere. Everywhere. It's not time yet. It's not like I sat on a porch reading four years straight, interspersed with trapping and shooting sundry beasts, dear Romes," he said.

"What *did* you do all those years?"

MK's eyes—already the deepest blue—turned an even darker blue, so dark almost black. Like water at night. Like the sun never shone on them. He did not answer.

I surprised myself, "And where did you go?"

You growled low, Dammit, but he didn't seem to care. He walked up and sat beside me on the floorboards, leaning against the wall.

He changed the subject. "You're not going to apologize?"

"For what?"

"Attacking me at dinner. Scaring the shit out of everyone?"

"No. You touched 'Deer.'"

"Alpha Romayo." He sounded offended. "Penny's sister's name is Cressida, by the way. Shits and giggles. You didn't see what was going on between them?"

"I don't see nothing but curtains," I said, thinking of how my busted eye looked through a curtain right now.

"That's your problem. You got to SEE."

"With people, I look through curtains all the time," I said. "Even when my eye isn't swole." I changed the subject. "When you were gone from the home place, were you—or were you not—sucking souls out of people?"

His face twisted, "I would never suck souls out of people."

"You grab them from behind and lean over them and—whatever it is that *is* them—you suck it out. Don't you remember?"

"I only remember how I feel before I do it. The next thing I remember is not feeling that feeling. Feeling what they are—bad. But not as bad as me. Not as bad as me."

How do you respond to that, Dammit? You muttered, "he who burns down his house knows the high cost of ashes."

"Something hurts, Clay," MK said. "People help me."

"You don't stay around to see what happens, and later, you conveniently forget."

"I don't forget everything, not on purpose."

"Pretty much. I'm always telling you later about the goddamn cougar. And you were there."

"I see by your language Granma's getting to you," He popped his knuckles. "*Tis in my memory lock'd, and you keep the key of it.*"

"'Hamlet,'" I said without thinking. "Stop changing the subject. I'm up two, and *you are only to yourself true.*" I choked, "what does — did — Craig know?"

"We are a couple nerds and I love it. Same play."

"Answer the question."

I knew he was thinking deeply because he did not say, "Hamlet, ha!" or keep score. He sighed and cracked his knuckles. Then he leaned back, crossed his lean bare feet over one another, pulled his twisting hair over his shoulder, and stuck his hands in his jean pockets. "The truth?" he asked. "You never asked about my peculiar problem."

"You never ate someone's soul out their ear."

"That's not how it is." He shifted on the floorboards. He never could sit still.

"Now you're just wasting time," I said, lighting another cig. I blew out smoke and pretended I was Pops. Tough-as-nails, full of stories, chop down trees with a single blow.

"You know how everything feels OFF?" asked MK. "Bad smells, stunted trees, drought for years?"

I thought of the dogs that tried to attack me, how Spring felt like it was fighting through a wall of dust here. I thought of writhing maggots in a peach, Penny's black eye, Ms. Swan's shadowy twisted self gibbering about tearing it all down, Big Jim's hand on my wuttus, the sobbing boys in the grove, the screams of the rabbit, and that deep-high vibrating Voice in the murder glade. I thought of all the blood I seen already, and wondered what blood was coming. *"Unnatural deeds do breed unnatural troubles,"* I said, and I shivered for the memory of that story.

"Exactly. Macbeth. Point for me. Actually, Macbeth works as well as any to tell you what I know: Sometimes I think I sleep and I walk, speaking of things maybe I have done. But maybe someone else has done?"

"Like the Lady with the blood on her hands?"

"I have no family, no one I can remember." He looked me straight in the eye, and it hurt bad like it always does when I actually look back. Like a black hole with a swinging hi-beam of ultra-black at the end of it.

That's how I knew he was true. No shifty gaze, no popping knuckles.

"I wander under the heavens and there is no light. It is very dark. The only light is memories taken. And you, Clayton. You are a light. The memories stay like a stiff drink. Long enough to numb. Short enough to need another."

"Who are you?" I asked, and you stirred on the porch, listening.

MK spoke as if he had not heard, "I seek something I cannot find. I fear I have done something terrible." Here, he paused, and it seemed he could not go on. "I try to look into that memory but when I look there, it is black as the night when it happened." His face turned upon itself misshapen like wax in the sun. A face unlike any I had seen before, though I seen Craig's staring eyes, and horror on the face of the nurse. Though I seen Penny's eyes after she stayed with Junior in the hallway. Though I seen light go from the eyes of the cougar in my arms.

"There is great pain," he whispered. He was somewhere very far away.

In truth, I realized, he was more real than my Momma or Dad (who were real only in dreams and surging memories). He looked lost, alone, like he was stranded on the dark side of a planet furthest from the sun.

"Pain," he said, hands like claws on his knees, turned towards each other like a prayer that can never be spoken.

I felt something for him, for the first time. A feeling stronger than companionship. A burning in my chest, but nothing like Penny's lighter. In that moment, if you asked me, I'd a grabbed Achilles by the neck for MK, I'd a jabbed Big Jim in the eye. It's like getting close to a campfire at night, and when you get there, you find someone waiting. Someone you been looking for a long time.

I reached for his hand, but he pulled it away and rubbed the other one.

"That is when I find anyone, and they help me," MK said. "They give me light and a *when* to live."

"Except they live in you, they possess you. You would rather live anyone's life but your own," I said, and as I said it, I knew it was true.

"It was a black, black night," he whispered.

I shuddered, remembering the writhing bodies I saw deep in the cave of his eyes. I saw Lady Macbeth walking in a dark hall, rubbing the blood from her pearl-white hands, always rubbing.

"Well, as for me," I said, "all I want is to find my Momma." I did not say "avenge my Dad," because I did not want to do that, Dammit. Or "be with Penny," because I did not want MK to know. "And it feels like everything is against me, and I'm stuck in someone else's story trying to get out and into mine."

"The wise monkey in the trap lets go the banana," you said.

"You are definitely stuck," MK said.

How true he was in that moment, Dammit. You know as good as me.

"*We* are stuck," I said.

He cracked his knuckles, black eyes returned to indigo, and he was fully back. But sadder. "Nah, just you Romeo. O Romeo," he grinned, and then said something that made me realize he knew me inside and out: "*Deny thy father and refuse thy name. Or if thou wilt not, be but sworn my love...* and I'll no longer be a naughty boy."

I was done with the TRG. I threw Pop's lighter at him and he caught it without looking.

"The dog is right, Romes." He flicked the lighter and watched the flame touch his middle finger which he pointed directly at me. "Let go the banana. Or burn the whole thing down to get in your own story," he said. "Or, I know. Fake your own death."

"Not what I said," you growled. "Grass suffers under two fighting elephants."

"Duh, everyone knows that, hound. Now, Romes, something is causing me concern; I need your insight."

Chapter 26

The Dammit Rule of Fighting

"I don't trust the ruler of this town to fulfill Her bargain," MK said.

"She gave Her word," I said.

"Ha! Word? Your girlfriends didn't fill you in, Romes?" He rolled his praying hands like they were a wave.

What is it about him, Dammit, I could go from friends to enemies in one knuckle-pop? Like I wanted to punch him so hard he'd fall off the porch. "I have no friends who are girls, Juliet," I lied.

He bowed mockingly. He could pull that off sitting on the floor and look graceful. Slender fingers. Sharp chin, high forehead. Long, crossed legs that made his cheap jeans look like a thousand bucks. Dad used to say that to my Momma every morning, Dammit. "You look like a thousand bucks, R.M.—a thousand bucks wasted on this bum."

"Will you keep your vow to.... Ms. Swan?" I could barely say Her nickname without blacking out.

"I always keep my vows." His eyes went pitch black for a moment, then cleared to indigo. He chewed a nail and stared at the brown lawn. "There are things I've been ordered to do today. Then, She'll tell me about myself. I need leverage if She doesn't follow through."

"What things?"

"Can't say. Remember, I'm doing this job for you." He smiled nastily. "If I told you, I'd have to kill you."

"You're doing this for yourself, lazy-ass, not me." It popped out without thinking, and his eyes went black, so I joked. "It's going to be *so great* to see you finally do some work. That will be a first." I reckoned I better ask him quickly: "Help me find out what happened to Dad, who did it, and I'll help you," I said. "Dad's ghost asked me to avenge him. Dad was murdered. I seen it in a dream."

MK's eyes flashed when I said, "Dad was murdered." Then he pretended to study the ponderosas along the street instead of looking at me.

I kept going. "Craig—inside you—told me my Momma's alive. You help me, I'll help you with leverage. Whatever the hell that means." Saying it out loud made it real. I took the lighter from him, lit a cig, and took a deep breath. This time I didn't cough. I watched the smoke rise.

"Deal," he looked at the trees like they were incredibly important. "Give me time. That's how vows with these Ancient Ones work. Follow through. Or else." His brow furrowed. "Else the kickback grinds you into nothing." He took the lighter back. "I just pretend it's a job and it's soon over. You know those cigarettes will kill you?"

"You know bad vows will too?"

"Bad vows, sure. And fast cars, and rabid dogs, and walnuts in your windpipe, and stingray barbs to the heart, and leftovers, and grizzlies, and vacuum cleaners used inappropriately, and cigarettes — mostly cigarettes — will give you cancer and kill you." He slapped his knees with both hands and looked straight at the rising sun. "Fuckit what do I care."

"Cancer. I heard about that. When abnormal becomes uncontrolled. That's what Mister Brown says monsters are."

His eyes went black. "Off topic. My fault."

"Are you one?" I asked.

"No. Worse," he said, and he was not joking.

I changed the subject to get away from his eyes, "Tell me about Craig, like you promised."

He leaned back, put his hands behind his head like he does when he's pretending to be calm, and closed his eyes. "What Craig knew about your Mom is fading away in me. There's less and less every day, only that he heard Rose-Marie might be alive." He yawned.

I hadn't heard my mother's name in so long. Dad would lay his hand under her hair and lift it up, until it was flowing out behind her back and she'd smile and he'd say — like it was a secret between them — "...dark as raven's wing my beauty, my Rosey, dark as the stoneflies under the waters and the trout that seek them in the deeps," and she would laugh and say, "only you would compare me to fishing, George," and kiss him. At some point, they would reach down and pull me in — "get in here Baby Grizz." Looking up through her hair, my face pressed against the cold brass of his axe-embossed buckle.

"What?" I asked.

"Good God. Again?" He smacked the floorboards. "Pay attention. I told you what Craig knew which is barely anything. I told you the plan. Just answer me this: What would you be willing to do to find your Mom?"

"Anything," I said. "I will do anything." Was my head buzzing from hope or the cigarettes?

"Good. New plan. Leverage. First step is you get Mister Brown to find that magic buffalo hide."

"What does he know?" I was confused.

"Jesus. Did you hear nothing? Promise me: Will you ask Ms. Swan to honor her vow? If you get a chance?"

I nodded but did not speak.

"The lizard nods his head," you said, scratching your ear, "but that is not a contract."

"I did not ask you," he said darkly, and your ears pinned back. "What do you know, dog, about surviving without parents? Or looking for what you've lost, like me?"

Your ears laid back, and for the first time I knew you were hurting too. "Lots," you said, and it sounded more like a growl. You stood up and stretched.

"Pick your fights," you said.

Down the street Achilles came walking stiffly, bowlegged. Twice as big as you, long as a yearling cougar, like he owned the street. He sniffed a lilac bush, and peed on it, glaring at us. It was a big stream. He peed for a long time.

"Hey catfucker," you said.

Achilles looked like a hand squeezed his middle and pushed all the linked-chain muscles to his shoulders. "The boy," he said, "I am here to rend his throat and drink his blood."

The only sound was the scrape of your claws on floorboards. You leapt off the porch, silent as a shadow. He saw you coming and barked. I know it took only a moment, but as you streaked towards each other I swear I counted every step on the porch—there are five—and couldn't believe you cleared it with one jump. I noticed the birds in the Ponderosas stopped buzzing.

You met him, chest to chest.

Achilles knocked you face-first to the ground like a fawn hit by a truck. But the truck staggered on his haunches, and you were off the ground like you were made of springs, and at his throat. He fell back and you fought, tearing up great clumps of dead grass.

He tried to clamp those steel-trap jaws, and you slashed like a swordsman. It was always you pressing him. Always a little faster to the counter-leap, a little faster to the throat. He skidded backwards into the middle of the street. Achilles snarled as he fought. You were silent as death.

He wanted to catch you, just once, and clamp down and choke you out. It seemed you were too quick, and he missed each time. But then he did it. (He caught you because you are a counterpuncher. You wait for the other fighter to open up their chest after a lunge—and then you leap.) But Achilles feinted. You waited on what you thought was a lunge, and leaped as he pulled back. He was ready and grabbed your throat. I thought it was over. Achilles' jaws closed like a vice. You hung from his mouth. Your back legs jerked, and I thought you were dead.

Then I saw he had missed and only caught you on the shoulder. With a lunge against him, you tore loose a chunk of fur and flesh in his mouth and then—no more counter punching—you came at Achilles in a rage of blood and fur and teeth. His jaws snapped like bear traps, *CLANG*.

But you were silent as a winter morning. Faster than a rattlesnake in the sun.

Then it was over.

Achilles lunged and his jaws snapped again *CLANG*—missing. Your muzzle curled, your fangs dripped spittle, and you crouched (but I saw it coming). His great neck stretched out for a single moment at the end of his jab. You leapt, slashed once. Blood from his throat sprayed in a fountain between your jaws. Achilles knelt in the middle of the street as if bowing to you. Then he fell between your front legs.

You stood over his body and howled, and the voices of dogs far away in the distance, all across Junction City—one by one until the howls came from every direction—joined you. When you were done howling you turned and came dripping blood from your muzzle all the way to the porch.

MK was gone.

You shook yourself from top to bottom and then back again like dogs do after coming in from the rain. Blood from your muzzle and bleeding shoulder spattered across the porch onto Granma's white walls.

I said, "You didn't need to do that." My ears felt hot, and my hands shook.

"Make mess or kill dog?" you asked grinning, and your voice was deep. Achilles lay in the street as if paralyzed, wheezing through his great open mouth. The wound on his neck bubbled. His pig eyes followed you to the porch.

"You said 'pick your fights,'" I said.

You looked at me, panting, with your head cocked and the old scar twisting your face. "Nope. Pick fight. Said, *'pick fight.'*"

"Ha. Is that a dog joke?"

"I tell you joke..." you grinned, waiting. When I said nothing, you said, "What taste like victory, smell like ass, be turd-brown and red all over?"

I shook my head. Nope. Not falling for it.

"Catfucker. Hargh."

So funny, so very funny. Dog jokes. Funniest thing ever. You laid your head back and howled for joy and every dog across town joined you again.

As I remember that day, Dammit, I don't want to forget how you cocked your head, how that scar made your grin mean and smooth as silk. How you would look at me like you would follow me into fire and death. Which you did. I don't want to forget the sound of that howl. Or your horrible jokes.

It was in that moment — as your enemy in the street gurgled out his life, kicking the gravel as he sought to run from you — that I remembered the line from The Riverside that haunts me still:

Caesar's spirit, ranging for revenge
With Ate by his side come hot from Hell,

Shall in these confines with a monarch's voice
Cry "Havoc!" And let slip the dogs of war.
"Maybe Granma should have named you 'Havoc,'" I said.

"Sure. Good name. But Clay?"

"What?"

"Don't care what name, care who loves me."

I nodded my head. After all, your enemy had a wonderful name and what good did it do him? "Fair enough," I said. "Achilles was a heel."

"Ha. Heel was weak." Then like an afterthought, but very seriously — dogs don't do sarcasm, that's for cats — you said, "You my lead dog."

"MK would call me the Alpha Romeo," I joked bitterly. "I care about you too, but I'm not cleaning up your mess."

"The broom likes the rain to clean, but the rain only likes the rain," you said with a shrug. And laid down and started wiping your face and licking the blood from your paws.

I walked to Achilles and — for some unnamed reason — laid my hand on his head. It was wide as a flat rock. There's nothing like that sweet tang of blood, that brooding incense drawn from a body. The unmistakable aftertaste of metal. I said, *"Thank you for your gift, that we may live."* I was not sure that was true in any way shape or form, but something at my core knew Dad would do this. Even for this beast, this enemy sent to kill me. So, I did it. *"Come to us brother,"* I said, *"and make your home with us on that day when all things are made new."* Achilles shuddered once more and was still, though his great chest moved ever so slowly. He was still breathing.

"Why you do that?" you called from the porch. "Those not in the pack run on their own."

"Exactly," I said. "Now he's in our pack, like it or not." I walked through the bloody pebbles and grass back to the porch, sat down, and put my hands on my head. "Everyone needs a place, Dammit, even bad dogs." I was shaking and smelled of dog and blood. But my heart felt right about it.

"Bad dogs don't deserve a pack," you said. "But yeah, sometimes they get one."

"I don't think it's about deserving. Anyways, I chose to give it," I said. "Thanks, Dammit," I said. "He'd a probably killed me."

"Fight pick you sometime." Blood still dripped from your jaws. "You wait. You can."

"I guess so," I said.

MK was definitely gone; without ever telling me about my Momma and Dad. I had more questions than before, that bastard a plague on him.

You shoved your wet nose under my hand until I scratched your ear. You looked at me with more fealty than any boy deserves.

"No guess so. Wolf inside you. Brave, fierce. Fighter."

"I hate killing." I rubbed my face. "I'm so afraid."

"Nope. Everyone afraid," you said. "Even Achilles here, him afraid. Afraid of me. Why him wait to bite? Because: afraid."

I muttered, "'*Tangle with grizz, get the claw.*' Dad used to say that."

"Grizz ain't so big." You lay down with a grunt — *"Hungh"* — looked at the body in the street and growled low. "Story tangled. Tangled bad," you said. Blood smeared from your muzzle and shoulder on the top step.

I reckoned the conversation was done. There was blood on my hands, and I wiped it on my pant leg.

Then you said something I still remember, still hold on to.

"Sometimes the knot needs only a knife," you said. "Bigger dog. Harder fall."

The whole morning had turned into a bad dream. The kind where you try to put on your pants, and you find out there are no pants, and you spend the rest of the dream naked—surrounded by a crowd of people pointing at your wuttus. And you're still feverishly looking for your pants. Every time I got close to learning *anything*, that bastard MK would disappear.

Now, it was just me and my blood-smeared, snarky dog. Knowing in the hollow spot behind my bruised ribs—the hollow spot that ached worse than any broken bones or bad dreams—this was just beginning. I flipped open Pop's lighter and lit another cig.

I didn't care anymore if it made my head spin.

"You think I'm done getting my ass kicked?"

"Nope." Slow dog-shrug, wide nasty grin.

Chapter 27

Flamin' Bag A Nuts

A shadow blocked the light. Big Jim's truck ran over Achilles' leg with a crunch and stopped, half in the street and half on the lawn. Achilles gurgled. The window rolled down and Big Jim's massive hand beckoned.

"What now?" I thought. "Bastard can't leave me alone." I shoved Pop's lighter in my pocket, told you to stay, Dammit, and walked down the stairs, rubbing Mister Brown's penny in my pocket. Praying for Granma to come.

"My sweet mmm. My sweet Achilles." Big Jim's face turned purple and blotchy, and he clicked his mouth. This time I saw green shadows come from under the mustache and curl back, fast. But I saw them for sure.

I pulled the penny from my pocket and started flipping it over and over. Catching it and rubbing it between flips. It fell into my hand, even when I didn't look. *Please, please work.*

"You're hanging with the wrong crowd, boy, flipping that penny."

I flipped the penny.

"That red-headed miscreant and his parlor tricks?"

I flipped the penny.

"How is it possible my dog lost a fight?"

I flipped the penny.

He gave you a look, Dammit, and I thought you would burst into flames. "I will deal with you later, cur."

I flipped the penny.

"I came to witness your bleed-out, boy." His voice got even more quiet than usual, which is how I know he was furious. "Instead, I'm forced to return you to Mistress for judgement. But first, Sengrim plays with you. You bad boy mmm. Get in."

I flipped the penny.

The pudgy baby voice: "I'll climb in you, boy, I'll find your fear spot."

One moment the penny was in the air. The next moment a penny-sized hole opened. My hand closed where the penny should have been. *Please*, I prayed, *Someone, anyone come. Please.*

Big Jim seemed not to notice. "Miscegenation of a fallen family. I scrape my boots every day mmm?" It was the deep voice, but so quiet I leaned closer to hear. "You're what comes off."

His hand — wide as a steak — wrapped around my elbow.

Sonofa spun around the corner spitting gravel. Granma Lina — blue cap pulled over her eyes, cig in her mouth like a middle finger — jumped out with a paper bag under her arm.

"Fuck ya doin' snake?"

Big Jim let go of my arm. I remembered my inventory from the night before and how badly I wanted to tell her I was sorry for jumping over the table and scaring her. "*To 'scape the serpent's tongue, we will make amends ere long.*" I felt my mouth open to say it, but all that came out was "*Urg.*"

Big Jim's hand squeezed the side mirror like a small toy. "Ah, Mrs. Bergmann. I hope you have all your mmm belongings out of the house."

She ground her cig out with her boot like it personally insulted her. Then she lit another with a plastic lighter and blew the smoke through his window. "Get off my property."

"Mmm, the letter? I've been designated the representative for The Oyster & Swan Company to make sure you leave *their* property."

"My land. Not going nowhere."

He spread his wide hands. "The O & S owns this house, and they've told you for months you need to be out."

"No shit, Sherlock," she said.

A line of trucks came around the corner as if summoned when he said, "out." One pulled a trailer, and on the trailer was a dirty dozer.

"You're NOT moving my house," she said, her eyes wide. "You're gonna knock it down."

"I am so mmm sorry for your loss," he said with a triumphant grin; the great mustache drooped, the mouth opened wide and made that horrible mashing.

Granma smoked like it was the only thing she cared about. The brim of her cap lay so low over her nose I could not see her eyes. One of the men started the dozer in a puff of black smoke, others wearing orange jackets grabbed shovels from a pickup. The street filled with the growl of the dozer backing off the trailer.

"Snake," she said quietly, and hawked a gob on his truck. She stomped her cig into the ground like it was a snake, and she was sending it to snake hell.

Big Jim's fractal eyes grew wider than any human's. "I've been trying to work with you, mmm, to help you find somewhere else to stay." So insistent, soft, kind.

"Why you LIE like that? For the boy?" She kicked a clump of dead grass. "I see through your bullshit. This's protected ground." She tried to light another cig. "You. Can't. Touch it."

If your hair could rise any higher, Dammit, it would have flown off your back.

"You're done Lina." The truck sighed and rose as he stepped out. I never seen anyone that big move that quick, or quiet.

"Where's the axe, mmm?" Big Jim asked.

Her eyes flickered to the house, but she stood her ground.

He ground his hands together like he was killing something. "Mmm. Oh I see. It IS here." He smiled and his giant eyes closed to thin slits. "I'm going to rip your mutt's balls out through his throat."

Granma snapped her lighter but could not get a flame.

"I'm going to take it all," he said.

The dozer turned towards the house in a belch of smoke.

"A life for a life," it looked like he was swelling, and she had shrunk, "your dog will die slow — I guarantee." Big Jim looked at you, Dammit, and I thought you would explode in a cloud of blood and dog fur.

You stared back, unafraid. Then, you said one word, and I knew you were the bravest one I ever knew (braver than Henry, Hamlet, Cordelia – even Paulina). Your claws settled into the floorboards *snap-snap-snap* like nails.

"Nope," you said.

Something inside me began to sing.

"Need a light," Granma beckoned to me. "Looks like you been smokin'. I seen that pack in your pocket."

I handed her Pop's brass lighter, and she lit her third.

The dozer tore up the grass in strips, getting into place beside the house to push over the porch. People came out of houses up and down the street when they heard the dozer. They stood watching, arms around each other. Not one of them came to help.

Granma Lina coughed, *hack*. With one hand holding the cig, the other hand beckoned, "Gimme that *hack* bandanna *hack* your Granpa's."

I watched the bulldozer and you, Dammit, and thought about how the power moved the wheels inside the tracks, and what kind of grease would make the squeak go away, and if it could push over a tree, and if so, how big a tree could it push over?

"GodDAMMit, Clayton Solomon Bergmann. *HACK.* Gimme the godDAMN bandanna."

It was in my back pocket where she shoved it the first day. I pulled it out, faded and blue, handed it to her and she held it to her face.

Thick, heavy coughs, clearing her chest.

"Clayton, you keep this snake off me," she said, and walked up the porch to stand next to you at the top of the stairs.

I couldn't make my legs move. I wanted to yell at Granma *"The axe is not here!"* All that came out of my mouth was a squeak like a chicken under a tire. *Bwaaagghhhk!*

Big Jim laughed, pushed me aside, and walked towards the house. A car with flashing lights on the top pulled up and a man came running towards us with a gun in his hand.

Granma swayed on the porch. She put her hand on your back, Dammit, to steady herself. Your lips drew back over dripping fangs. Your eyes were wild, bright, without a sign of fear. Big Jim's shoulders seemed to block out the sun as he walked towards the porch. He motioned to the man driving the dozer to turn off the engine.

Silence.

Granma's cig pointed out of her mouth to the sky. She held the bandanna in one hand, the brown bag in the other. Her voice was low, but grew louder until every neighbor down the street could hear her shouting around the cigarette that somehow never fell from her mouth.

"You GOD-dam sonsa-BITCHES gettin' on my case FOR YEARS." She blew out a cloud of smoke. "Destroyin' all 's good 'bout the world."

Her voice rose.

"You MOTHER-FUCKER." She pointed the bag at Big Jim. "AINT gonna GET my HOUSE over MY DEAD BODY."

Both arms raised in imprecation.

"You ain't gonna get my BEAUMONT'S AXE or ANY OF HIS STUFF you WIDOW-ROBBIN', ORPHAN-STEALIN', LYIN SNAKESinTHEGRASS SONS-a-BITCHES, (even louder) OVER MY DEAD BODY."

"Now, now, Lina," said the officer holstering his gun and holding his hands out. "Just come down off that porch."

Her eyes flamed. In a single flowing motion — she uncorked a bottle of clear liquid from the brown bag, poured it on the bandanna, shoved the bandanna into the mouth of the bottle, took a drag on the cig until it glowed, flipped open Pop's brass lighter and lit the bandanna so flames leaped from the top.

I could smell the alcohol from where I stood.

She held it high in the air for a single moment, flaming orange in the morning sun.

"MY house, MY home, cocksuckers," she said coldly.

Someone yelled "Noooooo," I think it was the cop, but maybe it was me.

She threw the flaming bottle through the open door. It broke against the dry walls. Licking flames streamed across the floor and up a wall. Something caught fire, flaring, in the kitchen.

Big Jim smiled at me *click click* and put his foot on the stairs. He didn't seem concerned at all.

You rose to meet him.

The house started crackling deep inside its bones. The sound of metal expanding and creaking for a split second.

BOOM.

It blew out the windows, knocked Granma and you clean off the porch — and Big Jim on his butt.

Granma landed on the lawn.

You landed on Big Jim's chest, fangs bared. *Cry havoc let slip the dogs of war!*

In a flash your jaws closed on his massive throat, but he ripped you off like a napkin and held you in one hand as he rose to his feet. He kicked you so hard — I thought he killed you. You landed with a thump on the burning porch. You tried to rise with fire in your eyes, but your back legs twisted behind you, your rear collapsed, and the pain caught you so fiercely that you screamed.

Granma pushed herself up on the lawn, dazed. She looked around like waking from a dream, grabbed her cap, shoved it back on her head. A siren far away began to scream, and it did not quit. It kept rising higher and higher. Then it cut out and started all over.

Granma rose on her knees looking at the house. Shock filled her face. Tears ran down her cheeks leaving trails through the dust and ash across her face. "Oh, Beaumont! Clayton," she waved at me, "Granpa's stuff!" She pointed up to the bedroom.

I was thinking about The Riverside, but it was too late.

"*Acuere!*" she cried. "Oh God... Dammit!"

Everything burned. The house was old and dry, like a box of matches dropped in a fire.

Big Jim swelled and seemed to grow even bigger; darkness hovered over the face of the house. He moved up the stairs with his fist raised, intent on smashing you, Dammit.

You pulled your broken body along the floorboards with your front paws. Too slow to escape him.

Something that sounded like an axe or hammer hit Big Jim square in the chest, *thunk*, and he went *OOF* and stepped back and sat down on the lawn.

You crawled to the edge of the burning porch and fell off.

Someone grabbed my elbow. I turned and it was Penny, grey eyes flashing green embers; she smelled like the back edge of a rainstorm in the sagebrush. She was crying.

The house made a sound like the breaking of a giant's back. There was an underlining bass roar as if a hundred trucks all started at once. The house expanded and contracted and then burned like a train running downhill.

Penny's eyes widened. Last night, I reckon the tension between her and Deer kept her from seeing how badly I had been beat up.

"OH MY GOD. What did they DO to you?" Her eyes lingered on the puffed-up flesh around my bloody eye, noticed my claw hand, and the bruising on my neck. Then she saw you lying among the broken boards and blazing cinders.

"Grab him," she said.

How long did I look at Penny? I don't know. You ever see someone with their guard down? I really seen her, Dammit: The wildest, kindest, smartest girl ever fashioned in the history of the world with a heart so goddamn big and open that every broken thing was like a nail punching another hole in her. It is hard to be *that* open to love the world because the world will fuck you up. Even in the midst of an inferno she was the most beautiful thing I ever seen. She had to punch me—and then push me to make me move.

I know you don't remember much of this, Dammit. I picked you up while Big Jim and the cop were shoving Granma in the cop car.

There was another *BOOM*. Flames belched from the windows.

Granma Lina's house burned straight up in the clear, still dawn. It burned orange in smoking flames from foundation to rooftop. Flames out every window. Flames pushing through sudden holes in the roof. Sparks and black smoke and big chunks flying up, up, up. Five pickups pulled up, one after the other. Men were everywhere pulling on big helmets and thick yellow jackets. But the fire was too hot for them to do a thing.

Penny turned the key in Sonofa, cursing and praying softly. She jammed it into reverse, and we backed down the street.

Granma leaned her face against the police car window as we snuck past her, mouth open, eyes burning. *"You go, Clayton Solomon Bergmann, you go quick!"* And banged her forehead on the glass.

Nobody noticed us leave. Especially not Big Jim — who kept getting knocked on his butt every time he tried to get close to the house. I knew what he was trying to find, and he would not find it there.

I laid my hand on your head. Your breath came in ragged gasps. Your legs lay straight out behind you like broken sticks. I knew you needed me, Dammit, and I let Penny drive us away. It was easy enough to do, I reckon, with all the mayhem.

The fire was so loud. People did not hear us leave, even with Pop's radio blaring and the man singing about a gang hiding in the darkness of a riverbed waiting for someone being chased.

Shakesbear would say, *"Exit, pursued by a bear."*

Yeah, we did.

Chapter 28

Dammit's Tale

"Romes, the dog don't look good." MK leaned over the seat. *"Diseases desperate grown by desperate appliance are relieved—or not at all."*

I ignored him, though in truth, we were in desperate straits. You lay on my lap like the steel was gone and all that was left was jiggly guts and hair. I could tell you were hurting because you were silent. I ran my hand over your head. You smelled horrible; you'd lost control of your bowels.

Penny drove Sonofa with her foot on the floor. She looked at road signs, blowing her hair from her eyes and muttering: "Big tree, turn left, where's Lupine road? Turn left again." Stuff like that. Then she said — as she yanked the truck onto a gravel road — "Hang on, I know where Doc Ranulf lives, maybe he can help."

MK started singing along with the radio, about a storm coming and someone blowing a feudal horn. Then he whispered in my ear, "I'll help the dog, for a smooch. With her. Just one? Say the word, she won't even feel it. She's the one with the heart we need, too, right? I won't do it without your say-so."

I shuddered. Is he talking about a kiss or ripping out her heart?

"No," I said, and I must have sounded angry because Penny stared at me and started to slow down.

"I HAVE to drive fast, Clay, or he will die!" she said. "Turn down the damn radio!"

"I was kidding, Romes. Geez," MK said. "And you *should* turn it down, I can't hear myself sing."

I turned it down, but I did it for Penny and not for him.

245

We skidded around a gravel corner and—standing in the middle of the road—waving us down was Mister Brown. Penny slammed on the brakes.

"Hey, hey WATCH where ya goin'!" Mister Brown smacked the hood with his meat-stick, skipped around to my side of the truck and climbed on the running board. When he saw MK in the back seat, Mister Brown's wrinkled his nose and spit on the ground.

"We gotta go, Mister Brown," said Penny. "Dammit's hurt, we gotta get to Doc."

"Yeah, I see this," he said. He rubbed your ear and tried to feed you a piece of meat, but you turned your head away.

"Sorry lil bruh," he patted your head, "looks like this is the end a the line." He clapped my shoulder. "You need to know Big Jim's comin', and he would know where to look. It's going down faster'n expected." He pointed at MK, "maybe that one could be helpful, but hard to say. Maybe you can ask him?"

Penny looked confused.

"Heh," said MK, "Happy to help, when requested. Though, presently on retainer."

"Erg," said Mister Brown with a shudder. "All I get from this guy is a sound like maggots in a shithole."

MK chuckled, and *that* sounded pretty bad.

I wanted to ask Mister Brown if he was serious about not hearing MK, but I couldn't find the words.

Mister Brown popped the meat-stick against the roof of the truck. He reached into the air and pinched a penny between his thumb and finger. "I see you flipped the other one. Heh." He pressed it into my palm. "Careful — last one." He smacked my shoulder with the meat stick. "I dub thee 'Flipper.' Heh. Stick with penny you be alright." He winked. "The girl not the coin, eh?"

Penny flipped him off, revved the engine and he hopped down.

"Now—go, go," he pounded on the truck. "Tell Doc to high tail it to the jailhouse where it's going down."

Penny jammed the stick shift and Mister Brown hollered at me, "Put that penny in your pocket or it will lose you!" He scurried into the trees like his body was too slow for his nose.

I shoved the penny in my pocket, and we screamed down a dirt road with ponderosas rising above patches of leftover snow; mighty cinnamon-orange columns in a shaded green hall that stretched far as I could see.

At the end of the road stood a two-story, many-gabled house of logs that could have fit ten of Granma's houses into it. Behind the house and its wraparound porch, a lawn swept down to a beach. Between the ragged trunks of the biggest ponderosas I ever seen — giants with tops so high I had to lean my head backwards — I saw ripples on the waves of the lake, touched by the rising sun, and a shoreline that curved back towards town. The breeze coming from the lake smelled of freedom and big fish and I felt a pang in my heart for the homeplace.

Doc stood on the porch, nose up, sniffing. Lips curled back from his teeth when he saw MK.

"Offer stands," MK said to me as he got out. He blew a kiss at Doc.

Doc spat on the ground, turned and held the door for us.

There was no furniture, just an old mattress with a sleeping bag in the living room. In the hospital-like kitchen I was somehow not surprised to see a stainless-steel table like a mirror; its surface shimmering with vistas revealed through floor to ceiling windows that opened towards the lake. A smell of raw meat entered my nostrils. Or was it blood? On the porch beyond the glass, a single pine-slat chair watched the water.

I laid you gently on the steel table with Penny's help. You stank. MK sat on a counter. Doc ignored him.

"I cannot heal this one," Doc said after he examined you carefully. You lay with your eyes closed, trying not to let us see how much it hurt. The deep panting gave you away.

Doc drew me to the side.

"He is, how you say it, *Gerbrochen*. The back. It is crushed. You must release him from the pain."

Penny grabbed my hand, "Do something."

I knew what he meant; I had seen this in a deer I shot poorly when I was too young to know better. The bullet missed the chest, went high, broke its back. It lay with wild eyes in a rank-smelling thicket until I slit its throat. As blood poured in a stream, I said Dad's blessing: "*Thank you for your gift, that we may live. Come to us sister, make your home with us on that day when all things are made new.*" When its eyes went from wide and frantic to — how can I say this any other way — gone, I knew that I had done everything I could to make it right.

I looked at you laying on the table, your eyes on me, panting hard so that you would not whine. Your back twisted at a strange angle and your dead legs hung sideways.

"No," you said. "No." Your eyes were fierce.

I understood you, but I also saw your broken body and I did not want you to hurt no more.

"There is nothing more to do, other than give the *berhuhigungsmittel*, the serum for the pain. And that, I do not have," said Doc. "You must hurry. It will not be long before the Big Jim gets here, and you must be gone." Doc, whose eyes were always on the edge of tears, was really crying.

He led me to a drawer and pulled out a long-barreled pistol.

Penny yelled, "No goddammit!" and tried to push the pistol into the drawer.

They struggled a moment, then I pulled her away. She wrapped her arms around my chest and buried her face under my arm. Her body shook, and I reckon I did not expect her to be so broken up. I could not say the word "kill" to myself, it felt far away and like something someone unknown to me would do. The closer I got to making it happen, the farther away something in me went. It was like there were two of me, and one was already out the door running through the lanes beneath the ponderosas.

"It must be done, he is in much pain," said Doc.

"Is there nothing we can do?" said Penny.

"Nothing," Doc said. "No more to do but help this vulf to eh... *beenden*. Use the gun. Better than knife, faster."

I took the gun.

Doc turned to lift you from the table. I suppose he did not want to cover his kitchen table with blood.

You snarled. Your front claws scrabbled against the table.

"Do it," Penny said, wiping her eyes. "I don't want you to."

"Outside," said Doc. "Quickly."

MK slid off the counter smoothly and came to stand by the table. "Fuck Ms. Swan and fuck the deal," he said. "She'll be mad, but..." He popped his knuckles, "Love is merely a madness, right Romes?"

Doc said, "*Ech*," and spat on the floor.

"I did not know I could do this until now," MK said. "And I don't know if it'll work. Put your hand on mine."

The hair on your back went straight up as he laid his pale hand on your head. But what were you going to do? You settled and breathed deep when I laid my hand on top of his.

"With the power vested in me, yada yada," said MK, his face inches from mine. "Name that one."

I could see there was no mirror in his eyes, just open holes.

"Do you believe?" he asked. "Ha. Just kidding."

I started to pull away, but he grabbed my hand and put it back, with his hand on top.

"Nah Romes, seriously. This isn't about believing."

He was being an ass. I almost shot him since I had the pistol in my other hand, but the bullet probably won't even go into him.

Then MK said something I still don't get, Dammit. "It's not about believing, it's about loving, Clay."

Doc Ranulf groaned behind me but did not move.

"Something I can't do," said MK, and his dead eyes did not blink. "At least not like you. So, this is all I can do. Use you as a conduit because you love him so much."

I tried to pull my hand away and his fingers were like steel.

"Romes," he said. "Will you forgive me next time you see me for what I will do? I'm not asking about helping the dog, I'm asking about what is coming." His eyes were dark as a night with no stars. "This? You're doing this. It's your love for this dog. Just remember, you did this not me." He stepped back.

Dammit, you know what happened way better than me. I wish you could describe what happened. I will try to tell it from my side.

I felt something like a river — but more like a snake—from my chest come out in a rush. Like the Spring rain that falls hard on the rocks on the side of the mountains and in a few seconds turns into a raging creek. The crashing snake pushed up my chest, through my hand and into your head and through you. So fast and hard that when it came out the other side — your tail popped straight like a flag.

Your eyes grew wide. Your ears went up.

You know how your back legs moved.

Slowly, tentatively stretching out as you felt your toes moving, one by one. Your legs that had been dead as two sticks, you pulled up under your belly. Your tail had been like a severed rope laying out behind you and off the edge of the table. Now it was a raised flag. It began to wave.

You took a shuddering breath, sat up on your haunches on the table, licked my hand and said, "For the animal with no tail, God keeps the flies away."

Penny screamed.

I dropped the gun on the floor, and it made a *thunk* but did not go off.

Doc stepped back, bumped against the counter, and said, "Oof."

When I turned to thank MK, he was gone, his strange request ringing in my ear.

After that, everything was a great goddamn flaming bag a nuts, as Granma says. You licked my hand and leaped off the table to the floor, jumped into Doc's arms and slathered his face with kisses, then ran around the kitchen in circles slipping and scrabbling on the wood floors, stopping every now and then to shove your head under Penny's hand.

Then doing the whole thing over again. Running and sliding and happy as a gopher in the sun with a mouthful a nuts.

You finally calmed down enough and stopped in a corner and lifted your leg and Doc growled at you and pointed outside and you were gone in a flash; running under the tall burnt-orange trees, stopping, tearing up clouds of needles with your claws like a bull. Running and jumping and hollering like a puppy in snow. It was a joy to see, and I'll never forget it, Dammit. Never.

Doc grabbed my arm in the middle of all this and said, "You must go. *Rennen.* Now."

Somehow, I got Penny — happy-crying with full abandon and looking at me weird — into Sonofa, but she couldn't drive because she couldn't see. I moved her over and started to figure out how to drive the truck while you ran in wider and wider circles through the open forest.

Some things come easy to me, I reckon. Things with logical processes and hierarchies and so forth, and this was no different. I already done inventory on Sonofa that first day. I knew what the pedals were for and what the stick was for, so the work was figuring out how they meshed. That took only a few moments. Also, stopping that beast and going around corners. That was tough, but I never drove fast enough to crash. I kept it mostly in first and second. One must consider the weight of the vehicle, how high it is off the ground, how much traction the tires have, and so forth. When I talk about these interesting things with MK, he tells me to shut up, so I will now.

You had reached a knob of boulders on a far rise and stood panting and raising your leg at everything gleefully.

I beckoned to you out the window.

I have seen many wild sights, and stranger ones, but the best was you running to me at full speed. Your ears laid back, eyes like fire, tail like a flag on a pirate ship, and that old scar pulling your mouth back in that half-open sneer that only I knew was a stupid grin. That was when it hit me like a grizzly bear coming down-hill.

Dad is a ghost and wants me to kill his killer.

I can't find my Momma.

I survived Big Jim's murder-worship glade.

Granma burned down her own house.

My dog was going to die, and I — or most likely MK — saved him.

Penny is with me, holding my hand, her eyes far-away fires in a storm started by lightning.

You leaped through the driver window, licked my face and snuggled Penny.

I stopped the truck, put my head on the wheel.

You put your paw on my shoulder.

The man on Pop's radio sang about no actor anywhere better than the Jack of Hearts. I started to feel like we would make it. That life is not just hurt every day when you wake up, and more hurt when you fall asleep and dream.

Chapter 29

I Rub Penny The Wrong Way

Penny stopped crying and started to talk: How scared she was for Cress, how she needed to find Cress to make it right, how she wanted to tell Cress the truth about Big Jim and Junior, how she was scared that Cress would not understand why she hung out with them for the last year. How all of us needed to get out of town. Get out with Granma and me and head to the coast.

I liked that part. Me tagging along.

I didn't understand her. Also, I was trying not to drive off the road.

I said, "I know how you feel," and she yelled at me about how I had no idea how she felt, and how it was better when I was quiet because everything I said was dumb, how she wasn't going to tell me about my Momma, and how I didn't know shit about her.

She clammed up and looked out the window.

Part of me paid attention to how angry she was. But I had another part that was thinking "Wow, I'm talking! It feels so easy to talk to her."

You said, "there is one who kisses and the other offers the cheek," which made no sense. All your damn riddles, Dammit. But I was glad that you were there and alive, so I let it go.

I reckoned if Penny was anything like MK, it would be a few days, and she'd start talking about the weather and act like nothing ever happened. But I didn't think we had a few days, so I tried again.

"You don't know what scared is," I said. "Did you lose your parents when you were twelve?"

She got real mad. "Fuck you, CS."

It's like she has no idea what it's like losing parents and living with a weirdo four years waiting for them to come back. Only to find out one is murdered and the other is lost. So, I said it again. "You don't know what scared is."

She looked straight at me, that one eye direct—a headlight into my head—the other eye pointed at my heart. Her lips trembled. "You ASS, you... you know nothing about me," she said.

I slowed where the road takes a curve by the lake downtown and she threw open the door.

I slammed on the brakes and stopped.

"You and I have time," she said coldly. "Cress doesn't." Her voice choked. "Junior bragged this morning. He's gonna get to her today. I need to find her because she doesn't know him like I do," she grabbed the door handle. "She hangs out here. Somewhere downtown."

"The mole says he goes inside when he sees the sun." You, from the back seat.

"I don't get it," I said. "Stay with me."

Penny climbed out and slammed the door. "No Clay, you DON'T get it. My sister hates me and thinks I'm stealing her boyfriend. She's wrong about everything. I can't stand Junior." She shuddered. "I HATE them all! Cress thinks Junior is her way out of this fucking town because he gives her attention. And what makes it horrible... horrible...." Her mouth drew down and her face looked like a mask with dead eyes staring through my head. "This last month...." She couldn't finish, instead pounded the door. "I'm all there is standing between him and her," her eyes flashed. "I have a plan. He's gonna pay. They're all gonna pay."

I didn't understand. But I remembered her page in my back pocket, and I pulled it out and waved it.

"Where's the rest?" she asked, suddenly angrier than before—if that was possible.

"I couldn't find the rest, what about this?"

"What about it? I'm too MAD at you right now. I'll explain later."

"When?"

"When I see you at your Granma's."

"It's all burned down."

"I know! Just GO there and WAIT for me. I need to find Cress; I need to make it right with her. You'll be fine." She walked away. Well, first she waved her middle finger at me and said, "Also, I forgive you for being an asshole." Then she walked away.

I let her go.

Of course, Dammit, you and I know that we should *not* have let her go.

You said in my ear, "a penny in hand is worth two in your pocket," and I should have listened to you. But I didn't. Instead, I put Sonofa in gear and drove slowly home with people honking at me from behind.

You also know we should have made her stay with us because three blocks down the street we found Owl with her big glasses, Trout with her spots, Squirrel with those teeth, and Deer who looked like the most-high God themselves had sucked up Penny and snorted her into a prettier mold.

"It's bungholio!" shouted Trout as I pulled over. "Commence the singing!"

They broke into harmonies, singing about bloodstained ground and rhyming it with "crown," and I lost myself and took my foot off the clutch, Sonofa jerked, they yelled, and the engine died. But they kept singing. Dammit, if you never heard music much that is sung by those who suffer—and then hear it—it is like a sword through your heart.

You joined them with a howl. Then you jumped out the window and took off chasing a cat like it killed your momma. I reckon you'd be running for a while.

"Watcha think?" asked Trout, bending to look at me through the window and popping Owl with her fist. "Not bad, huh?"

"Ouch, stop it." Owl crossed her arms, eyes like marbles behind her glasses.

"It's almost done," said Trout. "This song's got it all, even how to do it." She rubbed my shoulder with her long fingers and clicked her tongue. "Now, bunghole. If you listen."

"Thurender your crown on thith bloodthtained ground," said Squirrel, "take off your mathk." She smiled through buckteeth.

I could not understand her at all, it made no sense, so I spoke, surprising them (and myself too, damn you Shakesbear):

"This lighter burns so hot in my chest. *I love her with so much of my heart that none is left to protest.*"

Their jaws dropped.

"Penny's gone," I said. "She will not speak to me." In the silence, I realized they never heard me talk.

Then — all together — Squirrel, Owl and Trout climbed in Sonofa making sad noises like chickens bedding down at twilight. Except it was morning two hours after sunrise. Deer climbed in too, crossed her arms, and pretended I wasn't there.

I tried to say, "Penny's looking for you, Deer, and she loves you," but then I remembered her real name was Cressida; all that came out was *"Urgh."*

"There, there," said Trout. "You just got Pennied, that's all. She has big swings. She can be a little dramatic."

Squirrel and Owl snickered and smacked hands.

"It's gonna be OK," said Trout. "She'll swing around, you'll see."

Deer spat out the window on the ground. "Fucking boyfriend-stealer," she said.

"She's got her reasons," Trout said to her, but she did not sound confident.

"Turn right here," said Owl.

"Twooth ith an awwow," said Squirrel. A happy smile spread across her big cheeks. "Yull thee."

Chapter 30

I Will Take Everything

Granma's yard looked like a herd of elk had a fight, lit everything on fire and peed on it.

Trout said she needed smokes and Owl needed coffee so The Stray's took off. Their singing wavered through the trees long after they disappeared. I watched Sophelia in her ash-streaked nightgown digging in the mess as if someone died and she was picking their pockets for trinkets. Sonofa played a song about something funny going on, about dustups and feeling murder in the air. Yeah, I could smell it.

A police car pulled up and Granma Lina jumped out of the back madder than a mama grouse in a kicked nest. She raised her middle finger as the car pulled away and yanked down her cap.

"Cocksuckers made me fill a thousand papers. On purpose." Granma glanced at me; I must have looked horrible. "You OK? Where the HELL you been?"

When I said nothing, she gripped my arm, "Least your face is better. Boy, you heal FAST. C'mon. Get out."

I sat there in Sonofa and let the music play. I did not want to.

She waved around the yard. "Our home's gone. Protection's gone (I did not know what she meant, Dammit)." She pushed Achilles with her foot. "I remember when this dog was a good one and now, he's gone."

Silence.

"Where's Dammit?" she asked.

I shrugged, and she leaned against Sonofa's open window and began to cry.

She took off her blue hat and squeezed it in her hands. "You look just like your Momma. Handsome. Proud."

I tried to smile, but it hurt.

"Hated her. What she done. I needed George. Your ma took him. One moment he was here and the next he was gone. Never come back. Blamed her."

I just looked at her.

Granma shifted uncomfortably. "Reckon I shoulda told you sooner. Here goes. Blamed your ma for breaking us up, the centuries of our family calling. That curse our nemesis spoke before it died — it haunts our family. So does Pallas' prophecy:

'Never let thy seed to lie
With those who swim below the sky.
For rolling tides death shall fulfill.
Go! Seek your safety in the hills.'"

Granma wiped her face in the crook of her arm. "Jack Coeur De Montagne changed our family name to Bergmann; we been living in the mountains ever since. Tryin' to hide from our doom."

Something in me burned like dry timber struck by lightning.

"When George saw your ma bathing in a creek, way up there on the other side of the Shohesh summit (she come to visit her mother's sister's family) he fell in love. First sight. He wooed her then and there (that's a whole 'nother story, Clayton), but lost her in the wilderness. When he come home to us, he was heart broke. He swore to Pops and me he wasn't gonna rest until he found her. He would search the world. And he did. Packed up, handed *Acuere* to Beaumont, kissed me, and walked out the door. Left us and was gone. Years and years."

"Wish I could tell Rose-Marie sorry. For me bein' a bitch. Blamed her. She ruined everything. Nothin' was ever the same. George wasn't my boy no more when he came home. Pops got sick. It's just been Dammit and me these last years." She put her hand on mine. "And then, we found you." Her voice got rough, and she changed the subject. "S'pose you know that whole story, how George went through fire and water to woo your ma, to get her father's blessing?"

I shook my head. My Momma and Dad were silent about so much.

She twisted her frayed cap on her head. "Clayton, sometimes you need people."

Silence.

"It's not who's stronger, it's who keeps goin'. Out love 'em, out loco..." her voice choked, and her fierce eyes stared down the street. "You know I grew up like you, didn't have no one?"

I turned off the truck, got out, wrapped my arms around her and she started to shake.

You came romping down the street, Dammit, like the world was your party.

"Dammit you SONOFABITCH," yelled Granma from under my arm.

Sophie stopped a moment as if woken from a dream, waved at us, and then went back to digging through the muck.

You sniffed Achilles in the street, took a leap of joy straight into the air, peed on Achille's leg, then ran to the spot where the porch used to be, turned around three times, and laid there grinning at us in the ashes and charred boards. I'd seen nothing better than your head cocked to one side and that stupid grin like you stole twenty eggs.

Granma Lina looked up and her voice choked. "Thought Dammit was dead. How'd he....? Ah never mind, let me tell you somethin'." She pointed at the house, "Remember how that porch was built strong it never creaked?"

I nodded. It was a well-built porch, and the boards around the bottom had clasped it like a skirt.

"There's a reason for that," said Granma. "When your Granpa found me, I was worse'n a wounded cougar on the streets a Seattle. Down by the docks, in the hills, stealin' food, sleepin' in parks, crawlin' under decks and makin' a home for myself in cardboard and rags. And nobody—nobody—wanted me, not even the rottenest people that was left wanted me." She stamped her foot. "Pa was horrible to us girls after ma died. Not the boys, only the girls."

Her face grew dark. "Left home when I was thirteen, moved West, never looked back." Her face was peaceful. "Your Pops found me, an clothed me, an got me to quit drinkin', an told me he loved me. That I was special—the very best kind of special—which I didn't believe 'cause I thought he was just like all the others. By the way, he done that for three other street kids — got 'em jobs, and a place to live in the city — and never told nobody about it, just trying to help them get back on their feet. I watched him do that, and when he finally got me to come out of the darkness to talk, he asked me what I wanted. Can you believe it? What I WANTED. I just said to him, 'a home.'"

Her voice choked. "An he said, 'fine, but you got to leave this damn hellhole and start over,' (closest your Pops ever got to cussing), an I said, 'if you find me a home I'll go anywhere,' so he moved me out here an built me this house (though he never touched me) just to give me a fresh start. An I still didn't believe it. Then, there was this day when he said it to me without words: he built that porch and he put a thousand screws into the skirt around the bottom, and he called me out and just stood there smilin'. With those big hands just like yours, standing right there with that smile." She turned and looked at where the porch used to be, now a smoking ruin. "That is when I heard him say 'I love you' for the first time an it wasn't even with words (he been sayin' it for years; over an over an over. Just not out loud, the big lump)."

I'd never heard her speak so much.

"Few weeks later, Beaumont finally did speak. He said, 'we ain't people if we can't be brought back, and I love you...' and some other stuff, but mainly I heard 'I love you' because by then that was all I was hopin' for—to hear that. I ended up claimin' him — that's lovin' someone, Clayton — an we got married, an had your Dad, an a real good life. When your Dad didn't want to do our family's vocation and decided to run off an was gone for years with your ma, Pops got sick an started wastin' away." Her voice choked. "From the inside out. Pastor Issen come visitin', that's when it got worse." Her face darkened. "I knew he was a snake, but no one believed me. I jus went into a hole, bringin' Beaumont back over and over from the sickness 'till he couldn't do it no more, an now he's gone, an I was so busy taking care of him that's why I didn't find out 'bout your folks until too late." She took a shuddering breath. "But that's what I believe now: We're not people if we can't be brought back — That's what he said. Your Pops." Her face twisted. "But I couldn't bring *him* back."

I was listening, but I was also thinking about all the stuff that happened this morning, how me and MK brought you back, Dammit, and how Penny smelled and felt in my arms, why men treat girls that way, and why some people get joy when they crush the life in something. I realized the yard was silent, as if waiting. The only sounds were Sophie talking to herself and the tiny nuthatches creeping down the trunks of the ponderosas with their buzzing calls.

Granma pointed her blue cap at me, fierce as a mountain lion. "Let ME tell YOU somethin'. You *are* special, Clayton, the very best kind of special."

Something in my chest hurt because I remembered that was the last thing my Momma said to me.

"Don't you EVER forget you need people, fucked up as we be," Granma pounded my chest, "every one of us can be brought back, ya know. House an truck an clothes an books an everything else don't matter. It's people that last."

I shook my head. People die and are gone. Like a house of smoke and cinders, you're left to dig through the ashes.

She gazed at what was left of her burned-down house. "Oh, Beaumont what have I done?"

I wanted to be at the homeplace. With the river flowing in that sweet turn below the cliffs, and the sun coming up over the high ridge. I did not understand, Dammit, that a person can be all that country and more. Do you believe a person is a river running wild and free, rounding a bend of hills and sunshines and diving deep into the edges of its Ponderosa banks? Do you believe a person could also be a place, Dammit? Like the water that touches the sides of the mountain — changing and always the same? I did not know it then, but she was trying to tell me.

"Clayton," she said, and rubbed my cheekbones with her thumbs that scratched as she rubbed. She smelled like cigs and apples. "Your mine, set my claim on you."

I nodded like I understood, just to get her to quit, and tried to pull away.

"You are not alone," she said. Her pale blue eyes, so much like Dad's, blazed. She held on like we were in a storm, hard enough to make me wince.

Sometimes you bury it like a stick under leaves — you will understand this, Dammit — and the wind comes along and blows away the leaves and you see. (First you see exactly what kind of leaves: Western White Oak, I believe, or perhaps the rusty orange of the *Acer Macrophylum,* the Great Maple). And before you can grasp it, the wind blows not only the leaves but you away.

The wind drops you on a rock in a big river, and your Granma shouts from the far shore and you cannot hear all the words. But you hear some of them. Because she is shouting so hard.

"You are not alone," she said again.

Something like a piece of paper wrapped around Ms. Swan's hook in my chest, so I couldn't feel the barb as much. Something like scales fell out of my eyes. Like I wasn't looking through curtains for a moment. Or maybe it was just tears.

You whined and rubbed up between our legs.

Granma patted me on the shoulder for a long time. We stood there watching Sophelia digging through the ashes — dropping something every time she picked up something else.

Tires made popping sounds on the gravel as the black truck pulled up.

The hair went straight up on your back and a growl rumbled in your chest.

"I've been all over town looking for you." The mustache fluttered, his eyes were luminous and kind. "Mmm." Big Jim turned the engine off.

"You KNOW where I was, you fuckin snake."

I decided I would take inventory on the insults to keep my mind off the shaking in my legs. Point to Granma.

"I wanted to tell you: this is mmm this is just the beginning." His hand wrapped around the side-mirror and squeezed it like he was throttling a rabbit to death.

Point to Big Jim.

Her eyes flashed like she was stung. "Git AWAY from me ya *fuckin* tomb."

Point to Granma.

"Now Lina, that's no way to talk to your pastor," he said looking at the ashes of the house. "Where's that axe of your husbands?"

"No shepherd a mine. You're a grass-covered grave, an under it ... rotten bones."

Point to Granma.

"So, you lost the axe in the fire?" He pretended he had not heard her insult.

She turned her back to him so he could not see her wiping her eyes.

"Well, mmm not to worry. That is the only reason I stopped by, to see for myself. It is gone. Mmm." He sounded triumphant. "What protection you had is gone."

Sadly, I had to give Big Jim a point.

"No shit, Sherlock," she said, taking a deep drag from the cig.

Point to Granma.

I thought to myself, yeah — you fuck — if you only knew.

Point to Clay. I knew where the axe was.

"I see you healed nicely, mongrel," he said to you, and his hand squeezed the mirror again. "However it was done, it won't last." Point to Big Jim, barely.

Your hair went straight up.

"You and I have unfinished business, dog." The hand twisted the wheel and the wheel creaked. "When I am done with you your balls will be in your mouth and mmm your eyes will be pinned to the wall to watch how I do it."

Point to Big Jim.

I would a dug a hole and crawled into it, but you stared back at Big Jim like you were ten feet tall. I don't know what he had against you, but every time he saw you, Dammit, he got madder. Maybe it was you would never bend.

"Nope." If a dog can shrug, you shrugged. "Bigger dog, harder fall."

Two points to Dammit. One for looking him straight in the eye, and one for the comeback.

Whether Big Jim heard you speaking or not, I can't say, but he looked like he was going to explode.

"He do anything to you?" Granma whispered to me.

I shook my head. All he did this morning was give me a flappy book with girls in it, I didn't mind that, he didn't beat me up. I didn't like the rabbit thing with Junior, or that weird voice that wanted more blood, and I didn't like that he was messing with a bunch of little boys, and I didn't like that he tried to touch my wuttus, but I wasn't going to tell her any of that. It would just make her more mad. I didn't like him kicking you, Dammit, or threatening you just now, but I already made up my mind there was nothing I could do.

There was one thing I wanted. It wasn't "avenge Dad," or "find Momma" anymore. It wasn't retrieving the axe. Or anything else that would get me beat up more. All I wanted was to figure out how to get home to the porch. Get back to how it was. And I wanted Penny to go with me. Or Ms. Swan. Or both of them. But I reckon, Dammit, they would not agree to *that* plan.

Granma's voice was quiet like Big Jim's, but there was no softness in it. "If you don't leave right now," she said, "swear to jesusfuckinchrist I pull Beaumont's .45 from under that seat and blow out your evil heart. Blow you clean to hell."

Point to Granma for, well, do I really need to say it?

His big hand broke the mirror off and threw it so fast at you, Dammit, that it hit you with *THUMP*. He was aiming for your head, but you dodged, and it hit your shoulder instead. You leaped six feet straight up and came down growling like a pack of dogs.

Point to Big Jim for pure velocity.

"Hell?" Big Jim asked softly. "You don't know what hell is Mrs. Bergmann. But you will. Hell is being crushed with no reprieve. I will crush you. I will crush your boy. Mmm. I will crush your whole family. What is left of it. If there were fifty more of you, I would crush them too. One by one." His eyes glittered, a hundred mirrors. "I'd say 'dead' — but crushing is slower and lasts longer. The last of your kind."

My legs and arms felt heavy; he could have climbed out of the truck and grabbed me.

I wasn't thinking about no points no more, Dammit.

"Go ahead and try, B.J.," she said. "Bergmanns been fucking up your kind for centuries."

With one comeback, she brought me back.

Point to Granma. But also: retroactive point to Big Jim.

"I'd rather watch it happen slow," Big Jim smiled. "And watch *you* watch it happen. And when it starts," he said, "you will know the crushing is coming because it will feel bad enough to make you scared. Yes, mmm. I like *this* plan." He pointed. "And do something about my dog before someone reports you to the police. Ooooh," he said. "The police haven't questioned you about Craig's unfortunate accident?" His deep voice, compassionate: "Mmm. And which felony? Murder or arson? Or both?"

Point to Big Jim. Actually four, if I'm honest.

Granma just lit a cig and stood there smoking, watching him from under her cap.

A low snarl came from the bottom of your throat.

Big Jim ignored you, "Come to think of it—you committed arson on this property. It belongs to Oyster & Swans. Mmm. Convicted for murder *and* arson. I know the hanging judge rather well, as you know."

Point to Big Jim.

"I know Her," Granma said. "She ain't no judge and I'm not gonna hang. Why don't you just say *Her* fuckin name instead of that fancy bullshit?"

Point to Granma.

He frowned and paused.

Extra point to Granma for slowing Big Jim down.

Then he patted the side of the truck and turned on the engine. "Lina Bergmann, I promise mmm: you will be locked forever in a room with no air to breathe and no hope of escape." He smiled gently. "The death that does not die." The mandibles made that shearing, tearing sound. *Click Click.*

Two points to Big Jim.

Surely Granma saw them flare like silent lightning? Like braided fingers under the mustache.

"And *You,* boy?" His voice dropped to a murmur. "I promise you. When you least expect it, *I will take everything.*" His wide fingers — with no mirror to hold — curled into a giant fist. "Everything."

Two more points to Big Jim.

She sucked on the cig in her left hand and slowly raised the middle finger of her right hand through the smoke. Her right hand stayed raised, and so did the middle finger. Then she dropped the cig on the ground and raised her left hand and middle finger too.

A double farewell. And double points to Granma.

"Piss on you," you said. I was glad you finally said something, Dammit.

Point to Dammit.

"Get the fuck off my land," she said.

"When you least expect it," he smiled *Click Click,* put the truck into gear, and pulled away so quietly that the only sound – again—was gravel crushing beneath its tires.

Grandma held both hands high at the truck until it turned the corner. Then, she pulled in the fingers, dropped her hands, sighed, lit another cig and rubbed her face. "What an asshole. Screw him and his threats. Got to be five o'clock somewhere."

Final inventory: Big Jim fifteen, Granma eleven, Clay one, Dammit three. Including you and me on Granma's side, Dammit, it was a tie. But it did not feel like it. I was done giving points to anyone, Dammit. I just wanted to lay down.

Chapter 31

Achilles In A Field

"Sophie, sis, just stop. It BURNED down like hell stopped for dinner and ate everything." Granma kicked around in the ashes and charred planks and wet insulation and bed springs and cast-iron pans and soupy mud. "Flamin' bag a nuts. Let's get some food in Clayton."

"A house where all were good to me," Sophelia said in a voice like chittering juncos, *"comforting smell breathed, fetched fresh, as I suppose, off some sweet wood."*

"Ah, Sophie, I can't," said Granma, and they put their arms around each other's waists and trudged across the street to her trailer house. You snuck in the door before it closed and left me standing alone by Sonofa.

I realized I had not slept all night. I slid to the ground against Sonofa, one foot touching Achilles, and closed my eyes. Someone spoke, in a voice like rocks rolling underwater.

"Help me."

You know that moment, Dammit, when you enter a vision and see everything? A dead dog in the street in a pool of his blood. No one walking and no cars. No crows or small birds calling. No dogs barking. Inside my ears I heard the pull and push of my heart. It drew in blood, WHOOM, and then pushed, WHOOSH.

The sun changed like a ball picked up by a red hand, like a dying coal.

Then the voice spoke again, rumbling like rocks in a barrel.

271

"H-help m-me young master."

The sky went dark orange like when forest fires have burned for a month.

Achilles grew to twice his size. Around him the street sunk into a crease with dark houses leaning in like boulders. My rear skidded on pebbles at the edge of a ravine that opened around Achilles, the edge gave way, and I fell, sliding over roots and sand. I tasted something like the hot edge of a file. I had bitten my tongue. The blood on the ground was warm; I tried to pull my hands up and could not. Stuck like a fly on a web. I swallowed my own blood and it tasted like milk and bitter roots.

Achilles had grown to the size of a bull elk.

I felt something unmistakable for him. Sorrow.

Don't be angry with me, Dammit. You love the fight and pity is for losers. But pity's lack is what makes Big Jim a black hole. I cannot live without pity. All those like Big Jim are gangrenous veins. They exist to suck life into their dying hearts; dead seas in search of tributaries.

"Help me, young master."

Something in Achilles was still alive. I laid my hand on his broad head, a wide table of bone. What came next from my mouth was sudden and unlooked for, but when I said it, I knew it was right. "Be at peace. I gave you a place with me. Remember?"

A great sigh released from the wide chest, and his shrewd pig eyes turned to me and the look therein, Dammit, oh that look would have melted even you. It had more fealty than any man deserves.

"Master, thine own... father. I was there...," he drew a long, whistling breath, *"on the d-day the wave rider...was s-slain. Aaaaggghhh."*

Great clots of blood spilled from his mouth.

"It was... a b-blade in the back. My master did it at the meeting of the Families, when the Nisoi were c-come together to make peace."

When he spoke, his mouth moved no more, the body spoke from deep in itself, like the sound of the rocks when your head is underwater.

"Take my heart, son of the mountains, child of waters."

He was larger than ever; I had shrunk to the size of a rabbit.

"Take, thou, my heart, Lord, or thou shalt surely die."

The blood in my mouth would not stop running, and I spat a glob onto the ground and — then with a strange premonition — spat another onto Achilles. The dog had grown larger than the biggest bull elk. The blood I spat lay a moment on his ribs. Then, his hide drooped, and the glob fell through his skin into his chest.

"Take. My gift for the day of need."

I saw stars flash and swirl on the edge of my vision. I knew Achilles had lain all morning in the street waiting for me.

I plunged my hands deep into Achilles' chest. And touched a round-backed thing like a salmon, the size of a human head. I could barely hold it with both hands. A squirming new-born baby made of muscle. Each heartbeat was like the flutter of the wings of a dying insect, wings that trembled and lay still.

I ripped the heart from its cords and lashings.

A voice cried, *"Aaaaaahhhhhh."* As if freed forever from anchor and lifted on a sudden wave, the cry fled with great speed to the far horizon.

I broke the surface, took a shuddering breath on my knees before our burned-down house. In my clenched fist, Achilles' heart — now shrunk to normal size — hung in dripping black veins. Like a small purse filled with sawdust. Just the right size to fit in my hand with fingers closed and thumb over the top. Smaller than I expected. It shuddered once, *Thump.* Then stopped.

I saw him, Dammit. I saw Achilles one last time. I will swear this until the day I die.

I saw Achilles running hard in a field under green hills rising and rising to a moss-roofed cabin and a porch I know well. A porch with a cougar lying still, with quiet, wise eyes, watching him come. Achilles—his head a rock slab, his shoulder-muscles rippling cords of steel—running fast through high grass. Fast but drunken, like a pup on the first day finding his legs. I saw Achilles leap the steps, nuzzle the cougar, and stop and turn to look at me. Then the vision was gone, and I knelt in the grass by his dead body in a pool of blood with Achilles' heart in my hand.

"*Nothing is so beautiful as Spring,*" said Sophelia, peering over my shoulder. "Could you show me where the bathroom is, I really gotta go." Her white hair was a halo in the morning sun, and she peered at me like one of the wild sisters of the moor. '*Thrush through the echoing timber does so rinse and wring the ear, it strikes like lightnings to hear him sing,*" she said.

Somewhere a dog slumped on the boards of a porch with a happy *hmmphh* and looked down a sweeping valley with new-pup eyes, a green valley thickened by rains, on the cusp of the turn to Summer. A long curve of oaks traced a braided river full of secrets only dogs love to find. He had unmeasured years to know them. And he was grateful as only a dog can be.

Sophelia grabbed my hand. "Always good to have a heart in your hand when you go to war," she said.

She wasn't letting go, so, heart in hand, I guided her across the lawn and up the crumbling stairs into her trailer-house to go pee.

Chapter 32

Putting Mad Dogs Down

"God almighty, Clayton what the hell," said Granma. In one hand was a glass of something the color of honey. She took a deep draw on her cig and a deep draw of the drink. Then she looked at the ceiling for a long moment, blowing smoke out her nose.

"I DO NOT want to look at that BLOODY mess," she said to the ceiling, "and I DON'T want to know why you got it. Put IT in a cardboard box. Here." She handed me a small box.

I put the heart in it and Granma put the box on a shelf in the back of the fridge next to the milk.

Sophelia sat at the kitchen table in the cramped trailer-house with its thin fiber-board walls. "Who are you?" Sophelia asked me again. "Who is your friend? You need to know who you are."

"Already met 'im, Sophie. It's Clayton." Granma grinned bitterly. "After THIS morning, he's got no friends, 'cept mebbe Dammit."

"He is filled with talking," said Sophelia.

"Sophie, I swear to God."

"You," Sophelia said to me, "you come here. I see you right now, I see you. I see you hurting. Why you hurting?" Then she whispered with both hands on my face, "Why your pale friend hurting? Worse'n you, hurting so bad he got to steal breath to breathe, ah ah, like breaking all da mirrors so you can't see yourself ever again, ever, ever."

Words came to me in a rush of memory. As if all the words I had *not* said from the night before poured in a flash flood from the high-line of the mountains, though I had sworn, Dammit, to never speak in Shakesbear again. I said the words like they were my own, for at that moment, indeed, they were:

"Where words are scarce, they are seldom spent in vain, for they breathe truth that breathe their words in pain."

"HOLY shit," said Granma Lina. "King-James, old-timey, poetry-quotin' genius."

"Don't be vexed," said Sophelia, who with a deft twist of her hands rearranged her white hair as she looked in the mirror of my eyes.

"Talkin' isn't all there is anyways child." She patted me on the hand. "Nor is the pain." With her other hand she took something from a pocket in her ash-stained nightgown and slipped it into the big pocket of my flannel shirt. Sophelia's slate-grey eyes were suddenly keen as an eagle's and her little hand on my arm felt like it was connected to a lightning bolt. "Wisdom says you find yourself when you help your friend. Release your pain. Help your friend find himself, you are the only one."

I felt the short blade she'd put in my pocket, like a flat pencil, rough on both sides ending in a point. It was a file for sharpening tools. The ones at the ranch are useful for sharpening hoes, adzes, shovels, and so forth.

"Found in the ashes, the ashes we all fall down," said Sophelia.

I shoved the file in the pocket of my jeans and forgot about it.

"You gotta pee, Sophie?" asked Granma.

"Ye-yes? Maybe? No."

"Clayton, clean up in the sink forGODsake, your hands are a bloody mess, I'm gonna get Sophie to the bathroom."

You and me wandered down the shaggy green carpet to Sophie's bedroom. A silver ash spear leaned at the end of the narrow hall, its wide blade pierced the ceiling, and its butt hid in the carpet.

Resting next to it on the floor was a bronze helmet that could have held three of Sophie's heads. Sophie's tiny bedroom smelt like a barn full of owls with its tiny bed hidden under quilts. You jumped on the bed, turned around three times, laid down.

"What's with Achilles?" you said.

I laid down next to you. "I dunno, it was weird."

"Weird is normal to the platypus," you said.

"I wouldn't a thought a dog as tough as Achilles hurt so bad in his heart," I said. For some reason my thoughts turned to Doc Ranulf, and his weeping eyes, and how he stood at the door last night looking at me: *"...the true topography of the heart is vast, wrinkled with rivers and layered mountains. It is a most dangerous country."*

You interrupted my thoughts. "Sometimes tough don't mean soft," you said. "Means tough *and* tenderized"

"What about you?"

"Sure. Been around long enough to get hurt bad."

"Like what?"

You got quiet and looked at the wall. I scratched your ear and you groaned happy and leaned into the scratch.

"C'mon," I said, "I know more about Achilles than I know about you."

"Better that way."

"I guess you can't teach an old dog new tricks," I said, and you fake-bit me on my hand.

"Take a horse to water, can't make him drink," you said, and grinned so wide your face almost split open. But then you started to talk. And not in riddles or in bursts like Granma. Like something was pouring out of you and you needed to get it out or it would eat you up like acid. Trust me Dammit, I get it.

"I had a Momma once," you said. "Like yours, lovely, warm, full of fire. A she-devil in a fight and a warm, warm chest at night. She was full-blood wild and raised me and my three brothers and two sisters free. She taught us to sing at the moon and chase the great elk in the hidden glens. Our father was a farm dog and sometimes she would take us to see him when the farmer's truck was gone, and he would breathe on us and kiss her, and they would fake-fight pretending he was the mean farm-dog, and she was the wild wolf. They always kissed at the end, and we would romp beneath their legs."

Your ears laid flat and your lips drew back. "One day, the man was there. My Father tried to warn us as we came loping from the edge of the woods, he shouted 'BAD BAD' but my Momma thought he was play-fighting — the truck was not in the yard, you see, so she was unafraid — and we kept going. It wasn't until she saw that Father was chained and the man stepped out of the door with his gun that she turned to run. It was too late."

You started to shake, and I put my hand on your shoulder.

"All of them died. All of them, with my Momma the first to go. Blood, blood everywhere. The man had seen our sign in the earth of the farmyard, parked his truck in the barn, and waited for us. Until he could see our eyes. Then he shot us quickly, one by one. My Father in great strength tore the chain, broke the man's leg with a single bite — my father had great jaws and a face like a mountain — and ran to us. I was not fully grown and had never seen or heard a gun. I was standing over my Momma and my brothers and sisters, and my father knocked me flat until the farmer had to re-load. My Father took two bullets to his flanks and still managed to push me into the forest."

I said, "I know how you feel. If I could go back, I woulda got on that raft — and my Dad and my Momma would not be dead. Or lost."

"Sometimes I want to be dead and lost," you said.

"Me too," I said. "What did you and your dad do after that?"

"Too many tales to tell," you said. "Where you think I learned all my sayings?"

I grinned and realized for the first time the pain in my eye and cheekbone was gone — I could smile without pain — and my bruised hand could finally open and close. I reckon I heal pretty fast. *"Let Hercules himself do what he may, the cat will mew and the dog will have his day,"* I said. I scratched your ear with the healed hand, and you groaned in pleasure and kicked out a back leg. A leg that was a stick earlier that very same day.

"Where's your dad now?" I asked.

You rolled over and looked at the wall. "My Dad, he couldn't stay, him and me did not end well," you said. "Too much pain. Sometimes you got to put a mad dog down." You lay a long time with your eyes closed breathing slow. Then, just as I thought you were asleep, you said softly, "If we knew where death resides, we would never stay."

A knock hammered the front door. The whole trailer-house was so old, like Sophelia, the walls shook all the way in the back.

"Mrs. Bergmann? Officer Rall. Better for you to come out now. We need to ask you and the boy a few questions. Need you come down to the station."

Sophelia: "Let wisdom sing of gifted hearts like broken wings."

Granma: "Shit, shit, shit."

Sophelia: "It strikes like lightnings to hear him sing."

I thought about what Big Jim said about the crushing, how he was going to take everything from me, and how it would start slow—but we would know it. The light in the room dimmed and I felt a darkness falling over my eyes.

Officer Rall: "LISTEN. We can hear you. Come out. NOW."

Granma: "Shit. Fuck."

Officer Rall: "We know you're violent. Our guns are out. So please. Very carefully. Come out. Nice and slow."

Sophelia: *"Now the time has come, now the day is here, now the deed is done, now the way is clear."*

Exeunt Granma, Sophie, Clay, followed by dog.

Chapter 33

The Good, The Bad, and The Fugly

The jail smelled like a dead rat floating in a cistern. Across from me, in the corner of the waiting room, was the blind woman Big Jim had kissed earlier at the Oyster & Swans shop. The cuffs on her hands could not stop her thumbs ripping at her chest. She twisted on the floor slowly, her mouth open in a soundless scream. She stunk like pee. MK had said on the porch this morning that he "had a job to do." He must a got started.

The officer at the desk played with his mini-mustache, pretended she was not there, and took notes in a fat logbook.

Ministache had spoken only once to me: "I'm taking the cuffs off you. But I swear, you get off that bench, I'll shoot your ass."

I wished you were there, Dammit. But when we walked in the front door (to my left next to the bench) Ministache kicked you: "Fuck outa here, no dogs."

I hoped you went back to Sophie where the police left her on the porch.

A closed door with a small window was to my right. Behind it I heard Officer Rall: "Calm down Mrs. Bergmann."

"GodDAMmit, told you all I know. Interview Big Jim, he's the crook."

She begged him for a cig. Rall said there was no way he was interviewing Big Jim who was his pastor and also gave a lot of money to the police non-profit, and that he would give her one cig if she told him where the axe was.

"Why you looking for an axe? How about you do your job."

"We have witnesses that you did it. Calm down. We searched the ashes of your house and found nothing."

"You sonsa bitches. I'll call a lawyer."

"No lawyers in this town will work for you, Mrs. Bergmann. We'll let you off free, if you give me the axe. What did you do with it?"

"I used the axe to burn down the house. Ha."

"No, what did you DO with it. Was it in the house? Where did you hide it?"

"I know your mom and your dad, Richard. Knew you before this whole town got sick, before you sucked O & S dick — Dick."

"I'm just doing my job."

"Your job is to get to the truth and bring justice. And PROTECT widows and orphans."

He ignored her. "Let's start at the beginning. What did you do to Craig?"

"I TOLD you." Her voice began to raise. "He fell down. Figured heart attack. Brought him back. Checked him into the hospital. What more you want goddammit?"

"Let's go back to the beginning, why did you go to your son's place?"

"It was them nurses at the hospital let Craig die."

"Mrs. Bergmann. Please. What were you doing at your son's ranch? Is the axe there?"

"Pardonmyfrench Dick, it's NONE of your fuckin business. What you want with an ol' axe?"

"I'm the one asking the questions."

I closed my eyes and pretended I was in the forest, but the thumbs of the old blind woman went *scritch* against her chest *scritch* she was too close *scritch* I heard her in the trees. I tried to think of something else. Earlier that day I counted 23 different kinds of trees around Junction City. And then there was the Blue

Spruce with the sharp needles—where I'd hidden *Acuere*. I started to consider how I would organize trees. Biggest to smallest? No. Leaves. Porter said leaves was one way.

Ministache closed his big logbook. "How'd you get hurt, kid?"

Nope. Not answering. I can't think about trees jackass because you interrupted me.

"We found her wandering downtown." He pointed at the woman. "Big Jim's on his way. She's on some new street-drug. She can stew in it. Maybe she'll learn."

He stood up. "Did you hear me? I asked you, boy. How'd you get hurt?"

The Tamarack, also known as the Western Larch, *Larix Occidentalis*, is the largest of the species.

"Kid," he said, coming to stand in front of me, "I guarantee you'll talk to me before this is over."

Everyone thinks they can make me talk.

Ministache rubbed his mustache with one hand, fingering the fat logbook with the other.

The old blind woman in the corner turned like a worm dying, her thumbs bloody from scratching. Her white eyes rolled up in her head. I could not look in her glaring eyes, so I looked at her ear, instead, and saw the flash of an earring.

"GODDAMMIT, I told you TEN times," yelled Granma through the door.

"Where's the axe?" Ministache said.

Down at the bottom of my left pocket in the corner where one finger can reach was Mister Brown's penny. I pushed it up so I could hold it between my thumb and finger and tried to wink. I did not know what it meant — to wink. I reckon I just wanted to get out of there with Granma. The last time I winked Granma showed up. Then she burned down her own house. Whoa. I stopped rubbing the penny.

What would Pops do? I knew he was fierce. But also, kind. In the photos in the upstairs room, he had this look on his face like, "don't fuck with me," but also — "if you're a stray dog, I will feed you." His shoulders wide as a truck, hands like axe heads, thumbs always tucked in the pockets of his jeans. These jeans, maybe. My head throbbed from the lights. I had to get out. I started to rub that penny again, Dammit, like I could start a fire in my pocket.

With one hand Ministache held his fat logbook, with the other he fondled his mustache. "You hurt a man real bad. And now he's dead. Mebbe you're the one who did it. Killed himself? Suspicious." He examined my bruised face. "The nurses say he grabbed his heart out but that's stupid. They're lying. Are those good-lookin' nurses lying for you? You in on this together, with them hot nurses?"

I shook my head.

He swung the logbook and smacked me in the face.

My head banged off the wall and the cut below my eye opened. I growled.

"What are you, an animal? Some deviant's gonna pay. You or your Granma." He double-wiped his mustache and laid the bloody logbook on the desk. "Bummer, that cut broke open on the drive over here."

Granma's voice rose, "GODDAMMIT, am I BEIN' duh-TAINED?"

The door to the street opened and Penny stumbled in, crying, with her arms around Deer. The lighter in my chest went *POP*. Deer glared up at the hidden sun with an open mouth and streaming eyes. Like the blind woman in handcuffs on the floor. Like Craig. Deer's fingers were claws ripping her chest.

"Help us, help us," said Penny to Ministache, and then she saw me. "Ohmygod, Clay help us." Her wild eye looked as if it wanted to jump from her eye-socket.

"This is a jail not a hospital," said Ministache. "Get The Fuck Out." He went back to writing in the log book.

I jumped up and wrapped my arms around Deer. Every part of her strained. I had to clamp down like a vise. The whole time I held her, Dammit, she would not stop struggling.

"Cress can't see," said Penny. "She was there, talking to me for the first time in a long time. She was there, and then she was gone."

On the edge of my vision, I saw MK, though the door did not open. His dark blue eyes were not blue anymore. They were black holes, deeper than two wells at the end of the world. He popped his knuckles and said, "Ve'achron Romes!" Then saw the cut under my eye and backed against the wall. "Ugh. Blood. *Again?*"

"What's *she* doing here?" asked Penny, not noticing MK, and pointing at the blind corkscrewing woman in the corner. "Oh Clay," she said, and Penny looked at me with a strange look on her face. "Oh Clay, oh Clay, oh Clay."

I felt as if my mind was in four places yelling and none of them would listen to the other ones.

MK stopped smiling. His face changed and he looked at Penny.

"I want you to know I forgive you," he said to her. "I know it wasn't you, it was him. He hurt you, didn't he?"

Penny couldn't hear her, him, them. She was looking at me and at the woman in the corner in horror.

That is when I knew this whole thing — this whole flaming bag a nuts, like Granma says — was MK's doing. Because of his agreement with Ms. Swan.

Granma kicked on the other side of the wall and yelled like she was ten women, "Let me GO. Where's my BOY, godDAMmit!"

I kept one arm around Cress, stuck my hand into my pocket and squeezed the penny as hard as I could and wished for something to change, *oh, that this too solid flesh would melt, thaw, and resolve itself into a dew.*

The door opened and in walked Mister Brown flourishing his meat stick. Grinning like you, Dammit, when you got a steak in your mouth. He bowed deeply, "Young Master Bergmann, I presume?" He acted like we were neighbors on an evening stroll after supper and had bumped into each other. Except, a chaw of meat made his left cheek look like he had mumps, and his right eye winked.

"Penny for a wink, Mister Bergmann," and I dropped the penny in his sticky hand as he passed me.

Mister Brown spat at MK's feet.

MK said, "I'll just watch a moment, this will be fun."

Mister Brown stopped in front of Ministache and took a bite of his meat stick, "What's the meaning of this, officer?"

"Uh. Who are you?"

"When you address me, please call me Federal Marshall Brown. I'm here for your confession."

Ministache looked confused.

Mister Brown stuck his meat stick in his chest. "Does your superior know you like to watch girls through windows?"

"Uh," said Ministache, and his face flushed.

Mister Brown waved the meat stick and the room went *OOMPH* and jiggled. He drew a square in the air. "You can tell a lot about a man by the windows he looks through."

Ministache muttered, "You never seen me. No one knows."

"Ha!" said Mister Brown, "GOTCHA."

Mister Brown lifted the meat stick. "See this. It's my pass." The room jiggled again, and everything in it moved to the left about an inch. "Ever notice that after you eat a steak, the turd that comes out is round like the world?" When he said, "round like the world," he stepped behind the desk, and wiped the meat stick against the wall, a big circular stain.

Ministache's mini-stache trembled. "I'm careful when I go to watch."

"CONFESSION!" yelled Mister Brown. "And that's *Federal Marshall Brown* to you." Mister Brown saluted me sharply with his meat stick, grinning. "Remand these prisoners into my custody," he ordered Ministache.

"Sir, yes Sir."

"Did you, or did you not, thump the kid in the face?"

"Um, aah, yes I did."

"Federal Marshal Brown!"

"Federal Marshal Brown, I did. Yes, I did. I hit him in the face."

"Here's what that felt like," said Mister Brown. He back-handed Ministache with the meat stick *CRACK*. A red stripe rose across his face, ruffling his mustache, all the way down past his chin. His eyes filled with tears.

At this point, I was not thinking the pen is mightier than the sword and so forth. I will say that I had a craving to walk over to Ministache, pick up the logbook, and thump him HARD. Being with Mister Brown made you feel that way, like you could do anything, Dammit. Just for the fun of it.

The door with the tiny window slammed open and Granma struggled out with Officer Rall's big arms wrapped around her.

Mister Brown clucked his tongue like he caught two kids fighting on the street. "Let her go." He raised the meat stick. I know it sounds like three words, Dammit, but they were big rocks dropped in a small pool.

Officer Rall let her go.

Ministache wiped his nose and left a trail of snot across his beautiful mustache, "This is Federal Marshall Brown. We are remanding everyone into his custody."

Officer Rall shrugged his big shoulders and looked relieved. He pushed Granma at Mister Brown. "Please. Take her away. I can't stop her," he said.

"Duh," said Mister Brown. "No one can stop this woman."

Then MK put his hand on my arm, and it felt like the far side of the universe where the rays of *no* sun ever touch. "Hey Romes, no hard feelings, mkay?" He seemed genuinely sad. "Remember, I vowed to do this to help you. Just fulfilling the bargain. I kissed the wrong girl; they look so alike."

I did not understand what he was saying, but it was clear in the next moment.

MK stepped quickly behind Penny.

I had no time to act. No. That is not true, Dammit, and I know if you were there, you'd have done something. My peculiar preponderance. Stuck between many and various thoughts, you see. Each more persuasive, more particular than my conscience. It seemed quick, but I know the truth. It was me all along. Four different voices talking at once:

"Time is out of joint, O cursed spite, was I born to set it right?"

"Blood, Jackass, blood. A whole lot of fuckin blood."

"Run to the water Baby-Grizz!"

"Look at you, talking to yourself right now. Hesitater! The slow kid, the one who stayed behind."

Grinding to a stop, rust in my gears.

MK dropped his face over Penny's head — did he suddenly grow ten feet tall? — His flaxen hair fell over her face. He laid his mouth close to her ear, penumbrating, then stepped back uncovering some other new person. Penny's eyes turned towards the distant sun; her hands became rats. I yelled at him and tried to punch him in the face, but he grabbed my arm. The cold went straight up my arm and pierced my heart.

MK looked directly at me. "I love you Clay, you fuckin nerd."

He smiled, and was somehow more Penny than him, that unmistakable frowning-smile that made my heart heave. "I've loved you since I saw you in that stupid school. I loved you long before. When your momma told me about you all those nights we were kept in Big Jim's mansion, and we couldn't get away. I know how your dad died. Stabbed through the heart, said your momma. And I know...." MK's hand rose slowly, "I know your momma's alive." His long finger pointed at the blind woman on the floor, twisting in the corner. The woman with the silver swallow earring.

Granma Lina screamed the same godawful cougar scream when Craig lost himself; she fell to her knees beside the corkscrewing woman.

MK kept talking like he could not stop, like Penny's life depended on it. "She's here with me. Your Momma says remember to go to the water, remember to tell your stories so you're not afraid." His face changed. "Oh no, I can't be here. I can't be in here." His voice became frantic. "I can't be here, no, no, NO. I can't be in here with them!"

I grabbed Penny who was already tearing at her chest, and in that moment as I reached for her, MK was gone through a grey doorway with arching wings of shadow.

"Good Lord, that happened too fast. Even for me," said Mister Brown. He didn't sound scared, or surprised. Just amazed.

I could not look Penny in the eyes. I knew what I would see. I put my free hand on Mister Brown's bird-bone shoulder and squeezed as hard as I could, and he yelped.

"Mister Brown is trying, lil bruh," he said. "Trust me, I'm trying." He waved his meat stick in little circles at the officers who seemed stupefied. "Marshall Brown says, 'It's no big deal officers.'"

The room shifted a couple more inches to the left, my eyes rolled around in my head, and I dry-heaved.

When everything settled back, Ministache rubbed his lip-hair. He said proudly, "It's no big deal."

Officer Rall sighed. "Ahhhh. No big deal."

"You two sit over there," said Mister Brown pointing at the corner.

"It's Rose-Marie," said Granma in a choking voice. "Clayton, what your shirtless friend said. It's your Momma."

Now, Dammit, it wasn't until later I found out how Granma saw MK. I'll just say that with everything going on, I didn't notice.

"God knows what's wrong with her," Granma said. "Why she looks older'n me, and her lovely hair.... all gone. I seen her in town. God's truth I did not know it was her." Granma touched the old blind woman's face.

"No," I said, surprised at the words coming from my mouth like dry bones. "No. My Momma is young and beautiful. With hair the color of wild honey."

"Sweet Lord have mercy," Granma said.

I wrapped my arms around Penny and Cress. They fought me, strong as wildcats, but slow.

The front door opened. I have to say, Dammit, I was hoping it was you and I know that's stupid because dogs can't open doors, but I did not know what to do, and you always help me feel better because you are never scared. But it wasn't you.

Big Jim walked in, leaning on a silver cane that looked way too thin to hold his weight. He was quiet as a snake except that weird shearing-clicking, which had grown louder. *Click Click.* He had to turn sideways to get his shoulders through the door. He smiled at Mister Brown as if no one else was in the room. "Finally, mmm we meet, Reynard," he said softly. The smile was much too wide, much too mean, for his kindly fat face. "You find me much changed?"

"Nah, bruh. If it walks like a dick, and acts like a dick, it's still a dick." Mister Brown's voice trembled. "Even if it looks like a vaj." The meat stick lay quiet against his thigh.

The silver cane made sharp strokes and slashes like Big Jim was writing a new language in the air. A lot like what Mister Brown done with his meat stick.

"FOOL!" *slash* "...You..." *stroke* "...find..." *slash* "...yourself..." *stroke* "...in a tight spot." *Big slash*. The room shuddered and moved an inch.

I clutched the writhing girls. I kept resetting my grip, and they kept squirming out. I'll tell you this right now, Dammit: there is no way I believed the woman in the corner was my Momma. She looked nothing like her. Anyone can have silver earrings.

"I'm gonna take brown to the super bowl," said Big Jim, clicking his teeth. "And flush him down."

"Tryin' too hard, Jim bruh," said Mister Brown.

Big Jim gurgled low and long. It felt like we were in the valley of the skukm, and I could hear it coming.

Mister Brown hawked deep in his chest, spat a gob at Big Jim's feet. "Let *Lycaon* come," he said to the ceiling. "Anytime, please." He looked at me, "Uh, lil bruh, now would be a great time for you to remember how to do whatever it was you did last time? Dial him up." There was sweat on his forehead.

"Let him come," said Big Jim, "I'll tear him limb from limb. Like I tore his wife and two laughing daughters." He smiled under his mustache *click click*. "Mmm. Can you see I've changed for the better?"

"Ugh," said Mister Brown, "Same piece ashit."

"This is our land now," said Big Jim. "This town, these bricks. Mmm? The cement between each brick? Even the idea of a jail is ours. These women—especially that one—mine, breeding grounds," and he pointed at the old woman twisting in the corner. "Sadly ruined. My progeny who will grow like oaks to rule with me..."

Mister Brown laughed out loud, interrupting him, like wind in an old growth forest. "Gonna break a rib with all the chest-thumpin.'"

Big Jim didn't seem to hear him, "...A new line with no moral hang-ups like the old Nisoi. My spade cometh. I dig new ground." Then the pudgy baby voice: "Great oaks of every-changing darkness, planted in you, seeded by me."

He sounded so kind, so loving, I wished he was my Dad for a moment. I almost said yes, yes, we will all help you tend those oaks. I'll tell you, Dammit, of all the things Big Jim could do, that voice felt the best and most awful crawling around inside me.

"Oh GEEZ." Mister Brown laughed and waved his meat stick. "You been waiting a LONG time to say that, huh?"

I came back to myself. Big Jim is bad for you, I said to myself. Bad.

Big Jim gurgled and waved his cane, but nothing happened.

Mister Brown took a bite of his meat stick and grinned. "'You're not an oak, ya big nut." He waved the meat stick, but his hand shook.

I saw purple ropes flicker from Big Jim's mouth. "I'll show you mmm how a nut gets cracked." He tapped his cane against the ceiling. "All those years you used to trick me. Turn the tables, twist the endings, and get out free." He seemed to swell; his shadow filled the room. "No more. SHE is helping me. She thinks I serve her, but that is temporary. I have plans. I'm calling Someone. My spade. Too bad you won't be around to see."

"Yeah, yeah we know," said Mister Brown. "S'why I'm here." Mister Brown — who was already very small — seemed to shrink to the size of a squirrel, and Big Jim's head touched the ceiling.

Big Jim said, "I am gonna crack you wide open, fox. I'm gonna suck you dry."

"Come and suck it," said Mister Brown. The meat stick looked like a pencil in his fingers, and he backed against the wall.

Big Jim's cracked his knuckles and it sounded like far away thunder. "Your blood is exactly what I need to complete my cycle. Mmm."

None of us could move.

Big Jim tapped the ceiling *boom boom* with his cane and tapped the floor again *boom boom*. The room shifted, something pulled at my entrails, all of us groaned, I leaned over and threw up on the floor. Finally. But I felt no better.

Big Jim leaned his cane carefully in the corner, touching it fondly. "I'll be back for you in just a moment mmm," he said to his cane. The mandibles unfurled in a purple slither and went back to hide under the mustache. His great eyes shone like dazzling orbs, and he said, "Under the walls, the blood spilled to hold them up, that's ours too, mmm? All of the blood. And I call on it now. Mmm. Here. Break your measly tent of sticks and hides."

The floor went black. I felt like there was some kind of new blood coming up my legs out of the foundations.

Big Jim said it as soft as he ever said anything: "Get out of town, Mister Brown." The room lurched. "Mmm."

Mister Brown fell to his knees.

Big Jim grabbed him by the scruff of his neck like he was a stray dog.

Mister Brown's grin was a shadow, but he spoke clearly, "Bignut's a poet and he don't know it."

Big Jim twisted Mister Brown's arm behind his back, until *CRACK*—it broke with the sound of a gunshot.

Mister Brown grinned like the existence of the whole world depended on his smile. Sweat dripped down his nose. His arm bone grated under Big Jim's hand. In the silence — with everyone frozen — his bones sounded like tires going over dry twigs.

Big Jim glared at Mister Brown's arm like he was deciding how to split it and drink from the stump.

Then the front door swung open again.

"Someone call for *Lycaon*?" It was a snarl deep as the woods of the far north in Winter, where there is no sun, where the night is cold and lasts forever.

Mister Brown laughed. I think it was a laugh, anyway, through his gritted teeth, though he sounded like a wounded animal. "You come in, bruh, these walls'll pop off."

There was no Doc left in the clothes Doc was wearing. The thing inside of them standing in the doorway was something grown hairy on stories by the fire when the moon is full. Its face was long, its thin ears laid back, spittle dripped from yellow fangs, and it was covered in black hair.

This time, I had not called him. I *never* want to call him, ever.

Right about then things got strange. I know, Dammit, you will say they already were. But you have no idea how weirder they could get. Neither did I. Everything I'm going to say happened WAY faster than I can tell it here:

First, Mister Brown started to giggle. "*Zimilia Zimilibus!*" He yelled and waved the meat stick, "The quick brown fox jumped over the lazy dog!"

Big Jim roared, shook him, and Mister Brown screamed. Then Big Jim threw him against the back wall. Mister Brown reached

up and tapped the center of the circle he'd drawn earlier with his
meat stick, and I saw a window — in the shape of a perfect circle
— open where the grease-circle used to be. I saw a prairie of high
grass with a thousand wild striped cattle running towards a butte
in the distance, mountains rising like a reef behind it. Dust spilled
from their hooves. An indigo cloud flickered with lightnings over
the plain.

Doc snarled. Its dark fur had broken through what was left
of its clothing and grew long as we watched. At first it was sable.
But it changed to a grey like the walls of the jail, and I felt that
strange sense when you look for a wild thing in the woods among
the branches and all you see is its eyes.

Granma said, "Flaming bag a..."

But the beast interrupted her, "For Margaret, and for my
daughters." It was the sound of a pack of wolves telling you they will
pull you down and eat you alive, screaming. It shut the door and
turned. "You will pay," it snarled. It was angry and tired. But most
of all, ravenous.

Over my shoulder, I thought I heard that familiar voice, a
whisper: *"A whole lot a fuckin blood."*

Mister Brown crawled to me fast as a lizard in the sun and
smacked me in the face. I had no idea that little body could pack
that kind of power. My head rang, I let go of Penny and Cress. He
pulled me in a death grip behind the desk. "You'll thank me later, lil
bruh!" Then he shoved me through the circle and followed behind.

I went head-first, rolled, and came to my knees.

Pop's file in my pocket jabbed me and I hollered.

The window closed to the size of a large ball. I tried to stick
my arm through to push my way back to get to Penny and Cress
and Granma and the grey-haired lady, but Mister Brown put his
shoulder into me and knocked me back, and my arm came out of
the hole.

For one single moment, my eyes locked with Granma's on the other side. "Clayton, goddammit," she yelled. "RUN!"

Through the hole that was now the size of a child's palm I saw the grey wolf and Big Jim tearing each other's throats. I could not tell what Big Jim had become, but his mouth had grown too wide for his head, and whipping purple threads came from it and wrapped the wolf like muscled snakes.

Doc was a red-eyed slashing demon of spittle and fangs.

Mister Brown bent over — with the canvas of blue sky stretching over his head, the hot sun setting in the west, and wild cattle grazing in the distance — pulled his pants down and crapped into his hand. A very small crap, the size of a deer dropping and about the consistency too. He grinned that snaggle-tooth grin at me, squished it flat and thumbed it into the closing window as it shrunk to a small hole.

"Squeeze THAT penny," he said. "You know, in case that turd-burglar tries to come through, lil bruh, he'll end up in my hole. Heh."

He sat on the ground caressing his twisted arm, wincing, and laughing so hard that he cried. But he'd left his meat stick behind, and he looked alone without it.

Chapter 34

Revelations, Wink Wink

Grass higher than my knees rippled as far as I could see. It was midday in high summer, but it was not hot. The air was dry, tasted like dirt and smelled of cow pies. Mister Brown's turd hung in the air like a dirty penny. Then it was gone. I pushed on the air where I had seen the hole and I yelled for my Granma, for Penny.

A massive cow with razor-sharp horns and stripes down its back chewed its cud at the top of the little bowl in which we stood. All was silent, except for the sound grass makes in a light breeze, and cows chewing.

And me yelling.

Mister Brown patted the ground. "No goin' back, lil bruh, least not that way. If you stayed, Big Jim woulda chomped you with that clickety snakemouth."

I could see in my mind Penny's gaping face, her clawing hands, her staring eyes. And the woman writhing slowly in the corner who looked nothing like my Momma.

"Shush! Hollerin' gets the aurochs antsy. These ancient cattle are all dead back in your place. Here in my place, in my time, they're doin' just great." As if on cue, the aurochs at the top of the bowl stomped her foot and shook her horns. "Their favorite thing is twisting horns through your body. Second favorite is smushing people, eh? *Ignarii bisontis nomen dederant.* Heh heh." The aurochs snorted like it agreed with him. Bloodshot eyes the size of small plates rolled under its wide bony forehead.

I didn't care. I grabbed Mister Brown by the throat and lifted him off the ground. His neck felt like a twig. I closed my hand, his eyes goggled and he squeaked, "Gehhgg you don't have to choke me, I was gonna to tell you everything I know already, gahhg. Shhhh, aurochs!"

I dropped him, he landed like a cat and sat cross-legged rubbing his throat.

"Siddown. Why you think Mister Brown brought you here?" He waved his finger at me like it was a tiny meat-stick. "You wanna help Penny?"

The sky started to spin, and I collapsed next to him.

"The firmament is bigger than you think, and much further away from other loci in our universe. Breathe." He made me lean forward on my hands. "Now, find yourself a spot you love to be in your mind. Sit there. And breathe."

I thought of the porch at the homeplace. The ground stopped rolling.

"There ya go. Niiiice and slow." Mister Brown patted my shoulder with his good hand. "There, there, let it flow. It's a lot, dontcha know? Mister Brown forgets you're young as a two-day bug. Heh. It's your eyes. They look old in your mug. Foolin' me."

I realized I could see the veins on each blade of grass. And I could see the moving cells within every vein. The whorls of the prints of my fingers were sharp as knives. As if the old Clay was a shadow in Mister Brown's country. I leaned on my elbows in the grass, rolled over, and looked up. Deep in the center where the sky was a bottomless lake, I saw the Pleiades clear as I could see them at night. I did not have to look at them sideways. I blushed and sat up. These were no girls in flappy books. These girls swam and laughed. Real as my own finger pointing up.

"Best not to point, it's rude," Mister Brown said. "Though, from what I know, they don't mind you lookin.'"

Everything felt upside down. But clearer, more solid, with hard edges.

"Welcome to my place," said Mister Brown waving his good
arm in a big circle. He sounded happier than I ever heard him.
"Good spot for a breather. Ouch!" He cradled his broken arm.

I just want to go back.

He chuckled. "Oh, you will, you will."

How did he know what I was thinking?

"Listen lil bruh. Carefully. First and mebbe the only thing to
know about my place — besides don't make an aurochs mad — is
that we can talk with our mouths... or our minds." He flourished
his good arm at the sky and grinned. "*Zimilia!*"

I need answers, I need to get back....

"Yeah, yeah, Mister Brown knows you need answers," he said.
"See. This place is perfect for you. Don't talk, just think and I'll talk
back 'n wink, let your mind be open; don't shrink."

I hate his stupid rhymes.

"I can hear you." He grinned.

How come I can't hear you?

Mister Brown's grin got so big it crinkled his eyes shut. "My
place, my rules, lil bruh."

Why are we here? I was beginning to get the hang of it, the
silence, Dammit. It was great to not feel the cords of my throat
scratching out words.

"We need help," said Mister Brown. "Real, legit, bonafide,
butt-kickin', wise-ass help. Mister Brown's cousin. Him that told
me the skukm story. He's around here somewhere. Start walkin', I'll
start talkin, heh? That way." He pointed through a wall of aurochs
who had showed up, curious. "Mister Brown's gonna tell you so
much on this walk — your ears'll burn and your eyes'll pop." He
waved his good arm and an aurochs slowly ambled out of his way
and we came over the rise.

A range of mountains edged the prairie to the West like
upthrust walls. The sun was beginning to set behind them. A clear,

crystal orange I'd never seen where I am from, even on the clearest day of Spring.

"The sun has moved," said Mister Brown. "Mister Brown's Cuz is messin' with the timin'. His foul humor."

No shit, Sherlock.

"Smartass! Outa my way, ya big meat stick." He dodged an aurochs hoof. "We're gonna call this next bit '*Revelations, Wink Wink.*' Yeah, that sounds good." He waggled his finger at me but kept walking.

"Why are we here?" I thought again.

"I'm tryin' to tell you! Long time ago, when wishes were for wishing, aiming was for aiming, and sometimes both came true, Mister Brown and Lycaon had an old beef with that critter Big Jim – we hate him and he hates us—and we hunted that thing for centuries. Started across the pond, the land of your ancestors. Under the peaks of Gaul, the wilds of Caledonia, across the waters of the Northern seas. Remember, Mister Brown told you about the big ones having gravity—only it works weird and slips you sideways and you step in the river big as the Mississippi?"

What's the Mississippi?

"Big water that makes your river look like my pee stream. Heh. Lil bruh, you do NOT want to fall into the fat streams that lead to *them*. Thing is, with the big ones, the river does not flow *out*. It flows in. Try winkin', and — if you are NOT good — you'll fall in one of them rivers and get dropped at their feet. Stick with Mister Brown, turn your smile to a frown. Learn how to get through fences, ubiquit... uh, ubiquit... dammit, what's that word? Ah! Ubiquitous! Get through fences, ubiquitous training sequences. Heh."

"Anyways," Mister Brown said, "me n' Lycaon tracked him like big game fishermen and popped him and made him show himself like a shark with a hook in his gut. Spooked him. But he ran too fast on our line, and he was getting stronger. Made no sense. Then he disappeared out West a hundred years ago. Took us forever to pick up his smell. And he was different. Stronger, more like a man than the old wolf scent. With a hint of mud and bug. That floozy of an ancient goddess gave him a blessing — if you call being changed backwards a blessing." He spat on the ground. "Excuse me, dear lady, what I meant to say was 'lovely maiden sprung from the foaming waves of the sea.'" He looked at the sky. "Forgive me, dear lady, I did not mean to insult you. It's just that you are not yourself no more."

You look like you're going to get blasted.

"Wrong god, lil bruh," Mister Brown said to me. "But you never know what they hear and what they don't. Shut that brain up tight! Mister Brown can hear you breathin' heavy like a creeper in a jeeper takin' secret peepers." He grinned and was himself again. "Doc Ranulf fell in love with Margaret (a lovely lady of the lake, that's why the lake stinks now, she's not livin' in it no more). Doc quit the chase. They settled down in Junction City, he built her that home on the water. She was kind, fair, and helped him when he turned dark in the moontimes. Had two little girls looked just like him. Raven hair and wide brown eyes. Cold as a fish to the touch like their mother. I left that family alone to love one another and never shoulda, lil bruh."

Revelations, wink wink.

Mister Brown put his hands on his hips, wincing. "I'm tryin' to tell you a very serious and sad story."

I'm sorry. I didn't know about Doc.

He sighed. "We did not know it, either. We weren't tracking Big Jim – HE was tracking us. Big Jim found Doc's wife and daughters alone and skinned 'em alive, stretched their hides on the walls of Doc's house. Doc went mad."

I shuddered, remembering Doc's empty house and the blood I smelled in its pores.

"Yes. Lotsa blood, lil bruh. I don't know why he stayed in that house. Probably for the rage it gives him." He rubbed his face. "Mister Brown had to run Lycaon down in the wild. Took me years to get him back to himself — just to talkin' and wearin' clothes. By then Big Jim had killed your dad and taken over Junction City. Big Jim used to be dumb in the old days. More wolf-beast than human. I tricked him into losing his tail, heh heh, stuck it in the ice hole and froze, heh heh lil bruh," he thumped my shoulder with his good hand, "that was a good one. No time to tell it the way it deserves. But there's more revelations."

In my mind I saw two dead girls who looked just like Doc nailed to the wall of his cabin. Then I thought of Penny scratching her chest, and my Dad getting stabbed in the back, and I started to run down the hill.

I got to get out.

"You're goin' the wrong way!" yelled Mister Brown.

I got to get out, I got to get out.

He chased me and grabbed my arm. "Breathe! Mister Brown's still got to tell you about your family. You listening? Big Jim got himself involved with that goddess-whore — oops, I mean 'lovely as the foaming waves,' from now on Mister Brown will just call her "She" or "Her" — and Big Jim drunk Her golden mead and maybe did other things much worse, yech, and he's turning. Into something, bruh. Something I never seen."

I remembered the glittering eyes and mandibles like purple threads and shuddered.

Hurry. We need to hurry.

"Breathe! Almost there," he said. "He's turning into something, if he gets there, even She won't be able to slow him down. Not that She would want to anymore. Fat and lazy is what happened to Her.

And, She had an actual legit job to do. Makin' sure you fell in love with the right person and all that—but that hasn't happened for a long time. Why you think it's so hard finding your person these days? With Her help, in the old days...."

Mister Brown stopped and seemed to forget himself.

"Mister Brown had a person once. He will always be in Her debt." Then he shook his head slowly. "That Floozy let Herself go."

Don't talk about Her like that. I love Her.

"Go ahead, then. Say Her name."

He waited and I could not do it.

"There you go. You don't love Her, lil bruh, you just got dunked in the funk of Her lady junk. Heh heh. She's starts wars with boys like you." He looked up at the sky and down at the earth. "Excuse me Madam, but it's true. Just do your job. I'd say it to your face if you were here. Anyways, the story would be tangled enough. But there's more. Wink wink."

What about my family?

"Mister Brown's getting there. My Cuz and She started seeing each other, got along great. Looking to shack up, believe it or not. But She tried to steal something he cares about." Mister Brown plowed on. "When he caught Her, he didn't do a thing to Her. Just went into a funk and hasn't come out of it for a few hundred."

Days?

"Years. And by funk, I mean he really let himself go, lil bruh."

What does this have to do with my family?

"Ah, now you're asking the right question. Short version? How does rabbit find the brambles when the hawk comes down? Heh heh. Here it is: Your Pops comes from a line of men, eh, let's call 'em Conveners."

I know what we're called, but that's all I know.

"A Convener's someone wise enough, trusted enough, feared enough to gather factions, build trust, talk through stuff. Your line started doing this a few thousand years ago after the first one forged that axe. It made for a good reason to calm things down when they started to get hairy. When a Convener lay *Acuere* on the table it carried real weight. Mainly because it could cut us. And cut us deep. You'd get the full story, but time is like the lizard's tail today."

Long?

"Cut short. Heh heh. And scaley. Hey, I never thought of Time being long and scaly, but mebbe? Anyway. You think it's just people need help? No. Everyone does. All the beings. All the Nisoi. We're all trying to muddle through. It's not wise to let the worst ones get into altercations, makes for bad times for everyone."

When elephants fight, the grass suffers. Thank you, Dammit.

"Exactly!" He snapped the fingers of his good hand. "So. Conveners. For some reason long ago, they could see all us Nisoi for who we are. To most humans we're invisible. To a very few we're sensed. Like the passing of a light wind or the smell of another planet. Your ancestors weren't afraid to stand up to us and talk us down when the worst ones got out of control. Very helpful when powerful folk start seein' red. A clan of bad-ass, peace-loving, mountain men and women with one hell of a nasty axe who don't take shit from no one."

I take everyone's shit.

He sighed. "You'll get there. You're growin'." He sounded uncertain. "The firmament it is not so big as you think, and neither is it so far away from other loci in our universe."

You said that opposite, earlier.

"Yeah, yeah. Smart-ass. You got the world by the lizard tail." He went to wave his meat stick, realized it wasn't there, and lamely raised his finger at me. "Mister Brown says both are true, and when you get *that* you'll know how to wink."

Can we leave now?

He winked, but it was a sad, slow wink. "Nope. There's more. Your pops handed it off to your dad, and your dad was learning the family way but then he met your ma, run off around the world, and when they came back, they got into a fight with your Granma about the prophecy and took off."

The prophecy? The one about me killing someone I love? I had not thought about *that* for a long time, Dammit.

"Oops, um. Yeaaaah." He paused to rub his broken arm and seemed very focused on its pain. "Uh, lil bruh, Mister Brown sometimes exaggerates things."

I've noticed.

He started walking again and spoke over his shoulder. "So anyway, back to your parents. No one could find 'em. Pretty much figured they went back to your ma's people. She needs to be near water to be free and strong. None of us knew your pa had a secret place on the Salmon where they raised you and tapped out. None of us knew, and no one considered your Granma might have known all along (we should have) until your Granma tracked you down two days ago."

She didn't know either.

"Hold your horses. Your ma and pa came to town four years ago, your pa took *Acuere* and called a Summum to sort out the shenanigans (A Summum is a type of conventicle, a conference, a meeting, basically for the Nisoi). Who was there? My Cuz, the One you call Ms. Swan, Big Jim, me and Doc and a handful of others I don't have time to tell you about. But a day before the meeting, your ma and pa ran into Big Jim. Or, I should say, Big Jim ran into them. Your Dad made a mistake, he left the axe behind. A mini-truce, ceasefire, was in effect because of the Summum. He was unprotected."

That oath-breaking bastard. He stabbed Dad through the heart and stole my Momma. I started to shake again.

"How'd you know?" he asked. It was the first time I seen him look surprised.

I see stuff. Sometimes stuff that has happened. Sometimes stuff that hasn't happened yet.

"What stuff?" He was suddenly very quiet. His darting eyes became steady, and he rested his little hand on my chest again.

"Do you ever see it lil bruh, and then say it out loud and it happens?"

The hairs on his thin arm were dark and rusty like the mane that flew back from his sweating forehead. He was in great pain. I realized that telling me stories was a way to cover it. But I did not want to answer him. I got pain too.

So, I changed the topic with a question. I know how to do this, Dammit. MK was easy to move in conversation, and Mister Brown was no different.

Where are we?

Chapter 35

Winking: A Primer (Or, Some Riddles For You, Dammit)

Mister Brown wasn't listening to me. He was suddenly looking up. Across the backs of the aurochs about a mile away a truck-sized cloud hung in the blue sky. Soundless lightnings flashed as if a heart pumped within. Mister Brown pointed and clenched his good fist in joy.

"There he is! Let's go." He pushed himself through grass that brushed against his chest.

Now, Dammit, you'll like this next part. It's like Granma's pancakes, except it's riddles not pancakes. One riddle after another stacked on a steaming plate of riddle with a slab of great big melting riddle on top and slathered with a jug of juicy riddle pouring over the top and spilling over the sides. Maybe you'll get everything that Mister Brown told me about winking right away. You'll probably love it. Me? I'm telling you because I'm still trying to understand, and I will use words you don't get because I'm trying to describe that prairie as best I can.

Where are we?

"It's where.... and it's when," said Mister Brown.

I don't understand.

"This is the time that Mister Brown loved most *when* he was young. So, we came here. To my favorite *when*. When Mister Brown was a red-haired ragamuffin climbin' the backs of aurochs and runnin' up them mountains." He was in a hurry and speaking over his shoulder. It was easy for me to keep up. The grass only came to my hips. "Mister Brown really misses this *when*," he said and stopped so quickly I bumped into him. "Mister Brown doesn't get to come here much." He sounded happy. And very sad, at the same time.

Ok. So 'when' are we?

"Duh. I told you. One mirror over. In Mister Brown's time."

Which made no sense at all, Dammit. A phrase rose to my mind, unbidden, from The Riverside. *"The eye sees not itself, but by reflection, by some other things."*

"Exactly. Seeing — winking — is more than with your eyeballs. A great way to hide from monsters. They have a tough time with the *when*. They love the *what* and the *how*. They like everything clean and simple. They hate, absolutely HATE, the *why*. They think they know about the *where* but no, no, no!" Mister Brown danced his little jig until he winced. "They get confused. And the *when* lil bruh? The mirror of *when* held up to the face of a monster? It burns, it tears at its deathless nothingness. Don't you see: a monster is a monster because it has no soul (A soul, in part, is made of a whole buncha *whens*). Oh, but they want a soul. And lie to themselves about the wanting. If you show them that truth, hold up a mirror to it, it gets bad for them real fast. They can't figure out the *when*. That's part of what makes 'em monsters."

I thought about my homeplace and how it felt sitting on the porch in the sun in the morning that first day I met you, Dammit. It was definitely a *where*. But for me, it was more *when* than anything.

"That's it!" said Mister Brown. "You ever get a feeling, sometimes, living is a mirror? If you turned quick enough, you'd see what made the reflection?"

Like Granma's hand-mirror?

"Yep. Only there's more'n one mirror, so you got to look quick to catch the real deal, or at least the next reflection over. Mirrors facing mirrors, moving like the wavelets of a calm river touched by wind and sun. There are moments you feel it. Mebbe falling asleep. Mebbe watching something small do something real big.

Like watching bugs in the water. You catch a feeling that don't fit any other feeling? Or just know in your gut because of the memories?"

I seen myself in the river once, and there was a shadow around me. I looked like someone else.

"Yep, something changes from itself into something completely different, but it somehow remains the same too? Sometimes it is just a lonely desire pulling like a string between your heart and 'there is more? Look, lil bruh, we're talkin' about paradoxes, so if your head hurts a little bit, it's OK."

What's a para... a paradox?

"Two mooring spots on a river. Heh heh." He went to scratch his nose with a missing meat stick, missed, and then did not know what to do with his hand. "The world is full of paradoxes and people who try to resolve them. Which is the epitome of dumb. Something changes and yet stays the same — as if that's its nature to be both."

I'm not dumb, I get it. But I don't want to change.

"We don't have a choice, lil bruh. Heh, and there's more revelations. Humans lost the connection, but if you look close enough it's there. Under the littlest things."

I thought of the orange and grey insect I crushed — it felt so long ago — when Granma showed up. My namesake, the stonefly, long as my thumb. It must have sat for some time warming up in the sun after crawling from the water. And then it crawled right out of its own skin leaving it there on the rock like a paper suit. It was just opening its wings when I stepped on it.

I seen what's in the river. I seen the littlest things there.

Mister Brown stopped and looked at me like he was seeing me for the first time. "You're getting close, lil bruh. Around the edges of the biggest things too. Things so big you can't see 'em directly, so you look at 'em sideways. You see the next mirror there if you look long enough."

Dammit, I thought of the winged Mayfly Creature, which — of all the things I had seen — felt most like a dream. You're the only one I told about it. Yet, somehow, it felt bigger than the world and most real and solid of all things. So real, I was still looking at it sideways just to remember it existed.

So, I'm looking in the mirror?

"No lil bruh. Well, yes and no. We're mirrors away, being looked at."

I don't understand.

"You got to smile like a frown, lil bruh, to think upside down." He waved his good arm. "Like Penny's smile. Like this sky." I couldn't tell if he was joking because he was smiling both sneaky and kindly like that day in the library.

We HAVE to help Penny.

"We will, lil bruh – patience! You got to pretend you're on your back lookin' at the sky, and the sky's so high it's all turned round, and the universe flips, and dips, sets you on her hips, and you find yourself eatin' chips—with your head all up in the brown, lookin' down at the sky like a clown with a frown." He winked. "Think opposite! Making a jokey-poem or a poemy-joke of it helps too. Heh."

Upside-down in the brown. Maybe that's how he got his name.

He grinned, and his teeth showed. He looked meaner and wiser than a mangy street cat and I was glad he was on my side.

"Mebbe lil bruh. Mister Brown: he's not no pouty demi-god or freakin'-deakin' monster, he's somethin' else. You like to be upside-down? Go with Mister Brown." He smacked me in the chest. "Was a time I was on *my* side only, lil bruh, but I changed. I'm on this side now." He opened his palm at the wide prairie and crystal sky.

What made you change?

He ignored my question. "Anyway. Think opposite. If you can make the move, move the wink, each mirror's closer to the actual blink. That is: if you got good mojo and don't step in the Nisoi."

I don't understand.

Aurochs bunched around us, chewing, farting, dropping aurochs-pies. Curious and unafraid. Their eyes were larger and brighter than I expected, like no animal eyes I ever seen, Dammit.

"It don't matter that you understand! Mostly, it matters that we made it here in the nick of time, that this *when* exists." He pushed on an aurochs with his good arm. "My *when* is real. To me. And now *my when* is real to you." The aurochs' eye was the size of a plate, shining brown. Kinder than the first aurochs.

"One last thing," said Mister Brown. "It ain't all mirrors."

You mean there's more?

"Heh heh. That's how we started this talk. Always more, lil bruh."

I am lost and I can't get home, and that is all I want.

"That's what Mister Brown is talking about, ya goof! It ain't all mirrors forever. Where does the light come from, eh?" His hand had created a warm spot on my chest, and when he took it away, I felt a chill. I hurried after him, around another aurochs that would not budge.

We got to get back.

"Mister Brown told you: We need my cuz to wink out."

What's winking, anyway?

We came over a rise, and the mountains had leaped closer by fifty miles, rising over our heads like buttresses. Mister Brown shook himself from head to tail and his bronze hair stuck up all over. He waved his good arm, and yelled, "HOW YA DOIN' HOMEPLACE?"

The sides of the mountains were forested blue shadows in the setting sun. Their ridges bathed by a white dusting so pure that I felt I saw snow for the first time. The sky was close. If I reached out my fingernail I'd scratch it. The silence of the mountains was a question and I heard myself say something back. "Yes. You know I love you." Flat-topped buttes rolled in the vast space between. And under them, aurochs more numerous than the stars.

My knees buckled.

"It does DO this, sometimes," said Mister Brown.

The seed-tops touched my face, and I smelled red dirt and aurochs, sweet prairie grass, and the sun setting in a breeze that was so young I could taste its birth in the mountains. A part of me is still on that hill looking, Dammit. You would a loved it.

Wild grass feathered Mister Brown's chest and he pulled me to my feet. He was crying. I'm not sure whether from pain in his arm or what. "Winking," said Mister Brown with a broken smile, "is seeing the lovely *when*. Seeing, lil bruh, even when you're hurting. Seeing the sweet refraction between the *whens* and walking in them."

Like I use a special talent?

"Don't be a dumbass." He was suddenly angry. "All you humans think about is what you *do* with something. Winkin's more than using stuff or using what's in you. At its heart, it's not using anything at all. Life is not a lever stuck under a boulder to move it. Besides — if anything, it's the boulder moves the lever."

Mister Brown scurried off half-singing, "flip it around, go to town, smile like a frown, upside down," over and over, his head a bronze boat washed by waves of green, disappearing in troughs and rising against the crests of the wind-touched prairie.

I don't understand.

His voice trailed back, muffled by distance and high prairie grass so I only caught bits and pieces. "...Special in them makes them who they are.... the way to the real deal. Like this place, with the aurochs.... my *when* is closer to the real deal. When Mister Brown was a little ragamuffin aurochs was everywhere.... We got to make sure we don't run into me... 'Old World' and 'New World'.... that's B.S.... one old world getting made new. All of us. My cuz .... his own place, just didn't.... too easy for *Her* to find him, so he came to mine."

Mister Brown emerged from a swathe of thick grass and popped me in the chest with his good finger. "Look, lil bruh. Whatever you want to call it, there's something in you no one else got from Someone that everyone's got." The grasses mixed with the bronze of his mane; a creature of copper and verdure woven from the fabric of the land.

"Only there's no need for shouting. He's said his piece, see?" He waved all around, the grass swished his good arm.

I did see. *The strongest voice is often the most silent.*

"Devil ain't in the details." He paused to spit. "Louder the shouting, meaner the dude, lil bruh. Ah.... back to winkin'. It comes in all sizes. Like when you rubbed that penny, and I showed up. That's a little wink. I hear you. I move a few mirrors *snap* (he snapped his fingers) from my *when* to your *when*."

Oh, I get it. Like traveling through time.

"My *when's* nothing like that!" His eyes burned. "Haven't you been listening? Time is a construct created as a tool. But it's not." He grinned. "If anyone's a tool, it's you, lil bruh. Heh heh."

He started singing again. "A *when* is a *when* that *when's* your *when!* Whenedy whenedy whenedy WHEN! What Mister Brown's been tryin' to tell you this whole time: Winkin's just be yourself, only more." He snapped his fingers. "Easy, jackass."

Not easy. I remembered that when Dad called me "jackass" he never really was angry. It always sounded like "I love you."

"You coming?" called Mister Brown.

I wiped my face, and I got up and made my way towards his voice. I had to get my mind off my thoughts, so I changed the subject.

So, I can wink?

"Depends. If you got one of my pennies, then sometimes. Are you more like your Dad, your Mom, or something else?"

Of rivers and the chain-ed canyons free, a winding restless spirit I will be.

"Omygod," said Mister Brown waving at the sky and peering warily at the swirling dark cloud, which was suddenly much closer. "The boy is full of ancient words."

I read The Riverside for years; that one I made up.

"Actually, you're close to winkin'. Mister Brown saw your homeplace in your lyric. You *were* looking in the mirror. All you need to do is find the flash, the place where the light moves, that's the mirrored-door to the *when* of what you are looking for."

But that's not real, the Riverside and all that? They're just stories.

"How do YOU know?" he asked, and his copper eyes flared. He looked exactly like that day in the library. The keeper of treasures, the one who protected the stories.

Then Mister Brown froze like a dog on point, "I smell 'im!" He closed his eyes. "Ya don't bathe, ya get kinda ripe. This way."

What about closing the circle after you go through. Is there another way?

"You mean you don't want to stick a turd in the hole for funzies? Heh. Nah, anything'll do, lil bruh. Whatever it is, it's got to be hard for the one chasing you to figure out. And by hard I mean soft."

I pulled Penny's crumpled page from my back pocket.

Like this?

Mister Brown shrugged. "Pretty much anything. Whatever you shove in the hole has to be from the heart. Or butt. Heh." He looked up at the cloud and frowned. "My Cuz's been in a funk lately." He sounded worried. "Us librarians called it A.S.S. few years ago. Heh. Austen Suffering Syndrome. You know lil bruh, now we call it the 'T.T.' heh heh (he pronounced it *"titty"* with a grin). The 'Twilight Twitches.'"

A rose by any other name?

"Somethin' like that." He spoke softly to himself, "Of course the boy knows what you're talking about Reynard, he's stuck in one himself." He slapped his thigh which made him grimace. "You shut your mind, OK? Don't think too much, or he'll hear you. Probably hear you anyway. Let Mister Brown do the talking."

I shoved the balled-up page back in my pocket and followed Mister Brown down the hill. I tried to shut out the sight of Penny's face. I tried to remember what my Momma looked like. But all I saw was the grey blind woman turning like a corkscrew on the floor and Granma beside her. I would pretty much do anything to help them. At least that's what I told myself, Dammit, as I followed Mister Brown into the cloud.

Chapter 36

The Smell of Dirt and Rain Before The Fire

We smelled him long before we saw him. Like Mister Brown said, there's nothing like the smell of someone who has not washed in a long time.

Mister Brown's Cuz lay curled on a pelt by a smoldering aurochs-pie fire. It was almost completely dark, the air filled with smoke and a light mist. I thought of a wounded dog, waiting to die, Dammit. Although you might have bowed down to him. There was something about his shoulders that felt like a shrug could break a mountain. His teeth were like his cousin's, and the set of his eyes. But when Cuz sat up, I saw wider shoulders, larger hands, and eyes like rivers of earthy loam. His hair was longer than mine, golden-brown, dipped in black on the edges. Unlike Mister Brown, he had no beard. Bits of grass and dirt and aurochs-pie clung to his shaggy mane.

The smell was bad. Spit poured into my mouth turning sour.

"It's me, Cuz," said Mister Brown.

No answer.

"May your enemies lick your shining balls and may your friends share your bloody kills. Er... If I had to choose one, I'd choose the licking of the shiny balls," and Mister Brown paused for effect, "...who wants their *friends* lickin' their balls? Eh? Eh?" The flourish made him go *yip* and hug his broken arm.

Cuz didn't laugh. The smell was like we popped open a coffin. Mister Brown tried again. "Whoo. Something died. That you?"

Cuz rose, sighed deeply, and hugged Mister Brown. They sat without a word. The stink was so bad I tried to leave but Mister

Brown grabbed me and made me sit. Dry lightning flared. Deep lines ran from Cuz's eyes down to the gash that was his mouth.

"You gotta shake off this girl, Cuz."

He stinks like a graveyard.

I remembered what Mister Brown said about trying not to think. But it was too late.

Mister Brown glared at me and put his finger to his lips.

Aurochs gathered in a brown wall around us, a musky hut thatched with cloud. The fire throbbed and sweat came off Mister Brown's long nose. There was so much water in the air, it felt like it was going to rain.

More silence.

Mister Brown clapped his good hand on his thigh. "Forgot greetings! This is my Cuz, second-cousin actually. You can call him Mister Bay."

Mister Bay shrugged. "Call me whatever you want." His voice was deep and resonant.

"This is Clayton," said Mister Brown. "He's in a mess, Cuz. Worse'n you n' me caught up with them chief's daughters and you had to eat me, and we got through the hole in the skukm's ass." Mister Brown grinned at the memory. "Ah, those were the days, huh? You look alright. Little peaked is all."

Mister Bay grunted, "Ain't et in a while."

"Can't get her off your mind, huh?" Mister Brown spat in the fire. "Women."

"Uh huh."

"Sweet lovin' goddesses. Get us every time."

"Who's the kid?"

"Rose-Marie Stonefly's boy. You know, salt-water girl run off with the Convenor's son?"

"Hmph." He was the gardener, and I was under the brown earth and moldering leaves of a thousand years, growing roots.

Mister Bay looked at me a long time. Something in me eased. Like that feeling when you take off your wet socks at the end of a long day of work. He still stunk, though.

Mister Brown said, "Its time, Cuz. Time to pick up your hide, trick a monster, tell a big lie, pull some crazy shit. Do *somethin'*."

"Hmph," Mister Bay said again. It pretty much sounded like "no," but he reached over and felt his cousin's crooked arm. I heard Mister Brown sigh so deep I couldn't hear the end of it. The arm straightened, and Dammit, I had the weird thrill run through me like after your legs started to work.

"Aaah." Mister Brown wiggled his fingers. "Many thanks, Cuz."

"Yep," said Mister Bay. "You in a world of shit. What you done?" He sighed and looked up at the cloud that seemed to thump with his heartbeat and answered his own question. "You been waving around that meat stick. Got your ass kicked."

How does he know about the meat stick?

"Oh, I know about that stick. How he likes to rub it and wiggle it," said Mister Bay, and smiled for the first time. A scary sight. Jaggly teeth and red tongue. "Was me taught him."

Mister Brown looked sheepish and rubbed his nose. "Mister Brown's got mojo, but, eh, real magic he's got to borrow."

"Still callin' yourself 'Mister Brown' even though you ain't brown?"

"Shits and giggles, Cuz," said Mister Brown rubbing his arm and grinning so all his teeth showed. The aurochs moved in. I swear they were trying to hear better. "Can't go around calling myself 'Mister Red.' Heh heh. Lame! Look, I been helping the boy. They're out to get him, what could I do?"

"Let him die," said Mister Bay, as if he let boys die all the time. "It's *Her* world. I'm done. She don't want me." Mister Bay curled up on the hide and closed his eyes.

Rain fell in drops the size of silver-dollar pancakes.

"Stop!" yelled Mister Brown. "We're gonna be in a mud hole."

"So what," said Mister Bay.

"Please, Cuz," said Mister Brown. "Please."

"Second-cuz, you dumbass."

"OK, Second-cuz, is that better?"

"Yah."

The rain went back to a drizzle, but the ground was muddy.

Mister Brown explained to me, "My second-cousin's in love with She-Of-The-Golden-Vajina (may she reign forever). She spurned him."

Mister Bay spoke to the wall of aurochs. "She's no witch, She's better than all of us, She's the only *Her* there is. She's... She's more lovely'n the seven sisters with their clothes off dancin' to bring on the rain."

I've seen them too. I thought. *They like the water. The brightness of her cheek would shame those stars.*

"Whoo, them crazy-ass sisters? Really?" asked Mister Brown. Then he had an idea. "Hey, what about them sisters, Bay? Maybe we get 'em to come over, hang out a bit? Get you some PUSSY."

I did not know what Mister Brown was talking about, but it didn't matter because a bunch of things connected all at once. The buffalo hide. The one Ms. Swan wanted. It was right here. With this poor excuse for a second-cousin — whoever he was — lying on it crying his eyes out.

Mister Bay sat up and looked at me and his tears were gone. The drizzle quit too.

I forgot, too late, they could hear my thoughts.

"She say anything about me, kid?"

"Lil bruh, ya don't have to answer that," said Mister Brown uneasily.

"What did she say?" asked Mister Bay, and he put his long finger on my arm. I felt the howling of a thousand dogs, my eyes dimmed, and for a moment I was standing in the black throne room and Ms. Swan pushed her fingernail into my chest.

"Hmph," he said. "Got nailed. Can't help it, huh?"

I nodded. Like a barbed fishhook jammed in my chest. Like a lighter flame between my ribs and my backbone.

"Young. Dumb. Fulla cum," said Mister Bay to Mister Brown. "He's OK, too many old-time words, though." He sounded like Doc making a diagnosis. "Story's tied up inside. A knot that needs a knife. But. He's OK."

Mister Brown grinned, "Glad he's OK."

"Yah. He could break it all with a word."

"Him?" said Mister Brown, and he sounded amazed.

I said out loud, *"The brightness of her cheek would shame those stars,"* and I meant every word, though I wasn't sure which girl I was talking about. Penny. Ms. Swan. Those seven sisters who tried calling me down into my river so long ago.

"Monster Lord speaks," said Mister Bay, frowning—it was somehow also a grin. "You ever tell a story? Then we'll see."

"Slow down," said Mister Brown, sounding amazed. "THIS kid?"

Mister Bay ignored him. "Whatcha got in ya pocket? Is that a file—or you just happy to see me?"

I did not understand him for a moment, then I remembered. Pop's file in my pocket, and the painful bruise on my thigh from falling on it. Sometimes you forget the little hurts because the others are so big.

"It's my Granpa's," I said to him pulling it out and holding it up. "You want it?"

He held up long fingers, tipped with longer fingernails. "Won't do me no good kid. These fingernails is too hard. Don't you lose that. Come in handy sometime."

A file? I thought to myself. *What good is that ever gonna be?*

Mister Bay ignored my thought. "That file'll be more helpful than the other one, your long-haired friend. Stink's all over you, like you rolled with a skunk."

You're one to talk.

He ignored me. "Killed too many children. Seen too much blood. Not his fault, maybe, but he still done it. He ain't ever gettin' free."

"Mmhmm," said Mister Brown like he was just there to agree with anything and everything Mister Bay said.

Then Mister Bay put that knobby long-fingered hand with its jagged nails on my chest and started asking questions in my head, one after the other, like arrows:

"The pain, the pain, what you do with the pain?

What would you do if you WAS good, and your master good, and you loved him, but he asks you: 'go do this one thing?'

And it's a bad, bad thing he asks. What you do?"

A pang in my heart shot up to the stars for MK.

Mister Bay pointed at Mister Brown, "Even this one, his little feet been all over this world ten times, he knows the story, but he didn't hear the screaming." He shuddered. "But I heard it. Long ago. Enough children crying out all at once I heard it loud and clear across the desert and mountains and sea and everything between 'em." He scratched a sign into the dust. "So loud. I'd a heard 'em if it was on the moon."

Mister Brown asked, "What is he?"

"Huh?" Mister Bay returned from his horrible memory. "Dunno. Messenger of some kind mebbe? He's the one furthest *in* got sent furthest *out*. To do the meanest stuff. Not to one kid. Not to one family. A whole tribe. Of kids. Anyways, with all that blood spilt and life taken, he had bad mojo. It followed the Death Messenger everywhere."

I don't believe in mojo.

Mister Brown interrupted, "Mojo's real, lil bruh, where you think I get my pennies?"

Mister Bay flicked Mister Brown's ear. "From me, dumbass. Listen Stonefly. No one would take the Death Messenger in; he wandered the earth for a thousand years...."

Mister Brown finished the sentence, "And every now and then we heard rumors of villages of sun-staring zombies who dug out their hearts."

He knows about my Momma and Dad.

"You bet your life he does," said Mister Brown, "and that's why we come ...."

"Shush," said Mister Bay. "Not now."

The only thing that he's afraid of is blood. It makes him leave.

Mister Bay nodded. "Yeah, blood, even a little. That's what he fears. That's what hurt him so bad. That long night." He sighed, "All them dead children."

I thought of the question I'd been holding onto since I saw Craig dig out his heart: *How come people tear out their hearts after he takes their souls?*

"Not souls, curious one," said Mister Bay. "Different than souls. Memories make us who we are, but they're not all there is." He put an aurochs pie in the fire, and a flame reflected in his deep earth eyes. "That one takes the memories. What's left of the self don't like what it sees in the mirror without company of its memories, don't like to be left alone with itself. We're used to having lots of us from different *whens* hanging around talking at ourselves."

He put his hand on my chest. Mister Bay's fingers were knobby and cold. His nails were sharp. "On this side of the universe-wall it's too painful to see yourself with all the curtains pulled." The words he chose—and his tone—changed as he tried to help me understand: "And so it is that the self seeks solace," said Mister Bay. "An end to the pain. It tears out its own self."

Mister Brown whispered, and his voice shook, "Like a mirror looking at a mirror. With no one in the mirror. The self needs relief from the horror gazing on itself alone. They scratch and tear and rip out their hearts. The soul cannot stand to be alone with what is left."

A long silence, filled only with the sound of two cousins scratching themselves uncomfortably and poking a fire. I did not think it possible for anything to trouble Mister Brown, or to make him speak simply and clearly like a normal person, or to make him quit talking. But he stared a long time at the flames talking to themselves and would not speak.

Mister Bay changed the subject as if he'd been talking about the weather. "Want your folks back?"

I would give anything.

"Ain't gonna get 'em back like they was," he said, but it did not sound mean or heartless. "They're gone for good," he said. It came out like, "I'm going to the store," or, "hand me another slice of bread."

Mister Brown shouted, "Why you tell him THAT? He's not ready!"

Mister Bay shrugged, "Never ready for this kinda news."

I felt anger rising inside me, a black wave.

Mister Brown sighed and turned to me. "Well, my turn now. Lil bruh, thing is, your Ma. She's different." He tapped his finger on my chest. "You know this, right? I'm sure your folks told you."

No one tells me anything.

"One, she's a selkie. A maiden of the seas. Two, selkies are immortal. They live forever. Three, selkies do not have a soul. And yes, you can live a long time *and* not have a soul."

I never heard of a selkie before, Dammit, and my mouth dropped open.

"Close your mouth, lil bruh, it's open like a toad lost a fly. They didn't tell you?"

No one tells me anything.

"Well, telling ya now. Long ago selkies were given a gift that none of the other immortal soulless Nisoi received. That's a whole other story, but for the sake of this one, you need to know that selkies were given a special absolution. They're allowed to get a soul one of two ways: they borrow them from those that die at sea, or they marry a man — forsaking immortality — and the covenant binds a new soul into them. The immortality of the selkie isn't lost... yet. It binds to the couple; as long as the husband lives, they both live forever."

Goddammit no one tells me anything.

"Yeah, yeah. Ever wonder why they kept a barrel of salt around? Why she's always talkin' about rivers and oceans? I see the answer in your face. Heh heh."

No one tells me anything. I felt like Sonafa had run over me, then backed up and run over me again.

"Your Ma is a selkie. A selkie can have kids with a man, and those kids will have a soul because of the father, and because of the reprieve. But the immortal life of the selkie is forever tied to her man. As long as selkies stay married to their love, as long as he lives, they stay young as a morning rose. And their husband does too. That's the immortal bit, it gets bound into the marriage. Some men do that just for the everlasting youth. They sneak up on the selkie when she climbs out of the ocean and suns on land — they like to do that, selkies, they take off the hide and lay there in the sun for a bit. The bad men steal the seal-hide, keep the hide in a locked chest, and keep her bound to them. Pretty much slavery. But your Dad didn't steal no hide, according to what we heard. He won her heart. He done it for love."

Mister Bay said I would never see them again.

"That's not what he said to you," said Mister Brown. "Anyhow, if her husband dies by unnatural means – which is the only way that he can die—the selkie ages. All those years deferred come back upon her like the side of a mountain shearing away. Makes perfect sense, she's not immortal no more since she clove to him. By the way, immortal means 'live forever,' but an eternal soul is a special gift more'n that. Tell you more sometime, but not today. A selkie, once married, is given a soul and that means that she can die. That she *will* die someday, in order to receive her new body. However long it was that they were together, all those years return upon her all at once. A scary way to live, lil bruh, knowing what's coming. I reckon for love we'll do anything."

My fists balled up so hard that my fingernails cut my palms. *I'll find them if I have to tear out my heart to do it.* Then I thought of Craig tearing out his heart and started to shake.

"Give your heart, your arms, your legs, boy — it don't matter." Mister Bay was dead serious. "Say you brought your folks back? Ain't gonna be what they was." He shrugged. "They will be made new, but things never go back to what they was."

No one tells me anything.

In my mind I saw the grey woman corkscrewing in the corner of the jail. Her short hair and wrinkled face were nothing like my Momma. But it was her. Silver swallow earring and all. Dammit, I knew it right then. I had known it all along.

Something took me over. I was a flame, a blaze under a hot wind roaring up the canyon. My face felt like it would explode.

They weren't even paying attention to me, their heads close together, whispering.

"You gotta see the stars out here, Cuz! I just remembered: tonight's swimming night and it's clothes-optional." Mister Brown pulled Mister Bay up to his feet. "Get out from under this cloud, check 'em out! Mebbe we talk 'em into giving you a bath?"

"No," said Mister Bay, though he let Mister Brown drag him away.

I knew how Mister Bay felt. People trying to be helpful makes you feel worse. Like when he said, *You're never going to see your folks again.* It was like someone shoved a knife in my gut. Then twisted.

I pushed an aurochs out of the way. He smelled like a big dog just came in from the sun. I thought of you right away, Dammit, and missed you real bad. The circle of aurochs closed in. They pushed me back towards the fire. Mister Bay's buffalo hide lay on the ground.

Didn't Ms. Swan want a robe? It couldn't be this. It's full of holes and smells bad.

The aurochs pressed around me, shining eyes watching.

I surprised myself and picked it up.

I'll give it to Ms. Swan, she'll order MK to release Penny and my Momma, give Granma a new house, make Penny my one true love for life, and we'll go back to our home place. Hope is a funny thing, Dammit. It tastes so good then gives you the shits.

I put it on.

Everything went crisp and heavy. Like blades of grass on a frosty morning. Like I was smelling and hearing and seeing combined in a single sense. My eyes were long poles full of light. My heart thrummed within my chest like Sonofa climbing the canyon. Every cell in my blood skittered like ants on a sidewalk; the seeping cut below my eye closed up *snap* and the aching pain departed from my ribs and arm. I was strong as an aurochs and wise as Granma. Sneaky and funny as Mister Brown, bold and crazy as you, Dammit. And I knew I could do just about anything. I heard the cousins talking as if they stood next to me, even though they were fifty yards away. I tasted their words on my tongue, and they were wild thyme and hot iron.

Mister Bay turned and looked straight at me. His eyes rolled me like a seed between his thumb and finger. Plant me, tend me for years, watch me grow big.

When I finally crawled out of the earth — you understand, Dammit, Mister Bay didn't push me into the dirt there under the prairie, it was some other place I fell — he wasn't watching me no more. He had his arm around Mister Brown, and they were looking at the sky.

"Get me a bucket," he said. "I'll clean up."

"Lord! You need a river."

"Fine. Here," said Mister Bay. The aurochs parted, the meadow caved into itself, and a brook — lit by starlight, because the cloud had disappeared — came chuckling over stones past me through a little dry canal towards them.

"I'll be darned," said Mister Brown and there was awe even in his voice.

Mister Bay stepped knee-deep into his river and started to splash himself. "Hey ladies," said Mister Bay to the sky. "It's me down here."

"Ya better HOPE they can't smell good. Heh."

I pulled out Penny's page and threw it on the ground where the robe had been. *He likes girls, he can have it.*

The robe shook me like a rat in a dog's mouth and I fell to the bottom of Mister Bay's stream. I won't tell you what mad voices I heard down there, but it wasn't good. They wanted me to listen to them about *Acuere*, and I did not want to. I choked, crawled onto the rough grass, and lay, gasping, on my back.

The sky was a black lake. Bright dust-devils swirled towards me like the silt storm that rises after the passing of a great fish.

I had to look away. Mister Brown and Mister Bay were figures silhouetted against the night sky — grass waving at their backs, their feet in the new-made river — pointing.

I looked back into the sky, to where they pointed.

Whoo. Probably shouldn't a done that, Dammit, but I don't regret it. It sucked the air out of my chest. All them women. I looked away faster than a squirrel can scoot up a tree. You ever seen a whole star? Not just the part of her that shines—but the whole of her?

It was right then that I saw things clear and made the turn. I knew I been looking at women all wrong. Looking at the reflection off the water instead of the water, herself. A woman is deeper than a river, stronger too, and more wise, if you are willing to look. I suppose even bitches might be that way, Dammit. I'm sad I never asked you about that. The aurochs shook their horns at me for gazing up too long, like old women shooing a sight-seeing boy at a water hole. Can't be helped. Woowee. Them Starwomen so wild, and not afraid of it. Wise and strong and beautiful in all the right bits. With gravity in braids intertwined. And yet, just girls in a river talking to each other.

They laughed and pointed at me and said I was too young for them but that someday I would meet them and when I did, they would help.

Then I had a notion, like two rivers dropping out of the mountains and finding each other, surprised, when the hill disappears between them.

I did not need a penny to wink.

I *did* need Penny's page.

I picked it off the ground and shook the dust from its wrinkled skin. I closed my eyes, felt the robe on my shoulders, felt it open new senses in me.

I smelled the little river chuckling at my feet, the aurochs, the lingering throat-clenching unwashed man or animal or whatever it was that was Mister Bay, and the meat-stick smell of Mister Brown. Smelled the dirt, the grass, the nip of cold air coming down from the stars, and the tinge from Mister Bay's lightning cloud that reminded me of MK when he's mad. Heard them Starwomen laughing as if they were strides away, not galaxies. Felt the weight of Mister Bay's nasty-smelling robe on my shoulders and winked like I knew what I was doing. And I guess I did. *Of rivers and the chained canyons free, A winding restless spirit I will be.*

A very small circle opened at my elbow.

I crawled through when it opened wider, crumpled Penny's page into a ball, and stuck it in the hole as it closed behind me.

Chapter 37

Rivers and Robes

A wave of surges caught my feet. The gravity-river ripped sideways at my arms and legs; my lungs imploded.

I'm alone on the front of the raft holding the rope between my legs like I'm riding a bull. It is noon in high summer, I'm facing upstream where the river comes from, and my sixteen-year-old body—muscles and big hands and long hair sweeping in the wind – feels strong, free. I look behind me. A green slick leads to a yawning ledge; I can't see the drop. The oars bang against the oarlocks, catch in the current, rip off.

The raft spins, slides down a long slope towards a wave that blocks out the sun.

It is a concrete wall of water.

The boat buckles, I go flying. The river strangles me, then vomits me up and I break the surface, take a shuddering breath, open my eyes. And see a ponderosa laying across half the river, branches high. This means there are branches underwater too.

Dad said this one time, "Only two ways, Jackass: swim over it and grab a branch and climb out; or take the biggest breath, dive deep, pray to the river gods — a hare's chance among wolves — she curls you in a pillow of white water, pushes you down under the churn to pop out the other side."

I don't do either, Dammit. I hesitate.

A muscled arm of the current rips me down. My back scrapes the bottom and I scream – and tear my throat. Water enters my lungs. I'm pinned against a massive branch, pushed backwards. My head touches my thighs, my backbone snaps. There is no sound now but the current through the branches of my lungs. And a faraway grinding: my shattered vertebrae.

My skin rots, pale flesh trails away like fishing line in the current. I hear them mad voices calling to me, and this time, I cannot get out.

Something warm wraps me in its embrace. I feel a strength I've never known, feel myself drawn from the deeps of Her wildness. My head smacks off a hard floor, I see spangly lights.

I rose to my knees in the cloying smell of lilies in Ms. Swan's throne room. I'm not drowning underwater. *Flaming bag a nuts.* Mister Brown was right, the Big Ones make their own rivers, and I got sucked in. I pulled the dripping robe close.

Ms. Swan came from the darkness behind the black throne. One fleshy arm held Granma's shoulder — whose eyes were clenched tight like she thought she'd turn to stone if she opened them — and the other fleshy arm clenched the blind, grey-haired woman by the neck. I mean, my Momma. *Where was Penny?*

Ms. Swan was crying.

I knew Her true name because of the robe—but I won't say it here. You know what happens when we say Their names. A twelve-foot tall, violet ember woman of tears, surrounded by fires burning from the outside-in. She wore nothing but a shapeless white dress checkered with purple flowers.

And She was chubby. Mister Bay's robe let me see all the way, and it was the last thing I expected: Folds of gleaming ivory skin rippled over Her curves within the flames. She was exactly as Porter might describe, *flowers strikingly irregular, often spurred, inflated lip with petaloids like flames.* Simply, Dammit: She looked like a wild orchid, with petals like purple fire rising and pouring into a white center-lip. She was consumed with sadness that ate at Her like pine beetles gnawing the heart of a tree.

"You heard Our call," She said in a voice too deep for any woman.

The fingernail in my chest crawled around like a mouse in a grain bag.

Granma and my Momma looked like children compared to her. My Momma clawed her chest slowly and screamed in silence like a banshee with red streaming eyes looking to a hidden sun.

With Mister Bay's robe on me, I heard her never-ending scream:

You know when a spirit takes you over, they call it 'possession?' This was opposite. My Momma, dispossessed from herself. Do you know the sound of someone completely alone, Dammit? The worst part was that her self knew it. There are many of us inside, our peculiar human issue. To be cleft from our selves — to have a self split, kidnapped, taken from the others — is the greatest horror. Something you dogs don't face. Why wouldn't I claw out my heart?

I saw all of this in my Momma because of the robe. And a tiny creature of muck and water, and more I won't say here. To be true, Dammit, I had one moment — a breath that I could not take — an instant, to see everything I just told you. I gasped as if drowning, darkness pushed my eyes. My hand closed around Pop's rough, cold file in my pocket.

I took a shuddering breath.

Then Ms. Swan spoke directly at me — a word of command — and I almost broke in half. 10,000 suns poured from Her: "No-one SEES me THIS WAY and LIVES."

Violet fire spiderwebs blazed from Her hands against the floor. I felt nothing.

When the flames subsided, She looked stunned.

"I know Thee goddess." My voice was loud, and I startled myself. "I know how hard You give love, though love gives nothing back."

Ms. Swan trapped the women with a single arm and raised the other high. My Momma's fingers scratched the goddess's alabaster arms but left no marks.

Of course, I was thinking of The Riverside. I saw Shakesbear's page that described Ms. Swan clear as day. The words came out of me free and easy, as if I read them that morning on the porch, so I said,

"More thirst for drink than she for this good turn.
Her help she sees, but help she cannot get,
She bathes in water, yet her fire must burn."

Purple fire — again, it looked like cobwebs connecting and breaking apart — danced from Ms. Swan's fingers. But, instead of joining into a great web above Her head, they tore one another apart, falling in thick, smoldering clots to the floor. Her eyes glowed molten violet.

"TODAY YOU DIE," she said.

I felt my heart open, like a land of rivers and canyons; my voice rough and loud. "Die? None of YOU die." The words — so long behind a dam — were a whitewater wave: "You keep going and going, on and on and on. Hurting us."

Granma's eyes opened wide.

"Long ago You cursed love," I said. "Because of your loss, You cursed love to be fickle and broke us all. Who quits a perfect job?"

My voice rose. " *'Sorrow on love hereafter shall attend,'* You said. *'Find sweet beginning, but unsavory end.'* Now, look at You. The sorrow You cast is rebound and drives You mad."

Ms. Swan's eyes were frothing seas. Fire throbbed in her temples.

"Why did you feed the monster? WHY?" I shouted.

"You think we KNOW why?" She screamed. "We know nothing!" Centuries of fear in her voice. "Microbes. You — YOU! — know more than us. Insects. You have a *WHEN.* We have nothing. We're brimmed with power, stuck in this mirrored pond, waiting for someone to blow the dam." Her great voice shook with rage. "We have no when."

"A pond with no outlet," I said, "breeds a stinking creature."

Her eyes flashed violet fire.

"But this pond is pierced," I said, "and already refreshing." As I said it, I knew it was true. Then, ancient words spooled from the reel of my tongue like fishing line:

"So is your natal curse of love ...
Which in sorrow for Adonis thou cast free,
That which thou cast upon the earth,
Forsooth, hath cast itself on thee."

"HOW DARE YOU!" Folds of fat under Her chin shook. Violet fire fell on me.

I felt nothing.

The robe cast silver fire upon Her like a firehose on a cat.

She screamed, Her dress burning and sticking to her skin folds. Strangely, Granma and my Momma were untouched.

"Don't feel so good, huh?" I said.

Ms. Swan stumbled but still held Granma and Momma.

"You have betrayed us," I said. I saw Big Jim in my mind's eye, large as a house with slithering fangs. "Left without Your protection, every woman, every child, every animal in this town is tortured, abused and...WORSE."

Ms. Swan looked around as if She was lost in a forest and the wolves were coming.

Then Granma found her voice. "Clayton, help us!"

Ms. Swan shrunk from twelve feet tall to normal woman and collapsed. The flames around her subsided, and she was like any other stout girl in a shapeless white dress crying on the stairs.

A voice like a current vibrating at the bottom of a wild river had woken in me. From a place I did not know I spoke quietly, "Your rule is twisted. *This day will have blood, they say; blood will have blood.*"

Ms. Swan's hands fell, purple cobwebs sparking, rejoining and breaking, smearing the floor with effluent. Granma ran to me dragging my Momma. I wrapped my arms around Granma and felt my Momma twist slowly in her arms.

Hope rushed through my heart. I had an idea.

"If you will give me back my Momma AND my Granma, I'll give you this robe." My voice shook. "You, only You, can DO it. Give my Momma back."

Ms. Swan beckoned weakly behind her, and MK came out of the darkness.

He walked down the stairs shaking his head with that stupid grin. "Romes, Romes. I told you I could not help myself; I had a job to do." He sat down next to Ms. Swan on the stairs. "I am bound by the very words of my vow. To serve the ruler of this town."

"Give me back my Momma," I said to him. "In you. She's in you."

"Yes, ruler," he said obediently, then his face twisted, "Nah, she's in your arms." It was a nasty grin. "You don't have much time. If you want to help Penny," he said. "Which one do you want to help? Your ma or your girl? Can't have both."

It was right about then, Dammit, I reckoned whatever friendship we had was gone. He was on some trajectory, and I reckon he sucked me into it. Four years. All the jokes and pranks—lies. He had just asked me to choose between my Momma and Penny.

I hated him and said the first thing that came to mind. "Yes, I can."

MK's black eyes flashed. "Or what?" he said.

The door opened behind me, in walked Big Jim, turning sideways to push his shoulders through the doorway. He had grown larger. His hand encircled Doc's neck.

Doc's half-wolf face was battered, dripping blood, his jaw broken. His left arm drug on the floor behind him.

I remembered Big Jim loved that move: sneak up behind a guy, grab his arm, twist until it breaks.

Chapter 38

The Ruler of Junction City

"Mmm boy, now you see," said Big Jim.

And I did. I saw him fully as he was, revealed by the robe. Fungus grey as death writhed under Big Jim's rotting skin. Mandibles lashed from his mouth, two segmented tapeworms with writhing fangs of their own. His eyes were bigger, glowing orbs of refracted smaller lenses drawing all light to themselves.

MK took my Momma from me and went back to the stairs next to Ms. Swan.

Big Jim pointed at my Momma, a claw that dripped pus-like effluent. "She's mine, *click click* Death Messenger." Its eyes were a thousand dead candles. "Boy, I put your father out of his misery. Mmm then I took his heart." The tapeworms in his mouth writhed. "With the heart comes the wife. She's mine by the ancient law. Mine. Give her to me Death Messenger."

MK shook his head and held her close.

Big Jim snickered *click click*. "Why don't you tell the boy what you did?"

"I don't know what you're talking about," MK's face twisted. "I have no memory of this."

"Search your people, you'll see the deed. And the boy's father. He's in you." Big Jim's voice rose. "Why did you find the boy? Fool! The father in you—what remains of his shredded soul, mmm? – the father sent you."

"You lie!" cried MK squeezing my Momma close. "We're friends, Clay and me!"

"Who else would steal that fool Bergmann from himself, leave him muttering wild in the broad sunlight?" Big Jim cackled and sheared his jaws. "Stumbling and scratching his chest to get it out? Who, I ask you?"

Big Jim threw Doc to the floor. "I gave that Convenor mercy. I smote him through the heart. I finished the job you couldn't." Big Jim played with his mustache. "That's what I do, mmm? I finish. I took his heart from his gaping chest. Which, as you know by all that is bound by the ancient laws of battle, makes him my servant, all that is his becomes mine, allows me to keep the boy's mother as concubine. And mmm." The tapeworms slithered out and fondled his mustache. "Mmm."

"I'll tear you!" cried Granma, swinging wildly, and I grabbed her.

"If only Rose-Marie could see you," Big Jim tapped his head. "Too bad, even if she was in her right mind she could not see." He threw every word at us like spears. He was enjoying the revelations. "She blinded her own eyes when she found her husband dead and knew she was mine. Mmm. I loved that bit. Make someone choose to hurt themselves — the best part."

Doc — half wolf-beast and somehow half man — whined behind Big Jim, clawing the floor.

"Shut up fool," Big Jim said.

Doc mumbled, *"I met a young girl, she gave me a rainbow."*

Big Jim raised a clawed hand. "Give me my woman, Death Messenger." Black ropes of veins twisted through his sinews like ribbed snakes. And more: his eyes grew wide, something stirred on his back. I knew this creature. As a child, I had seen the husk of a dragonfly by the slough, its body-casing left behind when it tore through its back. He was changing. The robe let me see it all. I could see through his casing. I saw what was coming.

"I will give you this robe," I said to Ms. Swan, "for my Momma and my Granma. I vow it."

She smiled weakly and I felt her nail in my chest like a hot knife. "He doesn't love me anymore."

"He does," I said. "He still loves you."

"You promised me," said MK to her. "You made a vow. You promised to help."

Big Jim *clicked* and stepped back in confusion.

"So be it," said Ms. Swan. "Anything to beat him." She leaned, exhausted, against MK's leg and reached up. "A worthy wager, and your vow I will see. Now. I see your Momma," said Ms. Swan. With a long finger, Ms. Swan drew a glistening stream from MK's chest. Like sucking the snot from the nose of a baby. He screamed. The stream flowed from him and down into my Momma in his arms, and suddenly she was there – alive, and herself. MK let her go, and she stood swaying on the stairs.

My Momma looked around with wild blind eyes at far corners of the ceiling and gasped for air. She muttered, "Clay, Clay."

Ms. Swan said very quietly — but her voice filled the room like incense — "Now. YOU give me my lover's robe."

MK held his face, muttering to himself like a crazy person. In the stream of incomprehensible words, I heard distinctly, softly, "Don't do it Clay."

"Rose-Marie, we're here!" Granma yelled.

My Momma stumbled towards Granma's voice, tripped, and fell down the stairs. I lifted her and looked in her eyes. No longer red and streaming, filled with hope. Brown like the pelt of a seal, brown like mine but covered in a film. Blind and staring right through me. Her short grey hair matted in sweat against her forehead. Long, care-worn creases ran from her eyes and mouth. She looked older than Granma.

But there was more. The robe helped me see: a wild creature, with leaping joy for waves and deep dives and sunlight through water and all things hidden that must be revealed. The smell of the sea was on her breath, and I knew her for who she was. My Momma.

"Clayton, where is Clayton?" Her hands fumbled with my face.

The words came from my mouth in a rush: "*We two alone will sing like birds in the cage, when thou dost ask my blessing I'll kneel down and ask of thee forgiveness.*"

"Who are you?" She exclaimed. "Where is my son?"

I realized my voice was deep and rough. Not the boy she left in our river four years ago. I said, "*Of rivers and the chain-ed canyons free...*"

She started, as if struck by a sword.

"*... A winding restless spirit I will be,*" I said.

The smell of the sea swirled around me as tears streamed from her eyes.

"Baby Grizz."

"Momma, I'm right here." I lifted her up, light as a bird, and wrapped her in my arms. She wept, rubbed my face, and exclaimed how big I had become. She was much smaller than I remembered. Like holding a chickadee.

"Oh son, I'm sorry. I'm so sorry."

"I see that pelt you wear, boy," said Big Jim. "You will give it to me of your free will or I will break this beast, mmm?" and he reached down and squeezed Doc's throat until he screamed.

MK said, "Don't do it, Clay." He sounded exhausted. "Don't do it, take them and go. I've got this. Forgive me, I took your father. I did not remember. Your dad was the strongest thing I could tap into. To take the edge off."

"You stay out of this," said Big Jim. His voice trembled and I wondered if he was afraid.

I could barely stand. The robe was a world on my shoulders. My Momma, breathing shallow, passed out from shock. She was alive — tired but alive. I could see ALL of her selves back together, as if I was looking through a silver translucent curtain at a table where they sat facing one another with little knowing smiles and telling her that she was OK now. Something scrabbled under the table, but not before I saw its claws. It did not want me to see it.

I hugged my Momma and I looked at Ms. Swan expecting to see anger and power. Instead, I saw Ms. Swan, elbows on her knees, hands on her face, a girl crying on the stairs. She, the nurture and wellspring of love—bereft.

I let the robe slip from my shoulder to the ground.

I tried to pick it up to give to Ms. Swan, but my fingers could barely grasp the thick hairs. It was heavy as a boulder.

"*I would not — on the rack of this rough world — stretch you any longer,*" I said to Ms. Swan. For a single moment, I still saw the real person. Ancient as days and young as the first blade in Spring. Haunted by eons of service to love and making love and giving love away. Haunted by desperate centuries running from it. She was crying, like a small girl lost in the woods.

Big Jim chuckled *click click*. He picked up the robe and shook it like a blanket. "You thought She was strong enough to take it? Now? In Her mmm condition? Cursed by you?"

MK stepped towards him.

Big Jim said, "You touch me I'll crush your last shred of hope, mmm? Stand down!"

MK, with a strange look on his face — as if dazzled by the sun — stepped back.

Granma ran her hand through her short hair and sighed. Then she said something under her breath as if to herself. "Go on then, Lina. Jesus Christ, you know She needs it." She left me and walked up the stairs and knelt before Ms. Swan. Granma touched Ms. Swan's chin gently.

Violet flames ran up Granma's forearm.

Granma said in a wondering voice, "Why, you're one of my babies, you're one of my own children."

For a single moment something seemed to pass between them. Then, Ms. Swan jumped like a rattler and glared. She filled with fire and rose to her great height. The lost girl was gone. Beauty fell on me in waves. Fire edged her gigantic frame and rolled quietly, flickering purple, along the lengths of her fingers. Her eyes flared and Ms. Swan said proudly, "I am no one's child, I am offspring of the progenitor, the froth of the seas and the raging waves"

Granma backed down the stairs quicker than a gopher jumps in a hole, bumped into my chest.

My hand found the file in my pocket. I pulled it out. I'm not sure what I was going to do. I held it up in front of me, like I did with the blade Junior knocked away. I knew whatever happened next — when Big Jim put the robe over his shoulders — was not going to be good.

Big Jim was in his own world. Chuckling to himself, shearing those jaws, shaking out the robe.

Ms. Swan lifted both hands high in the air and screamed, then cast a wave of purple fire on all of us. It hit the file, the fire split two ways, crashed against the walls and ate the curtains hungrily. I felt nothing.

Granma did a shimmy and shadow-boxed the air, "Fuck yeah!"

I wrapped my left arm around my Momma and raised my right hand as high as it would go — pointed the file at the hidden stars — and tried to wink. It felt useless, I had no penny in my pocket, the cold iron was no weapon.

MK shook himself from head to tail; like you, Dammit, when you've come in from the rain. He looked dazed and stared stupidly at the incense-smoke that writhed around the floor. I reckon getting someone sucked out of you can mess with your head.

Big Jim grinned like a fat toad. *Click Click.* "Your mother is mine, boy." He reached out and put a big hand on my Momma.

He shouldn't a done that.

I stuck the file in his eye and yellow cream squirted and bounced off the wall.

He screamed, let go of my Momma, and fell on his knees.

I pulled the file out. Bugs from his yellow eye-juice crawled up my arm. The pus from his eye stunk like an outhouse. I flipped the squeaking bugs onto the floor and crunched them under my boot.

I was going to shove the file into his other eyeball, still shining and rolling with a thousand lenses, but he pulled the robe around his shoulders and then, Dammit:

All hell broke loose.

I heard Granma whisper, "Oh shit, oh shit, oh shit. Flaming bag a nuts. Oh shit."

Big Jim started growing, and the first thing that happened was his eyeball popped back into place like there was an extra one hiding in his head.

I spoke, trying to stay brave: "*The valiant taste death but once....*"

Big Jim interrupted me. "Shut up."

He wiped eye-juice from his jaw, grinned and pinched a creature that crawled from his face between his thumb and finger. It squeaked and popped. "A real mmm comedian? '*Cowards die many times?'* I knew that bitch before he was famous." He paused and relished the tableau. Each of us frozen in place, waiting to be crushed. "Conscience makes cowards, boy, that's why I don't have one."

It was right about then — when I pretty much thought it was over, Dammit — that I learned how tough Doc really was. While we were fighting over the robe, he'd slowly crawled towards Big Jim.

Doc grabbed Big Jim's leg. "Fly, Stonefly!"

Big Jim tried to kick him off, but Doc wrapped his arms around the leg like he was caught in a twister and the leg was a tree.

Big Jim grabbed the handle of his cane and pulled out a three-foot silver blade, narrow as a ribbon. Instead of pointing it at Doc, he pointed it at Ms. Swan. "Come to me, fire. Mmm." Purple fire came out of her and ran down the blade.

Ms. Swan yelled and collapsed.

Big Jim made a *thunk* like a giant egg inside him cracked open. He sucked fire up like a sponge. The whole room went black as the inside of a cave.

Then, only one sound.

Click Click.

Purple flames ran up the blade. Like lightning in the middle of a thunderhead. The smoldering curtains caught fire. The whole room smoked and seemed to breathe along with Big Jim. The sword glowed violet.

I shoved the file in my pocket and pulled Granma and my Momma close.

Big Jim stretched his shoulders and raised the smoking sword. Something popped out under the robe on his back, a knobby growth that began to open like fractal mirrors and spread out behind his head.

"Fly...." Doc moaned again; his face pressed to the floor.

Big Jim switched his grip on the hilt, so the blade pointed down. He stepped on Doc's head and ground it into the floor. Then he centered the glowing point of the sword over Doc's eye. He placed his other hand over the pommel and drove the sword in. The eye sizzled like butter under a hot knife.

Doc let out a deep sigh, and his fists opened into long-fingered hands – fingers with ragged claws on their tips that spasmed and then lay still.

Big Jim pulled the smoking blade out of Doc's head like a poker from a grate. It made a scraping sound.

I felt MK's hand on my arm, cold as a stone.

He said, "He's the ruler of Junction City now. I've got one moment before he realizes I'm his to command. Time to fly, Romes."

For once I was not mad about him calling me Romes. I held onto Granma and my Momma. MK grabbed my neck, and we were gone.

Chapter 39

A Penny's Worth

It was MK's voice, but I could not see him or feel him.

Just his voice chanting a long-forgotten song like a scared child. Dammit, I'm telling you — a child singing softly to himself, so he doesn't start screaming:

"Farewell happy Fields
Where Joy forever dwells: Hail horrors, hail
Infernal world, and thou..."

There are no gravity currents here from the Big Ones.

With Mister Brown — when we winked — I felt like I stayed myself the whole way and it was quick. With MK, it's like you're a salmon jumping straight up through a waterfall, going where you've always known you should go against the stream. But the water freezes and blows you into a million bits. The bits are taken by a giant hand and squeezed into a ball of ice, and the ball of ice — you — is squirreled away inside a pitch-black cavern.

A black so black that it is not the absence of light. It is the presence of black. A thick and velvet black like water that goes on forever around you.

With that lonely voice singing quietly to itself.

Then, you hear the others. Under his melody, a harmony of uncountable thousands. Every voice trying to describe how black feels. Each singing to itself, completely alone. A crowd stuck in a black cave with no way out, and no way in to each other. Every voice and every song alone on the edge of hysteria.

Thump-thump, thump-thump. A far-away drum in a jungle.

You realize you are stuck in his resonating soul and the thump is your heart. You think that you will not find the rest of your bits and pieces, and you will die here listening to these voices telling their memories to themselves so they don't forget who they are.

You know something else: like children singing in a dark forest, they are already lost. You start to wonder if you are one of the voices. Then, you *know* you are one of them, Dammit.

Because you hear yourself.

Bruise turn green, Cut turn scar,
Mister nut-man and the bay,
Breaking bones and holey jars,
Hurt won't hurt always.

Funny thing is that my song felt like it was a harmony to the melody MK was singing far above. And his melody was drawing me deeper some place where I could help him, but at what cost?

I went back to old Sonnet 146:

Poor soul, the center of my earth,
Why dost thou pine within and suffer dearth?

A toneless voice spoke next to me. "Hey Jackass. Your head's so far up Shakespeare's ass he can taste you."

"Dad?"

"Fuck no! Guess again."

It was a lighter voice than Dad's. Thinner and quicker.

"Here's a clue. You keep losing my book. When you have it, you don't read it. When you read it, you don't get it. You prefer the company of a fuckin dog and a good-for-nothing, dad-joke-telling, midget-librarian to me. You like kissing me. But you prefer that goddess and probably my sister too."

"Penny!"

"Jackass."

"That's what Dad calls me."

"I know, nerd. I learned it from what's left of your dad, who seems to think you'll avenge him."

"Where is he?"

"It's not like that in here. There is no 'where.' Just what is left of people's memories and desires holding on for their own reasons, getting culty with their sing-song chants. I hate it."

"What's 'culty?'"

"Being a coward ass — but doing it because you're in a group."

"The chanting. It's horrible."

"At least now we'll be together forever," she said. If her windless voice could sound any drier, it would have blown away. She said, "Clayton and Penny, sitting in a tree. Kay-eye-ess-ess-eye-en-jee. Exactly what I *always* fucking wanted." Same old Penny. Sarcastic, quicker and smarter than anyone.

I said, "I want to be with you forever. I'm not going anywhere."

"Of course you're not, jackass. You can't go anywhere in here."

"I mean I'm gonna stick with you no matter what."

"Don't. Just don't. After all your silence when we were out there?"

"Where are you?"

"Here. We can't touch obviously; all I am is a wad of my memories and a few leftover desires that refuse out of pure spite to let go. I think the more anger you have, the longer you last in here. Hence your Dad still hanging around. A big ol' wad of gum stuck to MK's soul."

"We got to get you back into your self."

"God knows where THAT is now."

"Penny, I got so much to tell you."

"Whatever it is — I already know. I was trying to tell you about Rose-Marie all along. Your mom and me are family for all we've been through together. She saved me from my bat-shit crazy uncle who worked for Big Jim, hid me when he came looking, and took care of me for weeks right before Big Jim killed your dad. They were going to bring me back to your precious home-place after the meeting with the Nisoi because I had nowhere else to go, but then all hell broke loose and this murdering-bastard-creature who we're stuck inside blew up the detente between the powers by taking your dad's soul or whatever it is that he takes, then Big Jim stabbed him in the heart, and the rest is fuckin history. *Which you would have known if you'd paid attention.* I knew about your mom, you just wouldn't listen to me, and I couldn't tell you straight because of Junior, and all his... his shitty friends...."

She paused.

The silence went on for a long time with only the moaning songs weaving through the nothingness that was MK's inner-well.

Then she said, "Let's just say me and Junior have a score to settle. And now I can't settle it. Because of you."

"That's why the book?"

"Yeah Jackass, the book. My secret journal."

"Oh." It all crashed over me. Why, Dammit? Why can't they just give you an inventory?

"Yeah — *'Owe'* is right. I owe your Mother. I was trying to find a way to get her out. So, I went back in. Pretended to like them, to want them, so I could get to her. The cure, worse than the disease. Then you showed up. Ugh. YOU.... I did not know that you were so.... you."

"Guess what?" I said. "We saved my Momma — Granma Lina and me and MK, we did it Penny!" It was like something opened in me and I couldn't stop: "But Big Jim killed Doc with his sword. He sucked purple fire out of Ms. Swan. She's chubby you know? Weird and strange, but still lovely as the early morning. Chunky as a bear after a summer eating grubs and huckleberries. I told Her why things are bad. And why She is so sad. I don't remember exactly what I said — it was a gush! I popped Big Jim's eye with

Granpa's file and stuff came out — bugs and goop and yellow pus — but then he stole Ms. Swan's fire and stole the robe and healed his eyeball and got bigger. And started to grow wings. And I wish Dammit was there 'cause I reckon we could have done it together. Beat him. But I couldn't do it."

"He can't be beat." A whisper I almost couldn't hear.

"He has the buffalo robe I stole from Mister Bay," I said.

"What?!"

"I took it from them when they were looking at the stars in Mister Brown's *When* where the aurochs roam, and I took your page...."

She interrupted, "Now you're lying."

I shook my invisible head. "You won't believe it, but I seen women stars swimming, and a wild thing who smells like he was there at the beginning of the world, and talked to aurochs (they're like an old version of buffalo), and they seem like they can understand me like Dammit but they don't talk, and..."

"I don't care about buffalo, or star women! Or Mister Brown — who talks big talk about flipping pennies but can't seem to help this one. Big Jim has the robe?" Somehow, her flat voice became even flatter. "We're finished. How'd you get away?"

"MK didn't take me like he does other people, he grabbed us in his arms, and we left there like a salmon jumping up a waterfall."

"So, you are you? Not like me or the others in here?"

"Yeah, I reckon. But I don't know about Granma and my Momma."

"Then you got a shot. A long shot. You need to get MK's attention and remind him that he's holding all of you in here and that he needs to let you go."

"How?"

"Don't worry, I know where to find him Jackass. He and I have been going round and round on some things."

I tried to grab her, but my nothing arms could not feel the nothing that was her.

I said as firmly as I could, "I'm NOT going without you. Tell him that. I'm staying here unless he lets you go."

"Bless your heart, Jackass."

Her voice faded and — even though there was no way in this world without air — it rang with a tone I'd grown to love. "I'm sure *that'll* really convince him."

Then she was gone.

The whispers began again. Their chant — hysterical, lonely — filled the nothingness around me with jumbled songs, hymns and nursery rhymes.

Chapter 40

The Whippers Are In Love

Was it ten thousand years?

Was it ten minutes?

It felt like both.

It felt right to join them, singing in the Black. Truth is, Dammit, the longer I was there the more I wanted to stay. Like Penny said, it was a little culty.

And once you go in a little way with all them voices, you go in all the way.

The other truth was harder to admit: hope in me was dying as surely as I was an uprooted wild mountain violet — *Gentiana Detonsa,* Porter called them — ripped out of the earth and thrown in a black cave far from the sun.

There was one moment when I thought I heard Dad. It couldn't have been him because it was someone apologizing. A voice without timbre, a zephyr blowing across velvet strings:

"It was my fault. I was too proud to ask for help, I went into battle alone. I'm sorry son. Promise me, you won't do that."

"Do what?" I wondered but kept singing.

I tried to sort out if the voice was Dad. How a glob of memories and desires could say it's sorry, and if this was a different Dad than the one who appeared to me under the streetlight. I started to wonder if I was now a different version of Clay, and if there were so many of me, which is the one that – like a forged blade in a fire—is truest?

"*The whippers are in love, Romes.*"

"Aagh!" I yelled and jumped, and of course, couldn't do it with an unfeeling body. It was MK and his voice was not a disembodied whisper like Penny's or any of the other thousand whispers singing around me. He sounded real, living, powerful. Speaking with real lungs. About six feet to my left.

I felt if I reached out, I would touch him. I shuddered. "Not creepy at all," I said. "Just sneak up and start talking. I should have known."

"*Ve'achron.*"

Silence from me.

"You're supposed to say '*Alafar Yaqum.*'"

"Fuck you, as Granma would say."

"C'mon Romes. Name it — the play, the passage, the person. *Whippers are in love.*"

"You're joking. Now?"

"Do you NOT remember my vow? I vowed! To serve the ruler of this town. We don't have much time. How long before Big Jim figures it out?"

It hit me like a wave the size of a house. *I'm an idiot. Why did I drop the robe on the floor?*

"Breathe," he said. "I know you wish you kept the robe, but I'm not sure you could have. You're human and humans can't wear it for long. Breathe. You're not like the others in here. If you don't breathe, you die. You're still connected to your body. Breathe."

So, I did, Dammit. And felt better right away.

"Name it," said MK again, "the play, the passage, the person."

"I'm not playing."

"It's all I got, Romes. Please." He sounded so sad, I almost felt pity. But then I remembered what he done to my Dad.

"I hate you, and I am going to track you down and kill you."

"Romes! I just saved your ungrateful ass."

"I wouldn't call being stuck forever in your black heart 'being saved.'"

"That's not where we are, by the way."

"I'd jab my way out of here if I could feel the file in my pocket."

"C'mon. *The whippers are in love.* Name it."

"It's barely a quote," I said. "Second: I'm never, EVER playing the TRG with you — EVER again."

"What if I give you the full quote?"

I could almost feel him grinning.

"*Love is merely a madness and deserves a whip for madmen.*" He stopped, and I thought he was done. Then he said, "*None of us is whipped and cured by the whipping — because the whippers are in love too.*"

Silence from me, Dammit, because — I mean why not? I'm good at it.

"Do you love her, Clayton Solomon Bergmann?"

"I've not been cured by any whipping. Unless getting my butt kicked by everyone counts."

"That's not what it's about and you know it." Then he asked again: "Do you love her?"

"Love who?"

"You know who. Do you love Penny?"

"I don't know what love is."

"You do. Does a fire in your heart rise at the thought of her? Do you feel most like yourself and so much more when she's around? Do you know in your bones that she is good for you? Do you have no control over your mind or feelings? Is she an ever-fixed mark, that looks on tempests and never shakes? Do you love nothing in the world so well as her? Do you feel like you're going mad?"

"*Forty thousand brothers could not, with all their quantity of love, make up my love.* Yes."

"Then you love her."

"Piss on you."

"You know what? Penny asked me to let you go."

What the hell, Dammit.

"Do you know she came to me and asked for you to be released? No one here has ever had the will power to find me, let alone talk to me like that. Until Penny. They're less than souls, they're wisps of memory stuck on my sole. I am god here, as I am of all interior lands. She found me. And *told* me to let you go. Didn't ask. Told."

Silence from me, Dammit — I mean, what do you say?

"Do you know how hard it is for anyone to find me in here? And no one talks to me like that. That is the baddest-ass woman I have ever met. And I know Jael, Cleopatra, Medea, Qin, Joan, Catherine, Rani, Amelia and a whole bunch of others unknown to history or you."

By the sound of his voice, I could tell MK was in awe.

"Do you know what it does to me if I let anyone — *anyone* — go? Except for one small loophole which has never been tested, I'm closed as a concrete grave. I tried to let someone go once. At the very beginning. I let a very small very young child go free. And it almost killed me. I'm already weak after She pulled your mother out. If I did it on my own — let someone go — I would wander, a wraith stripped of strength, for years."

"I thought that was you already."

"Ah, joker's back! There are levels of hell, dumbass. Just because you're already there doesn't mean you can't go lower."

"I don't care."

"You should care. If we measure love by measure, that girl just lifted the world on her shoulders to get you out."

"If you're gonna do anything, I want her to go free and not me," I said. As soon as I said it, I knew that is what I wanted more than anything. *More than anything*, Dammit.

There was a long pause. Silence. No response from MK.

"Her, not me," I said, thinking he had not heard me. "Let her go free."

Thousands of voices murmured through the velvet-black like mourners, close to hysteria, filled with ancient words, snatches of childhood songs, and nursery rhymes.

"Are you there?" I asked.

Then MK spoke, and his tone was like nothing I ever heard, Dammit. "That's what I was waiting for. The loophole." He did not sound triumphant. He sounded the opposite. He said it again. "Remember me, my friend. That's what I was waiting for. Adieu, adieu. Just remember, *The whippers are in love.*"

Then, everything changed.

The ball of ice that was me melted in a shower of rain falling upwards. You realize that you're not a salmon jumping up a long waterfall. You are the water, simply and only yourself. And the last thing about you that feels like a salmon are your feet flopping around in your shoes. The ground under your sole tilts like a wave over your head. Then the soul under the ground tilts and rises.

You find yourself standing in a forest looking at a clear blue sky. A small crow on a branch watches you curiously. He turns his head side to side, his eyes glaring blue. Hands, feet, head, heart — all of you is back to all of you.

It feels like the first morning on the first day of your life, and you breathe in and it tastes like home.

The next thing I saw was you, Dammit.

And let me tell you: nose up, ears back, piss on you! I wanted to holler! The inside of my head was clear, and the outside too: No more voices singing all around. I only had a handful of voices now. The ones I know well, that sit at that table and have squabbles. Until the quietest one, the one who's been through fire and water, shuts them up and says, "love one another."

And then, I was even more thankful.

I saw my Granma Lina and my Momma. And — wonder of wonders. I heard Penny in her real, living, sarcastic, mad-as-hell voice say, "What the fuck am I doing here, tied-up naked?

Chapter 41

The Very Best Bad Dog

I am in the eye of this storm, and it just got quiet, Dammit. So, now I will tell the rest.

But first, I watch the lightning—in foul and pestilential congregation of vapors, as Shakesbear would say—and feel the *CRACK* in my chest; like the purple-web lightning that ran down Ms. Swan's fingers, except these *CRACKS* are all around me, inside me, and I am the fingertip of this storm. *Ah now, let not this enterprise of great pitch and moment be turned awry in current; to arm against this sea of troubles, oh, let me not lose the name of action!*

I do not want to tell this next part. (Mister Brown told me about it because him and Mister Bay were watching through a wink-circle. More about that later.) But it's all I got. My stupid inventories and telling the story to you:

When I jumped through the circle in the wall of the police station with Mister Brown, you were outside having no luck trying to sneak in. You love a good dust-up and were hoppin' mad you weren't a part of it.

Cry havoc let slip the dogs of war.

The door crashed open, out came Big Jim with Doc clutched by the neck, Cress and Penny in the other arm. Junior pulled up in the black truck and they took off. You chased as fast as you could, but they hit the outskirts of Junction City and sped up.

You guessed where they were going — all the dogs in town knew — and you smelled your way there. I remember you said to me once, "nothing smells sharp as blood on the ground."

By the time you got there, things had gone from bad to nasty-bad, as Mister Brown says.

The truck was gone, and so were Big Jim and Doc. The girls lay naked, red-eyed staring at the sun; screaming in silence with their scrabbling hands tied behind their backs. Junior, his back turned to you, dragged Cress to the statue. Before you could do anything, he plunged his knife into her chest. He took the blood in big handfuls and wiped the stone statue. He didn't take out her heart. He just pierced her with his hunting knife and let the blood bubble out over the white skin under her breasts. Then he flipped the knife in his hand and disemboweled her from rib to pelvis. The glade filled with the smell of guts.

And blood.

"*Blood*," said that vibrating Voice that covered the lowest of low registers and the highest of highs. "*Blood, blood, blood. I am well pleased.*"

Cress lay serene as if she had gone somewhere else. Which, in a way, she was. One time, when you and I were talking on Granma's porch about dying, you said, "the river calls to the rain, and it is the ocean who answers." At the time I didn't know what you were talking about, Dammit, so I just went along with it and figured you were doing your usual "I'm-smarter-than-I-look-and-tell-riddles" act. Now I'm calling bullshit, like Granma says. *Gone to that happy resting place in the sky?* Blah blah blah. What a load of crap. When someone is gone, they're just gone. And they leave a hole that no one can fill. And if you fall in that hole and stay there missing them, you too are gone. That is it.

Junior was sobbing and begging. Rubbing the statue with Cress's blood. Over and over, up and down. Pleading, invoking some garbled Name, yelling: *"Enter! Enter!"* Then he stopped and cried, *"TAKE THIS!"* and did something so horrible, even Mister Brown had to stop a moment before he could tell me this part: Junior pulled down his jeans, grabbed what was hanging there, and gelded himself with one stroke.

The scream he gave was like the earth split open.

Mister Brown had to look away.

When he looked back, Junior was weeping uncontrollably and rubbing something in his left hand over the statue. Blood ran from his crotch down his legs.

Mister Brown told me later that him and Mister Bay heard that Voice, deep and high, like a man and woman talking together at once. The ground heaved, the statue cracked through the middle, and the sky went black.

And the Voice said, *"Granted."*

Mister Brown told me that him and Mister Bay never heard a Voice like that before, or knew who it was, "and lil bruh, like I told you before, I know everyone.

"I am coming," said the Voice.

Then," said Mister Brown, "almost as if someone ordered it, the mirror-circle we were trying to get through to you snapped shut. We had to find another way."

It was exactly at that moment that we — MK, Granma, my Momma, and me — arrived, and Penny said, *"What the fucking shit am I doing, here tied-up naked?"*

MK stumbled and leaned against a tree rubbing his eyes.

You saw me, howled with joy, and almost ran into a tree. A beautiful sight, you laughing to see me. A sight to make any boy smile. Even here, in a glade full of blood and death.

Junior screamed, pulled up his jeans, picked up the knife and came at you.

The good bit is we landed behind Junior. You saw us, he did not.

The bad bit is that something had worked — whether it was the rabbit earlier, or Cress's blood, or his own gelding, or all three. *Someone* heard him and granted his wish. He grew bigger. Not as big as Big Jim, but definitely changing like him. His neck throbbed with purple veins. His wuttus was like a brick in his pants.

I went from feeling like a hundred awesome versions of myself —seeing Penny, you, Granma and my Momma, my feet on solid ground, eyes that could see color — to shitting myself, as Granma says.

Well, that's *not exactly* what she said.

"OhmyFUCK he's GOTaknife!"

Junior stopped chasing you around the clearing and turned. The big hunting knife dripped Cress's blood – or his own—and he wiped it on his jeans.

He pointed the knife. "Big chief. Wherever you came from, I'm glad you're here. I'm gonna scalp you, tear off all that long hair. Then, I'm gonna chop off your balls and make you my bitch."

"You're the bitch," said Penny, "you sawed off your own balls, fuckhead."

Then she noticed Cress.

Cress's bleeding pale torn-open body.

Penny screamed and rolled to her knees; hands still bound.

Before this, I was so happy to see you and Penny—Cress lying there bloody and dead didn't sink in right away. Not like it hit Penny. Something about the jump from Ms. Swan's throne-room and through MK had also made Momma and Granma loopy as hell.

Except Granma never forgets how to cuss. "You fucking FUCK!" she yelled. "What did you do?!"

"Cressida," Penny called softly, as if they were playing hide and seek, trying to be quiet.

"Ha!" Junior laughed. "You promised I'd never see you cry. All I had to do was gut your sister... like a fish." His voice got quiet, and he pointed the knife at me again. "This fucking mute is next." His face shone with triumph, "I paid the price!" His bulging eyes looked like they would burst, and he waved the knife in a great circle. "A New One comes!" Slobber fell from his lips, and he whispered. "*The Mastress.*"

The statue split in quarters *CRACK* like a rifle shot and fell apart smoking.

"You," Junior turned to MK. "You, Death Messenger, don't need to get involved."

MK, looking weary beyond comprehension, still managed to stand shakily at the edge of the clearing with his arms crossed. Then he smiled that creepy smile. The smile that no one would ever want to see. And most never do. The smile that, if you *do* see it, you wish he would come and take your soul to make the smile be over. He was obviously fully visible to everyone. He was just himself, no other voices, no one else talking through his mouth.

Just MK: hungry as death, here for breakfast. The dark blue of his eyes drained away into black. "*Ve'achron,*" he said.

I whispered, without thinking, "*Alafar yaqum.*"

Junior stepped backwards.

"I see that you see ME, friend," said MK. "That is a horrible gift."

Junior closed his eyes and shuddered.

Behind him, Penny sobbed quietly. Snot bubbles and tears and dirt covered her face. She started to roll across the dry pine needles behind Junior towards Cress.

You ran to her to chew the ropes free.

Granma stamped the ground, not giving an inch. She wrapped her arm around my Momma.

Junior opened his eyes but did not move. He seemed mesmerized.

MK walked toward him slowly, like a cat towards a mouse.

My Momma got her hand in mine and squeezed it hard. Her milky eyes shone. "Where's the water, Clay? Anytime you're in trouble, get to your water."

"Ain't no water, Momma," I said.

She started to cry.

Granma said, "I see him now, Clayton, ohgodalmighty. I see him, your friend."

"Don't touch me," yelled Junior waving the knife. "Stay away!"

MK stopped in front of Junior and popped his knuckles.

I knew he was going to come through and finally be the friend and the familiar my Momma always said I would get. He knocked the blade from Junior's hand like it was a twig, and — bending over him, growing somehow to twice his size with his white-straw hair falling all around Junior's head and shoulders — wrapped his arms around Junior and hugged him close, whispering in his ear.

Junior struggled weakly. He whimpered one word, over and over. I could barely hear him.

"Dad. Dad. Dad. Dad. Dad. Dad."

MK let him go and stepped back.

Junior fell to his knees. He shook his head like a bull coming out of a river and opened his squinty eyes. They were shrewd. Wide as a turd, reeking with the stink of what he had done to Cress. "Haw," he smiled at MK, then began to draw lines in the dirt with the tip of the knife. "My dad is ruler of this town. He won't let you do it."

MK looked around the glade like he was a dog, and someone said "COME!"

"It didn't work and I'm sorry," MK said to me. "The boss calls. I'm so very tired. So very, very tired. I'm terribly sorry, Romes." He turned and stepped into — somewhere. A shadowy, winged doorway.

You gnawed the ropes at Penny's back.

I saw that Junior had drawn a fence, or a wall, in the dirt. He began to chuckle as he rose. He flipped the knife and caught it with one hand and laughed again. "Haw. Fucker's my dad's bitch now."

You gnawed furiously, her hands came free.

"My dad could beat your dad up. Any day," said Junior. "Oh wait. He already did." He waved a hand. "Yay, dad."

I pushed Granma and my Momma behind me and made them sit on a downed tree trunk.

"Don't worry Rose-Marie — Clay's big now," Granma said, and grabbed my Momma. "Stronger than Beaumont or George ever was."

My Momma smiled a big smile. It was right then that I really saw her, knew it was her without a doubt. That smile gave her away.

But when Granma said, "George," my Momma closed her wild white-eyes in her scarred face and began to weep.

"George, oh George," she said. "Does Clay know?" Then she turned to Granma: "No water? There's no water here?"

"No water. Gonna have ta do it himself."

So, I did. At least I tried to.

Up until now, Dammit, I have said little about Junior because, like his name, he was a shadow. I mean, when he beat me up behind school with his buddies he was real enough. But I reckon I did not "see him—see him." Like you see someone you love, or someone whose guts you hate; he was just an A-hole who hurt Penny, and then hurt me. That is all. Sometimes we don't see someone because we don't care.

This time, I really saw him. Maybe it was because I worn the robe. Maybe it was because I just been inside MK. Maybe it was that I first saw you in that glade, felt the rush of joy — like my head was about to blow open — because I was so happy. You and your half-cocked grin, that damn scar-torn ear, and how you looked back at me with your shining golden eyes. I knew you were really seeing me and loving me; so, I started seeing things more clearly too. Like you told me once, seeing someone — really seeing them — is smelling, and hearing, *and* seeing. All, at the same time.

Junior was a beast locked in a hot cage; smell of piss in the fur and spongy flesh pushed against bars. Eating shreds of flesh, shitting in a corner. Then someone opens the cage. His eyes were needles. He licked the blade of the hunting knife, and his pants ripped down the back and sides. I knew that he was not Junior no more. His bloody white underwear held a bulge so big it seemed out of place.

I felt Granpa's file in my pocket, but it did not make me feel better. The fear was acid eating my stomach.

When you know — no matter what you do — you will get your ass kicked.

Junior leaped and the knife passed my ear, missing me because I leaned back at the last moment. His charge took him past me, so I kicked him in the butt, and he smashed his face into a tree. He shook blood from his nose, roared, sounding like a cougar screaming.

I wished right then that I had the shotgun and that I could put him down like I did that cougar in the snow.

That is when you jumped him.

Cry havoc let slip the dogs of war!

I reckon you would have got his throat, but your shoulder was bad from getting kicked by Big Jim outside the jail, so you missed, and caught the side of his face.

He screamed and swatted you with the knife, catching your belly in a long, ripping slice that drew blood and bowels. He fell to his knees, dropped the knife, and grabbed you with both hands — hands grown wide and thick like tires — and tried to pull you off his face.

But you locked in.

Ears back, piss on you, locked in. I could see your jaw working slowly. Closing like a vice being turned. Like a steel bear trap with a spring that would not let go. Junior's wet eyeball squirted out of your jaws.

Junior screamed and pulled so hard I thought your head would pop off but instead it was the side of his face that ripped off in your mouth, and Junior hurled you against a tree where you bounced and lay broken.

"Dammit, NO!" Granma yelled.

You had Junior's ear and jaw and part of his eye and most of the hair from that side of his face in your mouth. You lay still, unmoving.

Junior crawled on his hands and knees towards me, snuffling big clots of blood from his nose. The side of his face hung in shreds. He wiped his face with a dirty hand, and it came away muddy with blood and snot and pieces of jaw.

He roared, a mad animal, and lunged.

I hesitated. I just stood there.

I should have been full of rage that my Momma was in danger, that my Granma was in danger, that a girl I loved was in danger. That my best friend, my dog, was hurt bad and in danger. But I there was no anger. Just coldness, like everything jammed up tight in winter. Dammit, I cannot quiet down my voices that argue about what to do. Of course, most of them want to run away. A few want to hide, one wanted to swim but there was no water, one wanted to fight (but I'm not sure if that was me or just Dad talking or maybe even you, Dammit). And one just wants to raise his hand to the storming sky and tell a story. I heard the quietest one say, "RISE!" But my feet would not listen.

I held my hands out in front of me and closed my eyes.

Junior screamed so loud the rusting train rails in the glade rang like tuning forks.

I opened my eyes and saw Granma at the beginning of a second swing at Junior's face with a tree branch.

Penny knelt behind Junior, eyes blazing, his knife in her hand.

Junior stumbled back from Granma's blow — and into Penny's up-thrust knife. As he turned, the branch stuck in his eye socket and ripped out what remained of his eye. Blood gouted from his socket, running down his ripped face.

Penny leaped to her feet and her second stab came from the side—into his liver.

Junior went *OOF* and fell on his back.

Then, there were too many stabs to count as she bestraddled him, naked, shining in blood, driving in the knife. She was somewhere far away. I saw it in her face like the sun. A face blazing in the distance, fierce with heat, when the early-morning clouds part. An arm rising over and over, thin as a razor, fast as the strike of a rattler.

I turned my face away, I could not tell what I hated more: the blood bubbling from his wounds, the ragged glare in Junior's eye, or the zeal on her face.

I walked to you, Dammit, and knelt beside you.

Your eyes opened and you spat out a mouthful of Junior and your tail thumped. "Piss on you."

"Poop on you," I said. "He got you pretty good."

"No shit, Sherlock."

"You're a sonofa bitch," I said. "But you're the only sonofa bitch I got." My voice choked. "You know the hurt, you know how deep it is, in the bones."

"Bone," you said softly. "Could use one right now." You grinned but it looked like a snarl. "Fetch me one, catfucker."

There was blood everywhere. "Dammit! You're gonna make it, you HAVE to make it you... you old bastard," I said.

"A scratch," you said. Your body spasmed. You tried to lick my face, but fell back. "No bastard," you said. "Stray. That's what I am. Until Granma." Your guts pressed out, purple, through the ragged tear. "Until you," you said.

I smelled the scent of blood mixed with offal. Rain fell on your face in fat drops from the sky. Then I realized it was me.

"You know this old dog loves a kid? More'n any grey wolf loves the chase, the leap, and the blood."

"One hell of a day," I said.

"Every day a dog day," you grinned at your stupid joke, and the pain made it look like a snarl again. "You and me, kid. Twist of fate."

"Fuck fate," I said. "You're gonna make it."

Your front leg twisted at an unnatural angle. Blood dripped from your ears. "Nope," you said. "The river calls to the rain, and the ocean answers."

"You still got energy for *that* riddle?" I said. "You're gonna be fine."

"Proverbs, jackass," you winced.

I laid my hand on your head. "I don't care anymore." Your head was warm. "Tell all the proverbs you want. Stay," I said. "Don't go."

"I'm a bad dog," you grinned. "I don't stay. Hargh."

"Shutup," I said. "I need you." I pushed my face into your black neck. "You fucking dog, you sonofa bitch. Stay."

"Nope," you said. "The river calls.... Look at me, kid."

I raised my head and looked you in the eye. That golden, blood-tinged eye.

"The river calls," you said. "And the ocean..."—your eyes flashed, *"NOSE UP!"*

I turned too late.

Junior — exploding with the force he called into himself with Cress's blood — had pulled the knife from his side and, with it in his hand, dripping blood from many wounds, had been crawling towards me the whole time you and I were talking.

I saw Penny kneeling in a trance looking at her bloody hands, then Junior rose above me so close that he blocked my view. I could smell his rotten breath. I could see the shattered eye socket. He raised up on one knee with the knife high and plunged it at my chest.

Dammit, you moved faster than any animal I ever seen. Faster than that cougar I killed so long ago. So fast. A flash of black tail and chest-blaze and face-scars and paws and shining teeth. I don't know how you did it with a broken leg and your bowels coming out, but you did, Dammit. You did.

The knife fell with full force—the sound of an axe meeting a tree — deep into your chest.

But not before you slashed his throat with your fangs.

Junior landed on his back with you on top.

He lay still, bleeding out like a bull-elk. God knows how he still had blood after Penny's stabs; it seeped past your jaws and his neck to pool across the ground. Your back legs twitched. Blood streamed past the knife lodged in your chest. Junior's hand slowly opened, releasing the handle, and you slid off his chest.

You winked. "Bigger dog," you whispered. "Harder fall."

No boy could ever deserve that look. A look so full of love.

"Release the dog of war," you said. "Time to go." One last wink. "Stay, kid." You took a shallow breath, shuddered, groping for air that you could not find. "The river calls to the rain...." you said.

I finished it for you, holding your face in my hands. "And the ocean answers."

Then your whole body shook like you were getting ready to sleep for the night, you snarled towards a corner of the glade as if to fight the very shade of death coming for you, said *"Piss on you,"* – to me, to it, to everything and everyone you'd ever fought for and against—and were gone.

What was left was a pile of bones in a robe of fur the color of midnight. And the leftover smell of courage like the tinge of smoke from a wildfire.

I pulled you away from Junior— he was sickly pale, seemed deader than a pile of lumber — cradled you in my arms, shoved my face into your thick mane, and howled.

Sonofa came roaring through the trees, knocked down a sapling in a cloud of dust and Sophie jumped out in a wisp of a pink nightgown with her white hair shining, a silver circle around the moon.

She said, in her bird-voice: "The nice man with the long flaxen hair told me to come get you. We gotta go!"

Chapter 42

Penny Flips

I laid you carefully on Sonofa's truck-bed, light as a fern-leaf. You stunk pretty bad, and I did what I could with Penny's leftover ropes to carefully tie your gut closed. I realized I was focusing on little actions, one after the other, so I would not have to think.

Sophie pulled a pink nightgown from the backseat and tugged it over Penny's head. Then she held her and whispered softly,

"Now no matter, child, the name:
Sorrow's springs are the same."

Blood soaked through the nightgown in spots like Penny was melting. Her arms crossed over her chest, and she rubbed them like she was cold, her eyes stared at some far-away place. "No, Cress!" she whispered. "No."

Me and Granma picked Cress up from the stained ground (The stench from her was horrid; we tied her closed, like we did with you, with the ropes that bound her hands) and laid her in the truck-bed next to you.

Penny walked across the glade and started kicking Junior's body very slowly and very hard. She did not stop until I pulled her away.

I turned to go make sure Junior was really dead, but my Momma grabbed me and in a whisper of a voice said, "Clayton, we MUST go now. NOW."

"You gotta rest, Rose-Marie," said Granma.

I wrapped my arms around my Momma, and she held me fiercely. "Your dad wrote a letter to you and didn't tell me what it was about," she said, struggling to speak clearly, "he just said it was important." She felt my face with her hands. "He had it with him when he died. Find him, you'll find that letter."

After a moment, she wasn't holding me no more. I was holding her.

She clutched her stomach, groaned, and slumped in my arms, unconscious.

"Clayton, get movin'," said Granma. "She needs salt-water."

I picked up my Momma who felt light as a shadow and laid her on the back seat. Sophie and Granma got in the front; Penny and I climbed in the truck-bed.

Penny held Cress's dead fingers for a while, but they were already cold, so she let go and held onto me. Penny was freezing to the touch. Granma pushed Sophie out of the driver's seat across the bench to the passenger side (*"Good God, Sophie, how'd your feet touch the pedals?"*) and drove us back to town.

Penny didn't push me away. The blood on her rubbed off on me.

You were not coming back, Dammit. Not like last time. There was no counting on MK to work some weird magic. He was serving Big Jim. I'm a jackass, but at least I can tell myself the truth. So, I made up my mind about two things: One, I was going to keep talking to you. I didn't give a damn. Like I told you at the beginning, Dammit, it's mostly for me since you been gone. But it's for you too. (Of course, I'm conflicted about all of this and try to make myself stop. Good luck with *that*, Clay.). Two, I was going to tell Penny how I felt about her.

By the time we got to Sophie's, Penny was done crying. I got a blanket, rolled you and Cress together (which did nothing to remove the stench) and laid you on the matted green shag-carpet of Sophie's living room. We argued, then lifted the two of you to the couch and covered your faces.

Then Penny pulled me down for a hungry kiss that almost made me black out. I had stars in my eyes when she pulled away. "Hey nerd, thanks for getting me out of the darkness," she said. "I owe you."

"I'm the one who owes you," I said. "You brought me back. *A chance that does redeem all sorrows that ever I have felt.*" As I said it, I thought to myself, how fitting you would remember that particular line.

Her eyes flashed. "Redeem all sorrows?" She hit me in the chest. "Redeem? You *asshole.*" Penny looked at her dead sister on the couch and her face crumpled. "You fixed Dammit's legs, why didn't you bring Cress back? I never got to tell her I was sorry."

I did not know what she was talking about. It was MK who helped you, Dammit. It was him who fixed your broken back.

She scratched my arms, her fingers red-stained claws. "*You!* You could have made her whole again. What's wrong with you?" Her face was a mask, she kept hitting me.

I held her away. How do you tell someone you're not what they think you are?

The anger drained from her face and the look she gave me was not anger, or care, or love. It was nothing I ever seen before. Even that one eye that looked sideways into my heart seemed to not care.

"Fuckit," she said. "I need to get out of this nightgown." She went in the back room.

While she was gone, Granma made us PB & J sandwiches on the counter by the sink.

My Momma woke up, gazed into nothingness with her white-hooded eyes, touched my face and kept saying, "Baby Grizz, the best kind of special." Every minute or so, she would groan and grab her belly in pain, so we talked my Momma into getting in the bathtub while Sophie poured handfuls of salt in the rising warm water. It was hard to believe this wrinkled, ancient woman was really her. My Momma squeezed my hand, leaned her iron-grey head against the edge of the tub, and fell asleep.

Penny came out of the back room and acted like nothing had happened between us.

The tension was a rope around my chest.

She wore a pair of Walter's over-size jeans cinched with a leather belt, a green pearl-buttoned shirt, and a pair of old boots. I'll tell you what, Dammit, Penny could make a garbage bag look good (Stop it, Clay, you got to stop talking to that dog). The shirt made the green in her eyes flash. I thought of those swallows in the canyon and wanted to go there with her.

"Come with me," Penny said.

We held hands on the creaking porch steps in the late-morning sun and ate our sandwiches.

"Your Momma needs the ocean, or she will die," said Penny. "She needs to go now."

I had not thought about this. I would give my right arm for a penny to squeeze and get some help from Mister Brown. I shuddered. Him and Mister Bay were probably hunting me down right now for stealing the robe.

"Pay attention, Jackass," she said.

I realized Dad must have worn off on Penny when she was in MK. I didn't mind. Anything that came out of Penny's mouth always sounded ten times better than anyone else.

"You're wandering again," said Penny. "We need you to come along." She sounded bitter. "Maybe you'll even figure out how to do that magic you did for Dammit's legs in time to help your mom. We can make it to the ocean in ten hours, maybe nine, no stopping."

The words came out of me easy and smooth (Penny always made me feel like I could talk). "Stay with me Penny, don't go," I said. "We can take my Momma to the homeplace. The river there, it will help her."

She stiffened and pulled her hand away.

I kept going. "You and me. Safe." The river rose up in me. Strong, ripping fast, stretched like a watery spine through the mountains. "Safe, at the homeplace with my Momma."

"Safe? There's nowhere safe anymore. Your mom saved my life," said Penny. "She gave herself up to Big Jim to try to save me. I owe her, OK?"

I looked at Penny, the words made sense, but I was far away. I felt the sun on my face, felt my feet find the path down to my river, felt my hand holding Penny's, and my other waving to my Momma sitting on the porch.

"Listen to me CS! I love Rose-Marie like she was my mom," Penny said. "Mine left a long time ago and was a bitch. Always chose her boyfriends over me. I have to help her."

Granma kicked open the screen door and handed us glasses of water. "What about that asshole who killed George?" Granma said. "Can't let Big Jim get away with it. This town is ROTTEN." She slapped her thigh. "My God. They're gonna blame Cress dyin' on me! We can't run off."

Through the door we heard Sophie sing, *"when will you ever, Peace, wild wood dove, shy wings shut, your round me roaming end, and under be my boughs?"*

"Sophelia, goddammit," Granma turned and went back inside, "get some clothes on!"

A bunny hopped from under a bush and started nibbling a dandelion a few feet from us.

Penny leaned back on her hands and watched the bunny. The stairs were narrow, our knees touched. "Your momma needs the ocean, Clay." Penny's eyes flashed, "Salt water's the only thing that will bring her back. Not a river in the middle of nowhere."

I did not answer her unasked question. It hung in the air.

The bunny started pooping on the lawn. It laid turds down, one by one; pebble-sized turds in a straight line. The bunny's eyes were wild in fear.

Penny kicked the rusty railing on the stairs with her foot. "Her breathing's ragged. She keeps falling asleep. She's barely conscious. Maybe she has a day. Maybe a week. She's been living on the bare hope that she would see you again." Penny smiled bitterly at the truth that my Momma would never see me again. "And now that she has.... She's letting go." Penny grabbed my shoulder. "We HAVE to get her to the ocean."

The bunny took off into the bushes like a hawk was after it. As plain and clear as writing on a blackboard, it's turds in tight letters spelled a message: "*Delayed. Squeeze a Penny.*"

Thanks Mister Brown. Glad you're OK and just delayed, I thought. I even smiled a little. I wasn't surprised anymore to see animals spelling messages in turds. What the hell kind of story am I in anyway, Dammit?

The kind of story where I talk to a dead dog.

"You think this is FUNNY, turds in a sentence on the lawn? Are you listening?" Penny shouted. "Do I have to ask it?" She drew a deep breath and finally asked: "Will you come with me?"

I knew we needed to help my Momma, but it was not the first thing on my mind. I mean, I knew already that I would say yes and that Penny and me were going to take Momma to the ocean, so I wasn't that bothered. I had something more important to say to Penny.

Why am I always off-track Dammit? All this time missing my Momma and now she was here and all I could think about was Penny mad as a hornet in that green pearl-button shirt. Pushing back her hair, her eyes flashing, full lips turned down frowning at me. Calling me a jackass. Which I was, Dammit. I was. Penny's way of talking in that scratchy voice. Penny's long fingers on her knees and how her eyes — both of them — saw right into my heart. Penny's curled lip when she said, "jackass," just like Dad.

I had thirty-seven different quotes from The Riverside to choose from. None of them were any good. I mean, Dammit, I reckon I looked at all of them in my head and none of them were good enough for her. When I spoke, it was the first time in my life — ever —that I sounded like my Granma *and* my Dad. Brief.

"I love you."

That is what I said, Dammit. With all the best lines about love in the world rolling around in my lump of a head I chose the dumbest.

She looked away, and I couldn't see her face, so I said it again, "I love you, Penny."

It was like I hit her with a two-by-four. When she spoke, it was careful. "You don't want me, I'm a second-hand piece of white trash, a lost fucking cause." Her mouth turned down. "I left something of me inside that Death Messenger anyway, and I'm not sure I'm getting it back. Stay as far the fuck away from me as you can."

"I love you, Penny. And I can't stop."

She said, *"I have no joy... It is too rash, too unadvised, too sudden, too like the lightning."*

Yeah, two can play that game I know. But I was not going to play it with her. I meant business, and I sworn off The Riverside.

So, I just looked at her.

Penny sighed and pushed her forelock back and her grey-green eyes looked deep into mine – well, one did and the other looked straight at my heart—and I thought for a moment she was going to change her mind.

"CS, understand. I'm your friend. I just needed a little help. I won't love you."

"Don't or won't?"

She said nothing — just looked across the street, past Sonofa, to the pile of ashes that used to be the house Pops built for Granma.

"Stay," I said. "Just stay and let me love you. I won't never love anyone else."

Ms. Swan's fingernail wiggled like a barbed fishhook in my chest. The lighter popped into a flame behind it. I remembered how my Momma used to say it to my Dad, and sometimes to me, so I said it to Penny: "You are special to me, the very best kind of special." That was all I had. But my whole self was in it.

She looked at me with that turned-down smile.

"That is THE lamest thing anyone's ever said to me," she said, but she was smiling. She picked a piece of grass off the steps and flicked it away. "You don't get it. I don't have love in me." Her voice turned bitter. "It was taken a long time ago." She got up, shook her head like she was shaking our conversation out, and put her hand on my shoulder. "You coming?"

She must have seen the look in my eye.

"Hey! Stop it, jackass!" She whispered, looking around, then rubbing my cheekbones. "We *have* to go. Don't cry."

The river had frozen all the way down in me and I was going to shatter into a million pieces. First you were gone, Dammit. Now Penny didn't love me and was leaving. I said — and as I said it, I got madder and madder—"What about holding hands? What about all the goddamn kissing?"

She shrugged, and for the first time, looked uncertain. "I kiss everyone," she said, her eyes grew distant. She turned and walked into the house.

The frozen river exploded. She didn't see me shaking in anger; the screen door slammed behind her.

I got up, went inside — still so mad I could barely see. Sophie was talking to herself in the mirror, combing out her long white hair. Granma was nowhere to be seen. I picked up my Momma who they'd changed into dry clothes, took her outside and laid her on the back seat.

Penny climbed in the driver's side and shut the door. "Trust me," she said, "we're better this way. Get in."

I wanted to break something. "I need Granma," I said. I even sounded almost normal. "I'll get her."

"Fuck Granma! She's probably buying a Fifth at Bill's Market. Maybe you didn't notice? Your Granma's a lush."

"I'm not going without my Granma," I said.

"Going gets tough, Lina gets drunk," Penny said, and started Sonafa in a crash and shudder and — like a bum in the rain begging for a dime — that goddamn singer started whining about bringing me misery.

My Momma curled up in the back like a sleeping kitten.

What was I supposed to do, Dammit? My hands trembled so bad I had to clasp them together like I was praying. No way I was going without Granma, my only family besides my Momma. Penny was bluffing. I reckoned two can play that game.

"You got to do what you got to do." My voice sounded cold and distant, "I got things to do here. Take care of her." I opened the door and kissed my Momma, but she did not move. "I love you Momma. I'll see you soon."

Penny banged on the steering-wheel. "Things to do? WHAT THINGS? Big Jim is going to CRUSH you. He's GOING TO KILL YOU if you stay here." Her eyes flashed and she looked more beautiful than the sun going down; a blazing ship through my tears dropping into the infinite waves of the mountains.

I just looked at Penny and loved her. But I was not going without Granma. I did not need to say more of anything. Also, and this is important, Dammit: I was sure that she would turn off the truck. I was sure that she was not really going.

"I'm not bluffing," she said. "Your choice. With or without you."

Truly, Dammit—I did not know it, then—this girl never bluffs. I thought if I gave her that look, she'd change her mind and stay.

I thought Penny would turn off the truck, walk around the front of Sonofa, stick those long fingers around the front of my belt, pull me down to her, and kiss me long and hard until I saw green like the fire in her eyes. I thought she'd kiss me until the lighter in my chest blew a hole through Pop's shirt. I thought we'd load everyone up in Sonofa — you too, Dammit — and high-tail it to the home place. I thought that my Momma would recover there in the river, why did she need the ocean? I wanted to dig a grave down by the river on that little bluff and lay you to rest surrounded by cliffs, flashing swallows, and giant orange and grey stoneflies rising from the river like winged pebbles into the sun. That's what I thought, so I didn't move. My mind must've wandered. What a jackass.

"You just STOOD there for ten seconds looking into nowhere," she said, revving the engine. The man on the radio sang something about friends disappearing. Penny's voice rose. "I'm SO glad you're present and paying attention." She backed up, smoke rose around Sonofa's tires. "Fuck you too," she said.

The engine revved like a storm.

She glared at me, grinding the gearshift. Then, she yelled over the radio, "JACKASS. I'll call you from the coast. I know Sophie's number."

Sonofa swerved away down the street, Penny's middle finger raised out the window, turned the corner and was gone.

Granma yelled from inside, "WAIT Penny!"

She came down the porch stairs and into the street, stamped her foot, threw her hat on the ground, put her hands on her hips and looked into the sky. "GodDAMMIT that girl is a PAIN IN THE ASS."

Sweat spread in stains under her arms. "Where's she goin'?"

Sophie came out of the trailer-house in a yellow sundress, "How you like this? I know, I know, I'm pretty. Wait for me." She tottered down the street like a flower-petal on a slow river.

"Sophie's goin' to get our wheels," Granma said. "Walter's piece-a-shit RV. Neighbor borrowed it last week. That's where I was. Getting the keys back. Was afraid Sophie would drive it in a ditch. Now I don't care."

Granma walked back to me and squeezed my shoulder. "That Penny."

Then she saw my face.

"Come inside, Clayton. She can take care of herself. And for damn sure, she'll take good care of Rose-Marie."

I didn't move. We watched Sophie go. It took her forever to disappear around the corner.

I looked down and saw my hands had torn the metal porch railing in two. Granma tried to pry the rusty steel from my fingers, but I would not let go. All I heard was that whining singer in Sonofa talking about bringing me misery.

"Come inside, Clayton. We got things to say to each other."

Chapter 43

Come Poor Jackself, I Do Advise

Inventory:

One girl, you love. In your head jackass, in real life she holds a grudge and left.

One dog, you talk to him. Also in your head jackass, in real life he's dead.

One Momma, found. And lost. Please be OK, Momma.

One Dad, dead. I wish you were here, Dad. You'd fix everything.

One friend, maybe familiar. Is he, though?

One Big Jim, enemy. Told me he was going to take everything from me.

One Granma, badass. Wraps her arms around me, tells me she loves me. Dammit, that last one is a total lie. Granma is NOT a hugger.

Inventory done.

Granma grasped my neck and said, "'*Your own heart let you more have pity on.*' Penny's gone, Clayton. Quit cryin'."

I did not understand what the hell she was saying – she sounded like Shakesbear, but I never heard that before – so I threw the broken railing on the lawn.

Her eyes burned blue fire. "I know you like Penny, son. Know you *loved* that dog. She's gone and he...." She choked, lit a cig, and took a long drag. Smoke and words came out together. "That dog in there loved you like his own flesh. But he is deader'n a door nail."

I shrugged. So what? What did that change about Penny not wanting me?

Granma dragged me in the house. The tangy smell of blood was like wading through high muddy water. The sheet had fallen from Cress's face and — though she looked more peaceful than she ever did alive — the room was full of death. It smelled like MK. Which is to say, like something was missing; a penumbra-tinged hole filled with the smell after lightning strikes.

Granma pulled back her shoulders. "Look. You got to brush off this thing with Penny. She's gone." She tapped my chest. "And Dammit," her voice got thick, "he's gone too. *My own heart let me more have pity on.*"

There was that line again.

"Gotta get this mess cleaned up." She rummaged through the cupboards. "And get our stories straight."

I folded my arms. I was so tired. Just hold on for a few more hours, Clay, I said to myself. The deal will be done. MK will be his own master. I was going to sit on the porch and wait for MK to be free and help me sort out this snarl. Then I was going to kill him. Out of nowhere I remembered what Dad said: "*.... only way to get to love is go through loco, Jackass.*"

Granma punched me in the chest. "Quit day-dreamin'!"

Something broke in me. "*True, I talk of dreams which are the children of an idle brain, begot of nothing but vain fantasy more inconstant than the wind,*" I said.

Granma bark-laughed like you, Dammit, lit another cig and said, "WELL. There he is. Talkin' and a course I can't understand."

"*This time, I dream things true,*" I said.

"Yeah, I know," she blew smoke at me. "Mister Brown does magic, right? Ms. Swan — that's what you call her — is not herself no more, right? Big Jim is turning into something else. Something with fangs and wings. And your bare-chest friend is a lying sonofabitch who isn't always in his right mind. Did I get it all?"

I was stunned, I had no words.

"Now let me tell you something." She poked me in the chest. "That long-haired hippie ain't your friend."

The look on my face made her laugh.

"HAH! Look at this cap. Pops gave it to me 'fore he died. I see 'em all when I wear it. All a them," she said, shaking her head. "All them crazies. All them powers. Hurting bad. Good Lord!" She took a drag. "You see 'em just like your ma, huh?"

I nodded.

"Godalmighty!" Her smile was wide and, somehow, also sad. "Well, she is right. You *are* the very best kind of special. Shoulda told you sooner."

I touched the faded blue ball cap in wonder, and she smacked my hand. "Yep. Sometimes Granmas know more'n you know. Sometimes Granmas got to hold their tongue. Got to outlast 'em, and out loco 'em. Patience!"

"Your... your cap is for seeing?" I asked. My tongue felt like a fish flopping in my mouth.

"All kinds a tools in this Convenor family," she said. "Pop's axe, see? Goddammit wish we still had 'er. That was a tool for choppin' trees AND keepin' peace. When he convened. They knew THAT axe could cut. Was no ordinary blade. Forged in the fire of an ancient lizard and cooled in the blood of a dying god. Oh, WHAT a thing that was. Now *Acuere's* gone forever."

She sighed. "Pop's cap, that's how he could see 'em. This." She pointed at the ragged, faded blue cap on her head. "This fabric was woven of the mane of the last colt that was born of the last of the Reyms. See. Here. How you think we survived inside your pasty friend?" She pointed at a strand of glimmering silver I'd never noticed that ran around the back. "Look, I got no time to START to tell you about the Reym. Just believe me — you're different, last of your kind, like the creature that grew this hair."

I tried to tell her *Acuere* was safe, but she cut me off.

"...And Pop's file you got in your pocket? So much to tell you about the job your Pops did, and I wished your Dad did that job too," her face crumpled. "But he's gone now. Gone!" She clenched her hands into fists, then came back to herself. "Stubborn as a mule and would not do it — but no time, Clayton, I got no time." She slapped her hands. "*WE GOT TO GO.*"

"I'm not going anywhere." My voice was thick. "I'm going to wait for MK."

She stamped her foot. "Never trust someone with that much pain who makes that many jokes. That fool may show you love — God knows if he can — he is a dozer with no steerin' wheel and no brakes." She opened Sophie's fridge and pulled out the box: "We need this before we leave."

I had forgotten Achille's heart.

She looked in the box. "Ech. Listen Clayton, somethin' about this heart — keep it. I seen your face after you dug it out. Like you knew something. You go to war—good to have a heart in your hand." Her nose wrinkled. "GOD that stinks!" She set the box on the counter.

We stood there looking at each other. Trying not to look at your body and Cress's on the couch, though the room smelled like a butchering shed.

"What are we going to do?" I pointed at Cress.

"Don't matter. What's done is done."

"I'm tired Granma. I'm so tired of nothing being what it's supposed to be. Of all the mirrors and all the curtains."

"No shit, Sherlock."

"Why does everyone I love — EVERYONE — get hurt or killed or leave me?" I finally asked her what I'd been waiting to ask for years: "Is it me?"

"Ain't you. Life happens," Granma said. "Love keeps us going."

"Why does it feel like I'm wading through high water?" Maybe for the first time ever, I told someone how I really felt. "Why does it feel like the light is dimming?" Then I asked the question, the one with the answer I already knew: "Am I bad luck?"

Granma's eyes sparked, "No, dammit! I forget you're just sixteen, Clayton. It's not about you."

"It IS me. Why does everyone I love end up dying?"

She put her warm, firm palm on my chest. "You wanna know what is what?" She pulled off Pop's cap and ran her hand through her short grey curls. "There is no answer. Not on this side. Not even with this hat. You look for clear, for the answer, you don't see the love." She put the cap back on her head. "We are what we look for. Clayton—you try too hard to hold on to the clear, you miss what makes us who we are. The human bit."

"I miss Dammit," I choked, and her face crumbled. I said, "He was a good dog."

"No," she said. "He was NOT a good dog. He was the very best bad dog I knew."

That is when I sat down, leaned against the couch, shoulder blades touching your body, and lost it. I did not think I had tears left. But I did.

I stared at the floor, and Granma stared at the ceiling.

After a long time, she smacked her hands on her hips, muttered something to herself that sounded like "help me do this right," and knelt down and grabbed my hands.

"Clayton," she pulled me to my feet. "You ARE the very best kind of special. To me. And it's not because of anything you do. It's because you're mine — I love you." She looked me in the eye and squeezed my hands. "It's just. You're stuck in someone else's story. Ain't your fault people you love, even dogs, keep dyin.'"

"I'm scared, Granma. SCARED. All I do is freeze. I know I should help, but I can't."

She patted my arm and lit another cig, smoked, and gazed out the window at the burnt ruin of the home Pops had built for her.

"Well, going to have to figure it out because if you don't figure it out — no one will," she said. "You think it's bad now? You're the last of this family." Her eyes twinkled. "You're one of a kind. No one left but you."

"You're left, Granma," I said.

"This ol' body got one last work a love, I reckon," she wiped her eyes. "But it ain't killin' Big Jim." She took a deep draw. "Things're changing. Always. And sometimes, things change into other things. Confusin' as hell. But if things change," she blew smoke at the ceiling, "it means there are things that do NOT." She pointed her cig at me. "Understand?"

I had no idea what she was talking about.

She rubbed your blood-matted ear. "Clayton, when you know what don't change you can look between the changes and find it there. Like breathin'. Everyone hears the words we say, no one hears the breath in your lungs between the words. But it's there. The breath that makes the words."

I must have looked confused.

"Look. It's why I'm not scared of you not talkin'. You're livin' in the breath. Which is just as real. Remember: Love never changes. Dyin's only one kind of change. Love is what lasts."

"Granma you sound like The Riverside."

"Ya mean that Shakesbear book them buttholes beat you with?"

"Now you sound like Dad."

"Where you think he got it, Sherlock," she winked at me, and took my hand.

"What if I can't do what Dad wants? What if I can't do what my Momma wants—take care of people?"

"Clayton, don't worry about them." She squeezed my hand. "Your Dad asking for revenge, that's not him, that's a dead man hurtin'. They lived their story, now you live yours."

"I can't, I'm stuck in theirs."

She rubbed her face. "You're right. But you don't have to let it make you afraid. Look, I got lots more to tell you. Where you come from. What our family is. Why it's us and not others." She wrinkled her nose and looked out the window again. "Just don't know where to start." Smoke curled in a line from her nose to the ceiling. She was quiet for so long I thought she had forgotten what we were talking about. Then she shrugged and looked at me with those eyes that seemed to bore right through me.

"Guess what?"

"What?" I said.

"You got other folks in you too. They make you who you are. And not just your Ma or Pa. You got your Pops. His strength. His whadyacallit? Conviction." Her eyes gazed deep in mine. Like she could see him in there. "He saw things clear, and he could follow through. I see it in you. You don't feel it right now. But you will. You got to talk to your feelings about what is real. Also," she said shyly, "you got me."

"You?"

Her face flushed. "You got my slow-burnin' fury. You got my love for animals. You got my love for people. I see it in you. I see how you look — each person — see 'em for who they are. Special. Lovely. You know what? It's a power of its own."

"It hurts."

"I KNOW. But Clayton," she shook my shoulders, "got to be friends with people too, not just dogs. AND you got to put a gov'nor on that rage. It will burn you to ashes — like I burnt my house." She lit another cig. "People're many selves, hard to love 'em all."

"Penny said she doesn't love me."

"Ah, that girl." Granma rubbed her face. "She don't love who she was without you, and can't cross the bridge to come back. We all got THAT problem." She patted my arm. "We GOT to go," she said. "But I got one last thing to say." Her eyes grew distant, remembering, and she tapped her cheek. "When I was little, before my Momma died, she used to sing to me. Like I sing to you — 'cept she sounded lovely, not like a chicken bock-bockin'. She'd be tired from the sickness and sit at the big window in the morning and sing to me. I still remember." She punched me, "Pay attention, Clayton!"

I was thinking about you, Dammit (not you on the couch like a curled shell). I was thinking about your eyes, and how they sparked. How your tail waved like a flag in battle. The very best bad dog.

Granma Lina closed her eyes and spoke in a sing-song voice:

"Soul, self; come poor Jackself, I do advise
You, jaded, let be; call off thoughts awhile.
Elsewhere; leave comfort root-room; let joy size
As God knows when to God knows what; whose smile
'S not wrung, see you...."

"Stop," I said. I felt like I was choking. The dead lay around us. Their bloody stares fixed on some lost memory, a *when* they could never go; their lips twisted in mockery of a smile they would never feel.

Granma pulled me close in a rib-cracking hug. "I'll never let you go."

"I'll never let you go either, Granma." I did not know Granma had poetry inside her like me.

"I'm not good as you," she grinned, "but I know a poem or two. Hell." She threw her cig in the sink and lit another. "Made up my mind. We're gonna run. Forget about stayin'. Fuck it. Big Jim owns the cops."

I hugged her back.

"We got to buy time," she said. "I'll take you back to the home place." She looked up at me, suddenly happy, as if making the decision to get out of Junction City lifted a weight. "No. This's what we'll do. We'll drive to Oregon. We'll find your Momma and your Penny—and THEN we'll hightail to the home place. How's that sound? We'll wait it out."

"I don't have a Penny," I said.

Granma reached out and rubbed my cheek with her thumb. "Don't you fear losin' love, and don't you fear death. He comes for everyone. Someday, someone will come for his ass."

Her face shone. It was as if Granma had taken a drink from a deep well and come back to herself. She started to sing the dark words of the old family lullaby Pops had taught her:

"Living words, wind and wave,
Comes the one who kills his blood.
Curse of death and open grave,
Vengeance mine and rolling flood.
Child of sadness, sings to save,
When all things new a-bud."

"Now I see it," she said. "Talkin' to you made me see it."

I realized in that moment I never really paid attention to Granma. I said to her as clearly as I could, looking in those shining blue eyes, "I'm sorry Granma Lina, I see you now."

And I really did. Her eyes were not mirrors anymore, they were windows. I saw deep within them a girl running in a meadow. A hidden meadow on the side of a mountain. I saw her open her arms by a mountain lake, surrounded by wildflowers and crags. She loved everything and everyone. I saw her — not for what she looked like — no, I saw her for who she really was. Not the belly and grey skin and yellow teeth. Not the age spots or the wrinkles that ran like canyons down her face. I saw her, Dammit, I really saw her.

She took a long draw on her cig, looking at me with eyes half-closed. "I see you too, you little shit," she said. "I seen you all along." She grinned. "If only you talked more yesterday. You sounded like my Beaumont, just now. Son," she reached out and wiped the water from my cheeks, "I don't need no hat to see your heart. You're a good boy. Mister talker." She blew smoke in my face and smiled so big the house filled with light. "My Clayton. Growin' up."

I took a deep breath, let it out slowly and felt my body relax.

A vision came over me: The two of us, in a rusty red truck. With Penny and my Momma in the back seat. Laughing, telling stories, driving down to the homeplace above the silver-flashing river, bumping down an old trail that twists like a bull snake on a hot rock.

MK said, from behind me, "*Marry, here's grace and a codpiece, that's a wise man and a fool.* Guess that one, it's touching—considering the tableaux." He chuckled and it sounded like ice breaking. "And by the way. That bit when you first started talking to her? Romeo and Juliet, Romes. To be exact, it's Mercutio. I'm up one. Also, her cap is special, for sure. Until it runs into me. It does nothing unless I say so. She can't hear me, or see me." He chuckled. That icy sound again. "Probably for the best."

Granma said, "Whatsamatter Clayton? You turned white as a sheet."

MK had been listening. Probably from the very beginning. He touched my shoulder, and his hand was cold iron. My body froze. This time it was not in my head. It was him. I could not move.

"Sorry Romes. This...." He paused. "Well." His voice was sad. "This will hurt. For both of us. Can't have you slowing things down."

Granma looked around wildly. "It's him? That no-good friend of yours!"

I wanted to say something. I could only, barely, move my eyes.

Her face went white.

I watched him walk behind her and turn to face me with his arms open wide. She was half his size and the blue cap shone against his pale-granite chest.

Her mouth set in a line, and she folded her arms against her chest. "Let 'im come. Not afraid."

"Romes, I'm sorry," said MK. "You know these vows get weird if you break them? Things start to back-fire, I could get hurt. We could all get hurt. Besides, she's old anyway. It's not like she has quality of life cleaning toilets for a buck, with no possessions, living in a friend's stinky, mouse-infested trailer-house." He grimaced. "That's neither here nor there."

I strained, but all I could move was my eyes, which felt like they were bleeding.

"You're welcome by the way," he said. "For releasing your Juliet. Penny wanted to be with you so badly I couldn't keep her."

A thrill ran through my body. The lighter popped in my chest hot as a flame. Had Penny been lying to me about her feelings for me?

"I have a message for you." MK cracked his knuckles uneasily. "Master says to remind you that he promised — and I quote, because he ordered me to repeat his exact words: '*When you least expect it, I will take everything from you.*' Master Sengrim summons you to Ranulf's cabin on the lake. Bring the maiden's heart and the axe. Or else."

He smiled bitterly. "I don't know what you're going to do about finding a maiden's heart Romes. That's a doozy. I know she's gone. I got no control over this."

It felt like my feet were fastened with spikes to the floor.

"I've been ordered specifically to do something else, and you are not going to like it." He shook his long waves over his shoulders. "And not like the others. There is a place inside with no voices."

Granma looked where I was looking over her shoulder and whispered fiercely, "Where is he? Where is he? I don't see 'im."

MK kept going like she was not there. "Take solace, Clay. She was old. This will be quicker than the usual way old people die — gasping in their excrement with no one to hold them." His eyes were black pools. "I will even let her say goodbye."

Granma Lina squeezed her arms. She held the cig between her lips, encircled by a cloud of smoke, and watched me like a hawk.

MK's face behind her jutted through the smoke like an immovable crag.

She crunched the cig under her foot and lit another.

I thought of Porter then, a perfect description of my Granma's eyes: "*Flowers often showy, perfect, the corolla of united petals, deep blue are their aspect.*"

Her eye-sockets seemed to glow beneath the cap, sparking like sapphires. Granma Lina smiled and opened her arms. Her body mimicked the shadow behind her. "Clayton, my lovely boy," she said, her eyes wild as *Gentiana Detonsa*.

Yes, I have seen them, Dammit, the wild alpine gentians that flower in late-summer after the snow is gone by the lakes in the high country. Deep blue is their aspect, and when you find them you find the source.

Her arms were wide. "Clayton, I love you so. So much." It was the little girl running up the meadow happy as a swallow chasing the wind. "Remember, Clayton," she said. "Bein' angry's OK. Bein' vengeful — THAT is not. The only one who can fix this mess is YOU." Her eyes blazed. "So, ya better fuckin do it." She pulled the blue cap from her head and tossed it at my feet, *"My own heart let me more have pity on."*

MK stepped forward until her head touched his chest.

She did not move.

My horrified eyes must have told her the truth.

She looked behind her, then looked at me. "You, boy," — and she pointed at my chest with her cig, smiled a crooked smile, and tears ran down through the coulees on her aged face — "You, boy, are special to me. The very BEST kind of special."

Every part of me strained. It felt as if hot blood poured from my eyes and down my face.

"Do NOT be afraid," she said.

MK wrapped his arms gently around her and dropped his mouth to her ear.

She shivered and raised her arms to enfold his head, as if she sensed his grasp.

"You no-account-bum, you lazy-good-for-nothin'-soul-stealin' hobo." She sounded like she was telling him she loved him as she tucked him in for the night. "I KNOW you still got good in you. I KNOW you want what's right." She leaned back in his arms. "You keep an eye out for my Clayton," she said. "You don't take care of him — I will hunt you down. I swear to God I'll find a way."

He raised his head and looked at me. "I will care for him, as best I can."

"I know WHAT you are," she said. "You take care of my boy."

"I cannot help myself," he said, so softly I could barely hear.

Maybe Granma Lina heard? All I know is she smiled that gentle, dangerous smile. Big as a meadow full of wildflowers at noon day. "Son, I'm already waiting for you under the healing tree. You do right. When it's your time to pass — you come find me. I'll be here."

MK's pale hair fell around her in a curtain.

Her arms dropped to her sides; the burning cig fell from her hand to the floor. Then her hands crawled like crabs up her belly, scratching their way to her heart.

MK stepped backwards into a doorway the size and shape of his silhouette — and was gone.

I leapt forward, stomped out the cigarette, and caught her as she fell.

Sophelia's empty tub had a ring of brown half-way up the inside and was still warm from my Momma's bath. I closed the door — the room was barely larger than a closet — and knelt with Granma in my arms. I took her cigarette pack and Pop's lighter which I slid into my shirt-pocket. Then I laid her fully clothed in the tub. I turned on the warm water and let it run. She did not move. Other than her hands, which began to tear ribbons of flesh through her shirt, damp with her blood. They weren't her hands no more.

I did not look at her eyes. I knew what I would see.

As the water filled the tub, I looked at my hands. I have long fingers, tendons like ropes. I never noticed how big they were, how her hands disappeared in mine. I made myself look at each finger and each thumb on its own.

Then the tub was full.

I pushed on her shoulders. Her hands clawed her chest like rats. The water swirled and settled into a curtain-less window over her face. I gazed through its rippled pane at the shuck of a river bug slowly curling into itself. What lay there made sounds like a wind passing through the chambers of an empty shell.

So, I sang to her. The same song I grown to hate because it was the only one she sang to me.

"*Bruise turn green, Cut turn scar,*
Mister nut-man and the bay,
Breaking bones and holey jars,
Hurt won't hurt always."

I made up more words because it took a long time for the hands to stop scratching. My Granma, she is strong. I sung about her dog. You would've fought for her, Dammit, if you were there. And I sung about her son. I sung about her daughter-in-law. And her tough-as-nails husband, her best friend. Whose axe lay hid under a blue spruce down the street, here in Junction City.

I sung about how good a cig tastes, and I sung about the hug of an old friend, and I sung about a table full of strays, and I sung about all the lost puppies she'd found and raised, and I sung about what it's like to see your grandson for the very first time.

I sung about all the nasty and the hard things in this world, and yes, Dammit, I found my voice. And I sung me a song of vengeance.

I felt Sophie's trailer-house shake. I sung, and sung, and sung. Until the water grew still.

Then, I took my hands away. And quit singing.

I wanted to say, "I love you Granma. I love you — all the way there and back again. You are the very best kind of special."

But she was already gone there and not coming back.

Chapter 44

I Cut My Hair, Dammit

I made the The Strays cut my hair all the way down until there was only a hint of fuzz (I remembered what Doc did when he lost his wife and daughters). At first The Strays were scared to do it because I was talking nonsense and most of it was in Shakesbear.

"I will have such revenges...."

I grabbed Squirrel by the hair and told her to find something to cut my hair. I waved Granpa's file at their faces like a knife until they did what I asked.

Trout ran next door and found clippers. Then, they held my hands and wiped the tears from their faces with their grubby T-shirts as Trout did her work.

Before they showed up at the door, I had grabbed Achilles' moldering heart in the box off the counter and shoved it into a tattered backpack lying by the front door.

The Strays walked in and smelled its funk right away and yelled at me about the stink and how I was an idiot and — dear god what is inside that backpack! — and that we needed to jam outa town before the Po-Po got there. Then they saw Cress and you on the couch because the blanket had fallen off her face. And they went apeshit, as Dad would say.

I said, "Shut up! Junior did it. I swear if you don't cut my hair, I will get my grandpa's axe and come back here and shut you up. One face at a time."

That shut them up pretty good.

"Cut off my hair," I said. "All of it."

They sat me down on Sophie's little porch and cut my hair in swathes. And they sang — in their sweet harmonies that lilted across rabbit turds that spelled "*delayed, squeeze a penny,*" across the dirty street and over the still-smoking ruins of my Granma's house — they sang about being in the mouth of a graveyard and rain falling hard.

I felt their song on me like rain. "*I will have such revenges... I will do such things . . . they shall be the terrors of the earth.*" I felt the waves of their voices crash my face, and I closed my eyes and let them cut off all of my hair.

It fell around my boots like black waters.

Then I told them to plague off. And they did.

I lit a cig with Pop's lighter. The smoke curled down into me, and I thought about her for the space of time it takes to go all the way in and then find its way back out. I thought of the smoke-clouds in Sonofa in the darkness of that first morning. Of the clouds that rose around her every time she was smoking and thinking or getting ready to do something.

She wouldn't want me lolling around. She'd want action.

I found a box of matches next to Sophie's stove. They were the big matches that you use to start a campfire. I lit one and watched it burn. Then, I dropped it on the floor and the shag carpet caught fire like a parched field.

"Goddamn flaming bag a nuts," I said.

Then I walked into the street.

I kept saying it, over and over, as I watched flames through the open door eat the shaggy carpet and lick, red and hungry, up the fake-wood walls. I watched it for a while. The flames captured me, and I decided that the yellow-orange you see when you stare at the sun was my new favorite color. I could see it in the heart of the fire. The flames turned into whips of curling smoke at the roofline, I heard the wail of sirens on the other side of town. It was time to go.

I walked to the blue spruce down the street.

"Hold fast," she said when her handle snapped into my hand.

My body was a blade. I could cut through anything.

"Hold fast," I said back for the first time ever, felt a shiver run up her handle. She hummed with cold rage, and I remembered the lines from Granma's song: *"...curse of death and open grave, vengeance mine and rolling flood."*

I remembered her singing that goddamn song. How did it start?

Living words, wind and wave,
Comes the one who kills his blood.
Curse of death ....

And then it came on me as I walked away. My Momma and Dad on that day they left in the raft. They told me there was a prophecy. Long ago. A prophecy.

About me killing someone I loved.

That is when I lost whatever it was holding me back from being like Junior. Or Big Jim. I had a poison in my bones. I was not myself no more. Maybe it was the look in my eyes that made people turn away, or the axe on my shoulder. No one running to the fire looked at me straight.

I had taken only one thing besides the cigs, the lighter, and Achilles' heart in the backpack. I'd grabbed Granma's blue cap. I pulled it on my head, sliding over the stubble, and clamped it above my ears. The brim curled over my eyes, and I felt safe. Like I was hidden in a cave with granite at my back. Granpa's file poked my leg through my pocket. I wrapped my fingers around it, felt its rough backbone, steady as a good friend.

I was gonna sharpen this axe until I could shave the hair off my arm.

Then I was gonna kill that fucking monster and his pretty boy, MK.

I was gonna kill anyone who got in my way.

Cry havoc, let slip the dogs of war.

I was gonna kill 'em all.

I flipped open Pop's double-bladed axe lighter, lit a cig, and felt a smile on my face. A strange, alien movement of my cheeks that hid my eyes. I was gonna break into the library at school. Mister Brown tried to tell me the truth the other day, which felt like ten years ago. I was gonna steal that slim book with the drawings of the monster-bugs. I was gonna find the truth. And then I was gonna kill the truth.

Chapter 45

Boogers and Barbless Hooks

Acuere came in handy busting the library window.

It was not a school day, I reckon, or I could have walked in. Instead, there I was crawling through a shattered window, falling on a shelf, and almost slicing my throat with the edge of the axe. That would have been a good way to start off my revenge-quest, Dammit. Bleeding out on the library floor in the entomology section.

Dragonflies of North America was not on the shelf. Just my luck. My legs buckled and I sat on the floor and read the note on the sheet of paper I pulled from the space where the book used to be. I knew who it was right away. A combination of overstating everything with repeated threats:

Boy,

I told you I would take everything.

I know many, many things now that I wear this robe.

If you bring me the heart of the maid first requested by my Mistress (no longer!) and you bring me the axe-head — your Grandmother burned up the axe-handle the FOOL!—I will fulfill Her promise to you and tell you where your father's body lies.

That is the easy way. And by that, I mean the way with the least pain IF YOU BRING ME WHAT I WANT. What is the hard way? I take the last thing you have: yourself. I will make you into one of my boys; I will get inside you.

Come. Bring the gifts. I shall tell you of your father. You shall die.
In my benevolence, the Master will grant mercy, a quick death.
Cordially,
Master Rev. Dr. James Y. Sengrim, Esq.

It could have been three sentences, and he wrote a page. I learned this from Shakesbear: villains like long titles; and love – *love* —to hear themselves talk. Plus, why tell me about Dad just to kill me? What a jackass.

Walking downtown on my way to Doc's cabin I must have looked like I escaped crazy-people prison.

It did not matter. Junction City had gone mad. I saw it happen first in mothers who started to yell and hit their children too hard. Then I saw men and women getting into quick, dirty fights that ended abruptly. The bigger ones would win with a punch that left the other's head bouncing off the sidewalk. Sometimes a smaller person — I even saw a couple of women — would dodge a punch and climb on a back and wrap their legs around the belly of the bigger person and choke them. I saw a woman sneak up with a pocketknife behind a big man (smaller than Big Jim by a couple hundred pounds, but still big) and slice his ankle tendons and fell him like a tree in the parking lot of the sporting goods store. She kicked him in the head until he quit yelling.

I saw the lake shining blue behind the hotel and reckoned sneaking through the alley would be a shortcut around the madness. I was wrong. Shovels and another one of Junior's gang were ripping the T-shirt off a sobbing girl. I lifted the axe to take their lives like rabid dogs.

Instead, I broke them with my fists. They weren't worth her blade.

I did not realize how strong I was until I heard the sound of my fists on their faces. Pretty soon they were on the ground and not fighting anymore. I took the shirt off Shovels, put it on the girl, told her to run, picked up *Acuere* and kept walking.

The strip of beach curved like a vast crescent moon into the haze of the first hot day of summer, framing an indigo universe spattered by stars on every wave tip. I remembered I wore Granma's cap, so I wiggled it and moved it around on my head, hoping it had magic to see beyond the glints and into the lake. Nothing. After a while, I took it off and shoved it in my back pocket, felt the sun burn my scalp. Good! Let it burn.

A tiredness came over me, as if some vital part was seeping out. I thought of Penny and what she said to me yesterday — a lifetime ago — in Sonofa. How she had so many holes punched in her that she would drain out unless she kept pouring something in; didn't matter what. I decided I would stop at the next shade, yank off Pop's boots and scrunch my toes in the sand. Mebbe just quit right there. I saw a ponderosa in the distance leaning over the water. Looked promising.

"Nice axe, lil bruh."

I jumped like I been shot.

Mister Brown in his flaming red shirt with the purple parrots climbed on a rock, chewing his meat-stick. He was scratching himself like a chipmunk, rubbing his neckbeard. "You got yourself in *serious* poopoo, baldy," he said.

Mister Bay rose from behind the same rock — in faded jeans, boots, and an old, brown-patterned pearl-button shirt that fit well against his broad shoulders — and climbed up beside Mister Brown and started picking his nose. Like two men on a city bench watching a parade.

"Where's my robe, kid?"

Fair question. But I did not know where to start.

"Little fuckin thief." He was grinning. "You been a bad boy." He looked rested and clean and happy. And not mad at me at all. He didn't even smell bad. "We know what happened, anyhow, Monster Lord," he said.

I didn't say nothing, Dammit. I stood there hoping he wouldn't burn me to a crisp with lightning from his eyes. His buckskin hair with its dark ends was braided and tied back.

"What'd you do to your hair?" Mister Bay asked. His eyes were black pools with a center-gem that gleamed like amber. Like if you looked in them too long, you'd start growing. Not for the first time did I wonder who Mister Brown's cousin was.

"Second cousin, dumbass," he said with a grin and more teeth than any mouth should have, "yeah, I hear you." He picked at a booger in his long nose, but it would not budge.

"Child, thy doom and joy, in word and sound," Mister Brown said, looking uncomfortable. *"For blood spilt on earth's sweet, hallowed ground."* He scratched his ear with his meat stick and coughed politely, "I was told to remind you of that."

"What're you doing here?" My voice surprised all of us. It was full of anger.

"Finally. He talks," said Mister Bay to Mister Brown.

"Ah, just sittin'." Mister Brown took a big bite of the meat stick.

"Phew," said Mister Bay wrinkling his nose. "Ya stink. Like dead dog. Watcha got in the backpack?"

"Lil bruh, what happened to your hair?"

"Your scalp shinin' bright as the moon," grinned Mister Bay.

"Be nice. He's mournin'," said Mister Brown.

"He ain't mournin', though his clothes are tore up," said Mister Bay. "If he was mournin', he woulda put ashes on himself."

"Well, how you know that? He wasn't taught that by his family. May they rest in peace."

"Ha. All a them resting or gone. Find yer ma and pa?" said Mister Bay.

I just looked at him.

Mister Bay grunted, "Told you to stay away from *that* ruckus with that old evil Nisoi but you went straight at it." He tapped his nose, pointed at me. "Mister Bay approves."

I was surprised at the weight that fell from my shoulders. Ever since I stole his robe, I carried the fear of what he would do to me.

"Take it back from Big Jim," I said. "You could fix everything."

"Don't work that way, everyone knows thief's rules. You stole it. You get it back." He dislodged the booger and flicked it. It stuck on my shirt pocket — *thump*. "Signed, sealed, delivered," said Mister Bay. "Approved."

I decided I was going to ignore that I had a booger on my shirt, maybe that would shut them up. Also, Dammit, very weird, as soon as the booger landed, everything slowed down. Except for my brain.

"That booger's goin' nowhere," said Mister Bay. "Eddy out, son. Slow down. Listen."

Truth be told, this next bit is real slow, Dammit. It drove me nuts at the time. I *wanted* to get going, let Big Jim kick my ass, and get the whole damn thing over. But I was stuck there like that booger on my shirt, until they let me go.

"Lil bruh, listen carefully," said Mister Brown. "You need to understand: this next fight ain't no dogfight. You got to be ready for a LONG fight. No slam-bam-thank-you-ma'am-get-outa-dodge-and-make-like-scram. Nope." He popped his shoulders, dodged his head, and punched the air. "We're here to get you ready for a knock-down, drag-out. A fifteen-round, heavy-weight pound." He snickered. "In the ground, ya hound."

Oh great, I thought. Not only will I get my ass kicked. It's going to last like my all-night nightmares.

"You could end it with one," said Mister Bay and Mister Brown elbowed him, then pointed his meat stick at the booger on my shirt. "You have no idea how much that means, heh, Bay don't do that for anyone." He looked at Mister Bay. "Cuz, what *are* you doin?"

"The boy'll need it, he's gotta thaw out," said Mister Bay softly, working on his other nostril. "Can't throw ice-cubes inna fire. Gotta go slow."

"We can't help him Cuz, we were told not to."

"Not helping. Just a boog."

"What ARE you doing here?" I asked again, trying to remove the booger. It was warm as a hot penny, sticky, and would not come off. I gagged and wiped my finger on my pants.

"Got a friend out there," Mister Bay pointed at the lake. "And he told us to sit tight and that you be comin' along. So, we sat tight. Dang, if you didn't come walkin' down the beach."

Sure enough, far across the water, there was a canoe I had not seen before and a silhouette in the sun with a fly rod casting a line further than I thought possible. Must be a man with an arm like a piston, I thought. An arm so strong it's more like a leg. That cast had to take him into his backing it went so far. Behind him, sitting elegantly in the canoe, Ms. Swan was a golden vision. Naked as a nymph in Her ivory rolls of fat under a see-through summer dress.

She smiled and waved at me and the fingernail in my chest flared like molten silver; like when you finally pull a sliver out. Except this sliver pulled in deeper. The canoe rocked as if it would flip, its back-end low in the water. She was a big, beautiful woman. Or something like that.

The cousins grinned in appreciation.

"Mm mm MMM. Sight to see!" said Mister Brown.

I was genuinely surprised. "I thought you were done with Her," I said.

"Done with Her? Never done with Her," said Mister Bay. "She thought She was done with me, but She ain't. We're all fixed up."

She blew him a kiss and he caught it—and released a yellow bird that flew, undulating like a wave, into the trees.

"Wish we had time to tell you. How She got better, how me and Her got OK. But we don't got time, at least not for THAT. We got stuff to say an' things to give," said Mister Bay.

"Believe me, lil bruh," said Mister Brown. "We been tryin' to get back to you ever since you run off."

"Been hard," said Mister Bay, "You closed all the doors. That page you stuck in the hole got strong magic." He pulled Penny's page out from somewhere behind him, unfolded it, and started to read:

"*I'll burn this I know it. I prayed last night for it to stop and for there to be justice, like you said to me 'a bruised reed he won't break, a smoldering wick he won't snuff out,' but nothing happened.*"

"DAMN lil bruh. She prayed for justice and here you are," said Mister Brown.

Mister Bay beckoned me over and handed me Penny's page.

"Not vengeance, though," said Mister Bay.

I remembered I had also written on it — it felt so long ago — early this very morning. There it was; my scratched sonnet:

In every light your eyes so constant shine,

With clear unwaver'd purpose to my thought....
I could read no more, Dammit. I saw Penny's eyes. And how they looked when she said she never loved me. I crumpled it in a ball and shoved it in my back pocket.

Mister Bay reached out and squeezed my shoulder and I felt — for a dark and shining second — the howling of a thousand dogs at night under the full moon. I felt like stealing the sun and telling a tale and flipping a story and riding a whale.

"I forgive you for stealing my robe. Tell your punk friend it is finished and for him to come home," said Mister Bay. "Tell him the fisherman says so." He squeezed my shoulder again and I felt like I could do anything, and I knew I was something that nobody knew about. But I did not have the words yet — even though I got all of Shakesbear bumping around in me — to say so.

I came back to myself and realized I'd fallen to my knees. I slowly got to my feet.

"Believe it or not, butterfingers," said Mister Brown, "we got bigger things than bringing *your* sticky fingers to justice. Heh. Big Jim's the tip of the iceberg. The tip. Heh." He sniggered, Mister Bay elbowed him.

"Anyways, you're in good company little thief," said Mister Brown. "The best ones know how to nick a little." He grinned. "Like the first one of y'all Coeur De Montagne's: he found the girl, he stole them chains, he forged the axe and gave it a name, he tore that giant's heart-bone out, he used it on that big ol' lout!" Mister Brown waved his meat stick happily.

My stomach churned; I realized I was real hungry and didn't give a damn about ancestors.

The fisherman picked up his line, threw it behind him in a tight loop that seemed to trail behind him forever, and cast again.

"Who is that?" I asked. "What is She doing with him?"

"Don't you mind her, She's got her own story," said Mister Brown. He waved to Her and She waved back. "Let's just say even gods hit rock-bottom. Even gods — especially gods — need a little help now and then. Why you think your family's around, anyhow?" Mister Brown scratched himself and Cuz nodded his head in approval.

"Yep," said Mister Bay.

"You make it out alive?" said Mister Brown. "Tell ya the whole thing." He took a bite of his meat stick. "Listen, don't mind who's fishing, lil bruh. He's a friend a Mister Brown's and Mister Bay's, s'all you need to know."

"Yep," said Mister Bay, happy to let Mister Brown do the talking.

"Every pack a cards needs a wild," said Mister Brown. "And every pack a dogs needs one too."

"Yep," said Mister Bay, and this time he tapped his nose.

"What can I say?" said Mister Brown. "When he's fishin', he's fishin'. Nothin' else matters."

"Until he come fishing for you," said Mister Bay.

"He told us we can't go with you," said Mister Brown. "But to tell you that you got everything you need."

"For example: lunch." Mister Bay beckoned with his booger-finger and pointed behind the rock.

I looked behind the big rock and saw a loaf and a grilled trout on a smoking flat rock on a bed of coals. I smelled garlic and butter. My mouth watered; the loaf and ketchup from this morning on Granma's porch felt like a year ago. I threw *Acuere* down and started tearing at the food.

"Slow down Monster Lord ya gonna choke!"

I crunched the head of the trout, eyeballs and all, and chased it with warm bread while Mister Brown and Mister Bay told me how they got to the beach through a "dog-sized mirror" whatever that means, including all that they saw with Junior and the girls and you before I got there. Basically, time here moves different than their time. They tried to explain *the whens* are like the difference between fish in the water and a man living above the water in a boat, but all I was thinking about was grilled fish crumbling in buttery bites in my mouth, and why warm bread tastes so much better than any candy.

I half-listened to them and half-watched the fisherman, but mostly zoned out. I reckon it was getting food in me, or maybe the booger on me. All I know is I felt calm for the first time in a long time. Like Mister Brown says, "Chill, but stoked."

The fisherman was long and lean and seemed to be into catching fish on a dry fly. He kept a couple trout, but most he threw back after showing them to Ms. Swan and talking to them briefly. Just a silhouette of a man in the late morning talking to a fish, face to face.

A weariness came over me, I closed my eyes and leaned against the big rock.

"Look what you done, Bay! He's falling asleep!"

Mister Bay punched me gently on the shoulder, and I opened my eyes.

"We almost forgot!" said Mister Brown. "Listen, lil bruh. You got to remember something." He pointed at the fisherman. "It's what he said for us to tell you." Mister Brown put his hand over his heart and spoke solemnly, *"The heart is simply this: A pump the size of your fist…"*

"I know," I said. "I heard this before. 'It's a most dangerous country. Those who venture there…' blah blah blah."

"Mm hmm," said Mister Bay. Those amber-gem eyes. I felt as if he was pouring liquid tree sap into my head.

Mister Brown said, "Don't forget the rest. Seriously. '... *those who venture there must be foolish, unafraid, or willing to suffer the trials of loss and grief far beyond any hope of return.'*"

"Tell him it's bullshit," I said. "I'm gonna get my butt kicked."

"You're getting so good using your outside voice!" said Mister Brown. "That's great! And so far as you getting your ass kicked: Well, mebbe you won't."

"Prob'ly will," said Mister Bay.

"Have you seen Junction City?" I said. "It's a mess." I thought of how fast the girl in the alley ran. "I'm the last of the Conveners — and Big Jim wants to wipe us out." My voice cracked. "He's been after me from the beginning."

"Not the only one been after you from the beginning," Mister Bay smiled sadly. "Anyhow. This Big Jim — mebbe he has my robe. But he don't know how to WEAR it. Two different things."

"I'm sorry, Mister Brown can't go with you, this is your fight." Mister Brown took a chomp of meat stick. "To win, or lose, lil bruh."

The silence gathered, broken only by the far-away sound of the fly-line lifting off the water and passing through the air. And Ms. Swan's excited and joyful chatter, just beyond the edge of understanding.

I broke the silence. "Granma said that to me too," I said bitterly.

The fisherman threw fly-line in swinging loops, and waterdrops from the line made rainbows over his head.

"Now, lil bruh, the second message from our friend." Mister Brown pointed his thumb over his shoulder. "He says, 'it's not about the tool. It's about you, and what you do with you.' Heh." He grinned. "The tool. Still, it is nice to have gifts and we DO have gifts for you." He reached in the air and pulled down a mirror small enough to hide in his hand. "Here ya go."

"A mirror? This is stupid." But I took it.

"Trust me, lil bruh, you'll be thankful. It's your Granma's," said Mister Brown. "Remember what I said in the Library? *'To catch a dragon that flies. You got to deal with its eyes.'* How you like that now?"

"Real helpful," I said. "Thank you so VERY much."

"Oh, he's coming around, he'll be just fine," said Mister Bay picking absently at his nose.

"I'm NOT gonna be just fine," I said. I threw the mirror at Mister Brown's head, but he caught it.

"You never listen, lil bruh," he said. *"Tokens and tools, misers and rules. It's the man who makes mantles, and mantles makes fools."*

"I'm not your lil bruh. Fuck your fucking riddles."

"C'mon, lil bruh." He was still grinning. "Give us a riddle, just a little one 'fore you go."

"I'll tell you a riddle *bruh*.'" My anger did not surprise me. "How does a boy who wants only to be left alone, to be by himself, get sucked into the WORST losing battle in the history of the world?" I felt Granma coming out as each word got louder. "How does a boy LOSE his parents for no fault of his own, and end up blaming himself for years while they are gone? How does a boy who HATES fighting have to be the one to avenge his father's death? How DOES a boy breathe? After he has to KILL his own Granma — and no one else is there to DO it?"

"That's not a riddle," said Mister Bay, and Mister Brown punched him.

Words came in painful jerks. "No one will DO anything. This bullshit. I look around and NO ONE will do it. So, I do it. GOD!" I rubbed my face until I saw stars.

When I could see again, I saw their eyes were big and they had reached to each other and held hands. Neither of them said a thing. The only sound was the *fwaap* of the fly-line being pulled off the water and the *fwip-fwip* it made in the air as it curled back and then landed the fly gently on the surface. It sounded close. But it was behind me, and I did not turn to look.

Ms. Swan said something in a whisper, like a zephyr, and the hook in my chest went *zing*. She said, *"Don't be afraid."* Did I really hear it? What do I know, Dammit?

My chest opened like a spring, "Why do I think you two could handle Big Jim — just the two of you — if you wanted to? With both hands tied BEHIND your backs. And a plague upon you too," I turned to the approaching figures in the canoe. "Plague you for fishing while the world is on fire."

The two figures in the canoe were no closer. It must have been some strange trick of the wind. The fisherman remained intent on his fishing, but I felt the weight of his gaze, warmer than the sun. Ms. Swan kissed the tip of her finger at me and a tiny bluebird came across the water, circled my head and took off into the trees. The canoe wobbled and she grabbed both sides and giggled.

"Fishes with barbless hooks," said Mister Bay.

"That's stupid. Let's them get away," I said.

"I see you've noticed," Mister Brown grinned, "how few he's caught."

Look, Dammit, the fisherman is weird. What is he doing in this story? Hell if I know. I got to tell it true so I can rip this rusty, tangled, sharp-edged story OUT.

"Lil bruh, everyone's got jobs to do," said Mister Brown, and he was smiling kindly. "And, like I already said, we're after bigger fish. Big Jim's a minnow in the big jimmy picture."

"A minnow?" I asked. "Then who's the shark?"

"It's *when's* the shark." A shadow crossed Mister Brown's face. "And you don't wanna know. Not today."

"Har," said Mister Bay. "No more old-timey talk from monster-lord?" His eyes burned. "*To be or not to be,* uh? How's the knot?"

"*Ground is ground, earth is earth,*" Mister Brown said. "*She makes us certain of our worth,*" he danced in a circle. "Remember that?" He grinned. "*Her garments woven ever new, But who's the weaver? Maybe You. Zimilibus!*" He waved his arms at the sky like he was calling down fire, but all that happened was Mister Bay let out a big fart. Mister Brown laughed out loud, cupped a hand under his armpit and farted back, then tapped my head with his meat stick, "Knot untie, stone'll fly," he said.

I knocked his hand away, pulled on the backpack and picked up *Acuere.*

"When do I get to be in MY story? I hate this one!" I kicked the coals from the fire, banged my toe on the rock. "Plague!" I threw it as far as I could into the lake, burning my hands. "Thanks for nothing!" I wiped my hands on my pants. They were red — but not blistered. "See you jackasses in hell," I said, and walked away not looking back.

"Remember, Stonefly," shouted Mister Bay after me. "Way you're made, ya never do it the same way twice."

I was weary to the core of my heart.

"Fifteen rounds, lil bruh!"

The sun shone on a thousand wavelets, vibrated off the pines pressed against the golden lip of the lake. Just before I went beyond hearing, Mister Brown yelled at me; a shout that echoed off the water and sent "wink-wink" back from the trees.

"You get in a tight spot, REMEMBER... to WINK."

Something burned my thigh through my jeans. I reached in my pocket and down at the bottom, under Pop's file — in the very bottom of Pop's jeans — was a penny. Like a flake of the sun. I couldn't bring myself to throw it away, though I wanted to toss it as hard as I could at the azure waves and watch it sink. Instead, I squeezed the penny in my pocket, burned my finger and thumb, and without turning — still walking away — I showed them my middle finger. Just like Granma would a done.

Chapter 46

I Talk To A Dead Dog, And So Forth

He will make me kill myself, Dammit, like he said in his letter. Why am I not running the other way? *I am punished with a sore distraction.* Well, one last inventory before I die:

One axe. Heavy as a tree, sometimes light as a feather.
    One hat. Magic, still smells like her.
    One file. Good for sharpening *Acuere*, poking monsters in eyes.
    One heart. Going sour, in backpack.
    One page. Back pocket, worthless. Except it reminds me of her.
    One Penny. She's gone, just gone.
    One penny. No longer hot, in my pocket like a cold rabbit turd.
    One booger. Stuck to my shirt, what the hell.
    One me. Mad as a cubless she-bear.

It is strange to realize you are closer to your family's enemy than your blood. Part of me wants to tear out MK's soul if he has one. The other part wants to ask him, finally, "ARE you my friend? Forget the vow — Couldn't you say 'NO?'" *I am punished with a sore distraction.* There is no floor to madness. Granma, you were right. The rage is burning me down to ashes like a house on fire. It is a pleasurable fire that needs no fuel, just a person who is alone.

    That is *not* the reason I'm talking to you, Dammit. I am fine being alone. Just fine. I'll die a stupid, painful death, squashed like a cockroach. No one gives a flying fuck about Rosencranz. Like him, I'm a parable in blood for a friendship gone bad.

It is strange how seeking answers can drive a man mad. Or is it chasing ghosts?

One last thing, Dammit, and I got it from you: I've seen Junction City full of dust and death and boys screaming for blood. Someone inside me looked around, saw no one doing anything, and — angry and ready to get it over, but with a winding, tender root hidden in the darkness, like a daisy pushing through a crack in concrete — said, *"Send me!"* It was more like growled. Maybe I'm making excuses, but I'll just say it: The damn dog made me do it. If there's a homeplace for catfuckers — like where I seen Achilles run — you're probably getting in dustups there too. And sticking up for the underdog. If you can do that, then I reckon I can try to *not* run, even if I'd rather be back at the homeplace... *Of rivers and the chain-ed canyons free, A winding, restless spirit I will be.*

I wanted this ass-kickin' at high noon to go quick like all your fights. But there's two reasons it did not:

One, Mister Bay's booger.

Two, me. Captain Hesitater.

Okay, three — Big Jim loves him a good villain speech.

Nose-up, ears-back. Stick with me to the end, it will be worth it. I promise.

Inventory definitely done. Like me.

Chapter 47

Culus Vivit Et Bene

And now, Dammit, the part I said was the worst part. Remember?

Doc's cabin rested like a still-life painting framed by ponderosas far up the lawn. A cathedral of trees, great pillars, marched into a distant haze under a ceiling of too-blue sky that crackled overhead. The air was thick, like a storm coming. Big Jim walked onto the porch, ignored – or didn't see—me and proceeded to flay the flesh from Doc like a garment. He threw the carcass on the lawn and turned to his task: pounding each nail into Doc's hide, once to start it and once to drive it in.

Bam Bam.

The worm twisted in my gut. *Oh, how all occasions do inform against me, and spur my dull revenge!* I told it to go to hell and walked forward to stand next to a curled husk with long claws; the seeping, raw corpse of Doc Ranulf, my friend, at the foot of the stairs.

Bam Bam.

"Did you know," murmured Big Jim to the wall, "Mmm. In the old days, farmers would do this to keep the wolf packs away?"

Bam Bam.

I said nothing. How did the hide on the wall have a head, and the body on the lawn also have a head? The body, white-eyed, with a face like a skinned baby? The hide on the wall with fangs, grey ears, and a thick tongue?

Bam Bam.

I could not find a word to say. My stomach felt like it was pierced by a hot poker.

Bam Bam.

No sign of wings on Big Jim. Just shoulders too-wide for any man and muscles that bunched like rock-piles.

"Fee, fie, fo, fum.... Mmm." He spoke softly at the wall through a mouth of nails. "I smell the blood of George's son." He wiped his drooping blonde mustache, and continued to nail the wolf head, working his way around the edges of the hide. One *BAM* to start the nail, and the second *BAM* to drive it in.

"Here you are, boy. In my trap. Mmm the last Convener." He chuckled. "I told you I'd take everything."

"Not everything,'" I said. My voice was rough as an unfiled blade.

He turned his head, looked at me for the first time; oh, those eyes! *O'er-sized with coagulate gore and large as carbuncles!* The fat on his face rippled, he dropped the hammer and swelled to fill the porch.

"It didn't burn?" he muttered.

"Hold fast," *Acuere* said. I felt, under her sudden weight, that I would smash through the grass into the earth below.

"Boy." *Click Click.* The garden shears snapped deep under his mustache. "Give it to me."

"Dream on, jackass." I surprised even myself, Dammit.

"You have brought me my wildest dream, boy. Before I came into possession of the robe, *that* was all I wanted." He closed a massive fist and smiled, and I did not like the smile because the fear was gone. His mirrored eyes flickered. "Did you bring the other item?"

"Yeah, right here," I tugged the strap of the backpack. "She was a goner anyway, so I dug it out and brought it." I *had* thought this out, Dammit, before I got there: If he didn't know that Penny survived MK and came back to her true self—if he thought that she was murdered by Junior—then he might believe I would tear out her heart. Monsters got no soul, which means they got no empathy, which means they can't walk in your shoes, ergo. Blind spot.

I reckon I'd give it a shot. "Right here," I said, and shook the backpack like it had a steak in it. "Now tell me what you done with Dad's body."

"Ah. The heart." He looked at me to see the effect of his next words. "None of us liked that cunt — arrogant. *Ugh*. Virtuous. I couldn't break her. All of us thought it would be fun to see you attempt. Two for one. Very pleasurable. Mmm. To break you — to break her. Is it pulpy?"

He stopped to enjoy my face. Then he murmured, "I don't give a damn about that bitch's heart." His eyes glittered, a thousand carbuncled refractions; the mandibles came out the whole way—for the first time—from under his mustache, dripping spider legs with razors at the tips. "Give me the axe."

I could not move.

He patted the bloody grey wolf-hide on the wall gently and spoke to it; but I knew he was speaking to me: "Old friend, mmm to flay you is an utter pleasure. Like taking the cover and leaving the pages."

I tasted sour in my mouth. My arm felt glued to my side.

"You *do* understand what flaying means?" he asked.

I could not move or speak.

"It is, certainly, a physical act. But more so, mmm and much better, an act upon the soul. To flay a soul is to take all the pages and leave the cover."

He walked down the stairs, pulled Penny's tattered book from his jacket and shoved it into my front shirt pocket. "I'll trade you," he said. "This last pulpy memorial of your dear Penelope. I'll trade it to you mmm for her pulpy heart and Beaumont Bergmann's magic axe, the bane of all powers, the power of all banes."

Why, what an ass I am, prompted to revenge, to act, I unpack my heart with words. I am punished with a sore distraction. I hesitated.

Big Jim snatched *Acuere* from my hand. "Oooh, that's hot," he said with that too-wide smile. His serrated nails scratched the handle as he raised it, effortlessly. "You thought this could hurt me? Mmm?" It looked like a twig.

My knees crashed into the lawn. I lowered my head.

"Dad, how do you keep from being afraid?"

"Look him in his red eye, son. Tell him..."

"Dad, I'm so afraid. I can't."

"You were born to do this, goddammit. Look him in his red eye, tell him, 'Go fuck yourself.'"

So, I did. My knees felt like wax. But I looked up at Big Jim's fat, wide eyes, and whispered so softly I could barely hear myself.

"Go plague yourself."

"Hold fast," she said.

"Mmm this is nowhere near as fun as I imagined," he *click clicked*, the spider-leg mandibles curled out from its mouth, and Big Jim raised Pop's double-bladed axe high in its massive fist. "Time to die." He swung my grandfather's axe down like lightning as if to split me in half.

Acuere rang like a bell, and I heard a *CRACK*.

Big Jim roared.

The axe-handle shattered into a thousand splinters.

He screamed, shook his hand, and pulled a foot-long splinter from his eye.

The axe head fell at my feet, smoking. Shards of blackened wood protruded from *Acuere,* its glowing steel burned into the grass; smoke rose like incense from where it fell with the scent of grass and burnt hickory and earth.

I felt nothing. Not even a prick of pain. I rubbed my head, it felt fine.

A ripple of fear and confusion ran across its giant face. Mirrored eyes flared and the mandibles sucked back into its great mouth. Big Jim backed up in confusion.

"Hold fast," she said, as steady and cold-hearted a killer as ever.

I picked up the axe head — cool to touch — and dropped it in the open backpack as he rubbed his broken hand. His eye dripped pus. A squeaking vermin like a giant cockroach crawled from his eye, fell to the ground, and I crunched it under my foot.

He sat down on the stairs with a thump that made them creak and snapped the fingers of the hand that still worked. "Come to me slave. Bring my robe!" He waited and nothing happened. So, he snapped his fingers again, and the sound echoed off the trees. "COME, SLAVE."

MK walked around the edge of the wraparound porch with the robe between a thumb and finger like it was a dirty diaper.

"*Culus vivit et bene*," MK said, "the ass is alive and well." He was grinning. "I am sorry to be late. Forgive me, master. It looks like young Clayton swallowed your promise. You are to be commended, Oh Master of the Bait."

Who was the ass? MK, Big Jim, or me? It was so like MK to show up with that smirk, two dirty jokes and a riddle on his tongue.

"Why ... why did it blow up in my hand," muttered Big Jim.

"Elementary, my dear master. *Acuere* was hand-forged to overpower gods and kill monsters, not boys."

"Why did it.... not destroy him," growled Big Jim, pointing at me with a giant, jagged fingernail.

MK rolled his eyes. "Do I have to explain everything? This lad, Clayton Solomon Stonefly-Bergmann, is neither god nor monster.

He is just a boy. Descended from a family of boys... who then became men. Hence the sad event of its breaking."

"Forget it! Give me my robe," muttered Big Jim, rubbing his broken arm.

"Even more sad," MK kept going, "is that you didn't think of the possibility that his ancestor may have forged the steel by his own hand and consequently, no steel thus forged could ever wound a descendant."

"What?" Big Jim struggled to comprehend. He rubbed his punctured eye and — like a dumb beast — picked the creatures off his cheek that crawled from the ooze, one by one. He pinched their heads absently until they popped. The blow from *Acuere* must have addled Big Jim in some interior way. He was sluggish, as if returned to a former, more brutish, self.

I looked at *Acuere*, still smoking, in my open backpack. I'm not dead, I thought. I'm not dead. I zipped the backpack shut.

"I'm not dead," I whispered, mostly to myself.

"Not dead yet, hesitater," said MK. But he was smiling.

I shook my head. My axe was broke. I had no way to destroy my enemy.

"Ah, Romes," MK popped his knuckles, the only way I knew he was nervous. "To be honest, I'm glad the axe is broke. That thing could have killed me. And I would've died, the unknown soldier, not even knowing my name." He laughed bitterly. "Ms. Swan, the snake, never did tell me who I am. '*Sometime am I all wound with adders, who with cloven tongues do hiss me madness.*' Name it, Clay, my undying favor will be yours."

"Caliban, jackass," I felt angry blood rushing to my face. "Act two, scene two." I had not thought of the possibility that *Acuere* could hurt him, or even kill him. I was in no mood for the TRG.

"Ah. Point to you. Favor to you, Stonefly. See, it's not so bad, laughing in the face of death. Especially if it's a buttface."

Not funny, but he's all the funny I got. "Dumbass," I muttered, but could not hold back a grin.

"I see you've found your tongue, Romes. And your smile. You should trust them both."

"Two points, plagueface," I said. "If we're playing the TRG—I named the scene."

"Fine," said MK. "Two points. Now it's your turn."

I hesitated.

Big Jim still seemed confused, rubbing his arm, and blinking in the noon sun.

I said the next thing that came to mind, but it was not Shakesbear:

"Living words, wind and wave,
Comes the one who kills his blood.
Curse of death and open grave..."

"That's not TRG," MK interrupted with a frown.

"Point to me, Jules," I said. "Three to zero."

Big Jim stirred. "GIVE ME THE ROBE, SLAVE!" It was a bellow that shook the ponderosas and rattled the windows.

"As you wish, master. As you wish." MK walked down and handed the robe to Big Jim. Then MK turned to me. His face changed and he said gruffly, "What are you doing away from the water, Jackass? Didn't your Mother tell you to go to the water in danger?"

I started to shake. I knew who *that* was.

MK said, "Whoops... here I am. You're the best friend I ever had, Romes. The only one. I would help you if I could, but to be perfectly honest, since your Mom got sucked out and I released Penny I have little control over the voices, or over this vow. Feeling a little wobbly." He turned to Big Jim who was wrapping the robe around his shoulders and crackling to life under its power like the sound aluminum foil makes when you squeeze it. "I'm sorry master, sometimes other people's words pop out of me." MK cracked his knuckles, and his eyes were so black I had to look away.

"Urg argh ugguuu argh," said Big Jim, crumpling in on himself. Wormy things chased one another under his skin and across his face.

MK's voice changed. "Forget revenge, son," he said. "I was wrong. All things change, Clay. All things die. Even me. I'm the ghost of a ghost. Don't listen to either of us! We've long since moved on."

"Dad!" I cried. "Dad, don't go!"

"Trust me," said my father in MK's voice as if reciting. "There is a change like a cancer that has no end. The larger it grows, the smaller — and tighter — the circle it swims. An in-bred swamp. This my father told me, and now I tell you, son."

I looked at MK, seeking my father, but I could not meet MK's eyes. They were cauldrons of black fire.

"Only way out is sluice it out," he said.

Then MK shouted, himself once again, "Forget revenge, Romes! RUN!"

Big Jim stood between me and the water and changed before our eyes. His body went stiff and turned to crystalline brown paper. His back ruptured. A creature climbed from the brown-paper husk. The creature had Big Jim's head and six arms with talons on the end of each. Four wings — like multitudinous shining veils of glossy paper — crinkled from its back and shook yellow fluid across the lawn. Its splintered eye was healed. Its thorax-chest—wrapped in the buffalo robe—swelled and pulsed a sick emerald green. A tail like a dragon's, except with pincers on the end, rose over its head. It had grown to half the size of Doc's house and no longer looked like a man. It was a dragonfly with Big Jim's head and massive many-mirrored eyes. The mandibles in its mouth clacked together like swords.

I know if you were there, Dammit, you'd be laughing at how stupid he looked. But me? I shoved my hands in my pockets and got ready to die.

My left hand touched the file and — beneath that — the penny at the bottom. My right hand closed around a square object, and I pulled it out.

It was Granma's mirror I'd thrown at Mister Brown. How it got in there I will never know, Dammit. I got a guess, though.

"To catch a dragon that flies," I heard Mister Brown say in my head. *"You got to deal with its eyes!"*

I had no idea what that meant, Dammit. But I was willing to try.

I held up Penny's mirror and pointed it towards the monster. The light of the noon sun blazed off the mirror's face and fell straight in the creature's eyes—then reflected back and forth between the mirror and its eyes in a stream of midnight black.

And I remembered what Mister Brown said on the prairie. *"...The mirror...held up to the face of a monster? It burns, it tears at its deathless nothingness."*

The black stream, like a hard gem wrapped in gold wire, arced and tore and raged. Hotter and hotter.

"The monster dare not look upon its own soul for it has none, and looking there-in, it vanquishes itself."

I grabbed the mirror with both hands, but strangely, felt no pain or heat. The mirror melted into golden oil and dripped to the grass. Big Jim screamed, eyes melting, shot black lightning from its rear hamulus at the porch, blew up the cabin, and began to burn from every orifice of its body in white-hot flames.

I rubbed the penny in my left pocket as hard as I could, winked with all my best intentions, wished for Mister Brown to come, for rescue, for home.

Wish, wish, wish.

Somewhere in my head I heard Granma say wryly, "...*wishin' don't wash out shit-stains, Clayton, only washin' does that.*"

I began to laugh; a deep laugh that welled from the bottom of my soul, from the skin of my feet, from the ragged stinking trench inside me where I feared most to go. As if all the fear and pain and sadness wrapped like a big chain around that laugh, and that big chain was cabled to ten dozers, and those ten dozers were all pulling together ripping the laugh out of me.

Of rivers and the chain-ed canyons free, A winding, restless spirit I will be.

I felt a tearing in my chest like someone was prying it open; my eyesight went black.

Chapter 48

The Riverside

Rough floorboards underfoot. Heat like an oven. I felt the warm press of the chair on the porch at the homeplace against my back and opened my eyes. My little river stretched below me, turning against the cliffs, deepening into the pool shadowed by the tall cinnamon-orange ponderosas and the flashing swallows. The sun was overhead. Heat vibrated off the meadow.

I knew this *when*.

My hand fumbled to the side-table and felt the spine of The Riverside. I was home. I took a deep breath. I could live here now. As long as I wanted.

And no one — no one — could find me or catch me.

I pulled The Riverside to my lap but did not open it. After all, everything in there was inside of me already. Its familiar weight pressed against my knees. I ran my hand across its cover dimpled and roughened by countless morning mists and four hot summers.

Then I heard my Momma. Clear as if she sat next to me: "*Let the stories find a good place in you, and then you find a good place in the stories. It's like learning to whistle. And don't be afraid of your dreams. You have a gift, son, let your dreams have their way even when they're bad.*"

I ignored her.

No one can find me. No one can catch me. I am here in *this when* and I will not be in a hurry for another when. You see, Dammit, sometimes in this conversation with you I talk too much about what's happening, I move too fast, I forget the best parts happen when you slow down and get outside yourself.

I forget to tell you how bad (or is it good?) the beauty hurts, if I can be so bold to say. So, I will stop on this sun-warmed porch, and do that here:

You know there are places that feel like a warm bed with a dog breathing slow on a cold night? You know how the sun captures a certain green in the river that matches the lichen on the rusting cliffs and then bounces from the violet-green backs of the swallows? You know how the rippling heat unveils silver pools on the hill? You know how the afternoon's touch on your brown summer-skin wraps you like a blanket? Knit special for you by some mighty hand? You know how the circling hills and rocks and ponderosas cling to one another under the cerulean sky as if they are family; and through this sage-brimmed, rusted heart there runs a river?

There. You feel a moment too deep for words. As if, to find words, you must fall in the water once again? It was here, on my porch, that I knew I was not afraid of the water no more.

My eye caught movement at the riverside and at the same moment heard a sound that made the hair on my arms and neck and shaven head prickle: the screech of a dozer coming down the hill. I saw the faint and distant silhouette of myself — long-haired and crouching — step around a boulder and look up at the hill. I saw the pale form of MK come to stand next to me on the sand. I screamed in anguish – not knowing why—and jumped over the side of the porch before they could see me.

I ran down the narrow coulee that curls and drops from the back of the cabin towards the river. I was unsure of the reason, but I needed to be near my other self. And away from the dozer and you, Dammit, and Granma and Craig. I think if I'd seen you again, Dammit, my heart would rend.

It wasn't until I was striding waist-deep through the river with voices tugging at my legs that I realized I had left The Riverside on the porch, once again. I was crossing in the spot where the pool gets wide and shallow before making the turn around the cliffs.

MK was walking up the hill with his back to us, and my other self's back was turned to me, watching him go.

I almost walked back to my other self and grabbed myself to run.

But a *BOOM* threw me against the other bank where I scrabbled and pulled myself behind a thick sagebrush under a ponderosa.

The Mayfly Creature rose from the water between us, and I saw myself across the river turn white in fear. We both faced it and felt ourselves cry out. For it was looking at me—as surely on this side—as it was looking upon me on the other.

I groveled in the dust and tried to hide myself as it spoke once again.

This time I heard all of its words as I watched my other self, unhearing, crawl upon the stones under the water. But its words made no sense.

I saw myself crawl from the water like a nymphal stonefly, saw myself break through what I was and rise to my knees with water falling down my hair and face and in my eyes.

I stood up and reached to him. I knew in the depths of my being what he was going to pass through, and I wanted to hold him and tell him that he should not go.

My other self knelt there, rubbing water from his eyes, and looking straight at me.

"... *You find yourself a good place in the stories,*" my Momma said.
I knew I couldn't stay.
"*...You let them find a good place in you,*" she said.

I knew what I had to do. If no one can find me, and no one can catch me, then the opposite might be true. I can find anyone, and I can catch anyone I want to catch.

The dozer broke the fencepost *CRACK* and my other self turned to look up at the meadow.

I stepped behind the ponderosa and peered around it in time to see myself rub the last drops of water from my eyes and shake my head like a dog — shaking the image of the shorn-headed stranger from my mind. I watched me rise to one knee across the river, cough, and spit, watched my face harden, my shoulders stiffen, watched me stand up, turn away from the river and walk up the hill to enter this story.

I knew what I had to do.

I closed my eyes and saw the wrinkle in the mirror. It was like catching a sudden glimpse of the sun through a lifted curtain in a dark room. A curtain billowed by a quick breeze from the mountains in the still afternoon heat before a coming storm. *Of rivers and the chain-ed canyons free, A winding, restless spirit I will be.* I rubbed Mister Brown's penny, hot as an ember, and winked. And felt myself rush in a thick and billowing stream through the mirror and curtains to when I needed most to be.

Chapter 49

Living Words of Wind And Wave

I found myself in the lake up to my hips; cool water below, hot sun on my chest. Voices tugged my legs.

The blinded monster raged far up by the crushed cabin. It swung its tail trying to knock me down, but I was not there. It became more vicious. It tore ponderosas from the ground like weeds and flung them across the lawn.

A tree fell in the water next to me and a green wall over my head blocked the sun. The wave knocked me on my back. I screamed underwater, felt my lungs exploding as a watery hand entered. I heard many things through the tympany of my lungs: a rising wail of voices, louder than my own heart's beating. The singing of seals, far away in the north under the ice floes where the light touches the deep.

I stood, vomited water in a flood, dry-heaved and fell against the steadying, rough bark of the ponderosa which now jutted diagonally from the lake. Its head in water, its cinnamon-orange trunk and muddy roots to the sky.

Never had sand underfoot felt so solid.

I beat him.

All I had to do was show Big Jim to itself. The monster was now a melting insect the size of a house tearing itself and everything to pieces.

I had won.

I leaned against the dripping bark and pulled Penny's soaked book from my shirt pocket. The back cover fell open. I saw familiar handwriting: "*I hope he remembers that any child whose mother is of the sea and whose father is of the mountains is he foretold from of old, living words of wind and wave.*"

I felt something in me ring, struck like an iron bell.

MK came walking slowly along the sand hands clasped behind him as if he had nothing better to do than see the sights after brunch. I threw Penny's book on the shore at his feet to dry.

Living words of wind and wave.

"That book, AGAIN, Romes? You need to run, not read."

Living words of wind and wave. Where had I heard that before? The sun glanced off the water like a thousand stars. I had spoken these words to myself, recently, I felt it in my bones, but I could not remember their meaning. My head ached. I knew I was supposed to remember, to feel the words in me and know where they came from, but the heat was a giant's hand crushing my face and I was unsteady from the wink to get back from the riverside. The words in me jangled around like rocks in a can.

The monster raged — still blind — a hundred yards away and laid waste to what remained of the porch. It wasn't dying like I expected. It seemed to be bigger, more angry. There was something I needed to remember. Something I heard before, a song? Something under the green wave.

"Why are you here?" I asked him. "Why did you come to me all those years ago? Why did you stay?"

He shrugged and cracked his knuckles and looked across the lake at the grey mountains. "We don't have time to do this, Romes. You have GOT to run. That thing," he pointed up the lawn, "...is NOT going to die. The robe will re-form its eyesight soon."

I felt a weight the size of Sonofa crush my chest. Darkness came over my eyes. "Fifteen-rounds," said Mister Brown somewhere in my head, and I felt my hands close in fists; if he was there, I would have ripped off his arms. "Who are you?" I asked.

MK's face seemed hewn from ancient cliffs. "I am the one who kept you safe."

"Keep me safe?" I shouted. "Murderer. I will HUNT you to the END of the earth." I felt the file bend within the iron grip of my hand. "What ARE you? Have you nothing to say?"

"Sometimes the children are too loud," MK said flatly. He was somewhere far away. Then he spoke slowly as if in a dream, "The knave, the knave of wind and wave," he muttered. "Run knave, run."

I could not move, even if I wanted to. A feeling began to vibrate, from the soles of my feet up through my body; a slow, growing, impending vibration that shook me like a squirrel in the jaws of a cougar—and blew out the top of my head.

I rang again like an iron bell.

And all I saw was Penny's words on that last page: *Living words of wind and wave.*

It was too late, anyway, to run. The monster had regained its sight, healed somehow by the robe it wore, and — in a storm of wings and legs — landed on the sand in front of us, laughing softly. It waved a pincer-hand and thick clouds came furling to block the sun and fill the air with water. Grey light filtered through the mist.

"I see you, mmm." The voice was quiet, like a baby's. "Didn't I promise I would take everything from you?" Its voice changed to the deep rumble. A heavy, wet twilight descended, damp with the smell of rotting bodies, and it spoke the ancient curse: "*When mountain's son and ocean's line betroth, surely water's blood is bloody end, and bloodied end the child of wroth.*" The beast shook out its glistening wings. "My curse fulfilled today," it said. "And now, no sun to shine from mirrors, boy."

I could barely see in the twilight. It felt like we stood on that shore by the river where the boy met the skukm in Mister Brown's story. And then I realized why.

I was the boy, and here was the skukm glaring with its glowing faceted eyes.

I saw every word on the page I opened in the library that first day: "*The face, a conglomeration of plates separated by seams. The compound eye is composed of nearly 30,000 lenses, with a quick turn of the head, they are able to scan 360. Their vision allows them to discern individual wing beats, which to us would appear as a blur, and ultraviolet light.*"

"I SEE you, mmm," it said again, quietly in Big Jim's voice through mandibles moving sideways like razor-doors. Its eyes glistened. "I see inside you. I will eat your heart in front of you while you watch me eat you. Kneel before me, worship!"

"Still the villain," I said, not knowing where the courage came from. "Still talking too much, boasting too long."

"Kneel!" It demanded.

"Nope." That was it. Would have made you proud, Dammit.

"Mmm... I wear the robe."

"You don't wear it — jackass." The words came from some unknown depth. "Only *one* wears *that* robe. And you are not him. Nor do you wear it well. Beware."

"You will kneel to me, you will worship me, you will die, and I will make you watch me and beg it all to end," it said quietly.

And then — still vibrating like a struck bell — I'm overcome by a memory. Sitting on Granma's porch with you, Dammit. I can see you: every detail, the old scar up your face that splits your ear, your golden eyes, and the fresh wound on your neck from the battle with Achilles.

I say, *"I feel like it's a knot, and it's too hard to untie."*
And you say, *"Sometimes the knot needs only a knife."*
And I finally get it. So, I say it out loud. "Sometimes the knot needs only a knife." I stand up proudly, feel my shoulders straighten. "I'm the knife."

The monster's eyes flickered in confusion.

What a jackass, I thought. Surprise rolled over me. I was talking like Dad! But I kept going: *"Thou art an envious emulator of every man's good parts, a secret and villainous contriver against me,"* I said, and it felt so good to get it out. "A plague upon you."

"Mmm?" The monster moaned.

MK, still standing on shore, pointed at me like he'd just seen something cool, and winked. He seemed tired, with a shadow of a smile. "Point to you, Romes," he said. "Remember the story you heard in the library."

For a moment I did not understand him. Then, I saw Mister Brown in the library slapping his meat stick on the counter and laughing at the horrified look on my face at his skukm story. And I got a crazy-ass idea, a fool's glimmer, a chance-of-a-chance-of-a-wish.

"You're nothing. You're weak," I said.

I thought of the wonderful boy and the skukm, and how the boy got the skukm to stick a finger in the crack in the tree.

"That buffalo robe's the only way you could ever finish me, jackass," I said. "You got no strength without it. You're old. And dumb. Fat, powerless."

"Mmm-aaaghh," It murmured, still gentle and soft as a woman nursing a baby, but behind the murmur was the awful sheering of its jaws — *click click.* "Speak not to me of strength, mmm I am FULL of it."

"Full of it. Yeah, you are," I said, trying to keep the tremble from my voice.

"I will crush you NOW."

"You need the robe to do it."

"I could CRUSH you with one finger. Without this robe!"

"Horseshit," I said. "Then show me. I don't believe you."

The monster paused a moment and I saw the thought pass his many-mirrored eyes plain as day. But he dismissed it — the thought that this boy was dangerous, the thought that there was some kind of hidden strength. There was nothing this boy could do to him. Not after the axe was broken and Penny's mirror melted. I must have looked like a drowned rat, standing there up to my hips in water. Like so many of the kids whose souls he'd poisoned in the rabbit-glade.

The grey above us began to drizzle, and it got real dark.

"I WILL SHOW YOU." Taloned arms ripped the shaggy robe from his thorax and held it to the side. Big Jim waved the robe and chuckled. Now, he didn't sound like a nursing mother; he sounded like the nursing mother's baby being murdered with giant shearing scissors — *click click*. "Fool," he whispered. "I will eat out your heart."

"Eat YOUR heart out dumbass," said Mister Bay, popping out from behind Big Jim like he been there all along. He yanked the robe from Big Jim's talon and put it on. Then he turned to me. "Many thanks, young one."

The monster screamed and stamped its foot. But it stepped back from Mister Bay; a flicker of fear played across its mirrored eyes.

Mister Bay winked, ignoring Big Jim. "Forget not how esteemed you are," he tapped his nose, "...to my nose." His amber-gem eyes glowed with laughter. He turned to MK, who did the strangest thing of all.

MK bowed to him.

"You may speak—but you are not to help anyone," said Mister Bay. "And you are constrained to this stratum." Mister Bay turned, tapped his nose once again at me, flipped his long braids over his shoulder, pointed where he wanted to go, took one step, and was gone. He didn't even seem to need a door like MK. One moment he was there — and then he wasn't. All that remained was a hint of the smell of warm prairie in the sun and an old buffalo hide.

The monster smiled and the spider legs came out towards my face. "Mmm...Aagghh. I need no feeble robe to crush you now."

I heard someone chuckle and realized it was me. "Methinks the poet doth protest much," I said.

MK grinned. "*Gertrude, Act III, Scene 2,* but you ruined it."

The monster *click clicked*, "Better yet, I promised to take everything from you. Mmm and I will do that now." Big Jim pointed a talon at MK, "Slave. Now you take his memories and his soul. Like you took his father's."

If there was a way for MK to turn paler than he already was, he would have. He looked stricken. Then slowly he came walking into the water.

I backed up. The lake touched my chest. "Don't touch me, murderer."

It was then I realized I never seen him cry, and even now there were no tears. He was surrounded by sorrow like a shawl, entombed as if he had died in the sorrow, and shaking. His gun-hole eyes were no longer black. They swirled with the distances of space. I saw within them far-off galaxies slipping over the edges of black-hole whirlpools. He smiled and cracked his knuckles. "Ah Romes, it's not as bad as it looks."

He spoke loudly; Big Jim heard him and grunted in approval. MK leaned forward until all I saw was those eyes.

Behind him I heard the monster chuckle, *click click*, "Yesss. You will take him, and he will lie there screaming with no sound and we shall watch him dig out his heart. Mmm one scratch at a time."

"I'm done," I said. "Do what you will."

"Clay." He used my name. His breath was that familiar leftover scent of lightning on granite. "First. Remember I swore to serve the ruler of this town? Well, the ruler of this town is the one with the robe. So."

A fire entered my heart and I understood.

MK continued, "Second. Remember that day we stayed out way too long in the snow waiting for the cougar? Remember what you did after you took his life?"

Of course, I remember. I can't forget.

"You were going to die of hunger. So, you blessed him and ate his heart there in the snow."

The memory came over me. The tang of iron on my tongue, the rasp of organ meat against my teeth.

"Ah, hesitater. You think you freeze — and yet you can act in a flash," MK said. "Why is that?"

I felt MK's presence around me like a dark mantle, and I could not speak.

Big Jim *clicked clicked* impatiently, "FINISH HIM."

MK paid him no mind. "It's not hesitating. It's waiting... for the right moment. Like your forefathers. You know it's true. And this. One last gift I give. You'll thank me, you will." He smiled sadly.

I clamped my eyes shut and waited for IT to happen.

He bent over me, his pale hair falling like a curtain on every side.

I expected to be staring through MK's eyes at the vacant body of Clay digging his heart from his chest. I expected, somehow, to feel my empty mind left behind in a gaping body. A loose boat. Marooned with one single desire. To chop a hole in its floorboards and let the waters in. Or let blood out. *Blood Blood Blood.* I expected to be up to my neck, in a river of blood.

"Remember this knave, when you come for me," MK whispered. "I could've taken your memories like I take everyone's. But I lied for you, instead. Clay." He said my name as if he were calling to me from a pit for help.

MK turned and said flatly to Big Jim, "He is resistant, there is something upon him I cannot touch."

The monster paused in mid *click*. Its mandibles hung like dead tapeworms. It looked surprised. Like it was taking a crap, and someone opened the bathroom door.

"END HIM. DO WHAT I SAY!"

"I can't do it. I'm still avowed servant of the one ruler of this town, and that happens to be... whoever wears the robe...." MK let the last word trail off as he watched Big Jim slowly realize what it lost. Rage, and then fear, twisted across the massive human-insect face.

MK popped his knuckles and turned to me. I could tell if he could cry, he would be. "Keep looking for the knave of hearts, Romes. You'll find him one day."

"I will find you, one day," I said, surprising myself. "And when I do, I won't be froze no more and we will end this."

"It is the one thing I'm counting on, tater," he said, and waded back to the shore.

"I've been waiting to say this for a while," he said to Big Jim, lifting his flaxen curls with a long hand to shake them over his back. "BJ — by the way, a great name, that — you know what you can do?"

"HUH?" said the monster. "What?"

"Suck my fat, ten-thousand-year-old chubby.

Chapter 50

I Am But Mad, North North-West

Big Jim made a sound like a bull moose lying down in muck. The same sound he made when he forced the boys to watch Junior stab the rabbit. "Mmm. Who cares if you're not usefull *click* but I know this: you're not to interfere."

"He's right, I can't help," said MK.

The monster laughed, "Suck on that Death Messenger."

"Forgive me, I will not stay to see this happen. Not to you." MK stepped into his doorway; unfurled wings of shadow. "*Love is merely a madness, Romes, and deserves a whip for madmen.*" His face disappeared in the shadow of his door. "Forgive me. A tired, old killer. You and I — we got something right."

"No," I said. "We got nothing. Liar, murderer," I threw words at him like stones. "Father-killer. I'm gonna find you. And take all your memories like you took my dad's. No forgiveness. I will track you down."

Big Jim popped its maxillae *click click*, and chuckled. It sounded like water going down a drain, houses on fire, and dogs getting kicked.

I felt it in my bones: It was time to die.

Then MK spoke from the doorway — someone's voice I would know anywhere, even if I was blind. It started quietly, a song I'd heard her sing before:

"Living words, wind and wave,
Comes the one who kills his blood.
Curse of death and open grave,
Vengeance mine and rolling flood.

Child of sadness, sings to save,
When all things new a-bud."

"Oh, my boy. You never was alone," said Granma. "Didn't I hear you say it? *Of rivers and the chain-ed canyons free, A winding, restless spirit I will be.* You don't need no gimmicks. My Clayton, the very best kind of special. Put on Pop's cap, see for yourself."

My heart spasmed. I took her cap from my back pocket and put it on my head.

Big Jim was a white grub, a legless pale hairless baby pulling itself with pudgy hands over a ledge towards me, leering. Behind the grub, in the no-home of its chasm, swirled pure nothing. Absence. A backwater of inbred self. I fell back in disgust, trying to get away, but it kept crawling. It was coming to crawl inside me.

Then I saw them. Everywhere around us. Watchers. Some with wings, some with eyes like flames, some like wolves with swords coming from their mouths, and some like men with great axes in their hands and beards to their chests. Women like wild silky creatures with black eyes like seals. None of them speaking a word. All of them watching.

I fell on my knees and the water closed around my chest. The voices in the green wave wailed. Rocks gouged my shins and I gasped. There was something here I was supposed to remember. *Living words of wind and wave.*

Big Jim's insect-arm swatted the cap from my head onto the sand. The crawling grub turned back into a massive insect; the watchers flickered and disappeared. If you were there, Dammit, you would have seen a lawn — turning black under swirling clouds — stretching away under a twilight mist. You would have seen a dragonfly with wings of diamond, refracting eyes, talons like spears, churning garden-shear jaws and slithering snake-probosces rising over a desperate boy. A desperate boy kneeling and crying in a black lake.

"You are right to kneel," it said softly. "I'm going to crawl inside you through that little window mmm. Crawl inside you and eat you, boy, from the inside. And turn you into me... and me into you."

The clouds grew black with rain; a dark mist rose from the lake.

"I know what you're afraid of, boy." Big Jim's voice fell. "Yourself. Mmm? You stink of it. You smell of self-hate. Aaah, there." He saw my face. "I see the window now and I'm coming in."

It took a step into the water.

"I'll tell you this, boy: the truth. *You* killed your parents."

My heart split as if pierced by the very sword he had pierced my father.

I felt him inside me, one grubby arm across the window of my soul pushing through shattered glass and feeling for the latch.

"It's your fault," it said.

"Everything's my fault," I said. "SO WHAT. I killed my own Granma, you plague." Hollow voices in the deeps rang against my chest. "COME ON. Climb in through that window."

It groaned, spread its mouth-labium wide.

I rose, muscles rippling like a cougar. *O, from this time forth, my thoughts be bloody, or be nothing worth!* I grabbed the pebble-sized booger that was somehow still stuck to my shirt — it peeled off easily, still warm, hard as a pebble — and threw it at Big Jim's face. I threw as hard as I could with all the strength I had left in me.

The booger burrowed into Big Jim's splintered eye like a hot rock into butter.

The eye caved in on itself *thunk* like a rotten egg dropped on the ground.

Big Jim groaned and clawed its face, slicing green flesh in ribbons. Wings like a thousand flashing mirrors rustled—then froze straight out like knives. It caught my throat in giant talons. The cratered eye flashed mirrored fires and splattered pus on my face.

"How stand I then," I thought, *"that have a father kill'd and mother stain'd? O, thoughts be bloody."*

Big Jim's monstrous mouth opened, and I saw side-grinding razors. From within the mouth and above the jaws, something fat, red, dripping. A tongue turned inside out, a naked eyeless baby. The tongue stiffened. The eyeless baby spat a stream of yellow mucous.

I screamed and plunged my burning face in the water. And felt myself pulled into a cool jade world, heard someone from within speak very clearly, and very quietly:

Stop thinking, just be.

The voices came at me in a wave, then, a rising chorus, and I finally heard them and understood what they wanted.

"Of rivers and the chained canyons free, A winding restless spirit thou shalt be." A musical bow pulled across wild strings; if the strings were old-growth ponderosa pines with 500-year-old roots, and ancient salmon rivers, and granite peaks far-ridged to the sky. *"Living words of wind and wave, Child of sadness, born to save,"* they sang.

The monster-dragonfly pulled me from the water by my shoulders. Its single good eye blazed. Its dead eye spattered pus. *"Boy,* there's always the old-fashioned way." It groaned with pleasure, "Mmm. Watch me punch a hole in your ribs and eat your living heart."

My body twitched. That familiar ball of fear. Numbness in my arms. Burning mucous tore the skin on my face. I closed my eyes, felt its mandible gently scrape the skin of my chest, feeling for a spot between my ribs.

A shout — *Zimilibus!*

The monster cursed, the mandible withdrew. I felt my body lifted and thrown in the lake once again. I sank to my knees at the bottom; I saw a fresh sea-green wave in the distance rushing at me. I heard her familiar voice upon it like the crying of a hundred seals. My Momma:

"Son, don't forget you're mine. Remember. Remember..."

I stood, gasping for air, and saw Mister Brown clinging to one leg of the monster like a monkey on a bucking bronco.

"Can't let you get all the glory, lil bruh. *Yeehah!*"

Clasped on the other back leg was the naked, raw, eye-less, bleeding Doc Ranulf.

"Fight," Doc croaked. His skinned skull-face with one staring bloody eye, fangs, and tongue. "*Gefeht!*" He howled. "Fight Stonefly... FIGHT and fight!"

Mister Brown yipped like a wild dog and waved his arm high, meat stick and all, "Awooooo. Fifteen rounds!"

Big Jim ripped Doc from neck to crotch and dropped the torn body on the sand. Mister Brown scampered up the lawn towards Doc's cabin, but the monster flashed its mirrored wings, rose in a storm, and cut him off. In the distance I saw Big Jim catch Mister Brown with a sharp talon through his chest, and slowly rip his legs from their sockets.

"NO!" I screamed.

I stared at Doc's bleeding body, half in the water and half on the sand. The body that kept coming back over and over because his spirit would not quit.

"*Fight,*" he whispered.

And then, quietly, whatever remained of him was gone. Like the moment after a song is finished, and you still hear it; like the smell of fire and smoke after the candle is snuffed. Replaced by torn shreds of tissue and the tinge of blood in a film across the water.

That is when MK spoke from the blackness of the winged door. "Ah Romes. Remember when I said to Ms. Swan I had to go Danish-prince-crazy to make this work?"

"*I am but mad north-north-west,*" I groaned. Two friends, torn to pieces.

"Shut up," MK said. "Can't you see I'm trying to say goodbye?" He held his hands towards me. "*Good night sweet knave, and flights of angels sing thee to thy rest.*" Black eyes inscrutable; dark mirrors of my own darkened face. "Name it," he said. "One last time, for a friend."

"Horatio, you fool," I choked, "the only friend he had." I went to push my hair from my face and felt rough stubble. "But it's 'prince,' not 'knave.'"

"Point to you. But you're wrong. You're the knave of wind and wave. You're the fool, the one to save. Still up three—and oh, so brave."

What a jackass. Even now, rhyming with bad meter.

MK's voice became gruff, a tone I knew all too well: "It's time, Jackass," said Dad. "Time for loco."

I was a twelve-year old standing in the water, waiting for his father to speak one last time.

"All them gods and monsters, them sonsa bitches, they know The Conveners, the Coeur De Montagnes. The ones who keep 'em honest. Every Nisoi knows Jack's axe. And everyone in the family – everyone but you—knows the family nickname: *'Jacksaxe.'* A name polished under the pressure of a thousand years like a river polishes a stone. Polished into *'Jackass.'*" The voice of my father faded to a whisper. "Our family name; the best of 'em all. Jackass," he said. "Hold fast."

I knew this was the last gasp of a memory stuck like gum to MK's mind, but it was still true.

"Us," Dad muttered. "It was us who forged *Acuere* from the bones." His voice was almost gone, a glistening line, a zephyr. "But know this: It wasn't the axe that killed the giant." MK's face was dark, inscrutable, and my father spoke clearly from his mouth: "Jack Coeur De Montagne had something else. He ripped the heart-bone from that giant's chest. And used it on him. No more thinking, Jackass. Do it!"

I pulled the file from my pocket.

Its whole length glittered like obsidian under a full moon. Its filing ridges were gone, replaced by a wide swirl moving like a snake. It was not a file. It was a bone vibrating with power, dripping black sparks. It must do that when it's around monsters. The heart-bone of a giant. Stolen by my great-ancestor who started this whole thing. It poked and bothered me for a full day. Like a seed stuck in the back of my mouth. Why had I kept it? Something in me must have known, Dammit, right?

"*Before my God,*" said MK in awe, "*I might not this believe without the sensible and true avouch of mine own eyes.*"

"You're not gonna HELP me finish this fight?" I yelled. "You're a BUM leg." I waved the spark-dripping bone at him. "A bum leg that gives out when I need it most. Just leave me alone!"

His eyes shone black the only way that *nothing* shines when you put a fence of *something* around it. The same two gun-holes I saw that day we left the home place.

"So be it," he said. "*Ve'achron.*"

"*Alafar yaqum,*" I said, and hated myself.

From the space behind the closing door the monster rose slowly. *Click Click.* It chuckled softly. "Oh no, no, no. Mmm what is this stick, this puny thing, in your hand?"

"No son of mine afraid of water," beyond the closing door, I heard MK whisper. "Jackass."

And I remembered what my Momma said. *"When you're afraid—go to your water."*

"Today you die," said Big Jim.

I stepped backwards.

The wailing in the green wave rose around my chest, I heard the singing again, and this time I knew the lyrics.

That is when I felt it. For the first time, ever, Dammit. What them voices been singing all along to me. Not just heard it; felt it. *Living words of wind and wave.* I tasted iron. The hair rose on my arms. I swear lighting was about to strike. The River of No Return that runs through the heart of the wilderness sprung from the soles of my feet and rose through my spine to my right hand. Something like black blood dripped from the heart bone.

Chapter 51

When Wishes Were For Wishing

"Of rivers and the chain-ed canyons free," I said. I pointed Pop's file at the sky. *"A winding, restless spirit I will be."*

Big Jim was a black shadow in the fading light. It raised its talons and called the storm in waves that crashed against my shoulders. Curtains of froth ripped from their crests into the storm like bats.

"I sing of waters, and I sing of land," I said, not knowing why.

Nothing happened.

Big Jim chuckled, "That little wand? Mmm." His voice gained confidence *click click*, "I have grown beyond the robe. This little land? I'm the master."

"No shit Sherlock," I raised my Grandfather's file. "You know your problem?" My voice was firm. "You got no homeplace, no land. How about you shut up and fight?" I summoned every power in me and winked. I saw black tendrils climb my arm, circling the heart-bone. I flicked a bead from the tip towards Big Jim but then — as if confronted by an invisible wall — it rose to hover twenty feet above its head.

"Uh - Oh," said Big Jim in singsong. "Premature ejaculation of magic, mmm a common rookie problem." He cackled.

My arm fell to my side. A wave knocked me forward.

"Plague you," I said.

Big Jim cleaned its mandibles like a beaver cleans its face with its paws *click click* "I'm going to climb in your window, push you in your trench, and live inside you. Teenage magic can't bind me."

"Then get it over, windbag." I prepared, once again, to die, or worse.

Click click.

I tried to imagine you, Dammit, wherever you are, running wild towards a swift sunrise.

Click Click.

And then: the memory of my Momma four years ago in the raft rose in me: *"It's like learning to whistle, Baby Grizz. You try and try. And then one day, it's just there."*

So, I tried one last time. And learned to whistle.

It is not an equation,
   Nor a hex, a hoodoo or charm.
   It is not a formula, nor incantation
   — though it does move as if
   breathed through by magic —
   Nor is it meant to do harm.
   It is not a conjuration, a bewitchment, a sorcery,
   Nor anything resembling a recitation,
   Or, whatever riddles one tells.
   If it is anything at all, then maybe
   It is an invocation, in first-fruiting — a spell.

Only in this sense, Dammit: that when I spell out the letters into words, and the words into lines, and those lines become a story – when I spell the story, I feel the wind and the wave and the living silver that runs through its heart. Something like that.

Click Click. The monster moves very close. Playing with me.

"*A long time ago, when wishes were for wishing and aiming was for aiming, and sometimes both came true....*" The story comes from me like a rolling stream.

Mandibles caress my forehead. "Mmm, boy," he speaks softly. "What foolishness is this?"

My voice quivers, but I speak, and the words are a smooth, unending line cast from the heart-bone into the storm:

"*A skukm was going there and he came upon a boy in distress, in need of aid. A boy whose heart was dark and sad as the skukm's and just as fierce.*"

There was a gurgling behind me like the sound of a giant drain.

I saw a shadow twist across Big Jim's remaining eye.

The water stirred, something rose from the deep: Vast, hairy, long as a Viking ship, wider than a house, covered in steaming hair like a yak with spider legs, thin arms long as oars and pale as corpses—with fingers like jointed crepuscular snakes and a mouth that would have swallowed Mister Brown's skukm whole. It was ravenous, ancient. It smelled of hunger like a broken, diseased carbuncle.

I knew its shape from of old. The shape in my dreams that killed all hope, the seeker of murderers, the darkness of vengeance, the long-dead nemesis of my family that stalked us for centuries. It was not a nightmare. It was *the* nightmare. I knew it well, for its image woke me screaming many a night and kept me awake until dawn. This was no image, no dream. This was the real beast. *The Terror*, my forebears called it—a title, an honorific, and a curse all in one—even my father spoke this name with a grey face: *Das Ungeheuer.*

It spoke and the waves died. *"Murdererrr. You raissse me from Hell for thisss?"*

The water became black as poison. And still as a mirror.

"The ssstench of murderrr risessss from you like incenssse."

I knew its language, somehow.

"Kin-killerrr. On your people'sss fear I fed, boyyy, on their long-held murderer'sss cursse, and you call me back? Your ancesssstorss who fought a thousssand yearrrsss to kill me would cursse thisss day." It crept forward and grass withered black on the shoreline. *"Shall I not feed upon yourrrr heart? I come for murderersss and you are one. I am justiccce. I ammm the end."*

Big Jim chuckled.

"Murdererrr." It spoke from a mouth the size of a cave that could swallow a house. *"A merccccy I pronounccce: If you give your heart of your free will, your sssoul I shall releassse. Thusss it is done. Thusss it has always been done. Thusss it shall be. And ever shall be. Let me feeeeeeed."*

Big Jim clacked its mandibles. "It's unfortunate, boy. You see, these ancient ones, they live by a code, and you got to pay. In blood." He laughed, bending over, clutching his thorax.

The Ungeheuer moved towards me.

"Mmm. Payment in kind, boy," said Big Jim. "And you have nothing to give but yourself." He pointed a talon at me, and his voice rose, triumphant: *"I TOLD you I would take EVERYTHING from you."*

"Not everything," I said, and took the backpack from my shoulders and pulled out the box.

The Ungeheuer paused, hissing.

The box was soaked and smelled of dried blood. Like iron and clay. I picked away the fragments of the box and lifted Achille's heart in my hand. "How about this?" I asked.

Big Jim went *click click* and I saw confusion. The Ungeheuer hissed.

"Is that my dog's heart?" Big Jim asked.

"Yup," I said.

"He belonged to me!"

"You should have belonged to him!" I yelled. "You don't deserve the fealty of this heart!"

"*Silence fooolllsss.*" The Ungeheuer came forward, dripping water from its yak hide. Its face I cannot describe to you, Dammit, except to say it has no eyes and is mostly a mouth and the mouth is mostly teeth, and the teeth are mostly jagged serrated swords except for the ones in back that look like snakes. It dragged a carpet of hairy mucous. Then I realized this must be its flaccid backside that rippled in the water like an algae bloom, like someone poured a tanker of shit into the lake. I saw creatures crawling upon the filth. Writhing worms and grasping ticks fat with blood. Maggots twisted in the sludge.

"Of all the things to call up for your death mmm." Big Jim settled on the sand at the edge. "And I get a front row seat."

The Ungeheuer reached out a mouth from inside its mouth, took Achille's heart, turned its eyeless face upon me and I shook.

But I looked it full in the face. I heard Dad somewhere in my head, "you better look it in the eye; you're the one that called it up." There were no eyes, so I looked upon its face and despaired.

"*Yesssssssss. A worthy recompenssse, the heart of an enemy onccce, and now a friend. Redeemed. You do well to give me the hearrrt of the sssservant of your enemy.*"

It ate Achilles heart.

Big Jim made a sound like a snail stepped on by a boot. "Why?" croaked Big Jim. "Why, why.... Why are you here?"

"*Sssssss.*" It sounded angry. "*You KNOW The Why. Thissss boy... he isss The Why. But the dog, the dog. The dog isss the how. You want to know how thisss heart I consssume changessss all?*"

"No, I don't want to know anything anymore."

I could barely hear Big Jim. He backed up slowly.

"*You ssseek to become like me, yet you do not ssserve. All of us ssserve. Great is your foolishnessss. Thisss heart tassstes of loyalty. Corruption, yesssss. But loyalty more. Thisss heart — evil as it wasss — gave itssself in final brrreath to one dessserving of itsss love.*" The Ungeheuer gave a shuddering gulp, and I saw Achilles' heart squeege and glumph down its throat — like a mole goes down a hole — into a gullet-crop like a chicken. The Ungeheuer belched and withered a stand of aspen fifty feet away.

"*Though you were thisss dog'sss liege, hisss massster you were not.*"

It turned its sightless and horrible face towards Big Jim.

"*In hisss loyalty the dog has ssserved his massster with one last gift — and thusss, when I reccceive the gift, I am sssworn fealty to him as massster.*"

Big Jim moaned.

"*Thusss it is done. Thusss it has always been done. And EVER shall be. Hisss servant I am, Hisss command I obey. This ssstone that fliesss.*" And it bowed its great head into the lake and its voice rose in a stench through the churning water. "*I worship thee. Maaassssterrrr. I worship thee.*"

Thank you, Achilles. You were more right in your death than you ever were in your life. Sometimes dogs are right.

If you were there, Dammit, you'd a said, "Always dogs are right."

Point to you, Dammit.

I turned to Big Jim. Its mandibles hung from its razor jaws and its single refractive eye blinked dully.

"Mmm," I said.

"You wouldn't dare," Big Jim whispered.

"Bigger dog. Harder fall," I said.

Big Jim looked puzzled. Then it roared—and leapt at me. The heart bone, directed by my hand, moved imperceptibly. The drop of dark magic that had hovered this whole time in the mists above Big Jim grew to a boulder and crashed down, crushing him like a cliff sheering off a mountain.

He flung it over his shoulder into the trees. Then he leaped straight at me.

But.

When Big Jim came flying at me, spraying water in waves, my Ungeheuer reached out a giant spider-hand, caught him, and squeezed him until he screamed. Suddenly, the wind died to a deathly still, the waves fell back. But the darkness grew.

Click click. Big Jim's mandibles snapped madly, sheering sideways like great swords, but they had no impact on the ghostly-white fingers that held him. "I should have crushed you the first day I saw you," he shouted. "Stabbed you through the heart. Argg! Like your father."

I felt the grin rise up my face, and said to my Ungeheuer, "Squeeze him hard."

My Ungeheuer bent Big Jim's head down with a finger. *"Worship the masssterrrr,"* it said. *"Bow to him and worship."*

"AAAAGHHHH," yelled Big Jim. "I worship! I worship!"

"I don't need your worship, jackass," I said.

I waded to the shore, picked up Granma's cap and removed a cig – somehow still dry—from inside the brim. I flicked open Pop Bergmann's double-bladed axe lighter, and the flame shone steady in the twilight. I lit the soggy cigarette, sucked in a deep wet drag and blew it through my nose.

On one side of Pop's lighter, the embossed double-bladed axe was a spitting image of *Acuere*. I remembered that I never *really* looked at the other side. I turned it over. Engraved on the back of Pop's lighter, a mustached man with a tiny smirk. Holding that double-bladed axe he forged from the bones of the first giant, surrounded by hearts rising like swallows to the sun, my missing face-card ("You'll find him someday" I heard MK say). It was The Knave of Hearts. Above him the ancient family name, *"Coeur De Montagne."* Curling around the edges, in silver filigree—like the heart-bone in my hand—dances the words: *"The Knave of Wind and Wave."* You know who this is ("Coeur," is just French for "heart"); it is your ancestor, and the smirking face is the spitting image of your own.

"I'm the son of George Bergmann and Rose-Marie Stonefly, grandson of Beaumont and Karolina, friend of Achilles and Dammit, the scion of a mighty house, the last of my line, the consummation of your very curse, a scourge... a plague upon you." I blew smoke in his face. "I don't need worship from anyone." The loudness of my voice surprised me. A deep voice: a man I did not know.

"Yessss Masssteer. Now you sssseeeeeeee."

"His bodyguards and silver cane were no match for the Jack of Hearts," I said. I pretended I was Granma and flipped the cig in Big Jim's face. "How 'bout that, jackass."

"That's not Shakespeare," he whimpered.

"Don't matter." I flipped open the lighter and watched the flame burn red in the twilight of the storm. For a moment all I could think of was MK on the porch cracking jokes about third base, calling me Romes, and burning his fingertips. "It's a game I play with MK. You're not a part of it," I said. "You're done."

Big Jim shrunk. All the monster parts sucked back into him. He was a small and pitiful little man the size of a baby in the hand of my Ungeheuer.

"Please. Don't kill me. What have I ever done to you mmm?"

My Ungeheuer turned its terrible flat eyeless face towards me. *"Masssterr, let me eat thisss traitorrr. He isss filled with murderrsss. The olderrr they are, and the more the murderrrsss — the tassstierrr."*

"Nope," I said. "Hold him."

Big Jim's refracting eyes and razor jaws were gone, sucked away somewhere. His pudgy body writhed with burrowing Ungeheuer vermin. He whispered softly, "You and I — we got nothing against one another, do we?" The voice became sweet. "I've been so alone. Will you be a friend to me mmm?" There was magic in the voice, the kind that makes you tired and willing all at once. The magic crept through a window into my soul. He was inside me, taking up the oxygen in the room. Quiet, insistent.

"I know you want your parents, I'll give them to you," he said. We sat on a small ledge within me; he placed an arm over my shoulder like an old friend. "Mmm. Come out of the water, boy, let me stay here with you." He had wise eyes — not an enemy at all. It wanted to be my friend, to stay with me forever. It pointed a fat finger at the trench that dropped below the ledge, and its other hand inched along my arm.

I knew my parents were down there. I let my friend take me by the arm and together, we leaned over the edge.

"Mmm, just here. Look."

I felt my far-away legs start to walk out of the water. My foreign mouth opened to order my Ungeheuer to depart.

"Zimilia Zimilibus!" Did I imagine a shout?

Then, I saw your golden eyes, Dammit, on that day on the porch with me at Granma's, confident, grinning like a sonofabitch. Once again: *"Sometimes the knot needs only a knife."*

I remembered who I am, remembered what I am, but mostly, I remembered when I am. *Of rivers and the chain-ed canyons free, A winding, restless spirit I will be.* Like my ancestor The Knave of Wind and Wave before me, I am the maker and molder of tales, a jackknife of many stories. I am The Jack of Hearts.

"You can't eat my soul, I am born of water," I said, and jumped through his last shining eye, a depthless mirror with no bottom. Found the wasting location of his soul-less, dead-star-sucking hole. Shoved him over the edge and heard him scream like a slaughtered pig as the monster fell into his own trench. When it tried to climb out, I raised my grandfather's heart-bone, summoned a prisoner's shackles, and chained that larva to itself.

"You're not crawling in me no more," I said.

Then I jumped out of the monster, found myself alive and strong, water swirling at my knees, and pulled the silver sword from the sheath at Big Jim's side. He never thought to use it in the fight. Now, it shrank to a hunting knife.

I told my Ungeheuer to hold Big Jim by the arms. You will like this next bit, Dammit. I castrated him.

He writhed and screamed.

I flung his shriveled bits – crawling with insects—into the mouth of my Ungeheuer.

The knife grew back to its full size. Glittering, four feet long. I thought to myself, "This is the sword that pierced my father's heart." Certainly, stolen, and not Big Jim's. As sharp as a morning mountain and straight as a sunbeam that cuts through mist.

"Your curse has fallen on you," I cleaned the blade in the water. "As curses often do." Then, I quoted the original to him so he could catch the twist, the final truth:

"When mountain's son and ocean's line betroth,

Surely water's blood is bloody end,
And bloodied end the child of wroth."

"I'm your bloody end, bitch." I shoved the silver sword through Big Jim's eye, grating on his eye-socket. "I'm gonna take everything from you." Then — with a wave of my swirling heart-bone like a splinter of the dark sun — I threw him in the maw of my Ungeheuer.

My Ungeheuer's tongues – many and various like worms – pinched the skin on Big Jim's head and tore it from his seeping muscles. Like pulling the skin from a squirrel, like Big Jim did to Doc, a slow and continuous flaying that forced a scream from Big Jim with every tug. Some of the tongues held him tight, and some of them ripped. It was like watching a hundred worms peel the sock from a foot, leaving a glistening, bloody afterbirth with blinded eyes.

My Ungeheuer gulped; its throat like a muscle slid Big Jim's skin down, down into its craw.

"Hold him," I said. "Hold him tight."

"Why?!" Big Jim whimpered.

I could have said, "Why? You killed my Dad. You ruined my Momma. You destroyed my family, consumed our town. You broke Penny's heart. *You want to know WHY?* My home is gone, my house is gone, my life is gone. My Granma's gone because of you." Instead, I flipped open Pop's lighter – did I imagine my engraved ancestor Jack winked? – thumbed the flint, and lit another cig from Granma's cap. Then I took a draw, felt the smoke go in, leaned close and blew it in the face of my enemy just like she woulda done.

"I'll tell you why," I said. "You killed my dog."

I shoved the heart-bone into Big Jim's face, it expanded in my hand like a tube filled with fire — contracted to freezing cold — and blew up in a thousand drops of liquid metal.

Big Jim fell screaming into my Ungeheuer's stinking throat.

I would have been destroyed by the blast, but my Ungeheuer put his hand around me like a shield.

A shit-covered vermin crawled out of Big Jim's butt as my Ungeheuer ate him. It was a complete version of Big Jim, down to the refracting wide eyes, razor mandibles and yellow mustache. It climbed up a jagged Ungeheuer tooth with its grubby, fat fingers, jumped on my arm, and tried to bite me.

I twisted its neck *click click* popped off its head and threw the jerking carcass into my Ungeheuer's maw.

"I'm the Jack of Hearts, jackass." I washed its snapping head in the lake, held my nose, popped it in my mouth, crunched it up and swallowed. That's how you finish a monster, Dammit. Eat or be eaten. Remembering Mister Brown's skukm story, I know he would a been proud.

Chapter 52

The Knave of Hearts

The sun shone bright and hot; mist rose from the wet lawn. I dug a hole under the branches of the biggest ponderosa I could find and buried what was left of Doc. And Mister Brown? He was nowhere to be found, not a piece of him remained. For all I know he blew up in a cloud of *Zimilibus*!

Remember that green ledge, Dammit? We made it through the whitewater; this must be what it's like to eddy-out. I am tired, so tired.

"*Massterrr, I watch and follow.*" My Ungeheuer laid a talon on my forehead (dropping a dark lens over my eyes) shrank to the size of a small animal and disappeared into the trees. I slowly dug through the remains of Doc's cabin, found clean socks and a pair of old jeans in a crushed bureau and changed.

They found me lacing dry feet into Pop's boots. I felt a grin twist my face watching Sophie's RV in a cloud of yellow pine pollen rumble up the lane and settle in the dirt like a creaking hen. Sophie floated down like a flower, eyes grey and keen. "Where's the nice man with long flaxen hair?"

I shook my head. Nope. He's gone.

"*Oh, the mind, mind has mountains; cliffs of fall, frightful, sheer....*" Sophie tapped my chest to the words. "You must leave now." She was insistent, pulled on my arm. "The rise, the hill, the onward is here."

"Don't even ask," Trout climbed out the driver's side. "She's SO fuckin weird."

I forgot how much Trout liked to cuss. It made me think of MK, and I hated myself for it.

"What the fuck happened?" Trout shook her head looking around. "Never mind. We GOT to leave. People went nuts in town, fuckin NUTS. Then, everyone went back to normal like waking from a bad dream. Except half a them are naked, and the other half bloody."

"In a rare moment of lucidity Sophie said they'll be looking for a scapegoat," said Owl. "I wish Elbedeefa was here, she'd know what to do."

"Yah, Elbedee," said Squirrel, and started to cry.

We lit out for the Oregon Coast to find Penny and my Momma. The Stray's idea.

I saw my Ungeheuer like a cat squiggle up over a tire and onto an axle. I threw the backpack behind the driver's seat (smoking because it held *Acuere's* axe-head and Big Jim's silver sword which I made shrink to jackknife size). I pulled Granma's cap onto my prickly head, but I saw nothing except that bronze helmet from Sophie's house and one other thing behind the seat. More about that later, Dammit.

I said, "let me drive," and drove us slowly through Junction City where people stood in dazed clumps. Some wandered down the middle of the road as if looking for something they lost. I thought of Junior and felt my shoulders relax. I'm glad he was lost, Dammit. Dead and lost.

The RV is way easier to drive than Sonofa. Brake, gas—try not to bust the big mirrors. We headed down the highway. The driver's-side window was stuck down. A breeze skiffled the trees and that smell of an oncoming storm, wild as the ocean, played across my face.

My hands started to tremble, and I couldn't make them stop. I turned off the highway and sat shaking like I had a bad fever. I told the Strays and Sophie to stay, got out and climbed over a barb-wire fence into a meadow, followed by my Ungeheuer. A rusty barb pricked my hand and blood welled out. A memory of hot afternoons working the fence line with MK jumped me like a wolf. The most pleasurable memory since Penny's kisses. Or having a dog. *Let Hercules himself do what he may, the cat will mew and the dog will have his day.*

"Well," I joked to the dripping blood from my hand, to the waves of grass against my hips, to the grey-slabbed mountains rising like fists, "I got a new friend now. This jackass."

"*Yessss, massterrr. Friennnnnd.*"

I topped a low ridge like a tongue across the valley, north and south rimmed by greater mountains; ridges like fangs with me in their mouth. A car twenty miles away turned on its lonely headlights as hail fell from a glowering black wall.

Poor soul the center of my earth.

Why dost thou pine within and suffer dearth?

"At least my feet are dry," I thought. I started to feel bad for myself, like old times before you were there — I mean before Dammit was there. You have GOT to stop talking to him, Clay. He is so dead and gone.

I'm like someone doomed, that old king or someone:

I tax not you, you elements with unkindness....

Then, let fall your horrible pleasure.

Dad said on that morning long ago that he didn't want me to pursue vengeance. My real Dad, my whole and healthy Dad — not the crazy vengeance-saturated wraith who met me later, or the one who spoke riddles from MK's mouth. I know that Granma, and my Momma—and maybe even Penny—would tell me to turn around. To just let it go. But I'm starting to lean towards wraith-Dad.

My Ungeheuer isn't *making* me look through his lens. I want it. All complications and questions resolve. I gaze from a cave, my focus narrows. MK is a far-off, granite-skinned shadow glimmering in a sepulchral light at the end of the tunnel. All I want is to hurt MK like he hurt me. Then kill him. It was him all along who took my Dad. It was him who took my Granma. Everything started with him. All my troubles. Vengeance comes on hot and has no eyes.

He is a mad dog, Dammit, and needs to be put down.

"Yessss. Mad dogsss. Put them downnn."

Something in me can raise a monster from the deep. I know that vengeance is not mine. And I know *it is.* I'm afraid, Dammit. I reckon I been a mad stray a long time. Life is a big lie. Like climbing up a canyon. Every time you think you are at the top there's another rise. Out of pure spite, I keep walking up the spine of the hill.

I remember Mister Bay said, *"He could break it all with a word."*

I know what that means now, Dammit. *Of rivers and the chain-ed canyons free, A winding, restless spirit I will be.* I'm supposed to be from a line of Conveners. Men and women who bring peace among the Nisoi. But I am a murderer. What I done to Granma. Murderer. It is a burning slag-worm in my guts. I cannot help myself; I hear her sing.

"Living words, wind and wave,
Comes the one who kills his blood...."

The sadness wrenches me over; I fall down. My Ungeheuer climbs on my shoulder and sits there licking itself. Except cats don't wrap a long snaky arm with fingers like spiders around your neck. I feel its hunger and aloneness.

"Massster, you are weepinggg. Do not weep. We will kill themmm allll."

The slag-worm in my stomach twists.

"The Masstresss. You mussst faccce The Masstresss."

"I will find MK, and I will kill him. For Dad," I ignore the truth that a horror worse than my Ungeheuer is here. "I will have my vengeance."

"Jussstice. Your Dessstiny."

"Not justice," I say. "Plague Justice. And I don't give a damn about that thing Junior brought."

And Dammit, I'm sorry. I know you are gone, burned up with Cress in that tinderbox. But I cannot help myself, I still reach out. I rise and climb the hill.

Chapter 53

Inventory

It is OK to feel many things at once, Dammit. Many things fighting in your head like enemies. Like this storm I see coming over the western ridge fighting with itself. I feel a war coming, and there is no way to stop it. But feeling many things does not make you crazy. It makes you human (I just remembered something Big Jim said, I reckon I know where Dad's body is. I feel Ms. Swan's fingernail in my chest and reckon She'll know where MK is. She owes me).

Sometimes you got to take a walk. Go over things real slow, change the pace. And sometimes — like Granma says — you got to say it true, say it out loud to yourself, take your time and get it sorted.

So, one more Inventory. And understand, I'm in no hurry. Let's take it slow.

Monsters.

I set my Ungeheuer down in the grass, he grows to the size of a man and touches my face with a long finger.

"Masssster, let usss go back. Thisss place isss not for you."

I tell him to leave me, to go back and wait for me.

He does.

"Don't eat them," I say, and he waves absently, slithering downhill through the grass, and I know that—for now—Sophie and The Strays are not in danger.

Women.

That down-turned smile; the memory of a kiss like fire in my chest. Penny would appreciate the atmosphere: A blue-black storm coming over the western ridges and up the valley. Sun-blaze in jets of gold crashing through rent clouds and tipping the peaks to the East with fire under a full moon.

"*Let fall your horrible pleasure,*" I'd say, and she'd laugh at me.

"You're way over the top now, son!" she'd say.

And I'd say, "I'm no son, I love you and I want to be with you for all times."

And Penny would wrinkle her nose and smack me and say, "It's a figure of speech. Quit cryin' CS."

And I would grab her like I wanted to and never did — she always grabbed me — and we would kiss. I would close my eyes and be there in the sage and the smell of the canyon in the sun after a long rain.

The ground rolls beneath my feet. Jagged peaks turn silver in the moonglow, inscribed with black lines, as if gods carve messages on their flanks. What tides push these mountains to crest? The moon is lost at sea. Her sails catch lighthouse rays, then disappear in a trough of darkness.

Vengeance.

I am sound and fury on a burning road. Old 146, you know Dammit, always rolling around in my head: *So shalt thou feed on Death, that feeds on men....* I know your name, MK. And I take it for myself. I am the Death Messenger, and I'm coming for you.

Friends.

"Sometimes, if you're lucky Clay — like a magic penny in your pocket — the story finds you, gets inside of you." I see Mister Brown slapping that meat stick on the counter — eyes shining like copper moons — telling his cousin's skukm story. Heh. Mister Brown, that red-headed jackass and his pennies.

"If that happens, WOOWEE! Watch out!"

How his eyes burned copper and my heart was white-hot under a rushing wind.

"If it's inside you, lil bruh? No telling where that river flows, where that line goes."

If he was here, I'd ask him one question. Do you know about this burning slag-worm? Like a bone-shaking flu, like a weight on my chest so heavy I can barely breathe?

He's dead too, Dammit, like so many others I have loved.

Mothers.

If I could ask for one thing, it would be for my Momma to be here, and wrap me in her thin arms and say, "Baby-Grizz, it's gonna be alright." I want to be with you at the home place on the porch like when I was little and listening to you read The Riverside, doing all the voices of the characters, and tickling me when I got scared.

"Sometimes the wave looks big, son. But if you face it head-on it will be fine. Sometimes you have to go under to get through."

I don't want to be a Stonefly. I don't want to have your blood in me that moves with the cycle of the water and calls back to the tidal songs. I don't want to go under no more. I don't want to be able to talk to skukms.

Wind and Wave.

The grassy ridge that rises before me to the mountains seethes under the wind like loose skin on a dog's back. I see Achilles running wild in a meadow like this, except he has sunshine. A rippling green meadow under a heavy sun. But not here.

A storm is coming, and I do not have a choice. I need to face the wave. I can almost hear Dad: "*Out last 'em. Out loco 'em. Out love 'em.*" Oh, Dad. That big wave took you down and you never came back up.

The meadow rolls like a whitewater river before the face of the storm that has brewed long in the southern seas, pounding the surf where my Momma must have swum through the waves at the coast. She must be there, she has to be there, swimming now. The storm comes across the high desert, scrapes the granite tops of the Eagle Caps in Oregon, sucks ice like a shawl around itself as it rips over Hell's Canyon and screams between the ridges of the Seven Devils. It is coming at me like green waves in a cold salty ocean I never seen. I am tired. My heart is rent with sadness. But I know one thing: I am not afraid of the green ledge pull no more. I have been in it, I have been under it, and I am still standing. So, bring it on.

I go blind — or it gets very dark. I keep walking, pressed against the wind, surrounded by sheets of water. There is someone I desire to see up here, but I do not know his name just yet. I walk a tightrope over darkness. And then, the hill blazes gold. The sun pierces the storm. My eyes spasm. Sweat in cold streams runs down my sides. For a moment there is no wind, only an echo whispering the grass. The sun drags her red-gold fingers across the hill. The meadow weaves and rebounds against my hips. First gold — then black as night. The headlights of the car in the valley disappear in waves of sleet. The real storm comes, and the light goes out.

I dig frantically in my pocket. I am searching for a penny that does not exist.

Memory.

And then it is exactly in this moment I realize: I am heads, *and* I am tales. There is no riverbank here, and yet, something within crawls through this storm of storms to a nameless shore, cracks open.

I remember the buried words of the winged Mayfly Creature when my face was pressed to the stones.

"Long wand'ring captive alone, the cost!
Thou, death's kiss for one in need.
Long sund'ring pain, long memory lost;
Thou, release the pris'ner free."

I remember the sound of its rustling arms, the sadness — for me! — in its dark eyes, its many-winged voices intermingled with the cracking of the rocks under the current, and a distant scratching; the soft and steady crawling of stoneflies to the edge.

"Ve'achron Al'afar Yaqum,
Though you lose each other, you shall never part.
Ve'achron Al'afar Yaqum.
When all is lost, you shall remember, dear heart."

Remember? Remember what?

The storm is a green wave, a stampede of aurochs. I got no one who loves me. No one who is for me. I used to think MK was the familiar-friend that my Momma talked about long ago (if he was, then he was horrible at it. A real A-hole). If that jackass were here he'd be popping his knuckles and cracking jokes about getting "familiar" with my "girlfriend," telling me he stole *Ve'achron* from the winged creature, or some other nonsense.

And that is when I remember the most important thing.

Love.

My Momma and my Dad hold each other. With me hugged between them. Me, the size of a baby grizz, and their love so much bigger than our little cabin. I feel Granma's rough hands on my face smelling like apples and cigarettes. Her eyes, popping and snapping like sapphires in a fresh-pine fire.

"Clayton, no matter how far down we go under — or how far away — we can always be brought back. Love does that. Nothin' does that but love."

Is it like inheriting something? A penny thrown into me, like I'm a wishing well and someone made a wish?

Yes. Maybe. Only deeper.

Stonefly.

Strength pours from my fingers so that I do not know where I end and where the storm begins. The muscles between my shoulder blades bunch as I pull mighty oars. I cross the green ledge. I ride a whitewater river-of-a-storm. I'm in the current.

I'm above the current.

My feet leave the ground. I catch a thermal and I rise.

"If it's inside you, lil bruh? No telling where that river flows, where that line goes."

It is right here — twenty feet above the ground in the storm — that I begin the story to you, Dammit. The story I needed to tell for both of us, to untangle everything. I begin, of course, with....

Inventory: The qualities of a "good dog...." Here, transfixed above this hillside, watching the storm-swirled moon cross beneath the dancing Pleiades, I tell the whole thing — all of it. Our story, from start to finish. An unstoppable spring-fed current. I am lost in it and live in it all over again.

The moon sinks on the other side of the mountains.

I speak the final line, "... *no telling where that river flows, where that line goes.*" And I sense my line in stronger hands. Only one thing remains. My thumb closes upon my outstretched hand, makes a fist. Blood squeezes from the barbwire cut in my palm, mingled with rain. I throw my arm like a piston. Up and forward, as if to cast a line. Something rises from my palm at the terminus into this never-ending storm, a feathered intention cast to the waters, a flickering from my heart. The efflorescent sun — hastening through the night — tinges the eastern mountains with a predawn silver-blue. She flickers like a dying lightbulb. First, dark brown. Then white. My eyes crackle as darkness rends like a torn curtain in a castle surrounded by day, and I remember the other words of the Creature, rising like mayflies breaking the surface:

"You are given a familiar, he shall come to you late.
Not around the wave you must go — but under, and through.
You shall be blessed to forget: for the sorrow is great,
Remember, beloved. Remember. Everything will be made new!"

Remember, Dammit, what I said at the very beginning? That I would not tell you my wish, because Granma says if you tell the wish out loud it doesn't work? Well, now or never, I reckon.

I am heads I am tales my feet touch the ground it is evening of our first day and we see living silver everywhere I we us them and they and everyone else within know who it is we desire to see.

Yes, we.

Under-wave the stone shall go,
Returning river to its way;
Ever-still the water flows,
Ever-watchful friend of stray.

We know his true name. And so, we call.

Havoc.

A long time ago, when wishes were for wishing, aiming was for aiming, and sometimes both came true.... Even before I finish, I see you, Dammit. *A long time ago, a dog loved a boy. And the boy loved his dog.* Only you are much, much bigger than I remember. And much, much wilder. *The boy called him by his familiar name, "Havoc, Come!"*

Running ragged down the hill to me with that goldang scarred-up ear and stupid, mouth-open, tongue-hanging grin. Running like the hounds of hell are on your tail — and you are the leader of the pack. Running like a grizzly through a gully of willows coming at a man. Running down that storm-laden, pre-dawn ridge to me in great bounds, your tail like a flag. The rising sun pierces the storm, I feel the ground once more beneath my feet and I see you for one instant. Flashing from black to gold, surging through the grasses to me, coming at my call and the surge of my singing heart.

As you know, the true topography of the heart is vast, wrinkled with rivers and layered mountains. It is a most dangerous country. Those who venture there must be foolish, unafraid, and willing to suffer the trials of loss and grief far beyond any hope of return.

My heart churns like a whitewater hole on the Salmon river, shaded by the marching waves of a thousand granite peaks that crest the Frank Church wilderness.

Of rivers and the chain-ed canyons free, A winding, restless spirit I will be.

What is this in my eyes? It must be rain. I cannot see you no more. That is why I know it is no vision; you are real. The storm transforms again from wind and dust to sheets of whitewater. But,

Dammit, I can hear you. Real as real can be. Flesh and blood. Familiar as an old red pickup – and big as one—with bad brakes crashing down the hill. Baying to me in the storm.

Cry Havoc, a dog comes!

Cry Havoc! Let slip the dog of war.

Inventory done.

Golden Stone is Coming.

Book Two completes The Pteronarcys Cycle

Sign up for updates at dustauthor.com: follow the author on his
social media and Substack

The author is a member of Seed Of Dragons Writers Collective:
www.seedofdragons.com
We tell mythic tales of darkness and courage from the dragon's lair.

Though we dared to build gods
And their houses out of dark and light,
And sow the seed of dragons, 'twas our right
(Used or misused). The right has not decayed.
We make still by the law in which we're made.
-- J. R. R. Tolkien

On Influences and Sources

I owe a debt of gratitude to writers too numerous, too luminous to recount here. But especially one: Gene Wolfe taught me if a story can shoot straight, it can ride whatever pony it wants. Most agents and publishing houses are still on the other side of the Mississippi trying to decide if the piano stays in the wagon.

Thanks are due to those who preserved and translated the folk tales found in *Fly Stone, Fly*. Especially, the incomparable D.L. Ashliman, with whom I've corresponded and received his permission to use and cite his work, who has shared much of his work on indigenous folk stories in the public domain (https://sites.pitt.edu/~dash/ashliman.html). These include the following: Jacob and Wilhelm Grimm, *Der Bauer und der Teufel*[1], *Kinder- und Hausmärchen, (Children's and Household Tales—Grimms' Fairy Tales), 7th ed.* (Berlin, 1857), no. 189. [The Grimms added this tale to their Kinder- und Hausmärchen with the fifth edition (1843).] The Grimms' source: Ludwig Aurbacher, Bücher für die Jugend (Stuttgart and Tübingen, 1834), pp. 249-251. Translated by D. L. Ashliman[2], © 2002.

The stories Mister Brown tells are in the common domain and a precious resource from the indigenous peoples of Europe and North America. Mister Brown, because of who he is, lends his unique flavor to their telling. In particular, *The Peasant and the Devil* is a much more extensive retelling with Mister Brown's

---

1. *http://gutenberg.spiegel.de/?id=5&xid=969&kapitel=30&cHash=b2042df08bbauer_te#gb*
  _found

2. http://www.pitt.edu/~dash/ashliman.html

unique twists and turns. If you don't know about *Reynard Fuchs*, do an internet search and enjoy!

The Clackamas Chinook skukm story that Mister Brown re-tells can be found in brief form in *Coyote Was Going There: Indian Literature of the Oregon Country,* Compiled and Edited by Jarold Ramsey, University of Washington Press, 1977. It is originally described in *Oregon Historical Quarterly, Volume 1, 1900, "Reminiscences of Louis Labonte."* Available online: https://en.m.wikisource.org/wiki/Oregon_Historical_Quarterly/ Volume_1 (Of interest due to the veracity of primary source material: Louis, Jr., born in 1818 was the son of Louis Labonte, Senior, a Montreal-born member of the Astor expedition who married the daughter of chief Kobayway near present-day Astoria. Louis, Jr., who spoke multiple indigenous languages, grew up in the Willamette Valley, and an interview with him in 1900 when he was 88 years old is a primary source for a number of folk tales of the indigenous people of the Pacific Northwest). My greatest desire is to be one voice (of many) to celebrate and support.

The Epigraph can be found here: Monograph Number 3, of *Studies in Entomology, "The Stoneflies (Plecoptera) of the Pacific Northwest,"* by Stanley G. Jewett, Jr., the U.S. Bureau of Commercial Fisheries, Portland, Oregon. Published by Oregon State College Press, Corvallis, Oregon, 1959. For all I know, I may own the only copy that remains, picked up in a used bookstore decades ago. Many thanks to Stanley Jewett, whose love for all things stonefly shines in his little monograph.

The quote about dragonflies is not from *Dragonflies of North America,* a book published in 1929 and very rare, but instead, from *Dragonflies of the North Woods, by Kurt Mead,* and can also be found publicly available on the webpage of The Minnesota Dragonfly Society here: https://www.mndragonfly.org/html/ biology.html I love Mead's descriptions, and hope that the reader will grow to know and love dragonflies (and stoneflies) as Kurt and I do.

Everything here beats to an inescapable rhythm from my Ghanaian childhood. There are other influences in the pages of this story, but I believe it worth the adventure – and a great deal of pleasure—in finding them on your own, if you so wish. For what it's worth, I believe listening to the music while reading the story makes it better. I enjoy a good game of 52-card pickup, plus joker. And, of course, *The Riverside Shakespeare, The Poems of Gerard Manley Hopkins,* and *Porter's Taxonomy of Flowering Plants* exist in this world as well as in Clay's.

I know this because, as I write this final line, I see them on my shelf.

Grateful Acknowledgements

We shall all be alike — brothers of one father and one mother, with one sky above us and one country around us... Then the Great Spirit Chief who rules above will smile upon this land and send rain to wash out the bloody spots made by brothers' hands from the face of the earth.
—In-mut-too-yah-lat-lat, "Thunder Traveling Over The Mountains" - Chief Joseph
"Public Speech at Lincoln Hall," Washington D.C., 1879

Fly Stone, Fly took about twelve years to finish, the same amount of time it took Clay to grow big enough to stand on his own. I was working full time. Also, we raised two daughters. If you're a maker of anything — stories, songs, poems, breakfasts, new lines of code, wooden bowls, whatever — find a way. That is pretty much all I can share about the creative purpose. Find people who believe in you enough to encourage you. In the end, all we have is the encouragement we received and gave—and a finished work or two. The encouragement may last longer.

In this endeavor where would I be without you, lovely Janette, friend and soulmate? You turned a bedroom into a study. You painted it and furnished it. You said, "go for it." You dealt with me rising early mornings and staying up late to pursue this craft. Thank you for showing me what love looks like, for letting this stone fly. You are the smell of sage and the sound of water coming off the hills, my own Riverside. I love you and our story.

Our daughters Lily and Zoe were a ready and encouraging support when I did not want to keep going. Lily was an "early-reader" to give critical, wise feedback that made the story stronger; Zoe would often ask, "Dad, how's the book?" and then encourage me: "Keep doing it!" To our grafted children whose perseverance is an inspiration, this story's for you too: Brandilee, Jen, Susan, Kim, Jacob, Amanda, Nicole. For Graham, Eric, and Stephen who were the first friends who believed in me as a writer: there would be no *Fly Stone, Fly* without you.

My parents, Danny Joe and Ella Mae taught me to work hard and love every person. Specifically, my mother nurtured in me a love for reading. My father gave me fire that can never be taken, true grit. These two radical children of the '60's whose gentle reputation was to get in trouble by helping others, gave me – possibly—the best gift of all: loving myself as a "TCK: Third Culture Kid," a rare and endangered animal. Their influence shines everywhere in *Fly Stone, Fly*, but especially in standing up for the least. My brother Kristofer is a stalwart believer in me, often asked how it was going, brought his encouraging smile and gentle spirit to our conversations, and only ever said, "you can DO this — so DO it!" My sister Kari's gifts in leadership and passion to make things right is an inspiration. Uncle Phil, Aunt Carla, Ryan and Darren Pfeifle: your gift to me at age seventeen letting me live with you and be part of your family is more precious every year. It was gold on the first day. I am forever in your debt and will always love you. Aunt Irene taught me that singing from the heart is what matters. Ken Loss, Gary Baumann, Alastair Davidson all welcomed me, your friendship matters. Cousin Kevin, you've always had my back. James Atengane and Alex "BB" Lanbon I am grateful for the length and strength of our friendship. My Ghana Uncles, Phil and Tim, showed me that a man can be strong, wise, playful, *and* love stories. Burt and Sarah Keplinger, your friendship and love for our family over the years is so appreciated!

I'm grateful for colleagues and fellow executive coaches, all encouragers: Paul L., Mike VB., Jenny M., Elena S., Jim S., Bob and Robin F., Susan L., Susan O., Marilyn A., Brynn H., Laurie

B., Kelsie W., Dick and Martha W., Dominic R., Joe R., Paul and Joy M., Paul F., Jim H., Amy G., Vanessa S., Michelle T., Tina J., and Jonathan R.. I'm grateful for the friendship of Bryan Capitano and your expertise with all things internet. I'm grateful for writing mentors who taught me less is more: Bob Baker, Dick Hill, and Simon Beames. I'm grateful for fellow writers who held the door open and invited me in: Sunyi Dean, Josh Salzberg, Cassie Moore, Eric Ortlund. I wish I had the words to describe how timely and calming your encouragements—and frank feedback – have been.

Special thanks to my very own fellowship of the ring, the members of MOAT (Men Of Alpine Trout) naturalist organization of Central Idaho, each of whom provided companionship, encouragement, and expertise on all things trouts and trout-bugs through the years: Graham, Matt, Tadd, Isaac, Daniel, Jerry and El Jefe. El Jefe, you are the salty kindness every young man hopes to receive from a mentor, and few actually find; a grace I cannot repay. The reliance on barbless hooks as a state of mind. Special thanks to Lily my "early reader." You were the first to give this story your attention. You asked me hard questions and told me which characters you hated and which ones you liked, which made the final version so much better. Special thanks to Graham my other "early reader." You asked questions for hours, in person and on the phone, line by line through the entire book. I had no idea how much I needed your help. It's a testament to your good heart that we're still friends! Also, special thanks to Graham and Tanya together: for the blessing of quiet summer mornings on your porch (filled with the sounds of Parker and Emmeline playing) that allowed me to finish *Fly Stone, Fly*. Special thanks to Cassie Moore as self-pub guru and first-responder to my dire publishing emergencies. The gifts of your time and skill and encouragement got this book to the finish line. Special thanks to Sunyi Dean a gifted writer and so much more: a light and fire.

You opened a door to the world of writers, and I'm forever in your debt. You are the most kind, thoughtful and encouraging person I've never met (someday I'll lift a pint to your health in person). Special thanks to Trevor of Seed of Dragons Collective: for believing in the soul of this book expressed in the cover art for *Fly Stone, Fly*. Special thanks to Eric Ortlund of Seed of Dragons Collective: They say write with someone particular in your mind, and I thought of you. No words adequately describe my indebtedness for your friendship at the campfire and the feedback you provided on each draft, and getting *Fly Stone, Fly* published.

A final and most important thanks to you, dear reader and to all booksellers and librarians who choose to display and sell this book. You are, literally, the end goal of my gratefulness. As an indie author, I am fully and ever indebted to your desire to read.

If you've made it this far, you may have caught a theme. Believe in others and love them. Let them love you. This is the rain that washes away the bloody spots. Granma Lina, herself, would be proud of that spare line, but not of the rest of my long-windedness. A final gratitude: Mixed metaphors don't always work in writing. But somehow, miraculously, they do in life.

All the best things
Seem at odds until you are
In them and feel them free.
Love is both shore and the river,
And one other thing
Caught in your current,
Tangled roots of your tree.

A Word on Your Influence as A Reader

Writers exist because there are readers. Readers who enjoy what we write and want to share it. Increasingly, you and I must choose between ethically-sourced (non-AI) fiction or lesser alternatives. I reckon there will be more and more "knock offs" by "writers" using AI. We are what we eat. There is great pleasure in taking time to make something beautiful, and great pleasure in knowing of that effort. I'm also a fan of independent booksellers and librarians because they are advocates for reading; they believe in good, human-created books and in the meaningful relationship between writers and readers. If you're not aware of bookshop.org, please check it out.

I hope you consider these next steps (what indie music fans have done for ages): Tell your friends about *Fly Stone, Fly*. Give a copy of this book to someone you think will enjoy it. Take one extra moment and leave a review of this book online (most writers agree this may be the biggest thing you can do if you like our work). Ask your favorite book shop and local library to order this book and other indie books you love. Tell them this novel is available on Ingram (the world-wide ordering system available to independent book sellers). If they listen, and they're usually great at listening, they'll order this book. You'll not only help *Fly Stone, Fly* live and breathe in the wild but you'll also strengthen the influence of indie writers of ethically-sourced fiction everywhere.

Know how much I – and writers in my position – appreciate you for being a reader. We also appreciate any actions you take to share our work.

Gratefully yours,
Dust Kunkel

About the Author

Fly Stone, Fly is Dust Kunkel's first novel. He grew up in Ghana, West Africa, a Third Culture Kid (TCK). With a mother from Montana and a father from Oregon, he returned to the Pacific Northwest at age seventeen and fell in love with a Northwest girl, and the rivers and mountains of the Northwest. He has taught literature, run a gear-boat raft on the Salmon River in Idaho, foster parented teens, managed outdoor schools, and directed student leadership programs at a university. He is most excited these days helping Ghanaian friends launch a new school.

Dust has a BA in Literature, an Msc in Outdoor Education from the University of Edinburgh, Scotland, and is an Executive Coach credentialed by the International Coaching Federation. Dust and his wife, Jan, live in Oregon City, Oregon, have two daughters launched from the nest, and two elderly retriever-mixes, Bowie and Percy, who will not launch from any nest. When he's not writing, Dust goes on adventures with Jan, plays live music, rafts rivers with friends and fly-fishes. For contact or bookings: dustauthor.com.

www.ingramcontent.com/pod-product-compliance
Lightning Source LLC
Chambersburg PA
CBHW032018110726
47901CB00004B/1124